CREATURES OF THE
IN BETWEEN

ALSO BY CINDY LIN

The Twelve

Treasures of the Twelve

CREATURES OF THE IN BETWEEN

CINDY LIN

HARPER

An Imprint of HarperCollinsPublishers

Library of Congress Cataloging-in-Publication Data

Names: Lin, Cindy, author.

Title: Creatures of the in between / Cindy Lin.

Description: First edition. | New York, NY : Harper, an imprint
of HarperCollins Publishers, [2023] | Audience: Ages 8-12. |
Audience: Grades 4-6. | Summary: "Twelve-year-old Crown
Prince Jin must travel far beyond his palace home and find a
mythical creature to bond with him, all before his thirteenth
birthday-or risk his homeland falling into chaos"— Provided
by publisher.

Identifiers: LCCN 2022021826 | ISBN 978-0-06-306479-9
(hardcover) — ISBN 978-0-06-332898-3 (special edition)

Subjects: CYAC: Adventure and adventurers—Fiction. | Mythical
animals—Fiction. | Fantasy. | LCGFT: Fantasy fiction. |
Novels.

Classification: LCC PZ7.1.L553 Cr 2023 | DDC [Fic]—dc23

LC record available at https://lccn.loc.gov/2022021826

Typography by Catherine Lee

23 24 25 26 27 LBC 5 4 3 2 1

First Edition

FOR STEVEN

WHISPER ISLAND, EMPIRE OF THE THREE REALMS

New Year's Eve

FASTER—WE HAVE TO BEAT THEM.

Masa clutched the thick, furry ruff around the kirin's neck. It snorted in response and took on a burst of speed. She did her best to hang on as the great beast galloped across the island's shore, trying not to slide around on the iridescent scales armoring the creature's powerful flanks. Its massive hooves flew over the wet sand shimmering in the moonlight, away from the celebratory bonfires and festivities of the village. A shout went up behind her.

"Come on, now!" Her brother, Mau, urged his mount to run faster. Masa glanced back to see Mau sitting atop the winged lion, its feathered wings shooting out and flapping a few times, skimming just above the sand. Masa rolled her eyes. Piyaos. They had such a penchant for showing off. And they hated to lose. But not as much as she did.

"No flying!" She glared at the creature and her brother, then turned back and hunched low against her own monster. *They're cheating*, she warned. She squinted through the kirin's antlers and saw the fire tree glimmering in the distance. *We're almost to the finish. Give it one last push!* In a few hundred paces she'd win the race and get her pick of beasts to work with in the new year.

But her mount had other ideas. It lurched to a stop and bucked, kicking its back hooves straight at the piyao. Masa tumbled off the kirin's back and heard her brother cry out as his mount shied at the last second, roaring in surprise. The piyao wheeled around, its forked tail raised in warning. Snarling, it lunged and swiped its claws at the kirin. The kirin grunted and tossed its antlered head.

"Control your creature!" Masa yelled. "Or I'll tell Father!"

Her brother ducked as a sharp antler barely missed him. "You control yours, or I'll tell him you started it!" Mau yelled back. He bent and whispered into the piyao's ear.

Masa scrambled to her feet. She met the kirin's golden eyes and held its gaze. With every fiber of her being, she commanded the monster to stop. *I know kirins don't like wicked behavior, but piyaos are hotheads. This is not the way. We were having a* friendly *race.* The great beast shook itself as if it heartily disagreed and danced back and forth on its hooves a few times before settling down with a disgruntled huff, exhaling a cloud of hot breath.

Okay, Masa soothed, stroking the kirin's scaly pelt. *It's okay.*

BOOM. An enormous explosion shook the island. Masa whirled in the direction of their village. The sky lit with flame and several more blasts went off. "Strange. Mother said fireworks wouldn't be till midnight." Then she frowned. "Those don't look like the usual display." Uneasily, she reached for the kirin and remounted.

"The elders would never approve of this," agreed her twin. "Something's off. We'd better go back."

A three-legged green crow streaked through the night, cawing over their heads. "Big fire! Big fire!"

Masa started to ask more, but an eerie wailing went up, filling her ears. Then a low mournful note sounded, long and urgent. It was the call of the shell trumpet, which was rarely used. "They're blowing the horn. Why? What's happening?"

"Those aren't fireworks," Mau said. His face was pale. "We're under attack."

Both the kirin and the piyao shifted restlessly with uneasy growls, their dispute forgotten. A chorus of cries and roars erupted from the beasts on the island, echoing the distress call of their caretakers. Masa's blood ran cold as the icy night air filled with piercing sound. All of Whisper Island was screaming.

CHAPTER 1

THE IMPERIAL BESTIARY

JIN KNEW HE WASN'T SUPPOSED to go into the Diviners' Salon, but he couldn't help himself. The imperial bestiary was kept there, and he'd been forbidden to look through its ancient pages for weeks now, even though he'd be turning thirteen in a matter of months. But on this spring morning, with everyone at the Palace of Monsters preoccupied with the biggest festival of the year, he might have a chance to take a quick peek. He strode through the long halls. As he neared the great doors of the Diviners' Salon, he glanced around—and stopped himself just in time.

"Your Brilliance." A trio of women swathed in bright silks bowed deeply. They were his grandmother's attendants. He slouched against a tall, lacquered pillar and assumed a look of boredom, giving them a curt nod. Looking like colorful birds in their shimmering finery, they swished past in a cloud of scented oils. They were hardly halfway down the corridor when their whispers floated back.

"Good beasts, I thought it was a servant at first," murmured one. "Why does he dress so plainly? In worker's trousers instead of robes! You'd never know it was the crown prince from the back."

"That hair doesn't help!" said another with a sniff. "Shouldn't it be tied in the proper court style? It's all chopped off like the bristles of a pig."

"Hush, Lady Opal! Lady Coral, I'm surprised at you," hissed the third attendant. "He's still a pup. His hair may stay short till he comes of age. And as a royal, he can wear whatever he likes."

"Huh. Tell that to Grandmother," Jin muttered. The three ladies-in-waiting turned their heads at his voice, but he cleared his throat and coughed, pretending he hadn't heard them. As they hurried away, he smirked. Keep people on their toes, and their service will remain properly attentive, his grandmother liked to say. Not that he'd ever berate them like she would, or worse, have her pet phoenix teach them a lesson. Though the empress dowager *would* likely agree with her attendants about his clothes, she would never abide their insolent comments. Jin adjusted his dark linen tunic, defiantly tightening its belt. As soon as the hall was empty, he slipped into the room of diviners' tools and treasures.

It was deserted at this hour, with carved wooden shutters closed tight against the sun. The room was dimly lit by tall bronze butter lamps that flickered with a golden glow. Jin hurried past dozens of prized artifacts used by the Bureau of Divination, past the chart of the heavens, the gilt fortune sticks in their solid jade shaker, the scrolls and scales used by the alchemists, the silver compass of the geomancers. His soft felt boots scuffed along the polished wooden floor, which gleamed with reflected light. He went around the long table that held the imperial bestiary and secured the doors connecting the room to the royal library. Then he turned to the jeweled case. It winked invitingly.

He stroked its gold brocade cover and smiled. "Reunited at last."

Jin unlatched the thick lid and lifted it with both hands. Larger than any other book or scroll that existed in the imperial collection, the bestiary documented every monster, every magical beast, every creature of the enchanted land between realms. He riffled through the giant case, nearly the size of a large footstool, and pulled out one of the enormous bound volumes, its soft worn pages covered in inked diagrams and highly detailed painted illustrations of the wondrous beings that had once roamed the palace. Though the cages of the palace menagerie were now dusty and abandoned, he still wanted to know everything he could about its former occupants. After all, the custom and the rule was he'd need to gain the trust and companionship of a monster if he was to ever become emperor of Samtei. There might be fewer magical beasts than ever before—it was rumored that his grandmother's phoenix was the only one left—but Jin wanted to be prepared. Pulling out a chair, he sat at the table and flipped idly through the pages, landing on the one about the kirin. He practically had it memorized but read through it again.

"The 'king of beasts' is so gentle it won't even bend the grass beneath its feet." He frowned at the illustration of the cloven-hoofed creature. It was certainly handsome with a scaly coat and shining antlers, but if it was afraid to bend blades of grass, then it must be the worst in battle. He could never understand why this monster was held in such high regard. Then again, several of the greatest rulers in the empire's history had been bonded with a kirin, including one that he'd been named after, Jin the Mighty. He eagerly moved on to the extensive section on dragons—winged, horned, sea-dwelling, mountain-dwelling, shapeshifting mirage-makers. Dragons were so much more *interesting.* They controlled water, bringing rain or preventing floods. Rumor had it that in some lands of the far west, they actually breathed fire instead. They inspired awe immediately.

His father's creature companion, or monstermate, had been said to be a dragon. But from what Jin had seen depicted in portraits, it looked suspiciously like an ordinary, if large, lizard. Perhaps that was why Emperor Jen only ruled a short while. Both the emperor and his empress consort had died not long after ascending the throne, when Jin was a baby. Though he'd pieced together bits and pieces from snatches heard around the palace, no one ever would tell Jin more. Not his tutors, not his old nurse, and certainly not his grandmother, who'd only stared at him with steely eyes the one time he'd mustered the courage to ask. "What's past is past," the empress dowager had replied. "You must think about your future. The fate of the Three Realms depends on it." She'd then looked at his tutor, at the time an elderly fellow who shifted nervously and twirled his white beard, and at everyone else in the room. "Anyone caught gossiping about the dead and departed will be punished for dishonoring their memory. If you are caught, my phoenix will happily take your tongue for a snack."

Jin dared not ask again after that. But it didn't stop him from wondering about his parents. For as long as he could remember, only he and his grandmother had lived at the Palace of Monsters, surrounded by servants, attendants, guards, and courtiers, but no other family. He was the last surviving scion of the imperial line. And yet his grandmother rarely saw him, leaving him to the care of nursemaids and a rotation of various instructors, each with orders to make sure he was taught in all the subjects a good ruler of the Three Realms must know.

If only they hadn't been so painfully dull. Political history, economics, war strategy, land management, agriculture— they put him to sleep almost immediately, especially during a tutor's droning lectures. The only subject he never tired of studying was monsters and the art of handling and communicating with them, commonly known as Whispering. For nearly a month now, he'd not had a chance to thumb through the massive book of monsters that he loved so much. His latest tutor, Master Sonsen, had told Jin that he was forbidden from going into the Diviners' Salon alone to look at the bestiary, on orders from the empress dowager herself, until he'd improved his scores on his other subjects. Being banned from the salon was almost as torturous as sitting through a lesson on crop rotation and irrigation principles.

Jin turned back to the volume he held and traced a finger over the image of a dragon. So many emperors had kept these magnificent creatures as companions, roaming the halls of this very palace. What if he was the next?

A rattle echoed through the room, and the paneled doors from the library shook. Jin's head snapped up.

"They're locked!" exclaimed a petulant voice from the other side. It was one of the ministers in the Bureau of Divination.

"Then we'll go through the corridor. Stop grumbling."

Jin sprang from his chair. If he was caught in here, it would immediately be reported to the empress dowager, and he might get a caning—a punishment reserved for when he went expressly against her direct orders. It had been a few years, but he still quailed thinking of the last time, when he was whipped for feeding pieces of sea cucumber to her phoenix from his plate. It didn't matter that he hated the rubbery delicacy, or that the creature had eagerly gulped it down without suffering any ill effects. He'd not been able to sit for nearly a week.

Quickly he slipped the volume he'd been reading into the bestiary's case, then hesitated. Better put it exactly where he'd found it. As he dug through the unwieldy volumes, perspiration gathered on his forehead and threatened to trickle down. He frantically tried to remember the proper order. There! Right between the volume on feathered monsters and the one on furred beasts. He wedged the book in place between the other volumes, then secured the latch on the cover just as the ministers' footsteps sounded out in the hallway.

Monstermuck, he swore silently. He couldn't run out now—they'd be sure to tell his grandmother, even if he ordered them not to. He might be crown prince, but her word was law. He searched about the room. No use hiding under the table or behind any of the seating arrangements. But framing the doors to the library were two tall folding screens, painted with a famous battle scene from centuries prior, when fantastical monsters had helped the Samtei people defeat their neighbors. Those who could control such monsters were hailed as heroes and protectors, and the Empire of the Three Realms—said to be the realms of humans, animals, and monsters—was born.

The doors of the salon opened, and Jin dove behind a screen just in time. He peeked through the crack between two panels to see several diviners bustle in, all dressed in deep blue robes with decorated sashes and enameled monster pins signifying their rank as high ministers. There entered the head herbalist, who specialized in medicinal potions, wearing a tall cloth hat nearly as narrow as his face and a silk stole embroidered with leaves; a stout, bespectacled astrologer, who read the stars, his stole and flat folded cap stitched with a pattern of the heavens in silver and gold thread; and the head Whisperer, his black hat bearing wide wings and his silk stole beaded with bits of polished tortoiseshell.

"I asked for tea and sweets in here," said the astrologer as he lowered himself heavily onto a cushioned armchair. "What's so urgent that it couldn't wait till after lunch? I heard there was going to be roast peacock to celebrate the start of the Monster Festival."

"We can't risk being overheard," warned the Whisperer. "Certain things are too sensitive to be discussed anywhere other than behind closed doors." He looked at the long table where the bestiary sat and frowned. Jin stifled a groan. He'd forgotten to push back his chair, which stood conspicuously away from the table. He held his breath as the Whisperer drew close, head tilted and tugging at his dark beard as he approached the chair. Then with an exasperated sigh, the man shoved it back in place and returned to where the other two ministers sat. Jin began breathing again, but his mind raced. What was so sensitive that they had to meet in secret? If the ministers caught him eavesdropping in here, would he be in bigger trouble with them or with his grandmother? How long would he need to stay hidden?

There was a knock, and then a servant appeared with a tray. The ministers grunted their approval as tea was prepared and dishes of candied fruit and sweetened rice cakes were laid out before them. When they thought they were alone again, talk resumed.

"So, is it about the borderlands?" asked the herbalist. He slurped his tea noisily. "Word is that raiders from the Empire of Hulagu are back."

"More like scouts—the Hulagans are in a never-ending quest for expansion. The stars tell it true; they are always looking for opportunities to strike," said the astrologist, his mouth full of gooey rice cake. "Which is why, treaties or not, Her Majesty wants to fortify the northern border. The Three Realms might do well to build a true wall between us and our neighbors. There are too many unguarded sections."

The floral fragrance of the tea wafted through the room, and as Jin watched the three diviners stuffing themselves with sweets, his mouth watered. He'd barely touched his breakfast this morning, intent on visiting the bestiary before anyone could see him, but now he was sorry. His stomach twisted and rumbled in complaint. He shoved a fist against it, trying to silence it.

"A wall will cost money. The treasury minister says taxes must be raised again. The floods and crop failures of the last several years have taken a toll," the herbalist said, his long face doleful. "The people will be in an uproar."

The astrologist shrugged. "If the Samtei are reminded of the danger posed by their enemies, all will remain united behind the throne. If not, the masses will direct their discontent inward at the empress . . . and all those who serve her."

"That threat has only grown over the last twelve years with Empress Soro in charge," agreed the Whisperer. "Not in seven hundred years has the Triad Throne been occupied by a woman for this long. It's unheard of."

The astrologer adjusted his spectacles. "Unprecedented!"

"Unseemly," sniffed the herbalist. "But she is only regent, holding the throne for Prince Jin. It's rightfully his."

"Yet the crown prince is still a child and therefore

unproven," the Whisperer replied. He shook his head. "He's a bit of a runt, frankly—much like that frail-looking new tutor of his. Each generation of this family seems to weaken."

A *runt*? Jin pulled away from the crack between the screen panels, insulted. He was nothing like Master Sonsen. He hadn't hit a growth spurt yet was all.

"Very true," agreed the astrologer, chewing on a walnut-stuffed date. "And how can he make his claim, with such a scarcity of monsters? Let us say what must be said. But for the empress dowager's phoenix, no creatures have been seen around here for years." He smacked his lips and licked his fingers.

The Whisperer sighed. "We might as well be the Empire of Two Realms now. It was difficult enough coming up with something passable for his father."

Jin frowned. What did that mean? He peered through the crack once again.

"But that leads precisely to what I wanted to discuss." The Whisperer glanced fearfully at the closed doors. "In less than six months, the prince will turn thirteen—and he has yet to find a monstermate."

The herbalist took another slurp of tea. "So what if he does not?"

"It has never happened before! No ruler of the Three Realms has reached the age of thirteen without bonding with a creature of the in between," spluttered the Whisperer. "Prince Jin cannot ascend the throne without the authority of a monstermate. Everyone else in the royal line has either been banished or has met an untimely fate—and without a clear order of succession, the empire will be in peril from within as well as without."

A sinking feeling came over Jin. His grandmother had always told him that if he prepared properly to be emperor, a monster would present itself at the right moment. It was why he'd studied the bestiary as much as he had. But this? This was much more complicated—and urgent—than his grandmother had let on.

The astrologist wiped a sugary smudge from his spectacles. "Could you shave a scaly pattern on a water buffalo and call it a kirin? Nowadays people wouldn't know any different."

"I suppose," said the Whisperer. "I've been loath to mention it to Her Majesty. But it's a looming problem."

"We must advise the empress dowager properly or things will only get worse," said the herbalist. "Come now, sirs, we head the most important imperial bureau in the land. Without us, the regent is but a mere woman."

A high-pitched shriek filled the air outside the room, and the men jumped. They sprang to their feet as the doors opened and the empress swept in, followed by a large, shimmering bird with a serrated beak. It sailed about the room on vermilion wings tipped in gold, casting its piercing yellow eyes on the three divination ministers. Jin shrank back as the phoenix came alarmingly close to the folding screen, but it banked hard before the wall and flew to the empress dowager, who held out a jeweled scepter shaped like a trident.

The monster bird landed by the scepter's three-tined head, grasping the thick gold handle with fearsome claws. As his grandmother drew the trident closer, her rouged cheeks pleated in a rare smile at the phoenix, her fashionably blackened teeth a dark crescent against her pale powdered skin. Her hair, the coal-black strands famously unmarred by any sign of gray, was pulled into an elaborate hairstyle, with nine flower hairpins worked in gold. The phoenix snapped at the tinkling golden flowers cascading from the pins, then began to preen its long, curling tail feathers.

The ministers had fallen to their knees, and their heads were pressed to the floor. His grandmother's smile vanished as her gaze raked over them. She adjusted her voluminous formal robes, took her seat, then curtly bade them to get up and return to their chairs.

"As I thought." The empress dowager looked pointedly at the spread of sweets and tea before them. "Indulging in refreshment between affairs of state?"

"Forgive us, Your Brilliant Majesty," said the astrologer. "We thought it best to move here to discuss a few matters before the Bureau of Divination, and we got a little parched." Bowing, he offered a cup of tea.

She waved it aside. "I don't remember dismissing you from the throne room."

"Begging your mercy, madam," said the herbalist smoothly. "We were under the impression that you were busy with other matters, what with the Monster Festival beginning tonight."

The Whisperer chimed in. "But speaking of monsters, we were just discussing the problem of their scarcity." He hesitated. "Perhaps . . . Prince Jin should pay Whisper Island a visit?"

Jin's eyes widened. Whisper Island? The sanctuary? Oh, that'd be far better than paging through the bestiary or even reveling at the Monster Festival.

Whisper Island had been established more than a hundred years earlier, after the empire's long-standing wars with its neighbors had taken a toll on its prized array of monsters. His great-great-grandfather had ordered Whisperers to spirit away creatures to an island off Samtei's coast, creating a refuge named after those with power over the uncanny beasts. Surely he'd find a monstermate there!

His grandmother sniffed. "That would be quite an undertaking."

"His new tutor seems to think that Prince Jin has immense potential with the Whispering powers of his ancestors," offered the astrologer. "He's shown great interest in the subject."

The gilt flowers in the empress dowager's hair clinked with a bright, brittle sound as she shook her head. "My grandson must focus on his other studies. The last thing he needs is to be distracted by the demands of a pet monster."

With a frown, the Whisperer stroked his beard. "The people are restive, my lady, and will not take well to the news of new taxes for a border wall. If they see the crown prince matched with a suitably commanding beast, they may be mollified."

"Which is why their attention must be turned to the true threats facing the Three Realms," his grandmother replied. "Even with a monstermate, a young boy is no match for the many enemies of Samtei. He will be too weak."

The Whisperer chuckled. "Weak? No, my lady. Not if the prince is seen with his own creature. It will show everyone there is a strong successor for the leadership of the empire! Isn't that what we want?"

The empress dowager cocked her head. "Are you in that much of a hurry to get my grandson onto the Triad Throne?" Her voice had become soft. Too soft. Jin cringed.

The minister's face paled. "Oh, no," said the Whisperer nervously. "We just got to talking about monsters because of the Monster Festival and thought there was a point of concern."

"I would have thought that my decisions were long beyond questioning by now," said Empress Soro after a long pause. "Yet it seems to me that you are not only challenging them but scheming to push Jin onto the throne." She delicately stroked the phoenix's crested head with a gilt-lacquered nail. "A reckless move, especially when he is not ready. Wouldn't you agree, my pet?"

With a shriek, the phoenix launched at the Whisperer in a blur of scarlet and gold. As the bird tore off the minister's hat and scratched at him with its claws, a streak of blood trickled down his forehead and dripped onto his silk stole, staining it with crimson. He yelped and covered his head to no avail, while the other ministers leaned as far from him as possible, looking pained.

Jin grimaced and averted his gaze. Whisperers were supposed to be able to handle monsters with ease, but with so few left, their skills were rarely put to the test. How in the realms was this man the head Whisperer? No wonder he was always jumpy around the phoenix. As the minister let out a catlike yowl, Jin snorted in disbelief.

Despite the commotion, the phoenix halted as if it had heard. It swiveled its head and leveled a piercing stare right at Jin. He jerked back from the crack between the screen panels. There was an agonizing silence, and Jin breathed as quietly as he could, his heart hammering in his ears, praying to the gods that the phoenix would resume bothering the minister. Then a rustle of silks drew closer and closer. Jin looked up to see the empress dowager standing over him, the phoenix on her shoulder.

"Well," she said, arching a painted brow. "What have we here?"

CHAPTER 2

TEA AND CONSEQUENCES

CROUCHED BEHIND THE FOLDING SCREENS in the Diviners' Salon, Jin flinched under the empress dowager's dark gaze. His mouth went dry. "H-he-hello, G-Grand-mother." The monster bird on her shoulder stared down at him with sharp yellow eyes. It must have alerted the empress dowager to his presence. With a few snaps of its beak and a toss of its crested head, it seemed to be laughing at him. His gut clenched.

"Get up," ordered Empress Soro, her voice edged with impatience. Awkwardly, he stood, trying to keep his chin high.

The three ministers came shuffling up behind the empress and peered over her other shoulder. Upon seeing Jin, they drew sharp breaths and exchanged alarmed glances.

"Prince Jin!" Though the head Whisperer bore scratches on his face from the phoenix and had blood running down his temple, he frowned at Jin, the attack by the monster bird temporarily forgotten. "Your Majesty, we had no idea the crown prince was here!"

"Indeed, indeed," huffed the astrologer. "This is most distressing."

The empress dowager stepped back with a curt wave. "Come out, boy."

Jin emerged from behind the screen and faced his grandmother, the three ministers of divination glaring at him like a trio of baleful owls. Nervously he fiddled with the end of his cloth belt. The empress dowager's lips were pressed in a thin line.

"I thought I made it clear that you were not to be in here," she said. "Were you looking at the bestiary again?"

The phoenix launched from her shoulder and Jin ducked, but the monster bird flapped past him and began circling the room. Looking down at his feet, Jin nodded meekly. "I'm sorry, Grandmother." His voice cracked, and he felt his insides shrinking as she examined him. Was she going to make him pick out a bamboo stick for his own beating? The first time that had happened, after the offense of not practicing for his instrument lessons, he'd made the mistake of selecting the thinnest stalk of bamboo—even thinner than the bow of his upright fiddle—thinking it would hurt less. Instead, the flexible rod had whipped painful cuts across his back. Though he'd known to choose thicker stalks after that, there was no escaping their sting.

It would do no good to beg for mercy. But in a sudden burst of desperation, he tried to explain. "I haven't looked at it in ages, really. I just didn't want to forget anything that I've learned." His voice cracked again, and he cleared his throat. "You always say that study is important. If I'm to find a monstermate, I need to be ready."

With a screech, the phoenix glided toward the empress dowager. Without looking, she held out her scepter, and the monster bird landed neatly on the carved handle. As the creature cocked its head at Jin, his grandmother regarded him with eyes as dark as obsidian. "I see this is a matter to be discussed privately." She glanced at the tea and sweets that the ministers had been devouring. "Come. While I take refreshment in my quarters, I should like to hear you defend this breach of my orders."

The herbalist narrowed his eyes at Jin. "If you like, my lady, I can come up with a special tea that will compel obedience."

"Thank you, Minister Jandi, but that won't be necessary right now," replied the empress dowager. "Get along, boy."

He was doomed. With a last longing look at the bestiary, Jin followed his grandmother out of the Diviners' Salon. Standing just outside were two of her personal guards,

Imperial Beaststalkers, looking almost like monsters themselves, their helmets shaped like snarling lion heads. The elder Beaststalker, Old Fang, had been there for as long as Jin could remember. His grizzled cheeks creased in pleased surprise at the sight of Jin. Jin grimaced. An understanding expression crossed Old Fang's face, and he stepped up to flank the empress dowager.

Trailing a couple of respectful steps behind his grandmother and her guards, Jin kept his eyes on the train of her robes as the empress dowager glided through the pillared corridors and sunlit courtyards of the palace, her golden slippers whispering along glossy wood floors, colored tile mosaics, and polished stone. Everywhere they went, servants, guards, and courtiers bowed low. "Tea for the crown prince and me in my apartments," she said as she passed a prostrating pair of servants, who scrambled to their feet to do her bidding.

The phoenix fixed an eye on Jin and screeched. He flinched. The empress dowager might have ordered refreshments, but it couldn't distract him from what might be forthcoming. Thinking of his grandmother's temper and her unpredictable monster bird, Jin's stomach flip-flopped with dread.

They reached the pavilion that housed the empress's chambers. Guards flanking the entrance opened the doors and saluted as they passed. Jin collided with a cloud of incense smoke, the perfume heavy and sickly sweet. He sneezed.

"Your Brilliant Majesty," chirped his grandmother's attendants. They bowed to her, and then Jin. "Your Brilliance." The ladies-in-waiting descended upon them like a flock of bright parrotines and settled Jin and his grandmother onto wide carved couches, offering padded stools for their feet.

The phoenix launched off the empress dowager's scepter and landed on an ornate metal stand, a twisted leafless tree made of pure silver. It proceeded to pick irritably at its feathers, plucking bits of crimson and gold that floated to the floor. Patches of pale down on its breast peeked through where it had plucked itself nearly bare. The empress dowager frowned and pointed her scepter at the monster bird. "Stop that," she hissed. The phoenix jerked its head up, then grumbled and started sharpening its beak on a silver branch. Satisfied, the empress dowager set down the jeweled trident. She produced an enormous shining pearl the size of a plum from her robes and began idly playing with it, hefting it in her hand and rolling it around on her palm as she studied her grandson.

Several servants hurried in with heavy trays and began preparing tea, filling a low table between them with small plates piled high with delicacies. Jin welcomed the interruption, but his appetite was long gone. As a servant placed a dish of savory dumplings before him, he looked up to see it was a young girl. Among the palace staff, there were always a few children who'd been offered by their families to serve the throne. Despite their presence, Jin had never been allowed to play with them. Still, he couldn't help but notice anyone close to his own age. This girl looked to be a couple years younger than he, though her face was unfamiliar. Her thick hair was tied back from her round cheeks in tight pigtails, and the oversized kitchen smock she wore was still stiff and new. Nodding his thanks, Jin smiled.

Dimples appeared in her cheeks. She picked up a steaming iron kettle and began filling a teapot with hot water. In the corner, the phoenix stretched its wings on its silver tree and gave an ear-splitting screech. Startled, the servant girl jumped, splashing hot water onto the table and on Jin's leg. They both yelped. One of the empress's attendants smacked the back of the girl's head with a folded fan.

"Look what you did, clumsy fool!" scolded Lady Opal. "You've burned the prince!"

The young girl flushed, her lip trembling. She dropped to her knees and pressed her head to the floor. "Forgive me, Your Brilliance."

Lady Opal smacked the girl again. "Clean up this mess! Your Brilliance, shall we ask the herbalist for a poultice?"

As the girl scrambled to wipe up the spilled water, Jin

blotted himself with a napkin. "No need. Most of it just hit my trousers without even touching the skin. I was taken by surprise, is all."

"Still, this is unacceptable." The lady-in-waiting was unsatisfied. She whirled on the servant. "You're new, aren't you? What's your name, girl?"

Her dimples long gone, the servant's wide eyes reminded Jin of a frightened deer. She stood mutely until Lady Opal clucked disapprovingly. "Bingyoo, my lady," the young girl whispered.

"Well, Bingyoo, you clearly haven't been trained properly. How the kitchen could send someone so green to serve Their Majesties is beyond me!" She glanced at the empress dowager, who merely sipped at her tea, watching in impassive silence. Puffing herself up like an angry hen, the attendant pointed at the hapless new servant. "Who's been training you? And for how long?"

Jin rolled his eyes. "It was just a little water. I'm fine. Nothing's broken, either. Can't we just have our tea without an interrogation?" Annoyed, he reached for a delicately fluted cucumber cup stuffed with minced shrimp and popped it in his mouth.

Nonplussed, Lady Opal's plump powdered face scrunched into dozens of folds. Then she bared her blackened teeth. "I suppose so, Your Brilliance," she simpered. Her smile vanished as she glared at the servant girl. "Well, what are you gawking at? Haven't you done enough?"

With a hasty bow, Bingyoo stepped back from the table with her empty tray. Bowing again with the other servants, she hurried out of the room.

"I'm sorry you had to endure such incompetence, Your Brillant Majesty," Lady Opal began.

"And not for the first time." The empress dowager put down her cup. "Leave us," she ordered her attendants. As Lady Opal glanced back at Jin, he made a mocking face. Snapping open her fan with a huff, she swept out of the room after the other ladies-in-waiting. Jin smirked, but sobered and sat up straight as his grandmother turned her attention to him. "Let's talk about what happened. Now, I expressly forbade you to waste time with the bestiary, did I not?"

Jin swallowed and started to answer at the same time. A bit of shrimp went down the wrong way, and he coughed violently. He could feel himself turning bright red as he fought to clear his throat. His grandmother wrinkled her nose in distaste. Finally, he could speak. "Yes, Grandmother." He bowed his head in contrition. "It was wrong of me—I have no excuse."

"I thought you said it was because you wanted to prepare for a monster of your own," she said dryly. "I'm well aware that your birthday will be coming soon." Her lips curved at the corners in a tiny smile.

His heart leaped. Maybe she finally saw that he was old enough to be taken seriously. "That's true, too, Grandmother," he said eagerly. "And I couldn't help but overhear the ministers telling you that they thought that I might go to Whisper Island to find a beast. Don't you think that's a good idea?"

"Mmm. Possibly."

Possibly? Jin beamed, ready to make his case and convince her. The dangling gilt flowers in her hair clinked as she tilted her head. "What were they talking about before I arrived in the salon?"

He stopped and frowned. Some of what the ministers discussed might set his grandmother off, especially the complaints about her being on the throne, and their fear of the empire's decline. They might be pompous and far too satisifed with themselves, especially that useless head Whisperer, but they at least seemed to understand the importance of him finding a monstermate. "They were worried about the borderlands," he said carefully. "They thought the people might rise up if taxes were raised. And uh . . . they said monsters were hard to find nowadays."

His grandmother's eyes grew keen. "I see. And what else?"

"I—I don't know. You came in right then."

"Ah." The empress dowager stabbed a glazed sour cherry with a bamboo skewer. Her mouth puckered as she chewed.

"Interesting as that is, you should not have been in there. Regardless of what the ministers think or said, *I* know what is best for you. Your focus should be on studying and preparing for your future."

"But doesn't studying the bestiary count?" protested Jin. "How else should I prepare for a monstermate? You've always said if I studied hard enough, one would appear as my reward. Well, I'm ready. Ask me about a creature, any creature, and I'll tell you about it."

"Only knowing about creatures is not enough," sniffed his grandmother. "A worthy ruler doesn't just have control of a monster. If that were the case, any Whisperer could rule the empire. No, you must learn about the administration of power, and what an empire needs. I should not have to repeat myself about it. As punishment, you are barred from attending the Monster Festival this year. You will remain at the palace for its duration, and write me an essay instead."

"An essay?" Jin stared at his grandmother in dismay. Just moments before, they had been talking about Whisper Island. The conversation had taken a terrible turn. "About what?"

The empress dowager raised an eyebrow and dabbed at a corner of her mouth with a linen napkin. "You could write about the Monster Festival." She picked up her pearl ball, looking pleased with herself, and began rolling it in her fingers again. "Include its history, and its importance to the people. You will learn something useful and pay the price for your disobedience at the same time." Her lips thinned. "And if you disobey me again, I will personally make sure that you wish you hadn't." Her monster bird screeched on its silver tree and snapped its serrated beak when the empress dowager tossed it a dumpling. "You may be excused."

Jin sat there, stunned. Then he swallowed hard. "Y-yes, Grandmother." He bowed deeply and hurried to leave her chambers before she could see his expression.

Silently seething, he strode through the halls of the palace. His jaw was clenched so tight, Jin could barely nod an acknowledgment as courtiers and servants bowed and greeted him. Not only was he now barred from looking at the bestiary, he was banned from attending the biggest festival of the year. To have to write an essay about it without going? "This is pure monstermuck," he muttered.

"Your Brilliance!" said Old Fang as Jin rounded a corner. "How was your tea?" His weathered face beamed cheerfully from below his snarling lion helmet. A veteran of many wars that had been waged by the empire, he had served under both Jin's grandfather and Jin's father before becoming the commander of the empress dowager's personal guard.

Jin scowled. "I was given my punishment for sneaking into the Diviners' Salon. No festival for me."

"Ah," said the Beaststalker knowingly. "Well, you know your grandmother doesn't take kindly to being disobeyed. At least you didn't have to kneel on uncooked rice while holding the bestiary over your head. That thing is so big it would crush you in an instant."

"Don't give her any ideas," warned Jin, but he cracked a half-hearted smile. "I feel like I'm getting a lot stronger, though. I've been working on my boxing form like you showed me." He stepped into a fighting stance, curling his hands into fists.

The grizzled guard gave him a critical once-over. "Shoulders down." He pushed at one fist. "Wrist straight and firm. Knuckles flat across, thumb tucked over the fingers, not inside them. You remember why?"

"So I won't break my thumb if I hit something. Someone." Savagely, Jin punched at an invisible foe.

"Good," grunted Old Fang. He reached into a leather pouch at his waist. "I was saving this for your birthday this year, but maybe it'll cheer you up now. Open your hand." He placed something hard and cool in Jin's outstretched palm.

Jin examined the small metal object, looped on a waxed black cord. "A padlock?"

"It's a lock charm forged out of sky metal—the iron that comes from fallen stars," said Old Fang. "Your father gave it to me long ago, after I got him out of a whisker of trouble. It's for luck and protection. To lock the bearer to this realm and guard them from death. I've just been waiting for the right moment to pass it on to you."

"This was from my father?" Jin stared at the lock in wonder. No bigger than his thumb, it was shaped like a dragon on a cloud, a straight metal shackle connecting the monster's head and tail.

The commander smiled. "He used to wear it himself when he was your age. It's quite old—I'm sure it's been in the family for a long time. It was a sign of gratitude when he gave it to me, but I think he'd be even more gratified if you wore it."

"Does it have a key?" Jin asked, pulling at the shackle and peering at what appeared to be tiny keyholes.

"I was never given one." Old Fang's eyes crinkled. "But if anyone can unlock it, I'm sure it's you."

With a grin, Jin reached into his pocket and pulled out a small silken envelope. Inside were thin metal pins that he and Old Fang had hammered flat. He tried to insert one into the lock, fumbling with the minute piece.

"Keep your touch gentle," coached the Beaststalker. "Nothing is ever truly locked, but broken locks can't be picked no matter how good your skills. Hmm. We might have to make some narrower picks."

A voice called out from behind him. "Commander Fang? May we speak to you?" Jin hastily stuffed the picks back in his pocket and peered over the commander's shoulder. The astrologer and the herbalist from the Bureau of Divination stood at the other end of the corridor. Upon spotting Jin, their faces seemed to sour, but they bowed deeply.

Jin acknowledged them with a sardonic wave. He thanked Old Fang, who excused himself before striding off to talk to the diviners. Jin turned aimlessly down another corridor and through a courtyard, not really watching where he was going, entranced by his new present. A weathered bronze color, it didn't look like much—not a speck of gold or inlaid gems anywhere. It just looked like an old beat-up lock. But that was exactly why he liked it. That, and the fact that his father had once worn it. "Luck and protection, eh?" he said out loud. "I could really use both." He stopped to put it around his neck. It didn't completely take away the sting of being forbidden from attending the Monster Festival, but he did feel better.

He looked up and noticed that he'd wandered halfway through a quiet garden. Before him stretched a winding walkway leading to the old palace menagerie, which had stood empty for decades. Whenever anyone caught him near the menagerie, he was quickly steered away, but no one was around now. "She didn't say I couldn't go *there*," Jin muttered, and made his way to the giant wooden gate, its once vibrant paint now peeling, an imposing iron padlock dangling from the doors. He reached for his lockpicks.

Inserting first one pin, then another into the lock's

keyhole, Jin pressed and wiggled until the padlock's thick shackle sprang free. Success! He was getting better and better at this. Triumphantly, he removed the lock. With a furtive glance around, he pulled open the doors, their hinges creaking in protest, and slipped through.

CHAPTER 3

THE PALACE MENAGERIE

AT FIRST GLANCE, THE MENAGERIE didn't look much different from other gardens on the imperial grounds. Jin followed its winding stone path, which surrounded a lake with a small tree-covered island in its center. Pavilions of varying sizes and shapes flanked the broad walkway, the late-morning sun gleaming off their curved tile roofs. Wooden tea houses stood at intervals, their fine latticed shutters closed to the elements. A man-made waterfall spilled over a rock formation and fed a meandering stream lined with irises. All appeared tranquil and still.

But on closer inspection, the pavilions were encased with iron bars and screens that obscured overturned feeding troughs and rotted straw within. They were cages, and the elaborate tea houses were abandoned outbuildings that had housed smaller creatures and supplies for monster care. More than a century ago, when most of the empire's surviving monsters were taken to an island sanctuary by skilled Whisperers, a collection of the most prized creatures was kept in a menagerie at the palace to remind people of the throne's power.

Now the fine wire mesh that tented the empty lake had gaping holes and was rusting. The trees on the islet, bushy and wild, poked their branches through the mesh. Overgrown weeds bordered the pathway, sprang up around the cages, and emerged from cracks between the stones.

Jin walked purposefully toward the far end of the walled garden, which he had yet to explore. He'd managed to sneak in a couple of times before, but it was so large that it was impossible to see everything in one visit, even with the creatures now gone. As he passed by each cage, he looked at the mounted signs that indicated what had been held within. The poisonfeather bird pavilion had a metal swing that creaked gently in the breeze, while the structure for lion-dogs had a giant old ball covered in teeth marks. The kirin pen was two stories tall, for while the most common kirin was said to be powerfully built like an ox, there were some varieties that were more deerlike, with impossibly long, thin necks. And of course, there were the antlers to contend with.

Seeing the doors ajar, Jin impulsively entered the pen. Peering up at the roof sheltering the structure, he saw a feeding ball, looking like an abandoned, rusty bird cage, mounted from the rafters for the long-necked kirin. What a sight such creatures must have been!

In his wanderings around the menagerie, he never tired of finding unusual features that had been installed. A massive splintering perch on the lake for the kunpeng, a winged fish monster that transformed into a fierce bird out of water. Heavy blocks of marble for dragon-headed turtles, which liked to carry them on their backs. The peaked roof and water-collecting system around an enormous crystalline tank for tiger-headed fish known as shachi, which had a tendency to summon rain clouds.

When he reached the stable for winged horses, he tried the door, its handle shaped like a pair of feathered wings. It opened easily, and when he went inside the multistory tower, he looked up the central shaft ringed with paddocks. Horses would fly to their stalls, while stairs winding along the walls allowed for their human handlers to walk back down. The stale air smelled faintly of old manure. He climbed the stairs and poked around the stalls, hoping to find a giant feather, reciting bestiary tidbits about the winged horse. "'Under the hand of a talented Whisperer, it can travel a thousand miles in a mere day.'" But try as Jin might, he couldn't find a single feather left behind.

Bong. Bong. Bong.

In the distance, bells chimed from the great water clock in the palace's central courtyard. "Muckety muck," Jin grumbled. It was time for afternoon studies with his tutor. If he didn't head back, people would start looking for him. He hurried out of the menagerie and snapped the heavy padlock back in place, then ran back toward the heart of the palace complex. As he skidded around a corner, he smacked straight into a servant carrying a towering stack of bamboo steamer baskets. They went flying, fresh steamed buns scattering everywhere, while Jin and the servant tumbled to the ground.

"Bungling beasts! Why don't you watch where you're going?" cried the servant, her voice indignant.

Dazed, Jin didn't answer, the wind knocked out of him. As a domed lid rolled and spun to a stop by his head, he lay on the floor, staring up at the ceiling. Muttering angrily, the servant began gathering the fallen baskets and their contents.

"Unbelievable. At this rate I'll be fed to that monster bird by nightfall. I already near scalded the prince. Crickety creatures . . . what's next? Hey—you going to lie there all day? Help me clean up. You made this mess!"

The servant picked up the lid by Jin's head. It was the new girl, Bingyoo. Her eyes met his. "Holy beasts," she gasped. "I didn't . . . I thought you were . . ." Scrambling to her hands and knees, she pressed her forehead to the ground. "Forgive me, Your Brilliance! I swear I'm not trying to kill you."

Jin burst out laughing. He pushed himself up. "Are you

sure about that?" he teased. But Bingyoo remained as if she were stuck to the floor, bowed and frozen in fear. He softened.

"I'm kidding. I know it was an accident. With making tea—and here too." He leaned over. "You're right, you know. I was running and wasn't paying attention. Please get up. It's all right, really."

Slowly, Bingyoo rose and looked about. "No, it's not." She bit her lip. "The cooks are going to boil my hide."

He picked up one of the steamed buns that had scattered across the ground. It was squashed and dirty, its filling oozing out. He shook his head. "This is probably why I'm not supposed to run through the halls. Here, I'll help you." As they gathered up stray baskets and fallen buns, Jin's mouth watered. They still smelled amazing. His stomach growled, loudly.

"Was that you?" asked Bingyoo.

He coughed in embarrassment. "I didn't actually eat much with my grandmother."

"I would offer you one of these if they weren't ruined." She wrung her hands. "These were supposed to be part of an offering ceremony at the Monster Festival tonight."

"Well, if that's the case, then I'm glad they're ruined," Jin said sourly. Then he saw her stricken expression and stopped himself. "I don't mean to get you in trouble. I'll send word to the kitchens that I caused the accident, if that helps."

She nodded, relief crossing her face. "Thank you, Your Brilliance."

"It's just . . . I've been looking forward to the festival, but now I'm not going." Jin sulked. "I've been ordered to stay in and study."

"But everyone gets to go—even us servants. You're the prince!" Bingyoo stared at him in surprise.

He shrugged. "I have to do as my grandmother says. The whole reason I can't go is because I disobeyed her."

"What a shame." Bingyoo's eyes were wide with sympathy. She picked up a lid knocked askew on a basket, and her dimples appeared. "Look! Here's one that survived!" She handed him an intact bun, warm and fragrant. "It's not as good as going to the Monster Festival, but at least you'll get a taste of it."

Right in the middle of the corridor, Jin plopped himself back down and bit hungrily into the soft, sweet bread. Savory juices from the minced meat-and-vegetable filling ran down his chin. "Thanks," he said, his mouth full. He devoured the bun in several bites, then wiped his face with the back of his sleeve and gave a satisfied sigh. "I needed that."

"Your Brillance!"

They swiveled at the sound of the voice. Jin's tutor waved from across the courtyard. He hurried over, his long, winged sleeves flapping. "There you are," said Master Sonsen. He blinked at the scene, his eyes owlish behind round spectacles. "Is everything all right? What happened here?"

As the servant girl began to stammer, Jin cut in. "I was on my way to see you, Master Sonsen. But I was late, so I started running and caused a big mess." He gave a cheerful shrug.

"Oh dear," said Master Sonsen. "The empress dowager won't like this."

Jin snorted with more bravado than he felt. "So don't tell her." He got up and brushed off his pants, smiling at Bingyoo as she hefted her stack of steamer baskets. "Listen, I'll send someone to the kitchens to explain. But if the cooks give you any grief, tell them to come to the library and I'll set them straight personally." Shyly, she bowed and hurried away. Jin turned to his tutor with a sigh. "All right. What fresh torture do you have for me today?"

Master Sonsen blinked and gave a nervous laugh. "I'll try to make it as painless as possible. I heard from the ministers about your run-in with your grandmother. If you wanted to look at the bestiary so badly, why didn't you tell me? We could have done a quick review together."

"It wouldn't be the same," muttered Jin. Glumly, he followed his tutor to the palace library. They settled in at a long table covered with scrolls and stacks of bound volumes, tall butter lamps throwing a golden light over it all. As Master Sonsen laid out writing brushes, tools for preparing ink, and sheets of rice paper, Jin propped his chin on his hands and stared morosely at his tutor. He had been Jin's primary instructor for several months now. A slight young man, sallow and pale from hours spent indoors poring over books, he was prone to nervous fiddling with the trailing ends of his scholar's sleeves and going on too long when lecturing on a subject. But if that was the worst of his qualities, then Jin couldn't really complain. His last tutor was a sour old man who didn't hesitate to whack Jin's knuckles with a bamboo pointer, crown prince or not.

"Now then," Master Sonsen began. "Let's talk about the Monster Festival. It takes place in late spring here in Shining Claw and signifies the start of the festival season."

"No kidding," said Jin crossly. Every week in the summer, towns and villages across the empire would hold their own local festivities, attracting visitors eager to partake in each one's unique celebrations, like the Cherry Festival, where there was a contest for spitting cherry pits, and the Mosquito Festival, where offerings were burned to the god of insects with great ceremony. This would protect everyone from bites. "I already know about all the festivals. The best and biggest is the one they're setting up just outside the palace gates—and I should be going."

His tutor pushed up his spectacles. "Yes, I heard. Which is why I thought we could work on your essay. It's all well and good to experience something, but there's value in reading about it too. If I may ask, how many times have you attended the Monster Festival?"

"I've gone since I was a baby, and I'm turning thirteen the season after next. Eleven, I guess?" said Jin. "This is the first year I'm missing." He glared at the tortoise-shaped ink-stone before him. "Blasted beasts. I can't believe this is my punishment." He sloshed some water into the shallow well in its back and snatched up a stick of pressed ink. He rubbed it furiously into the wet stone, so hard that his tutor cleared his throat.

"Are you trying to break that?" Master Sonsen asked with a titter. "I understand you're disappointed about the festival, but let's look on the bright side. The more you know about it, the more you'll appreciate it. You'll never look at the festival in the same way once you learn about the meaning behind it. Let me show you!" He flipped through some books excitedly till he found an illustration of a line of Whisperers marching up to the Palace of Monsters with beasts in tow. "The very first festival came about after a parade of monsters was brought to the new capital of Shining Claw to present to the emperor. It was because of these powerful beasts that Samtei was able to defeat its neighbors and establish the Empire of the Three Realms."

As Master Sonsen talked about the history of the festival celebrating the importance of monsters to the empire, Jin found he was listening in spite of himself. But as he followed his tutor's bamboo pointer from page to page, looking at all the drawings depicting festival traditions, Jin felt a spark of rebellion flare up. All that fun was beginning tonight, and he was being denied it only because he wanted to learn about the very monsters that this palace was named after. It was pointless and unfair, and he wasn't going to stand for it. He continued to nod and occasionally dipped his brush in ink as if he were taking notes, doodling a monster or two on the rice paper. But silently Jin plotted his next move.

The flame in the butter lamps began to sputter, and his tutor put down his pointer. He took off his spectacles and polished them with the tip of a winged sleeve. "I think that's our sign to stop. I'm sorry about you missing the festival, but I hope learning about it makes it seem less far away."

"That's one way to look at it." Jin stood up and stretched. "I guess I'll turn in early tonight. Work on my essay in my room."

"Why don't I request something special from the kitchens for your evening meal?" suggested Master Sonsen kindly. "Perhaps some roast peacock or lobster? We can eat together, if you'd like the company."

Jin shook his head. "I'm not that hungry," he lied. There were festival delicacies to look forward to, and no time to waste. Bidding his tutor good evening, he hurried back to his quarters.

To go unnoticed at the festival, he'd need to blend in with the crowd. Fortunately, he was already dressed in the clothes that his grandmother claimed made him look like a monk or a day laborer. He grabbed a jacket and a soft black cap to ward against any evening chill, and counted a string of coins into a drawstring purse before shoving it into a pocket. The first thing he was going to do when he got to the square was buy all his favorite festival sweets.

He set out across the grounds, trying to look as if he were just out for an evening stroll. The sun was sinking below the high stone walls of the palace, and dusk was fast approaching. Servants began lighting lanterns around the palace grounds, while other workers headed to the gates, finished with their duties for the day and talking excitedly about the festival, which began at sunset. Jin tugged his felt cap down and hunched his shoulders, trying to disappear into his coat. It was the plainest jacket he had, in a drab shade of gray, but the buttons and trim were silk, and fur lined the cuffs and collar. Nervously he tucked in the edges, hoping no one would notice in the fading light.

His excitement rose as he neared the palace's Dragon Gate, on the eastern side of the massive golden brick wall surrounding the palace complex. Closest to the kitchens and stables, it was designated for deliveries of food and other supplies, its bright blue doors attended by several palace guards bearing sharp tridents. In all his twelve years, he'd never walked through this gate—and certainly not off palace grounds by himself. Whenever he'd attended the

Monster Festival in the past, he'd always left through the main gate on the southern end of the palace, escorted by an entourage that would take him to a few approved locations. Everything outside the wall might as well be a foreign land. Oh, there were yearly trips to the Summer Palace in the mountain lake district when the heat of the capital grew too oppressive, but he'd always been in a palanquin or carriage, and he was never allowed to go anywhere on his own. If anyone saw him now, word would quickly spread through the palace, and his grandmother would order someone to stop him. He couldn't let that happen.

His eyes darted about. The men in front of him appeared slack and tired from their day of work, their shoulders stooped. Instinctively he lowered his chin and imitated their posture. The gate guards looked bored, shifting ever so slightly as palace groomsmen, gardeners, and other workers streamed past.

Another guard hurried up to the gate, the tall peacock feather adorning his helmet quivering. "You hear about the dead bird they found outside the western wall?" he asked one of the gate guards. "It had three legs!"

"Come now, it only looked like that because they mangled it with a bad shot," replied the gate guard with a snort. "No such thing as three-legged birds anymore."

The other gate guard sniggered. "How stupid are they at the Kirin Gate?"

As the guards guffawed, they never even glanced at Jin as he shuffled by in his plain clothes and simple cap, looking for all the world like another laborer. Once safely outside the palace walls, he allowed himself a triumphant grin, though it faded quickly as he turned around. Now where should he go?

Jin wandered away from the Dragon Gate and soon found himself in a warren of small alleyways and narrow lanes, crowded with people who jostled him as they squeezed past. Everyone was eager to go to the festival, it seemed. Shopkeepers were preparing to close for the day, sweeping clouds of dust out from their storefronts and shouting last-minute bargains. Overwhelmed, he gawked at the sights and wrinkled his nose at the pungent smells of sweat and garbage. A couple of ragged boys hanging about a doorway eyed him curiously, their faces drawn and sharp. Jin looked away and walked a little faster, trying to look like he knew where he was going.

Think, he told himself. The Monster Festival was in the city's great central square, which lay just before the main imperial gates. He only needed to follow the palace wall till he reached the square, right? But where was the wall? Jin tried retracing his steps, but everything looked the same to him. With every turn, he felt like he was going in circles. Finally, he caught a glimpse of the distinctive pale golden bricks, and his heart leaped. He had never been so glad to see that wall as he was then. Making his way to it through the throngs, he trailed alongside the moat ringing the stately barrier and realized that everyone around him was headed in the same direction. Rounding a corner, he saw the great square at last and gasped at the sight.

CHAPTER 4

THE MONSTER FESTIVAL

GIANT GLOWING CREATURES IN ALL sorts of vibrant colors—a green dragon, an orange phoenix, a turquoise kirin, a golden tortoise, a red winged lion—towered above the square. Made of paper and silk stretched over bamboo-and-wire frames, the uncanny beasts were lanterns the size of great buildings, and the people milling about looked like ants swarming at their feet. In every direction, stalls and tents of all shapes and sizes were set around a raised round platform of packed earth roped off in the center. Rows of paper lanterns overhead lit the night as bright as day. A broad avenue led away from the square into the rest of the city, and it was filled with men, women, and children all heading for the Monster Festival.

Shouts and laughter swirled around Jin, and a dozen different smells came at him at once. There was the smoky scent of grilling meat and burning charcoal, and a heady sweet perfume around a stall where a vendor was pulling strands of sugar into silky clouds of dragon's beard candy. The sizzle of savory flatcakes on an oiled metal sheet turned his head as he passed, and at another, batter was poured into molds shaped like kunpeng, with dabs of sweet bean paste tucked inside the fish-monster-shaped pancake.

His mouth watered. Though the palace kitchens produced delicacies far more refined than anything at the festival, none of it seemed half as enticing. He watched two scruffy street sweepers eating deep-fried, greasy sausages wrapped in dough, and reached in his pocket for his purse. But he was soon distracted by a stall selling skewers of toasted rice dumplings glazed with caramelized brown sugar, and bought a stick of those instead. Biting into the warm, chewy dumplings, he licked sticky syrup from his lips and fingers. The evening air was filled with laughter and chatter from the crowd. He strolled around the square, browsing the stalls selling trinkets and snacks, watched street performers entertaining small knots of people, and observed contests like cricket racing and tugs-of-war pitting a sleepy-looking ox against anyone who wanted to try resisting its pull.

When he'd attended the festival in the past, there'd been no wandering about by himself unnoticed. He'd never been alone in such crowds. But now, no one knew who he was, no one was watching him, no one was reacting to his presence by bowing or hurrying to clear his path. A grin spread across his face, the disappointments of the day forgotten. Already this was more fun than he'd had in a while.

A crowded stall caught his curiosity, and he stopped, craning his neck. "Capture a baby dragon turtle and you'll get to keep it," bellowed the vendor. "That is, if you can keep the strongest creature in the land from tearing your net to shreds." Jin peered over a shoulder and saw a shallow tank of water perched on a low table. Inside the tank, tiny ordinary pond turtles swam around like bobbing green plums. Several children were crouched beside the tank, holding small round paddles and bamboo cups. One small boy, his tongue sticking out in concentration, slid his paddle underneath a turtle and tried to scoop it into his cup. The paddle quickly disintegrated into nothing but a bamboo hoop and bits of wet paper, and the boy began to cry. "I want a dragon turtle!"

Across the way, a similar tank teemed with small bright flashes of movement. They were regular goldfish, but the hawker at the stall challenged people to capture one, claiming they were monster tigerfish with the ability to summon rain. "Get your own shachi! If you can catch one, you'll never be thirsty again!" Festivalgoers huddled over the edges of the tank with their cups and paper paddles at the ready, watching the fish swim by like hungry herons about to strike.

A quartet of boys and girls around Jin's age watched nearby. "These games are impossible," one girl commented.

"I've only seen someone scoop something up once, and I'm pretty sure they cheated."

"It's a great way to lose your money," agreed the other girl.

"No it's not," blurted Jin. "It's really quite easy."

They turned and looked at him, skeptical. The two boys they were with sniggered, but Jin was unfazed. He pointed. "It's all a matter of sliding the paddle in at an angle and doing it quick enough that the water doesn't rip through. I've done it lots of times."

"Prove it," said the first girl scornfully.

Raising his chin, he stepped up to the stall hawker. "I'll take a paddle and cup."

The stall hawker held out a callused palm. "I'll take your coin, then. One bronze eye."

Jin produced a short string of coins from his pocket. There was a surprised murmur from the girls, while one of the boys exclaimed. "Crickety creatures, that's a lot of cash!"

Self-consciously, Jin removed one, a thin bronze piece with a hole in its center, and handed it over to the stall worker. He was often given money by his grandmother but rarely had a reason to spend it. It never occurred to him that the dozens of coin strings and banknotes sitting in a lacquered box in his room were something unusual. He removed another coin and nodded at the first girl. "Want to give it a try?"

The girl shrugged. "Sure, if you're paying."

Jin gave the man the coin. The hawker placed cups and paper paddles in their hands, baring his uneven teeth in a ragged smile. "May you have the touch of the Whisperers!"

Crouching beside the tank, Jin watched the fish wriggling by. The girl knelt and dipped her cup into the water, preparing to flip a fish inside with her paddle, when the hawker barked at her. "The only thing that can touch the water is your paddle!" Startled, she raised her cup, splashing water on her paddle. It quickly disintegrated. "Blasted beasts," she fumed, standing up with a huff.

Bringing the edge of the cup as close to the water as he dared, Jin wiggled a finger as if it were a worm, but none of the fish seemed interested. He finally spotted a fish darting closer, and slid his paddle after its tail. Keeping his paddle angled, he gently nudged it behind the fish, then prepared to flip it into his cup. But as he lifted the paddle beneath the wriggling orange fish, a hole opened up in the wet paper and the fish fell back in with a plop. His onlookers jeered.

"So close," boomed the stall hawker. "Another coin for another paddle?"

"That's odd," Jin muttered. He'd always managed to catch things with a paper paddle before, and his paddle always stayed intact. Then again, as crown prince he'd never had to jostle with others at this game, and the vendors had always insisted on giving him what they called a "lucky" paddle.

"The 'lucky' paddles were *silk*!" exclaimed Jin in sudden realization. He looked up and saw the stall worker staring at him impatiently, while the girl and her companions had already turned away as if he were nobody. "Er, no thanks," Jin said to the man. He watched the little group of friends strolling off, teasing each other and walking arm in arm, and a spark of indignation flared. A part of him wanted to call out, "I'm Prince Jin!" An odd pang twinged in his chest. More than ever, he wished for a monster to call his own.

Feeling strangely deflated, he wandered about the festival grounds, the excitement of being there alone now gone. He idly approached one of the giant creature lanterns and was examining the domed shell of the golden tortoise up close when a low voice addressed him. "Your Brilliance? Is that you?"

Startled, Jin turned to see Bingyoo, the new servant girl from the palace. She sucked in a breath, blinking, and began to bow.

"Stop that!" Jin hissed. "Get up, or people will start looking." He yanked his felt cap down, pulling it low over his brow as she straightened.

"I'm sorry. Wh-what are you doing here?"

"What does it look like? I'm checking out the festival. You can't tell anyone that you saw me." Bingyoo nodded solemnly. Jin glanced about. "Are you here alone?"

"Not exactly," said Bingyoo. "The head cooks let us

go early for the festival, so I came with some of the other kitchen kids. But they all split off into little groups."

"And left you?"

She shrugged. "I'm new. Besides, I'm one of those whose families sold them off. It makes the others uncomfortable."

Jin didn't know what to say. "Well, seeing as we're each on our own, we might as well stick together for a bit."

"Yes, Your Brilliance," she said, bobbing automatically.

"No bowing! And don't call me that here!"

Biting her lip, Bingyoo gave a stiff nod.

Mollified, he relaxed. "If you promise not to bow, I'll buy you a snack. Have you had anything to eat yet?"

Her eyes brightened and her dimples appeared. "Not yet."

They set off for the food stalls but didn't go far before coming across a curious tent with a boldly painted banner. "'Bureau of Divination: Celestial Foresight and Fate Calculation,'" read Jin.

"Isn't there a bureau of divination at court?" Bingyoo ventured. "They're always asking the kitchens for food to be brought to their salon."

Jin snorted. "I believe it. But this booth's full of common street fortune-tellers—they're just using the name of the bureau to sound more important." He paused. "At least that's what I've been told. I've never actually been in one."

"Let's take a look," said Bingyoo, and ducked inside.

As he followed, Jin was hit with the powerful odor of incense. He wrinkled his nose against the thick smoky air and looked around the tented space, lit with rickety butter lamps with flames that sputtered against the shadows. There were several elderly men dressed in double-collared blue robes similar to the ones the diviners wore at the palace, only they were clearly of rough-spun hemp, the black collars shabby and faded. Each one was seated at a low table, their customers on short stools across from them. There was a reader peering at a man's palm and examining his facial features, poking and prodding at his nose and ears. An astronomer fiddled with a circular cosmic board that featured a sky map and a rotating plate, while another fortune-teller shook a battered bamboo cylinder filled with worn wooden divination sticks—a far cry from the jade one with gilded sticks at the palace.

"Come discover your fate, children," a creaky voice breathed in their ears.

They jumped and turned. Behind them stood a wizened old woman, her hair tied in a kerchief. Her sunken eyes peered at them from her doughy wrinkled face like fermented black beans in a pleated steamed bun. She motioned Jin and Bingyoo to her station just by the entrance and waddled to a rickety stool, where a flat box perched. Picking it up, she sat heavily on the stool and put the box on her lap. "Choose a monster—and find fortune in more ways than one."

Jin leaned in for a better look. The box was covered with a sheet of paper marked off in squares, each square numbered and brightly decorated with a picture of a different monster. Some of them had been punctured, revealing an empty compartment beneath the paper. He frowned. "So we pick a square and what happens? It might hold nothing?"

"Oh, there will be something," rasped the old woman. "For a bronze eye, you shall see."

"I've seen these before," said Bingyoo. "But I've never had the chance to try."

"You might not like what you find—or it may bring you boundless delight," the old woman told her. "That's where the fun lies, little chick. The unknown!"

Jin reached for his coins and counted out a couple into the old woman's papery palm. "All right—let's both get a monster fortune."

Bending down and squinting in the dim light, they examined the grid of monsters. "You go first," Jin told the servant girl.

Cheeks dimpling, Bingyoo pointed to a monster bird with brilliant green spiked feathers, marked with the number eight. "This one."

"Looks like a poisonfeather bird," Jin observed.

"That it is," said the fortune-teller. She waved Bingyoo closer. "Go ahead, give it a rip."

Gingerly poking a finger through the bird image, Bingyoo wriggled it aside. "Oh!" She pulled out a shiny piece of sugar-glazed apple wrapped with a folded slip of paper. Unfolding it, she looked up. "I can't read. What does this say?"

Jin peered at it. "A great deal of sweetness is in your future." He looked at the candy in her hand and grinned. "I guess it's not wrong."

"That's not a bad fortune," said the old woman. "The person before you got a piece of salt fish jerky and a prediction that he would be desperate for water."

Bingyoo giggled. "Now you try!" she urged Jin.

He scanned the grid of monsters, and his eyes landed on a majestic-looking dragon, its scales painted bright red and its beard and antlers tipped in gold. "Number 34."

"Go on, then," said the fortune-teller.

Decisively, he punched his fingers through the dragon. Jin felt around and pulled out a rough, pale pebble and a flat piece of metal no longer than his thumb. It was shaped like a curving snake, its surface cross-hatched to look like scales, with a hole where its eye would be. He stared. "What's this?"

"It's a firestarter!" said Bingyoo. "You strike the rock against the metal and get sparks. It's handy if there's no flame nearby."

"Don't forget the fortune," said the old woman. "That's the most important part."

Jin fished inside the compartment and found a folded bit of paper. Opening the fortune, he read, "'Fight the darkness with a light in hand.'" He looked at the steel snake and the chip of quartz in his palm. "Ha—I get it. Very funny."

"Oh, there's nothing funny about these," intoned the old woman. "What you've chosen is a sign of your future." She waggled a crooked finger. "But whether it's good or bad is up to you."

With a smirk, Jin nodded. The paper grid was clearly a child's game—the whole tent was. None of these fortune-tellers were real, he thought, looking at their cheap imitations of the palace diviners. He thanked the old woman, then turned to Bingyoo. "Let's go."

Ducking out of the tent, they emerged to find the festival busier than ever. Bingyoo nibbled at her candied apple. "Want some?" she offered.

Shaking his head, he studied the metal snake and pebble again and was tempted to toss them. They looked so ordinary. Besides, there was never a need to start a fire at the palace—lamps and braziers were everywhere. Experimentally, he struck the steel with the sharp rock. "This doesn't even work."

"I've used those," said Bingyoo. "Don't just bang them

together like that. Run the edge of the stone against the steel when you strike it."

Jin tried a few times again, with Bingyoo making corrections, until a small bloom of sparks appeared, flying harmlessly into the air like tiny fireworks. "Look at that!" Maybe they were worth hanging on to after all. He shoved them in his pocket, next to his lockpicks. "Where to next?"

In the distance came the sound of firecrackers and crashing cymbals. All around them, heads turned. Bingyoo's eyes lit up. "I think that's the Monster Parade!"

The crowd in the square surged toward the broad avenue that bisected the capital and led to the palace gates, eager to catch the approaching parade. Firecrackers sizzled in the evening air, and the clash of cymbals and pounding drums signaled that something big was coming.

Jin and Bingyoo hurried to watch. The street was already lined with spectators, and city guards patrolled up and down, shouting good-naturedly for people to make way. "Get back! If the dragon eats you, it's not our fault!"

Peering into the distance, Jin saw bobbing lanterns and a moving, shimmering swirl of color. Sparks and flashes went off with the crackle of fireworks, and glittery round shapes bounced up and down. As the parade drew closer, he saw they were giant lion-dog heads made of painted paper pulp covered in sequins, their mouths snapping open and shut, their bodies a wriggling tube of cloth. Each had two pairs of legs dancing the head and body about, and when one lion-dog head popped up and blinked coquettishly at the crowd with long tinsel eyelashes, Jin spotted the men operating the giant lion-dog puppet, one forming the lion-dog's body, the other holding the head. They danced toward the sidelines and opened the lion-dog's mouth as spectators "fed" the creature gifts of sweets and coins, which were collected in a bag inside the head.

A team of acrobats somersaulting and cartwheeling alongside the lion-dogs set up a course of towering ladders in the middle of the road. The lion-dogs leaped onto the laddertops, dancing back-and-forth as easily as if they were on solid ground. The acrobats then rolled giant balls into place, and the lion-dogs jumped onto them. Working their legs furiously to balance atop the balls, they rolled away to hearty applause and cheers.

The sound of drums and cymbals grew cacophonous as a group of musicians inched past, beating wheeled drums as they pushed them down the street, the cymbalists marching alongside them. Right behind the musicians was a dancer wearing a mask and carrying a round white lantern on a stick. Representing a Whisperer with a giant pearl, she danced before an enormous dragon head with fierce glowing eyes and flowing whiskers. Its scaled cloth body was as long as a city block, and dozens of legs ran in a snaking line behind the head. The dragon's mouth opened for a fearsome roar, and water sprayed out, to squeals and laughter from the ducking crowd. "It got me!" Jin chuckled, wiping his face.

"Me too . . . Oh, look at all the dragon dancers!" Bingyoo clapped her hands.

As the sinuous body undulated past, they caught sight of several sweating men beneath its heavy golden fabric, raising and lowering poles that propped up the dragon's body in time to the pounding drums and clashing cymbals. "Real Whisperers used to lead actual monsters through the streets to present to the emperor each year," Jin told her. "But as creatures became rarer and fewer Whisperers were needed, decoys and substitutions were made for the parade. A live magical beast hasn't been brought into the city for decades. I've been told my grandmother's monster bird was among the last ones."

A flock of phoenixes came floating through the air after the dragon. "Hers doesn't look anything like these," said Bingyoo. Made of paper pulp and feathers, they were attached to bamboo poles carried by a group of young women, who swung the poles about and made their phoenix puppets swoop around and around in a bright blur of color. Several children nearby laughed and reached up as the puppets' tails of long feathery streamers swept over their heads.

"These are a lot less ragged looking," Jin observed. "And they won't try to take off your hand."

Bingyoo nodded. "Or deafen you."

More fantastical creatures followed, either as giant puppets or as dancers carrying masks of wood pulp. There were kirins, winged lions, and fierce-faced shachi that were a far cry from the goldfish he'd tried to scoop up with a paper paddle.

The crack of a whip turned heads. Brightly decorated oxcarts, laden with cages, rattled over the paving stones of the broad thoroughfare. As the carts rumbled past, the animals in the cages were on full display: scarred dogs with stubs for ears, large roosters with metal spurs on their feet, rams with thick curled horns, stocky horses emitting piercing neighs, grim-faced monkeys staring blankly through the bars, a giant boar with long tusks. There was even a bear, its fur patchy and matted around the metal collar at its neck. Excited chatter spread through the crowd.

"The competitors are here!"

"Look, the fighters!"

"Here they come! I wagered all my money on last year's champion."

Bingyoo looked over at Jin in dismay. "I don't like this."

"What, the Monster Fights?" He frowned. "They're the highlight of the festival, even if uncanny beasts are so hard to come by that they're staged with ordinary animals now. People raise them especially for this event."

"Well, I think it's cruel," said Bingyoo. "Ordinary or not,

why should they be hurt for people's entertainment?"

He opened his mouth, then closed it. He'd never really thought about it that way before. The last of the carts passed, and then the crowd surged around them, following the procession. Jostling and pushing, Jin and Bingyoo fought to stay upright and together.

"I don't want to see the fights!" she said, dread crossing her face.

"I don't think we have a choice," shouted Jin, and they were swept along with the rest of the spectators to the main square.

CHAPTER 5

THE MONSTER FIGHTS

THE MONSTER FIGHTS WERE ONCE a great show demonstrating the powers possessed by creatures of the in between. Each year, after the parade of monsters through the capital, a few were made to fight before the citizens of the Three Realms and their emperor. Dragons against dragons, or a winged lion against a horned one, it was a spectacular show that awed all who witnessed it, and the stories of the empire's control over the mighty creatures spread far and wide.

Now ordinary animal fights had taken their place, as a way to honor the legendary monsters that had led their empire to victory in the past. Throughout the land, beasts great and small were made to fight by their masters, to the enjoyment of many. Even children would capture crickets or beetles and pit them against each other. A saying became popular: "If you can handle a beastie of any sort, then the blood of Whisperers runs in your veins." Over the years, as prize money and betting on winners became popular, the fights had become deadly, with animals bred and trained specifically for viciousness. At the Monster Festival, they were brought from all over Samtei for the biggest contest in the empire. Dozens of matchups were scheduled, and the tournament now spanned the entire festival.

In the past, Jin had only been allowed to watch matches from a distance, sitting sedately in the tower above the main palace gates. But even from afar, the energy of the teeming crowds had been unforgettable. Now, among the people who rushed to secure seats with an open view of the ring, the feeling was irresistible—excitement zinged through his bones.

"Let's not stay," Bingyoo begged as they reached the square. "They're too horrible to watch."

But the crowd pressed them forward, and Jin was transfixed as handlers in heavy gloves and thickly padded jackets began moving the cages into place around the raised earthen platform where the animals would face off. He'd read plenty about the true monster fights of old, and was well aware of which creatures were the best fighters, which beasts you wanted at your command, which monsters could turn lethal when cornered. This scarred, ragged collection of farm and forest animals hardly compared, but the thrill of the gathering throngs was hard to resist. "Just one match," he suggested. "I've never seen it from this close before."

The servant girl looked miserable. "Yes, Your Brilliance," she murmured.

Jin flinched at hearing her use his royal address, but a quick look around set him at ease. Everyone's attention was fixed on the fighting ring, where a man in acid-green robes held a loud-speaking horn in one hand and a brightly painted paddle in another. He raised his paddle, and quiet fell over the assembled.

"Welcome to the Monster Fights!" he bellowed through the horn, and the crowd roared back. He chuckled, sending his extravagantly embellished hat aquiver. The ringmaster was supposed to represent a Whisperer in the Bureau of Divination, though he was in far gaudier costume. "We have a great many competitors this year, but only one will be named the Imperial Monstermate! Are you ready to see battle?"

Hoots and shouts of approval rang through the evening air. The robed man did a little stomping dance and raised his paddle with a flourish, signaling the start of the fights. They began with smaller animals first, pitting pairs of gamecocks against each other, then monkeys, then dogs. The animals were set loose on each other, prodded by their trainers, and would fight until one either ran away or dropped from its injuries. The ringmaster would throw up his paddle with a verdict, and the masses would give a frenzied cheer. Seeing it up close, Jin felt a strange pit form in his stomach. Some of the matchups were especially hard to watch, like a small squat dog against a giant lizard that took off the dog's tail before the dog managed to clamp its jaws on the lizard's throat, and the match was called for the dog. The packed earth of the ring became dark and slick with blood, and more than once, Jin had to shut his eyes. With the crush of people all around, screaming and yelling, it was hard to breathe. Their feverish delight in exhausted, desperate animals tearing each other apart made him queasy.

Glancing over, he saw that Bingyoo's eyes were fixed firmly on the ground, her head bent so low that her chin was nearly on her chest. Jin nudged her. "You were right. Want to get out of here?"

A burly man beside them overheard and gave a hearty laugh. "Bored already, are you? Come back for the final fight! That's when the biggest animals are in the ring—there was an elephant once. Pity there's only a bear this year. But don't worry, the carnage is always spectacular."

"Spectacular?" Bingyoo fumed. "More like spectacularly cruel. Those poor animals are killing each other, and you think it's fun!" She spun on her heel and began pushing and squeezing though the throngs of people around the earthen platform.

"Wait!" Jin followed, trying to keep her in sight. He

wriggled out of the crowd just as two rams began charging at each other, cracking their horns together with a sickening crash.

He saw Bingyoo heading back in the direction of the palace, only to stop short by the carts that had brought the animals to the square. He caught up with her to find that the carts weren't empty. Some cages, holding the survivors of earlier fights, had been loaded back onto the carts. "Oh, you poor thing," said Bingyoo, peering into a bamboo cage that held a potbellied pig with a gash across its back. The next cage over had a listless badger, its striped face streaked with blood.

"It was a lot harder to watch up close," Jin confessed. He uneasily eyed a cage holding a lizard, which tasted the air with a forked tongue, and then a cage where a giant python was coiled in a pile of glistening scales, patterned in striking patches of brown and black. Its body bulged with the swallowed remains of its opponent, and he shuddered, remembering the hapless crocodile.

Bingyoo looked around, then reached out and unlatched the door of the pig's cage. "There you go," she crooned.

"What do you think you're doing?" Jin clapped a hand on the door.

The servant girl glared. "Freeing him. He shouldn't be locked up for a life like this." She pulled the door open and beckoned the pig out, then opened the door to a cage where a forlorn monkey sat licking a wound on its arm. It stared at the open door, while Bingyoo moved on to another cage. "Are you going to help me or not?"

The crowd roared, and Jin heard the terrible scream of a wounded ram. It made his gut clench. He ran to the next cart and found that the cages there were padlocked. He pulled out his lockpicks and poked one into a keyhole, jimmying the lock until it clicked free. In triumph, he swung the door open for a small dog with a bleeding tail stump and helped it to the ground. Fast as he could, Jin picked every lock he got his hands on, while Bingyoo removed them and opened the doors. Animals began to climb out, leaping off the carts, crawling down, trotting off. The cages were emptying.

"Run, little one, run!" cried Bingyoo as she opened the door for a bleating goat.

Jin ducked as a fierce-looking gamecock emerged with a flurry of flapping wings. "Find your freedom!" he shouted.

They grinned at each other, then kept on working.

As the liberated animals dispersed through the square, startled shouts and frightened screams rang out. It wasn't long before several animal trainers raced up, followed by half a dozen city guards, surrounding Jin and Bingyoo. The trainers brandished the long hooks they used to corral their animals, while the guards had their truncheons drawn. "Stop right there!"

Strong hands grabbed Jin, knocking him off his feet. He

struggled to regain his balance, but the armed guards on either side of him didn't seem to care as they dragged him and Bingyoo away from the carts holding the animals for the Monster Fights. The last few bedraggled beasts staggered off from their cages while the rest of the freed animals ran through the square, terrorizing festivalgoers.

"Ow!" cried Bingyoo. She was in the grip of a guard squeezing both her arms behind her. "You're hurting me!" Eyes wide with fear and indignation, she kicked and stomped on his feet, trying to free herself.

As they neared the north edge of the festival grounds, the palace gate tower looming overhead, Master Sonsen ran up, his long sleeves fluttering like wings. "Stop!" In the nick of time, he dodged a fleeing boar barreling by, flailing his arms and knocking his scholar's hat down over his face. He pushed the hat back, revealing a furious expression. "Take your hands off him—that is the crown prince!"

"Right, and I'm the empress dowager," said one of the guards with a sneer, tightening his hold on Jin's arm. The other guards laughed, and Master Sonsen shook his head.

"This is no joke, sirs. I am the royal tutor, and that is Prince Jin that you're mishandling. If you don't believe me, perhaps Empress Soro will persuade you, on pain of your death." He pointed to the gate tower. Jin saw with horror his grandmother seated on an overlooking balcony, surrounded by her attendants and several of her top ministers. She was wearing her elaborate phoenix crown, unmistakable even from a distance. How could he have forgotten that she'd be watching the Monster Fights? He ducked his head, praying that she hadn't recognized him.

The guards exchanged an uneasy glance. Their grips slackened as they looked uncertainly at Jin. He wrenched himself free and straightened his clothes before turning to the man holding Bingyoo. "Let her go," he ordered imperiously. "She's with the palace too."

The man hesitated, peering at Jin, then at his fellow guards. With a shrug, he pushed Bingyoo away. She stumbled, and Jin caught her.

"Are you all right?" he asked.

She nodded and winced as she rolled her shoulders. Master Sonsen hurried to them, his face pale. "Your Brilliance! You're not supposed to be here! What in the realms have you done?"

"We were trying to help," said Jin.

Several palace guards emerged from the gate and walked over, trident spears in hand. One of them wore two feathers in his helmet, signifying his higher rank. "What seems to be the problem, Master Sonsen?"

The tutor pointed at the city guards, then nodded at Jin. "Please inform these men about the esteemed person they've roughed up here."

The palace guard lieutenant peered at Jin, then made a

strangled sound. He turned on the men angrily. "What did you do to the crown prince?"

Looking stricken, the guards fell to their knees and pressed their foreheads to the ground. "Forgive us, Your Brilliance."

A small crowd had gathered, and when they saw the guards bow, a gasp rippled through them and they began following suit. Jin groaned. So much for being in disguise.

"Your grandmother will be furious," fretted his tutor.

Jin bit his lip. "Has she seen me?"

Incredulous, Master Sonsen swept an arm around the festival grounds. The freed animals were running amok, and the area around the fight platform was full of chaos. Several handlers ran after the bear, which lumbered purposefully toward the food stalls while people screamed and darted out of the way. "Do you think she *didn't* notice?"

Unable to answer, Jin looked down and scuffed a toe against the stone pavers of the square.

"The gods help me, this will be laid at my feet," muttered Master Sonsen. He sighed. "We'd better face the empress dowager straightaway." His voice cracked a little, and he swallowed. "The longer we wait, the worse it will be."

Jin nodded glumly. Nothing good lay ahead, but there was no avoiding it now. He left the circle of prostrating guards and spectators, and as he trudged out of the square, festivalgoers stopped what they were doing and bowed low as he went past. Even the animal handlers chasing after the wayward animals paused to pay their respects. Clearly he was no longer anonymous. He felt his face flush at all the eyes upon him, and heard whispered snatches of commentary.

"Wait, who's that?"

"It's Crown Prince Jin—keep your head down!"

"Why's he dressed like a common laborer?"

He longed to pull his hat down over his eyes and hide, but Jin squared his shoulders and raised his chin. He leveled his gaze at the main entrance to the palace grounds, the Phoenix Gate. It loomed before him like a standing giant, the crimson doors swung wide open to allow courtiers and palace attendants to enjoy the delights of the festival. But as the escaped animals raced around the square, the guards at the entrance rushed to shut the gate, pushing and pulling the double doors closed, five men to a side. They halted long enough to let Jin and Bingyoo slip through, followed by the palace guards and Master Sonsen.

As the doors shut behind them, the chaos and cacophony of the square were immediately muffled, and the stillness of the palace grounds at night swallowed them like the eye of a storm. Old Fang was waiting for them at the base of the gate tower. He approached Master Sonsen, and they conferred in hushed tones, grim-faced. The Beaststalker nodded and turned to the palace guard lieutenant. "Take them to the

Hall of the Jade Haitai."

"Wait in the throne room," Master Sonsen instructed Jin and Bingyoo. "I'll have to report to your grandmother first." He hurried off after the commander, who was climbing the steps of the gate tower to where the empress dowager and her courtiers were watching the Monster Fights.

There were thousands of rooms and hundreds of structures in the palace complex, and as Jin and Bingyoo were escorted across the grounds, it felt as if they were being paraded past every single building. Ceramic monster figures stood guard on their gabled rooftops, glistening in the moonlight, their mouths open wide as if they were laughing at Jin. He slumped as they neared the central part of the palace, dragging his feet through manicured gardens, courtyards, and lacquered colonnades in silence.

A small sniffle beside him made him look over. Bingyoo was wringing the edge of her smock, her eyes bright with unshed tears. "Don't cry," he told her. "I'll tell Grandmother it's all my fault. I was the one who unlocked all the cages."

"That won't make a difference," she whispered. "You're the crown prince. You'll never be punished like me."

"That's what you think," Jin said. "I've been whipped plenty of times."

Her tears spilled over. "That's even worse. If *you* can be whipped, then they'll just kill me!"

"I won't let them," Jin promised. "Like you said, I'm crown

prince. I do have *some* standing around here."

She wiped a sleeve across her face. "I'll believe it when I see it."

He gave her a reassuring smile. "Don't be scared."

But when they reached the Hall of the Jade Haitai, Bingyoo looked no less terrified, her red-rimmed eyes wide. Here was where the most serious business of the empire was conducted, including the handing down of verdicts for criminals. They halted by the entrance flanked by two enormous haitai, scaly unicorns said to impose justice by skewering evil men with their horns. Carved from green nephrite and gilded, they stared down at Jin impassively. While the guards opened the doors, he sagged for a moment against one, feeling the cool stone against his cheek, a knot in his stomach. Everyone dreaded the empress dowager, but only Jin had to face her disappointment as her grandson.

They entered the throne room where his grandmother held court. It was empty and nearly pitch dark with decorated panels over the latticed paper windows. The only light came from the coals of a brazier, as everyone had retired for the day and was either at the festival or their own quarters. Automatically Bingyoo took a flame from the coals and lit the butter lamps. Their glow spread across the great hall and bounced off the golden columns and gilt lacquered ceiling, and the dragon scales inlaid in the window panels glittered in the light. The old monster nooks and perches built into the walls and rafters still gleamed as if new, though there was only one creature left to use them.

Nervously Jin leaned against the edge of the high platform supporting the Triad Throne. It was a splendidly carved chair, so wide that it was nearly a couch, covered in thick silk cushions embroidered with swirling patterns of dragons, phoenixes, and kirins. A matching three-paneled screen behind it concealed a nesting area for the emperor's monster. Jin had always wondered what that hidden area looked like, but he'd never been allowed back there. He was about to take a closer look when a screech sounded and the phoenix flew through the doors. The empress dowager swept into the hall, followed by her attendants, a passel of ministers, Master Sonsen, and a retinue of Beaststalkers, Old Fang at the head.

Bingyoo bowed low, and Jin scrambled to follow suit. They held their positions as his grandmother mounted the platform, assisted by her ladies-in-waiting, while her phoenix swooped onto a perch nearby and began picking at its feathers. In agonized silence, they waited for the empress dowager to speak.

CHAPTER 6

GRANDMOTHER'S WRATH

BEFORE THE TRIAD THRONE, JIN knelt with his head bowed, feeling his grandmother's disapproving gaze burning a hole in the top of his head. He scarcely dared to breathe.

"Sit up." The empress dowager's voice was sharp as an icicle, and her eyes were glittering shards of obsidian, even darker than her teeth. "Commander Fang and Master Sonsen briefed me, but I saw enough for myself. There are no words for how appalled I am, Prince Jin. Openly disobeying my orders not just once, but twice—in one day! Going outside the grounds without proper escort!" She stared pointedly at the head Beaststalker, and Master Sonsen, who twisted his sleeves with a miserable expression, while Old Fang's jaw tightened. The empress dowager's lips thinned. "And not only were you forbidden to go to the festival, but you and this servant girl caused utter havoc! There hasn't been a security breach of that sort in years!" Bingyoo let out a whimper and swallowed it when the empress dowager cut her a look.

Jin tried to explain. "The animals in the Monster Fights were suffering. They're not real monsters, they're just ordinary beasts. They aren't meant to fight like that. We—I was just trying to help them."

"Help?" The nine phoenix feathers adorning his grandmother's crown quivered. "You endangered citizens of the capital! The festival grounds have been upended, and people were hurt by rampaging beasts."

"But it's not the animals' fault—they were being tortured," protested Jin.

"Your Brilliant Majesty, if I may say something to that," injected the head Whisperer. The clawmarks the phoenix had left on his face had been patched up and he had changed out of his blood-stained robes, but he still looked rather beat-up. The empress dowager waved permission at the minister, her fingers covered in ceremonial gold nailguards that resembled claws. He bowed and addressed Jin. "Creatures of the in between are no longer readily available, so we must make do with what we can. Torture is a rather negative term, Your Brilliance—we prefer to say it's a sacrifice."

"An ennobling sacrifice," intoned the treasury minister, a well-fed man with a florid face. "The sacrifice of the ordinary makes them extraordinary. And sacrifice is needed for the good of the empire."

"Indeed!" chimed in the herbalist, stroking his beard. "Without things like the Monster Fights, the people will be unhappy."

"It's all just a distraction." Jin felt a flare of temper. "That can't work for long. People are already unhappy. You diviners said as much today."

The ladies-in-waiting gasped and fluttered their fans anxiously, while the divination ministers blanched. "Surely you misheard," blustered the herbalist.

A muscle by his grandmother's eye twitched. She raised a hand and clicked her long jeweled claws together. The phoenix flew obediently from its gilded perch to the arm of the throne. There was a deadly quiet as she stroked her monster bird's head. Its golden eyes fixed unblinkingly on Jin, as if it wanted to fly off the throne and strike.

"What do you know of discipline, of control, of *distraction*? Effective rulers must have all such tools at their disposal." His grandmother's voice was even. "I thought I'd give you another chance this morning, after you couldn't even follow the simple direction to keep away from the imperial bestiary. But then you chose to defy me once more, while your tutor did nothing to stop you. Pity—I thought this new young scholar might be a good influence." Master Sonsen's sallow face seemed to turn a distinct greenish hue, though he moved not a muscle.

Jin shook his head. "Don't blame him—it's not like he

knows what I'm doing all the time."

The empress dowager leaned forward and peered at Bingyoo. "Aren't you supposed to be in the kitchens? What made you think you could follow the crown prince around?"

"Forgive me, Your Brilliant Majesty," squeaked Bingyoo, trembling. "I never meant to."

"She did nothing wrong," Jin insisted. "I made her stick with me because I didn't want her telling anyone she'd spotted me."

"So you admit to your mischief." His grandmother sat back and rubbed her phoenix's beak. "I'd thought that forbidding you from the festival would be an effective punishment." She turned to her ministers. "How are we to get through to him?"

The ministers practically fell over themselves to advise the empress dowager. Jin scowled as one by one, they weighed in importantly with suggestions.

"Perhaps he should wrestle with some of the animals from the Monster Fights, madam. That might well serve instead of tracking down a monstermate."

"Your Brilliant Majesty, allow us geomancers to reconfigure the furniture in our young master's quarters according to the principles of directed energy. It shall curb Prince Jin's restlessness at once."

"May I concoct a daily elixir to increase his concentration, my lady? Also a change in diet—more fiber would surely do him good."

"None of that would be enough," she said wearily. "I should have just ordered a whipping." Jin swallowed hard and bowed his head, waiting for her to announce the number of lashes. He dreaded being caned, but if it spared the others, then he would grit his teeth and bear it.

But the empress dowager continued. "It's clear you are woefully inadequate for what lies ahead, Jin. I've always suspected it. All your life you've run wild, dressed like a commoner, failed in your studies, shown no great talent. I admit I considered the ministers' recommendation to send you to Whisper Island, but I see now you can't possibly go."

His head snapped up. "But I'll be thirteen soon. I'm supposed to have my own creature by then, and it's the last place in the empire with any creatures at all. You keep saying to prepare for the throne, but the most important part is having a monster. No ruler of the Three Realms has been without one!"

"It's far more than that," his grandmother shot back. "How many times have I told you? *Nothing* in life is for certain. Not even for emperors. That is what you prepare for. You've not been listening—and you clearly won't until you stop daydreaming about monsters. There will be no going to

Whisper Island, perhaps not ever, if you can't demonstrate proper readiness."

Jin was incredulous. "Are you saying I'll never be crowned?"

"Just because you expect something doesn't mean you'll get it," the empress dowager retorted. "You must earn your place. Unless you do as you're told and prove worthy of your title, you have no privileges. Fall short again, and you will be stripped from succession and banished from the palace."

It felt as if the ground was shifting, sinking beneath him. He threw himself facedown, forehead pressed to the floor. "Please, Grandmother. Beat me for thirty days straight if you must, but give me another chance. I can improve my scores, I promise. I'll study and stay away from the bestiary and do whatever you say. Just let me go to Whisper Island, please."

But the empress dowager was unmoved. She picked up her scepter, the jeweled trident. "In the name of the Beast of Righteousness, judgment is rendered." She pointed the three sharp tines at Jin and invoked the words traditionally uttered whenever a sentence was handed down over a crime. "In accordance with the laws of the Three Realms, the Hai-tai has decided."

No one else spoke up to defend him. Not that anyone could. As he looked at his grandmother's attendants hiding their smirks behind their fans, the portentous ministers gravely stroking their beards, ashen-faced Master Sonsen and Bingyoo, and the stoic Beaststalkers standing at attention by the Triad Throne, Jin felt utterly alone.

After the festival, the Palace of Monsters seemed even quieter and gloomier than usual. Jin was confined to his chambers at first, not even allowed to go beyond their doors. While his spacious quarters had multiple rooms and their own garden, he'd always been free to explore the palace grounds. Now, despite his luxurious surroundings, he was trapped.

Each morning, he was made to kneel on stony ground for half an hour with a heavy textbook above his head. Every time his arms began to wobble and sag, Master Sonsen would whack him with a pointer, though not before warning him. "Apologies, Your Brilliance," he would whisper to Jin before bringing down the thin bamboo stick. Gritting his teeth, Jin would raise the book high again, almost wishing he'd gotten a caning instead. Those were over faster.

He was allowed to go to the library for lessons with his tutor, but there was always an observer from one of the ministries there, keeping an eye on them both. If he wasn't in the library studying, he was forbidden to roam the rest of the palace as he usually did. Instead, he was escorted to his quarters by a rotation of guards keeping watch outside his doors. He was brought perfectly sumptuous meals from the kitchens, but never by Bingyoo. Whenever Jin asked about her, the servants would shake their heads, reluctant to speak. It was as if she'd ceased to exist. "Is she okay, at least?" he'd prod, desperate to know, but they would only shrug and hastily back away, leaving him to contemplate an array of covered dishes, his appetite gone.

His grandmother kept busy presiding in the throne room, huddling with her ministers, receiving petitioners or being entertained by courtiers who kept pet birds in imitation of the empress dowager with her phoenix. It was as if she'd forgotten about him entirely. Jin began to despair. His knees were badly bruised, and his arms and shoulders were horribly sore. In addition to that torture, being shut in, unable to go out as he pleased, see a friendly face, or talk to anyone freely was maddening. When would it all end? Just a week of it felt interminable. To make matters worse, he had to dress in proper court clothes and could no longer wear the simple rough-spun trousers and tunics he preferred. In his bright silks and embellished robes, he felt constricted and highly visible, as if he were on display, and he hated it. But he did all that was ordered of him without complaint, hoping that the empress dowager would eventually change her mind.

One day, as Jin was on his way back from the library after yet another long droning session on mining methods and iron ore extraction, Bingyoo appeared in the corridor outside his rooms, carrying a large covered basket. His heart leaped. Jin hadn't seen her since the night of the festival.

"Bingyoo!" he shouted. As he hurried toward her, trailed by his usual guard escort, she bent low in a respectful bow.

"Your Brilliance." She straightened up with a mysterious look of excitement on her face. "I've brought some fresh linens and was going to fetch your laundry."

Jin gestured for her to go into his quarters. "Go right in. I have some things that need to be cleaned." He stepped through the doors and shut them firmly behind him, leaving the guards to stand outside as always. "How have you been? No one ever tells me anything when I ask about you. I'm sorry about that night of the festival . . ."

"That's exactly why I'm here," Bingyoo interrupted. "Look who showed up on the grounds!" She set down the basket and pulled back the covering. A small head popped out. "A refugee from the Monster Fights!"

"Crickety creatures!" exclaimed Jin. "I remember you!" It was the dog—the one that had barely survived being lizard bait. Its broad face was surrounded by a ruff of golden-brown fur reminiscent of a lion. Jin stretched out a hand, and its short flat nose sniffed it. The tail that had been mauled in its fight was now a neatly bandaged stump, which began to wag. Jin stroked the dog's head and scratched carefully behind its black-tipped ears, which were folded like little purses and scarred from all the fights it had been in. "Where in the realms did you find it?"

Bingyoo grinned. "I went to throw out some scraps from the kitchens and found this little one hiding by the refuse heap. Best as I can tell, she'd sneaked in the night of the festival, because her wounds were still fresh, and she was scavenging food. But she was in terrible shape. Commander Fang helped me clean her up—we had to remove the mangled part of her tail."

The dog made to climb out of the basket, and Jin lifted it out. It wriggled in his arms and licked his face. It was so small that it could easily hide in one of Master Sonsen's long sleeves. Despite its size, its body was muscular and stout. "Little but strong," Jin said. "You're a big lion in a tiny dog." He put it down, and the dog began to explore its surroundings. It spotted a stuffed monster toy that had fallen to the ground. Made of brightly colored damask stitched with gold, it was a miniature baku, or dreameater, with a long floppy nose like an elephant, and nearly the same size as the dog. The dog's hackles rose, and it lunged at the stuffed baku with a growl.

"No, no—that's not for fighting," said Jin quickly, and snatched it away from the dog's jaws. Bakus were said to defend against nightmares, and Jin had slept with this toy since he was a baby. He set the stuffed dreameater carefully on a pillow, and the dog continued investigating the room.

"So what are you going to do with her?" asked Bingyoo.

"Me?" Jin turned in surprise. "You're not keeping her?"

"I think she came looking for you," said Bingyoo, her

dimples deepening. "You freed her, after all."

Jin looked at the dog sniffing in a corner. It squatted, and a small puddle began to spread on the floor. He chuckled. "Looks like she's making herself comfortable already." Bingyoo let out a cry of dismay and hurried over to wipe it up. He followed and picked up the dog. It snuffled happily and wagged its stump. "Well, no one, least of all my grandmother, ever said I couldn't keep a regular beast as a companion."

Bingyoo gathered up the soiled cloths she'd used to clean up the dog's mess, along with some of Jin's laundry, and smiled at them both. "It's settled then. What are you going to call her?"

The dog sat back and scratched at the thick ruff around its neck. If Jin squinted, it almost resembled the lion-dogs in the parade. He grinned. "Shishi."

They soon became inseparable. No one dared take Shishi away from him, and while his grandmother hated dogs, Jin never saw her anyway. Master Sonsen convinced the empress dowager that the dog would take her grandson's mind off finding a monster. Shishi accompanied him to the library for his studies and napped at his feet or gnawed on bones that Bingyoo brought from the kitchens. While Jin was still forbidden to go near the bestiary or the abandoned menagerie, he was allowed in the small garden adjoining his quarters and took Shishi there regularly.

The dog proved to be quite smart, quickly learning not to relieve itself indoors and performing tricks that Jin taught it. "Do the lion-dog dance!" Jin would order, and it would rear up and turn in a circle, its stumpy tail wagging all the way. "Greet the empress dowager!" he'd tell Shishi, and she would lower her front half in a bow. "Give me some gold!" he'd say with a palm extended, and the dog would place a paw in his hand.

For the first time in memory, he felt less alone, thanks to the little lion dog. It lessened the sting of his confinement somewhat, and made it easier to ignore the tittering whispers from attendants and courtiers when he passed by. But then the otherworldly screech of his grandmother's phoenix would echo through the halls, and a stab of longing would strike him. If only he were allowed to go to Whisper Island. As good a companion as Shishi was, she was no creature of the in between. Jin would never become emperor with an ordinary dog at his side.

CHAPTER 7

HATCHING PLANS

AS THE WEEKS WENT BY, the stultifying heat of summer settled over the capital like a thick blanket. Jin no longer had to start his day with the punishment of kneeling while holding a heavy book overhead, but his time was taken up with lessons, with hardly a friendly face around, save for his dog. Though he was surrounded by guards, he never got to see Old Fang's grizzled smile among them. Bingyoo was kept toiling in the kitchen, not permitted to bring Jin meals.

His grandmother's phoenix would occasionally fly through the grounds until it found Jin. The monster bird would perch nearby and fix its bright yellow eyes upon him, as if it were watching him for the empress dowager. Shishi took to barking in a frenzy whenever the phoenix appeared, and Jin had to hurry to scoop up the little dog for fear of the monster bird's talons carrying it off. But at least he was getting some warning.

He wished he could say the same for his sessions with Master Sonsen. Officious ministers from the empress dowager's advisory council would often appear with a litany of suggestions to his tutor.

"Have you taught him the tricks of accounting and rapid calculation yet?" asked one from the ministry of finance. "I shall be happy to talk about my own family's role in saving the crown prince's great-great-grandfather from overspending the treasury." The minister puffed out his chest.

"I can't understand how you didn't cover the vital uses for animal dung in crop rotation and fuel conservation!" scolded a minister from the agricultural bureau. "How can Prince Jin pass his exams without knowing all the details of dung?"

"You must ensure that all seven hundred eighty-six precepts about warfare have been memorized," intoned the minister of military affairs. "As long as there is hostility on our borders, His Brilliance must be prepared to fight—and one cannot fight unless one knows the precepts."

Jin rolled his eyes. He didn't see how memorizing a bunch of rules and prescriptions written hundreds of years ago on war would make anyone better at it. If that were the case, wouldn't fighting have stopped a long time ago?

Fortunately, Master Sonsen seemed to feel the same way, though it didn't keep him from giving Jin the lessons that the busybody ministers insisted on. When Jin complained, his tutor shook his head ruefully. "They merely want you to succeed, Your Brilliance. After all, the sooner you pass your subject exams, the sooner you can make the case to go to Whisper Island."

But no matter how hard he tried, Jin couldn't seem to absorb his lessons. He would get distracted and drift off, silently making lists of monster categories in his head. Flying. Scaled. Furred. Venomous. Multiple tails. Multiple heads. Though he wasn't allowed to look at the bestiary, he'd memorized enough of it to entertain himself. A part of him feared he'd never do well enough on all the exams to satisfy his grandmother. Which meant he'd never be allowed to go to the monster sanctuary. He would never match with a creature of his own, and he would never ascend to the throne. And if he was never going to be emperor, then why was he bothering with any of it? What would become of him? It all got to be too much one day, when a list of practice examination questions sent his brain reeling. He shoved it all aside and shredded his paper in frustration, ripping it into tiny bits.

"Why don't you go for a walk around the courtyard?" Master Sonsen suggested. "Get some fresh air, do some stone viewing, and then we'll try again."

Jin pushed back from the table, a shower of paper falling from his lap like flakes of snow. "Fine," he grunted, and stalked out of the library. With Shishi at his heels, he paced around the courtyard garden, brooding. He was utterly stuck. Stuck at the palace, stuck in the library, stuck studying horribly boring subjects while the one he actually understood was off limits. He felt as if he would explode. Something had to change, but what?

The late afternoon heat was stifling. Shishi soon flopped on her belly against the cool tiles of the walkway, panting and wheezing. "You want a break?" Jin asked. "Poor furry thing, I bet you do."

A carefully sculpted tree sprawled over a small carp pond in the middle of the courtyard, surrounded by enormous twisted rocks meant for viewing and stimulating the mind. Imperial scholars would come out of the library to contemplate their unusual shapes, and return to their work refreshed and full of new ideas. Jin lifted Shishi into his arms and went to sit in the shade of a tall viewing stone. He trailed his hand in the coolness of the pond while his dog lapped at it thirstily. A jagged rock, said to be shaped like Whisper Island, was set in the middle of the water. Jin leaned forward, gazing at the miniature hills, valleys, and plains that made up the landscape of the rock's surface. Fat golden carp swam lazily around it like sea monsters. If only that were really Whisper Island. He'd go there right now if he could. He flicked at a dead leaf floating in the water like a tiny boat.

On the island, he'd find his creature—and once he had

a companion of his own, his grandmother would no longer dictate what he could or couldn't do. Despite what she said, the true mark of being fit to rule wasn't a bunch of exam scores. The proof was in the acceptance conferred by a creature of the in between—and nothing else. He'd be treated as a true heir to the throne, no longer whispered about by the court, thought of as strange or inadequate, or as a nuisance by the empress dowager.

Approaching murmurs turned his head. Two ministers spoke quietly as they moved through the covered walkways around the courtyard garden, as if they were afraid of someone overhearing them. Jin shrank back against the towering viewing stone as they drew near.

"It's too late," said a gravelly voice. Jin recognized it as the minister of the treasury. "The imperial seal on the decree makes it law. The new taxes will raise a fortified wall in the north."

The other man gave a grunt. "She isn't even listening to us anymore. The border is not the real problem." It was the head Whisperer.

"I don't disagree, but what can be done?" asked the treasury minister. He sighed. "If only the crown prince were given a bigger role. Isn't he nearly of age for a monster?"

"Time is running out, frankly. It's best to find a match with a creature at a young age, as it solidifies the bond, but that's hard to do when they've all but disappeared. There are no records of a royal heir matching with their monster after they turned thirteen." The diviner clucked his tongue. "I can't believe she's barred him from Whisper Island. That was our best hope. But Her Majesty insists that she's teaching him a valuable lesson, and that the monstermate is nothing but symbolic tradition."

The treasury minister scoffed. "We saw how that worked with the last emperor. If the prince does not find a creature to back his reign, then what?"

"He'll have no claim. And without a proper successor, the Three Realms will not hold. It will be the ruin of us all."

"Surely you're exaggerating."

"I wish I were. Without imperial dragons, droughts and floods are wiping out crops more than ever . . ."

As the ministers disappeared around the corner, muttering in a furious back-and-forth, Jin stared at the rock in the center of the pond, trying to absorb what he'd just heard. If he did not find a monstermate by his birthday, it'd be too late. Hardly more than three months were left till then.

He had to go to Whisper Island, and soon. The future of the empire depended on it.

But how?

Absently he stroked Shishi's ears, trying to think. Master Sonsen was always telling him to work backward from a problem. To reach the island, he needed a boat. Could he hire one? That would require money. He had some of that, at least. But the island refuge was not the sort of place people often visited. It was the exclusive domain of the throne, and special permission had to be granted to set foot there. The words of the ministers came back to him: "The imperial seal on the decree makes it law . . ."

That was it! He scrambled to his feet. He would draw up a decree and borrow his grandmother's official seal, and then he could go wherever he wanted. Jin looked down at his dog and grinned. "Come on, Shishi. We've got work to do."

Buoyed by hope and determination, Jin began by making a list of essentials for a trip to the island. He soon conceded to himself that there was much he didn't know. Where precisely *was* the island? Was it heavily forested, grassy, or rocky? How long was the journey from Shining Claw? What sort of boat could bring back a creature? What was on a royal permit? There was much to find out.

Prowling the royal library, Jin found an expansive selection of maps, most of them bound in large folios. Several detailed the coastline of the Three Realms, and to his delight, one folio contained a rare old map of Whisper Island at its founding. He was fascinated to discover a village called Beastly on its western coast. He knew all remaining Whisperers with any true talent had been sent to Whisper Island long ago to operate the monster refuge—both to keep the creatures safe and to keep them from wandering off the island—but hadn't considered that there would be an entire settlement of them. How marvelous it would be to meet truly skilled Whisperers who could help him. Jin wondered if Beastly had monsters wandering freely about, like the palace once had.

He studied all the maps carefully, feigning a newfound interest in geography. In the guise of practicing mapmaking, he traced a number of them onto thin rice paper and secreted a copy of the Whisper Island map away.

Poring over the records on the sanctuary, he searched for accounts of previous royals securing their monsters there, and found paintings of welcoming ceremonies for visiting royalty, including his grandfather, who had set off on his quest for a creature from the village of Beastly. Jin supposed he would do the same. As crown prince, Jin's grandfather had come back in triumph from the sanctuary, bearing a dragon as a monstermate. With so few months to go before his thirteenth birthday, Jin would be thrilled for a monster of any sort. But a part of him still dreamed of bringing back a great dragon, and that would require a good-sized vessel.

To discover the cost of hiring one, Jin pretended to be researching the empire's ships and their value. The ministry of maritime affairs was all too eager to share. "The finest ships are beyond the reach of most, so it's common for a group of fishermen or a consortium of merchants to pool money when hiring vessels for the season. A fishing trawler runs around twenty gold claws—the equivalent of two thousand silver scales or twenty thousand bronze eyes—which can be paid off with one good catch. A cargo ship runs at least three times that."

Counting all the banknotes and strings of cash he'd been given over the years, Jin figured he had nearly enough money to hire a boat that could get him to Whisper Island and back with a monster. But reaching the royal monster sanctuary required more than money. He still needed permission papers stamped with the imperial seal of the Three Realms.

The seal was no small thing. The large block of precious stone was heavy as a sack of rice and took two hands to maneuver. Created for the first emperor of the Samtei people, the handle was pure gold, while the rest was grass-green jade of such rare quality that it was clear as crystal. The bottom of the seal was inscribed with the words *Great Three Realms of Samtei* in ancient, stylized script that was nearly unreadable, and darkened with dried ink red as blood. Three of the Sacred Beasts of the Compass—the tortoise of the north, the dragon of the east, and the kirin of the west—were carved on each of the remaining sides, while the fourth, "south" side, which ordinarily would feature a phoenix, was left intentionally blank, representing a space for the emperor. That side would face the sovereign as they placed their approval on a document, whether decree, treaty, or contract, ensuring that the seal wouldn't be accidentally stamped upside down.

Jin had seen it by his grandmother's side whenever she held court and had noticed its mark on plenty of documents in the imperial library. Beyond that, he'd never really given it much thought, as it was just another thing that had always been part of the trappings of the palace, around for as long as he could remember, no more remarkable than a butter lamp or a decorative screen. But once he tried to figure out how to borrow it without anyone knowing, he realized how much of a challenge it'd be. It was always within the sovereign's sight in the throne room, except at night, when it was kept in the heavily fortified building of the imperial treasury.

Pretending to be gathering information for his exams, he probed for intelligence from the head treasury minister, who was all too happy to hold forth on all topics related to his position.

"Oh yes, I dare say the Repository of the Golden Piyao is the most important building in the entire palace, if not the empire," boasted the minister, rubbing his round belly with satisfaction. "It holds not just coins of the realm, but imperial jewels, heirlooms from the beginning of time, rare gifts from other kingdoms, and all the royal seals."

"All?" asked Jin, thrown. "There's more than one seal?"

The minister's belly jiggled with laughter. "Of course! There's the Money Seal that's stamped on all banknotes, the

Security Seal that goes on letters and packages sent from the palace, the Appreciation Seal that marks all books and scrolls owned by the throne, the Blessings Seal for promotion documents . . ."

Jin shook his head, trying to hide his dismay. "I just thought there was the one—that big jade block that sits by the throne when my grandmother holds court."

"Ah, the Royal State Seal," nodded the minister. "That's the one that can only be used by whoever sits on the Triad Throne. The other seals are used in the name of the empire. I myself am in charge of the Money Seal." He pulled out a wad of paper bills that displayed a prominent rectangle of red stamped in the center, with an inscription and an image of a winged lion. He peeled one off and gave it to Jin. "See that piyao on this banknote? It represents the treasury— they used to have real live ones guarding it, you know."

"Crickety creatures." Jin pretended that he didn't know about the monsters that once guarded the treasury, but he was more excited about the bill in his hands. It was worth ten strings, and a full string held the equivalent of a thousand bronze eyes, a hundred silver scales, or a single gold claw. According to Master Sonsen, most people in the empire labored all year to make even one complete string. With the addition of this money, Jin would surely be able to hire a larger boat. He held the banknote close and bowed. "Thank you, sir! I'll study this well." The minister's smile faltered as Jin stashed it in a pocket. "My grandmother will be so pleased that you're helping me to pass my exams."

The minister recovered and bared his teeth in what looked more like a grimace. "Consider it a gift for good luck," he said, and hastily tucked away the rest of his bills.

"Coming from you, it should bring the best of luck indeed," Jin said admiringly. "After all, you're in charge of the most important building on the grounds! With so many precious items in there, how do you even manage to keep it all safe?"

The treasury minister chuckled. "There may not be piyaos around to guard it anymore, but we've found ways. Each room in the repository is secured with a locked metal door, and only two sets of keys exist. One set is kept by the ruler on the Triad Throne, and the other . . ." With a little self-satisfied smile, he patted his pocket, which jingled tantalizingly.

It didn't take much flattery for the minister to show off the keys, and Jin quickly figured out upon examining them that he could pick the locks with the right tools and enough time. The building itself was windowless and built in the style of a traditional grain storehouse, with extra thick walls. "It's very well constructed," boasted the minister. "But more importantly, it's surrounded by guards, so no one can go in or out without notice."

Instead of trying to take the heavy seal, Jin decided the

best option was to bring his forged papers to where the insignia was stored. He ordered extra writing equipment—soft rice paper, ink, brushes—to be brought to his quarters, and began practicing his calligraphy whenever he had a spare moment. He had to perfect his brush skills before writing out the fake documents on official watermarked mulberry paper, which was harder to come by. He managed to get a few sheets by saying he needed it for writing a letter of apology to his grandmother and the organizers of the Monster Festival. Hunting in the palace archives for historical papers, he examined the wording of old royal decrees and orders and copied the official language he'd found on them to come up with one of his own.

After multiple drafts, Jin got what he thought looked like a reasonable facsimile of a travel document and decrees giving him permission to set foot on Whisper Island's shores. Carefully, he inscribed everything on the special sheets of thick mulberry paper. Even his flourishes looked rather convincing, he thought proudly. All that was needed was the official crimson stamp from the Royal State Seal.

It was time to go after it.

CHAPTER 8

BREAKING IN

ALL OF JIN'S PREPARATIONS TO sneak off to Whisper Island had an unexpected side benefit. His apparent diligence and fervent studies of history and geography garnered praise and approval from Master Sonsen and the ministers, and they proudly relayed Jin's growing interest in the workings of the empire to the empress dowager. As a result, after weeks of obedient studying, Jin was no longer confined to just his room and the library. Guards were still posted to keep an eye on him, but tended to do patrol checks instead of standing outside his doors for hours on end. It hardly mattered to Jin at first, for he was preoccupied with crossing off each item on his list. But now, as he got ready to break into the imperial treasury, he was glad for the easing of the guard.

After sunset, he rolled up the fake documents he'd forged and placed them in a small travel tube made from a hollow segment of bamboo. He changed into his old indigo-dyed cottons, for they were much easier to get around in and didn't rustle like the stiff silks he'd been forced to wear lately. He tied the tube and a few tools in a square of cloth, then fastened it to his waist. In his pocket, he tucked away his trusty lockpicks and the firestarter he'd gotten from the festival fortune-teller.

Worrying the lock charm around his neck, Jin watched the water clock in his sitting room. A series of cups collected dripping water from a sphere enameled in deep blue and gold, representing the celestial heavens. When a cup was filled at the quarter-hour mark, it tripped a lever that slid an empty cup into its place with the tiny peal of a bell. Gilded metal arms indicating the time clicked forward. The whole thing rested on the back of a carved marble turtle with a fierce dragon head. When the clock chimed midnight, he went to the doors and listened for footsteps. He'd been tracking the recent schedule of the night guards outside his chambers. Instead of standing at the doors all night, they patrolled the corridors at a leisurely pace that left his rooms unattended for nearly a quarter of an hour at a stretch.

When the sound of boots faded, Jin stuck out his head. The backs of two guards grew smaller as they moved down the hall. When they disappeared around the corner, Jin slipped out and hurried off in the opposite direction. His soft-soled shoes were silent as he ran through the corridor, and he was almost to the adjoining building when he heard the familiar clicking of toenails and a heavy snuffling. He turned. "Shishi!" The dog trotted up to him triumphantly, stump wagging. Jin groaned. He scooped up the dog and scurried back to his quarters. Sure enough, the doors were ajar—he must not have shut them properly. He deposited Shishi inside the doors and was making to close them when the little lion dog began to whine in protest. "Hush!" Jin begged, then relented. She had never been left behind before. He slung the dog over his shoulders and closed the doors more securely, then ran back down the hall and out into the night, Shishi panting happily in his ear.

Avoiding the corridors and colonnades that blazed with lantern light, Jin kept to the shadowy gardens and court-yards as he crossed the palace grounds. He hid behind a thick column upon nearing the treasury and peered at the building. It was once guarded by actual piyao, fierce winged lions with immense clawed paws, forked tails that could snake around an intruder and hold him fast, and short ant-lers as sharp as their many teeth. They were particularly fond of gold and would do anything to protect it, so they made excellent guards for treasure. In the earliest days of the empire, when magical beasts roamed freely about the Palace of Monsters instead of being kept in a menagerie park, perches and lairs were built all throughout the palace for them. The imperial treasury was the special domain of the piyao, and there was an attached den where they slept and were fed. It had long been boarded up, padlocked and forgotten, but Jin had worked it open months ago when he'd first started picking locks and exploring all the sealed-off parts of the palace.

Now a team of palace guards stood at intervals around the treasury and flanked the entrance, their tridents gleaming in the moonlight. Jin took a deep breath. "Keep quiet," he warned Shishi, and darted for the piyao den at the rear of the building, some fifty paces away in a darkened corner. Bushes obscured the door, and creeping vines had been allowed to grow over it, but he still remembered its location. Carefully he pulled away boards he'd loosened on earlier visits, pushing aside the thick vines. Shishi jumped off his shoulders and watched as he made short work of the padlock with his lockpicks. He cracked open the heavy wooden door. A whiff of stale air floated out. "Go in," he whispered to Shishi. The dog sniffed and shook its head. Jin nudged her with his foot. "Hurry up!" But Shishi snorted and whined softly, then ran off into the night.

"Monstermuck." There was no time to chase after her now. He had to go in and be quick. Jin slipped through the door, leaving it ajar. In the dim light, he untied the cloth at his waist and fumbled for his firestarter. After a few tries, he sparked a small flame onto a bit of twisted cotton wool and lit a small butter lamp that he'd brought. The den was just as he'd remembered it, spacious enough to hold a pair of winged lions, with straw-lined sleeping nooks and a deep trough for water. A low stone tunnel, sealed over with brick, led to the treasury. But Jin had brought a chisel and hammer he'd secured from a groundskeeper. Quietly as he could, he chipped at the mortar. Dislodging the first brick seemed to take forever. But after he pulled the first one out, it became easier to free others. He stacked them in a small pile until he'd made large-enough hole for him to climb through.

For fear of fire, the treasury was kept dark, its lanterns lit only when needed. Jin raised his little lamp and peered down a long corridor lined with locked chambers. Signs above each door indicated their contents. "Silks." "Jewels." "Ceremonial Weapons." "Precious Metals." "Coin and Paper." At last he found a door near the entrance of the building with a sign reading "Imperial Seals." He pulled out his picks and worked them in the door's lock till it clicked open.

The chamber was tiny, practically an alcove, with just enough room for a couple of people to stand in and a large, locked cabinet carved of fragrant cedar. Jin placed his butter lamp on the ground and made short work of the cabinet's lock. Lined up within were a number of lacquered boxes in varying sizes. He opened the largest one to find a porcelain container of ink paste and a heavy leather pouch. He untied its silk strings to reveal the gleaming gold handle of the Royal State Seal. At last.

The flame in his butter lamp began to sputter. Holy beasts, it was already running out of fuel! He had to hurry. Jin removed the forged papers from their bamboo tube, then spread them out on the stone floor, weighing down their corners with whatever he could grab—the pieces of his firestarter, his lockpicks, his shoes. He pressed the seal into the ink paste, then held his breath and placed it carefully onto the first document. When he lifted it off the paper, he frowned at the red imprint left behind. It was uneven, and not all the characters were clear. Too late, he realized that the rough surface beneath the paper was a problem. He needed padding of some sort, like the felt blotter that always lined writing tables. This document was ruined.

Fortunately, he'd brought an extra blank sheet. He grabbed the leather pouch that held the imperial seal and smoothed it out as a base for his paper. The next imprint came out perfectly, a bold square in vermilion ink. The light in his lamp flickered ominously—he didn't have much time. He stamped the remaining documents and blew at them, trying to speed their drying. As he rolled them up, the flame in the butter lamp grew so small that he could barely see. He shoved the seal back in its pouch, heaved it into its box with the ink paste, and rushed to put everything back in place. As he clicked the door of the cabinet shut, his lamp went out, and Jin was enveloped in total darkness.

"Muckety muck!" He stared vainly into the blackness

of the windowless chamber. He couldn't even see his hand before his face. That butter lamp had been far too small—or he'd taken too long. Jin leaned against the solidness of the cabinet, trying not to panic, and sucked in a deep breath. All he had to do was retrace his steps back out of the treasury building. Groping about, he found the lamp, still warm but empty of fuel, and put it in his pocket.

He shuffled for the exit, hands out in front of him till he bumped into a wall. Using it as a guide, he eased out of the chamber and closed its doors. Unable to see the lock, he searched for it gingerly, then inserted his picks and wiggled them, going by feel and sound. The lock snapped back into position, surprising Jin. It was almost easier in the dark. Placing a hand on the wall, he blindly walked down the long corridor till he reached the closed-off tunnel to the old piyao den. The faintest light came from the hole in the wall that he'd opened.

As he crawled back into the den, a sliver of moonlight from the grounds gleamed invitingly from the cracked door. In the dim light, he returned the bricks to their place in the wall as neatly and quickly as he could. With a sigh of relief, he exited the den, trying not to rustle the creeping vines around it. As he was securing the boards that normally barred the den's entrance, a voice behind him made him jump.

"Your Brilliance!"

Jin whirled to find Bingyoo standing with Shishi in her arms. "What in blazing beasts are you doing here? You scared me," he hissed. "Both of you." He glared at his dog.

"Whatever in the realms are *you* doing?" asked Bingyoo, perplexed. She rubbed Shishi's round head as the dog wagged its tail nub.

"Nothing that concerns you," he said curtly. He pulled a cloak of creeping vines securely over the boards. "How did you know I was here?"

Bingyoo nodded at Shishi. "I thought it was odd that she was running about so late, and was going to take her to your room, but she led me here instead."

Frowning, Jin peered through the bushes that surrounded them. The palace guards were still standing at attention by the treasury building. "Did anyone see you?"

"No, but if they did, I'd tell them that your dog had run away and I was bringing her back to you."

"Good thinking," said Jin.

She shrugged. "It's the truth. Now, what are you doing sneaking around here?" Bingyoo tilted her head. "Where does that door go?"

Jin scowled. "It's nothing you need to know about. Just don't tell anyone you saw me."

"Like I wasn't supposed to tell anyone you were at the festival?" Bingyoo scoffed. "You're clearly up to something."

He hesitated. He hadn't breathed a word of his plan to

anyone. No one could be trusted—not his tutor, Old Fang, the ministers, nor the servants. Even his dog had given away his location tonight.

"It's nothing, really," he said finally.

Bingyoo raised an eyebrow. She looked so skeptical that Jin nearly blurted that she'd be better off not knowing, but he bit it back and said nothing more. "Fine," she said shortly, and deposited Shishi into his arms. "Here's your dog. You'd better get to your chambers before you're found missing." She turned on her heel.

"Thanks!" said Jin, but Bingyoo disappeared into the night without another word or a second glance. Shishi gave his chin some enthusiastic licks, and he gazed at her with exasperation. "What am I going to do with you?"

The next morning, he unrolled the forged documents and examined his handiwork by the sunlight streaming through his windows. Only his first attempt featured an uneven and patchy crimson seal. But he had the stamped blank sheet. As he wrote out a new decree on the properly stamped sheet, he congratulated himself on thinking to bring an extra. He had everything he needed now.

Jin packed items he thought useful into a small knapsack, tying the precious documents and all his cash in a separate bundle. Besides a change of clothing, he added his lockpicks, the firestarter, a bone-handled knife, and several maps that he'd copied from the library archives. He picked up the stuffed toy baku on his bed and considered it for a second. He'd slept with it every night for as long as he could remember. Stroking its floppy long nose, Jin took a deep breath and put it back. Where he was going, there would be *real* dreameaters. He couldn't wait to meet one.

CHAPTER 9

A COSTLY BARGAIN

JIN GRITTED HIS TEETH, TRYING not to fidget as Master Sonsen droned about the Tea and Salt Wars. His original plan was to show up at morning lessons, get through the first hour, then announce he was feeling unwell and that he would need to rest undisturbed in his quarters for the remainder of the day. That way no one would question his absence. He'd have plenty of time to sneak down to the docks and find a boat. But he was so eager to be on his way that he feared he wouldn't even make it through fifteen minutes.

He just had to be patient for a bit longer. Fantasizing about his triumphant return to the palace, he pictured himself with an impressive monster in tow. Hopefully he would arrive in grand style on the back of an enormous dragon.

"Is something amiss, Your Brilliance?" The tutor blinked at him curiously. "You seem to be far away."

Jin decided it was enough that his tutor had laid eyes on

him, if only for a few minutes. He furrowed his brow. "Sorry, Master Sonsen. I'm not feeling all that well." Tenderly, he held his stomach for good measure.

"Merciful beasts. Are you in pain? Shall I call for the court healers? Or ask the kitchens to send some herbal soup?" He fussed over Jin, peering closely through his spectacles. "I daresay you look a bit peaked."

"I didn't sleep all that much last night," said Jin truthfully. "I was thinking of going back to my rooms to rest. Could we go over the Tea and Salt Wars another time?"

"Of course," said Master Sonsen, twisting a sleeve. "Is there anything else you need? Boiled root tea? Gingered rice porridge? Stewed bird's nest?"

Jin smiled wanly. "I'm sure I'll bounce back after a good long nap. If you could ask that I not be disturbed for the rest of the day, that would be so helpful." He hurried out of the library with Shishi at his heels and went in search of Bingyoo.

He found her outside the kitchens perched on a stool, scrubbing at a long white radish in a tub of water. A pile of dirt-crusted root vegetables sat nearby. Shishi ran up to her, stump wagging, and she wiped her hands on her smock to give the little lion dog a scratch. Seeing Jin, her dimples faded. She stood and bowed stiffly. "Your Brilliance."

"I need you to do something," Jin said quickly. "Can my dog stay with you for a little while? I just need someone to look after Shishi and keep her out of trouble. It wouldn't be for very long."

She frowned. "How long, then?"

He rubbed at his lock charm, calculating. A few days' sail to the island and back, plus a few days to find a creature. Surely once he found the right one, he'd bond with it in no time. "A week or so? No more than two, I'd think." Jin saw the burning curiosity in Bingyoo's eyes and pressed his lips together. "I have some things to do, and she'll get in the way. You saw what happened last night."

"Did I?" she retorted. "If I recall correctly, I didn't see a single thing."

"Exactly!" said Jin, relieved. He scooped up his dog. "Here you go. Thank you, truly. Can you tell the kitchens that I won't be needing any lunch? I'm . . . probably going to be napping for most of the day. I didn't get much sleep." He winked and turned with a wave, intent on taking care of one more thing before leaving.

Not far from the old menagerie was the palace temple, where the royal family went to pray and perform sacred rites. Known as the Temple of Gods and Monsters, it was a tall building with multiple stories, its curved eaves decorated with the figures of dozens of creatures. When Jin reached its wide courtyard, the priests were cloistered away in meditation as he'd expected. He looked up at the giant stone dragon that stood before the temple as if it were guarding it and patted its stony scales.

Seeking the ancestral shrine at the heart of the temple, Jin went straight to the elaborately carved altar and lit sticks of incense in a tortoise-shaped brazier. He placed them before gilded tablets featuring his parents' names and watched the smoke waft toward the high ceiling. Among the painted portraits of his ancestors staring from the walls, Jin located his mother and father, both looking so young, their expressions serene. Would they hear him if he asked for their protection?

"Mother," he said out loud. "I'm going to Whisper Island for a monstermate." Jin felt for the lock charm around his neck and clasped it as he prayed. "Father, please help me bring back a dragon like you did. Let me show Grandmother that I'm your rightful heir."

When the incense had burned away and the last of the smoke dissipated, Jin turned to leave. He thought he heard a familiar whine. "Shishi?" But when he came out of the temple, the courtyard was empty, save for the towering stone dragon coiled at its center. He heard the bells of the palace water clock. It was already mid-morning. He headed for his quarters, anxious to get going.

The guards patrolling his wing saluted as they marched past him in the corridor. In his rooms, Jin immediately shed his princely finery. In embroidered silks, he'd stand out on the docks like a phoenix among pigeons, and he knew better than to try capturing a monster in a long, fancy robe. Donning the simple peasant garb his grandmother detested, he immediately felt more comfortable. Jin retrieved his pack and reviewed the contents, then slid open one of the back doors to his private garden terrace and looked out. No one was about.

He slipped out and shut the door quietly behind him. Beneath the veranda, he'd stashed a burlap bag with a gardener's weeding sickle and conical worker's hat. Pulling its broad straw brim down low, he shoved his pack inside the bag and slung it over his shoulder. He walked through the grounds with the sickle in hand, looking like an apprentice groundskeeper with a sack of weeds. As he neared the Dragon Gate, he felt his heart pound and lowered his chin. The last time he left through this gate, things hadn't ended well. But it seemed safer to go through the gate typically used by the workers than the main gate. As soon as he exited the palace grounds, Jin breathed a huge sigh of relief. Now to the docks.

The city of Shining Claw was built between the banks of two rivers—the Horn River and Serpent River—that converged into a greater one, the Horned Serpent, leading out to sea. Ships traveled up and down its rippling slate-gray waters, said to look like the scales of a snake, bringing goods and wares from all over to the city. While copying maps of both the capital and the empire, Jin had figured that it would take him a couple of hours on foot to get to the docks, and several days to go downriver from the city to the great bay that sheltered Whisper Island.

What he hadn't expected, however, was how hungry and thirsty he would get just trying to reach the docks. The streets of the city were congested, noisy and smelly, with shouting vendors, haggling buyers, gossiping neighbors, squabbling children and scolding parents, clattering wheels, neighing horses, lowing oxen, and barking dogs. Even the Monster Festival hadn't felt this chaotic. He pulled out the map he'd traced on delicate rice paper and tried to make sense of his surroundings, so unlike the quiet serenity of the palace grounds. But it was one thing to look at lines on a map, and another thing entirely to figure out where you were on that map. Why hadn't this ever been taught to him in his lessons? He shook his head. Whenever he went beyond the palace gates, transported by servants or accompanied by guards, he'd never bothered with directions.

After being jostled for the umpteenth time, Jin glumly rubbed his shoulder. At least the Monster Festival had familiarized him with thick crowds. He found a half-eaten sweet biscuit that he'd stuck in a pocket and forgotten about, and nibbled at it slowly while he trudged along. The late summer heat was easing somewhat, but he was becoming terribly thirsty, and the stale, sugary biscuit didn't help. He spotted a line of people collecting water from a city fountain and got behind an old man carrying a wooden bucket with a bamboo ladle. As he waited, he studied his map again, frowning.

"Excuse me," said Jin to the old man. "I'm trying to get to the docks. Could you tell me which way I should go?"

The old man turned. He had one eye that was rheumy and covered with an opaque white film, while the other was dark and sharp. His good eye looked Jin up and down, then at his map.

"New to the city, are you?" he rasped. "Let's see now. We're here, near the Palace of Monsters." He stabbed the paper with a stubby finger, his knuckles knobbled and thick. "And you want to get to this part of the riverfront, yeah? If you take this street to the next boulevard and turn right," he indicated with a gray-stubbled chin, "then you should reach the docks by following that road all the way down to the water."

Jin was dumbfounded. "We're still near the palace?" he asked, dismayed. He felt as if he'd been walking for hours. "How long a walk would you say it is from here to the docks?"

The old man's dark eye twinkled. "For a young pup like you? No longer than it would take for a dragon to eat a water buffalo."

Jin calculated. "Ten minutes?"

"Maybe a herd of water buffalo, then," chuckled the old

man. "It shouldn't take you more than another hour or two—you'll get there before sundown. Me, on the other hand . . ." The old man shook his head. "I'm not as fast as I used to be." He reached the fountain and began filling his bucket. Once it was filled, he turned and smiled at Jin, revealing a row of silver-capped teeth. "May the best of beasts guide you!"

Jin thanked him and cupped his hands under the carved stone spout, an open-mouthed shachi just like the tiger-headed fish on the roofs of palace buildings. He splashed his face and drank the cool water thirstily, appalled that he'd made so little progress. How could he have miscalculated like this?

But the old man had spoken of the docks as if they were within easy reach. He wiped his mouth on his sleeve and followed the directions he'd been given. His feet began to hurt and his legs ached, unused to walking so far, but he kept going, anxious to find a boat before the day was out. At last, he spotted the masts of ships in the distance, water birds circling over them. He hurried closer until he saw the rippling waters of the two rivers conjoining into the Horned Serpent. Jin glanced at the sun, dipping toward the horizon. He didn't have much time.

He pulled out the bamboo tube that contained his travel documents and began searching for a vessel that could take him to his destination. There were several single-masted boats docked on the riverfront, crewed by a handful of wiry fishermen. Jin watched them unload their catches for the day, wrinkling his nose at the powerful smell of dead fish. The fishing boats looked rickety and incapable of carrying a decent-sized monster. Even a small dragon would sink one as soon as it climbed on. They would not do.

Jin noticed a couple of river barges being steered into dock, their covered decks filled with passengers eager to disembark. While a barge was certainly big enough to carry a creature, it was flat-bottomed and slow, not meant for the sea. He'd never make it to the island in one of those.

A double-masted merchant ship flying the banners of Samtei caught his eye. Its crew was busily unloading cargo, and its hull looked sturdy yet streamlined, with bamboo-battened sails that promised speed. He approached two sinewy men carrying baskets down its gangplank. "I need to talk to someone about getting onto this boat."

"Want a job, do you? Captain's over there," huffed one man, jerking his chin in the direction of a hefty man. Smartly dressed in seagoing attire, he was reading through a manifest as the crew moved the latest shipment onto waiting carts sitting on the dock.

Jin marched up to him and took a deep breath. "Sir, I'm looking to hire a boat." His voice cracked, and Jin swallowed, feeling like his mouth had filled with sand.

The captain had a dark beard and eyes to match. They regarded him skeptically. "You want to be hired on a boat?

My crew is full—I don't need scrawny hatchlings like you on board. You wouldn't last a day."

"You misunderstand me," said Jin. "I mean for this boat to take me somewhere."

"And where is this somewhere?" asked the captain, folding his arms.

Jin removed his hat and looked the man in the eye. "Whisper Island."

The captain exploded with a hearty laugh. "Have you a death wish? That island's strictly forbidden territory. Anyone caught approaching its shores will be executed by the Triad Throne."

"Not everyone." With a flick of his wrist, Jin unfurled the documents stamped with the imperial seal. "I have permission to go from the empress dowager herself."

"Let me see that." The captain snatched the papers from Jin and examined them closely. "'The bearer of these documents has my express permission to visit Whisper Island and bring back a creature of their choosing.' Bring back a creature?" He peered at Jin. "You?"

"I'm a Whisperer-in-training," Jin said. "I've been studying with the Bureau of Divination. There aren't any creatures left on the mainland, so they're sending me to the island for one."

"Why don't they just send you on an imperial ship?"

Jin thought quickly. "It's . . . part of my assignment," he

offered. "To see if I can find my own way."

"I'm surprised there are even creatures left there. I thought it was a myth." The captain riffled through the other papers. "Well, even if you've got permission from the throne, no one'll take you there for free. You got money?"

"How much?" asked Jin.

"How much you got?" countered the captain.

Putting a hand in his rucksack, Jin fingered the pouch holding his cash. "Around fifty strings. That ought to be enough."

"You can't possibly be carrying that much." The captain's eyes grew keen. "Let me see."

Jin hesitated. Then he pulled out the sack. Before he could blink, the captain snatched it out of his hands. He rummaged through it, whistling softly at the gold and banknotes. "You weren't kidding. Thanks, boy." He rolled the documents up, then tucked them and the pouch inside his jacket.

"B-but . . . I haven't ag-agreed," stammered Jin. That was all the money he'd brought—and his papers too. He lunged at the boat captain, but the man only grabbed him and squeezed his arms so tight that Jin gasped. "Ow!"

The captain leaned in so close Jin could smell the stewed eggs and pickled onions on his breath. "Here's what I'll do. For your fifty strings, I'll take you to Whisper Island. And if there's any trouble at all, I won't hesitate to drop you over the side as monster feed." He bared his teeth in a blood-red smile, stained from chewing quids of sweetwake. Jin recoiled. The little bundles of sweetpalm nuts wrapped in wake-leaves were banned at the palace after they'd become popular with guards on the night shift, to stop the spread of red spit stains.

His arms felt as if they were caught in an iron vise. Jin looked despondently at the spot in the man's jacket where his money and documents had disappeared. If he called for help, would anyone come? Panic seized his gut. If word got back to the empress dowager about his unsuccessful attempt to go to Whisper Island, he'd be done for. Failure was not an option. Besides, he was the crown prince. It was his *right* to go. Desperation and fury flooded through him. How dare this man? Jin glared and raised his chin. "All you'll drop is onto your knees if you don't bring me there and back. And not just any spot on the island—I want you to take me straight to the village of Beastly on the western shore."

"Beastly?" The captain sneered. "No one's sailed there in ages. They don't even bother to include it on maps anymore."

"If you're as good a captain as you seem to think you are, I'm sure you can find it, and I'll remind you my papers are from the Palace of Monsters. You think they won't notice if I don't return in one piece?"

"I didn't see your name on them documents—they just say whoever holds 'em has permission," said the captain, waggling his thick eyebrows. "So I'm going to keep 'em, because they might be worth a lot more than fifty strings."

"You can't take what's mine without earning it," Jin growled.

The captain guffawed and released him. "You may be scrawny, but I like your spirit, boy. It'd be wasted if you ended up in the sea. Well then, I'll take you to the island—and if you survive that nest of monsters, I'll let you hitch a ride back, just like you asked. What say you?"

Jin rubbed his arms and scowled. "Fine," he spat.

With a red grin, the captain gave a mocking bow. "Captain Pan at your service. What's your name, boy?"

"Uh, it's Fang." He didn't dare give his true name.

A wiry man with leathery cheeks and hair tied back in a long braid approached, eyeing Jin curiously. "What have we got here, sir? New recruit?"

"Actually, this hatchling's given us a nice sum for passage," said Captain Pan. "Find him a bunk, will you, Wako? Storage hold's fine." He hawked and spewed a stream of red juice on the dock. "Follow the first mate on board, Fang—he'll show you where to go."

Jin climbed the gangplank onto the boat, looking around curiously. It wasn't the finest or largest vessel docked on the riverfront, but it was well-kept, with a small crew of weather-beaten men who looked at him with sullen expressions.

The first mate jerked a thumb at Jin. "Say hello to our

new passenger, lads. Fang, is it? Where are we taking you?"

"Whisper Island," said Jin.

The crew members let out exclamations of surprise.

"Did he say what I think he said?"

"Claw me now. That misty hellhole?"

"I'd rather eat my shoe."

Wako's leathery tanned cheeks were ashy. "The isle of monsters? The captain said yes to that?"

Seeing the outrage in the crew's eyes, Jin was bewildered. "He did. What's so bad about Whisper Island? My—I mean, royal ships used to go there all the time."

"Used to," Wako repeated flatly. "It's been years since anyone's come back from that place. Why do you think all monsters were sent there?" He shoved a sweetwake quid in his cheek. "And why do you want to go there?"

Jin puffed out his chest. "If you knew anything about monsters, you'd know that they're the most blessed beings to ever grace the Three Realms. They're why the empire even exists! The palace is sending me as a Whisperer-in-training."

"Or because they want to get rid of you," guffawed a crew member with a flying fish tattooed on his neck.

"I'll talk to the captain about this, lads," said Wako. "You come with me for now." Looking uneasy, the wiry little man gestured for Jin to follow him along the deck. He stopped at a hatch door and flipped it to reveal a bamboo ladder. "Go on down." After climbing into the hold, Jin found himself in a cramped dim space that held barrels of rice wine and crates of supplies. Several dusty shelves had a few desultory items stored here and there. Wako stuck his head through the hatch. "Clear yourself a spot, and that'll be your bunk." As Jin shoved baskets together and moved a box from the wide wooden slats, the first mate shook his head, muttering to himself. "Whisper Island. Beasts preserve us." When Jin finally made enough space on a low shelf to lie down, Wako grunted in approval. "When you hear the bell ring three times, that'll be mealtime. Don't go pawing through anything in the hold that's not yours, unless you want a lashing."

He left, leaving the hatch open, and Jin sat down on his makeshift bunk, looking around. There was a small porthole letting in light from the outside, and he went and peered through the smudged, wavy glass. The dock was just below eye level, as if he were resting his chin on it, and the first thing he saw was a pile of crates and baskets waiting to be loaded. Crewmen moved back and forth along the gangplank, bringing aboard the cargo piece by piece. A pair of small feet appeared, and then the person crouched behind the pile of crates, low enough for Jin to see who it was. He yelped and clapped a hand over his mouth, staring up at Bingyoo.

CHAPTER 10

ON THE HORNED SERPENT

THE SMALL FIGURE CROUCHED ON the dock by the waiting cargo, as if she were hiding. Her face was partially covered by the low brim of her straw hat, and a satchel slung across her shoulder obscured the rest of her, but there was no mistaking Bingyoo's kitchen smock. In the ship's hold, Jin was about to knock on the glass porthole to get her attention when shouts at the hatch opening stopped him. "Put it all here in the forward bulkhead!"

Jin climbed out onto the deck and hurried to the side of the boat. Quickly he scanned the dock and the dwindling pile of crates and baskets, worried Bingyoo had been discovered. But she was nowhere to be seen. He rubbed his eyes. Had he just imagined her? Squinting through the fading light of dusk, he looked up and down the riverfront, but didn't find her anywhere. Jin wondered if he was hallucinating. That porthole *was* a grimy mess. He watched the crew load the rest of the cargo on board while the captain barked at them to get ready to set sail. "I want to get this next leg over with," he bellowed.

The merchant ship was freed from its moorings and the gangplank pulled up. As they pushed away from the riverbank, the gentle rocking of the vessel shifted. Jin looked down the river, its current flowing toward the sea. When he glanced back, the ship was already a good way from shore. Battened sails of woven rattan rose to catch the breeze, and a team of four men steered a giant rudder back and forth. Jin peered over the side and saw a flat board protruding from the keel. It swung from side to side, helping to stabilize the boat as the crew worked the rudder and propelled it into the deeper rushing waters of the river. Captain Pan barked out orders, punctuated with an occasional swear word.

The rank, stale air of the capital docks dissipated as they drew farther away, leaving the shouts and activity of porters, fishermen, and traders behind. Jin took a deep breath and began to relax. At last, he was bound for Whisper Island. In the west, the sun sank behind the rolling green hills that cradled the city. He watched the skyline of the capital recede in the dusk, its curving rooftops of tile and their stone monster guardians becoming a dark smudge punctuated by pinpricks of light.

Jin shivered slightly in the gathering dark. He'd brought a light jacket that was in his pack. Hoping his makeshift bunk hadn't been completely filled with cargo, he opened the hatch of the storage hold and climbed down. As he suspected, his spot on the shelves had practically disappeared, his hat and pack squashed on a remaining sliver of plank. Sighing, he began to shove aside the encroaching boxes, then stopped at a strange whimper and a shushing sound.

In disbelief, he looked around. Was he losing his mind? "Who's there?"

The top of a large basket lifted, and Bingyoo's sheepish face appeared. "It's me, Your Brilliance." Shishi's furry head popped out beside her, and the dog began to wriggle with excitement, panting happily.

"What in the realms are you doing here?" Jin was furious. He hadn't hallucinated after all. "You're supposed to be at the palace. I asked you to take care of Shishi!"

"And I am," said Bingyoo. "She's fine, see? I overheard you praying this morning and had to follow. I couldn't believe you'd do anything this foolish."

"What do you mean?" said Jin, outraged.

Bingyoo looked exasperated. "Every time the empress dowager forbids you from doing something, you do it anyway—and worse—and get yourself in deeper trouble!"

"My grandmother hasn't given me much choice." His jaw jutted. "If I don't match with a monster soon, I might never. How can I be expected to take up the trident scepter without a creature companion? As soon as I come back with one, she'll see how wrong she was."

The servant girl raised an eyebrow. "I hope you're right. No one else at the palace would dare defy her the way you do." She looked around. "So this is where they've put you? Do they know who you are?"

"No, and I'd rather they stay in the dark about it," said Jin. "I don't need the palace discovering my whereabouts." He frowned. "Speaking of which, aren't you afraid they'll notice you're gone?"

She shrugged. "It's not like it even mattered to my own family. They actually got rid of me. So why would it matter to the palace if I were missing?" Bingyoo stared at him defiantly. Jin didn't know what to say.

"I'm sorry about your family," he said after a pause.

Her face tightened. "They sold me off so there was one less mouth to feed. I did eat better once I started in the kitchens, so I guess it's a good thing no one cared."

"Don't say that," Jin protested, but she only looked away. Awkwardly he tried to change the subject. "I can't believe you sneaked on here."

Bingyoo threw up her hands. "It wasn't planned. I followed you because I didn't know what else to do." She climbed out of the basket, an empty satchel slung across her chest. "Shishi came along in this bag. After you got on the ship, I was just trying to find a way to check whether you were okay. It looked like they were kidnapping you."

The sound of singing filtered into the darkened hold, a rhythmic chant that came from the ruddermen on the deck. Jin shook his head. "Not exactly, but the captain isn't to be trusted. He took all my money and threatened to throw me overboard." Shishi pawed at Jin and whined. He picked her up and ruffled her thick fur. "You two need to stay hidden. I'll bring down what you need."

As they sailed down the Horned Serpent, Jin worked mightily to prevent the crew from discovering the two stowaways in the storage hold. On deck he hung about near the hatch door, which he kept closed, and volunteered to fetch things whenever anyone made a move to go in. At meals he would squirrel away part of his portion, whether salt fish and gruel or jerked meat and rice crackers, and take it to Bingyoo and Shishi. He began helping First Mate Wako around the boat so that no one questioned when he was seen emptying buckets of waste overboard or carrying pans of water. When he heard barking, he'd quickly attempt to sing a snippet of the work songs that the ruddermen liked to chant as they steered the boat. Invariably the deckhands would laugh at his mistakes and correct him, setting off rounds of raucous singing that would distract from any unusual sounds from the hold.

At night, when most of the crew was asleep, he'd open the hatch door and let the breeze in. He and Bingyoo would sit near the base of the ladder and look up into the starry sky, talking in low voices. Jin described the monsters they might find on the island. Sometimes he'd take out his lockpicks for another attempt to spring the lock charm that Old Fang had given him. He tried teaching Bingyoo to read, using the words on the maps he'd copied. And he'd tell her what he'd seen from the deck as they traveled along the great river. The surrounding countryside near the capital was mostly rolling farmland full of verdant growth and vast orchards of fruiting trees, earthen dikes keeping the rushing current at bay. But as they traveled farther downriver, the landscape began to change, the settlements and fertile fields diminishing in size and scale, with townships and villages giving way to desolate wilderness and a disconcerting change in the air.

"There was a strange smell on the wind today," Jin reported. "And there was a gray haze on the horizon ahead. Wako says we'll be passing Paddlepaw tomorrow."

Bingyoo grew very still. "That's where I'm from." She stared at down at Shishi, splayed out between them. "The whole town stinks—the mills fill the air with smoke."

"I guess that's why it smelled so odd up on deck," said Jin. He hesitated. "Do you ever think about going back?"

"No," said Bingyoo brusquely. "There's nothing to go back to." Curling up, she hugged her knees. "How long do you think it'll be before we get to the island?"

"I read that it was three days' sailing from the capital, but that was with imperial ships." Knitting his brow, Jin estimated. "A boat like this might take a couple days longer. But it's big enough to hold a monster."

"I've always wondered—why are they called creatures of the in between?" asked Bingyoo.

"That's what they've always been called," said Jin. "In Samtei, the throne rules over humans, monsters, and animals. Those make up the three realms, see? I think the creatures bridge the gap between humans and ordinary beasts."

Bingyoo yawned. "Where did they come from?"

"Supposedly the Uncanny Wild," said Jin. "It's a forest in the Far West, where the mountains meet the eternal sea. It's said to be where all magical creatures originated, eons ago. The Palace of Monsters was once crawling with them."

"Now there's just your grandmother's," she observed. "Do you truly think you'll find any on the island?"

"Absolutely." He reached out and scratched Shishi's ears. "The real question is, what if I can't connect with a creature? It'll be dangerous if I can't. We'll have to rely on the Whisperers to protect us. Or sing 'The Beastie Lullaby' the whole time."

Bingyoo laughed. "What's that?"

"It's an old nursery song that's supposed to charm monsters. *Yawn, beastie; Calm, beastie; Tuck your fangs away . . .*" Jin sang it softly, then slumped against a crate. "I know, it's ridiculous. Claw me now."

With a little whine, Shishi climbed into his lap to lick his face. Bingyoo shook her head stubbornly. "You'll be fine. Look at how much this creature loves you. It won't be any different if it's one from the in between. You know more about monsters than anyone I know."

Jin rubbed Shishi's short nose and sighed. "I hope you're right. According to my grandmother, I'm nothing but a troublemaker and a failure."

Getting up, Bingyoo stretched and went off to the corner where she'd been sleeping, hidden by strategically piled crates. "So you'll prove her wrong." Her dimples appeared briefly. Then she ducked into her hideout.

The next morning, Jin emerged on deck to find a thick, ghastly haze blocking out the sun. Through a smoky miasma, he saw the banks of the river lined with mills, their chimneys belching dark clouds, their pipes spewing sludgy wastewater into the river, while their water wheels churned the Horned Serpent. A frothy, oily, black slick spread across the river's surface, and the water was a muddy soup that gave off a sulfurous stink. Jin coughed and pulled his collar over his nose, trying to filter out the noxious smells. His eyes watered.

"That's no use, boy," said the first mate. He handed Jin a slightly grimy kerchief. "Tie this around your face." He demonstrated with his own, wrapping a strip of cloth around his nose and mouth so that just his eyes showed.

"Thanks, Wako," said Jin, his voice slightly muffled. "I never knew it could be so hard to breathe."

The first mate nodded. "Can't smelt steel or make fire-powder or process flour and lumber without these mills, but they do make a mess. The capital gets to enjoy everything good that comes out of these mills, and none of the bad." He sniggered. "See, Shining Claw is the mouth, and Paddlepaw is the rear end. And we're right in the toilet!" Wheezing, Wako slapped Jin on the back, then headed back to the bow, still chortling to himself.

After they passed beneath a bridge, the captain shouted for the crew to trim the sails. "Ease the sheet!" As the battened panels rose, the ship picked up speed, the wind and the currents taking them away from the foul air and cacophony of the mill town. Though it became easier to breathe, the water remained a sickly shade of green streaked with fingers of rust red along the lifeless riverbanks, which were lined with twisted tangles of dead trees. By the time the sun was high in the sky, the mill town was far behind, but conditions seemed even worse. The harsh sunlight revealed flooded plains, abandoned villages, and dead livestock. The bloated body of an ox floated by them in the river. The thatched peaks of farm huts peeked above the waterline like little straw islands. "What happened here?" Jin wondered out loud.

"Broken dike," said a voice behind him. He jumped. Captain Pan nodded at the crumbled remains of an earthen wall alongside the river. "They say dragons used to dredge the land and prevent flooding. But now this sort of thing is happening all over the empire. The farther you get from the capital, the worse it gets. Things are falling apart, and the crone on the throne won't do a thing to fix 'em—just keeps squalling about the Hulagans and squeezing us for taxes." The captain spat a stream of red juice. "So we all need to take care of our own. I've been thinking, Whisperer Boy. If there really are monsters still on the island, then why don't you bring back a bunch? Keep the one you want and leave the rest with me. I'll give you ten strings back."

"You want monsters?" Jin gaped at the captain.

"Don't look so surprised. A real monster could bring in a fortune. If it means so much to you, I'll give you fifteen strings back. That's fifteen gold claws, plus you get your original deal."

Jin was insulted. "First of all, that's only a fraction of what I gave you. Secondly, monsters aren't meant to be bought and sold! They're won. They're sacred."

"Ha! Sacred, my toe. The Triad Throne uses 'em same as they use everything else—for their own gain. Magical or no, monsters might as well be cattle to the royal family. But they're worth something, and there's no reason why we can't get a piece of it, what with your ability and my boat. We'll both win. How's this—I'll give you half your money back. Twenty-five strings." Captain Pan tapped his head. "Think about it. Let me know before we reach Beastly."

Disturbed, Jin stalked away. But he couldn't shut his eyes to what he'd seen, and the captain's words haunted him all throughout the day and into the next. He thought about the Palace of Monsters and its gilded opulence. However rundown and neglected the old menagerie and other parts were, it was nothing compared with what was happening throughout the empire itself. Jin rubbed the lock charm at his neck. Was the captain right about the throne? Was it corrupt? And if so—was it worth saving?

Yes. Of course it was. For things would be different when *he* was in charge. Jin tucked the charm under his collar, resolute.

Toward the end of their fourth day on the water, the river began to broaden till the banks were barely visible in the distance. Before them was wide-open sea. The waves lapped at the sides of their vessel and a wind stiffened their sails. It rushed into the hold when Jin opened the hatch door.

"Do you smell that?" asked Bingyoo, inhaling deeply.

He grinned. "I do!" He could taste the salt in the air, and with it the promise of Whisper Island. Jin scrambled back out onto the deck and looked around. Pink and orange tinted the sky as the sun began its descent. The boat turned onto the open water, leaving the river delta behind. Seagulls swooped overhead, their eyes sharp and curious, searching for something to eat. He felt a rush of excitement. They were but hours away from the island, and his creature was waiting for him there.

It had to be.

Jin was sure of it.

CHAPTER 11

CITY ON THE SEA

THE TRIDENT CREST OF THE Three Realms danced above Jin's head, the empire's standard snapping and fluttering in the briny breeze. He stood on the prow of the small merchant ship as it cut through the ocean waves, the rocking of the vessel stronger than when they had been on the river. He breathed in the crisp air, then hurried back down into the hold with a newly emptied bucket, where a seasick Bingyoo was lying prone in her hidden corner. Shishi curled sympathetically by her side. The sour smell of vomit penetrated everywhere.

Holding his nose, Jin gave her the bucket. "I'll come back to check on you, but if I stay down here, I might start throwing up too."

"Thank you, Your Brilliance," Bingyoo said weakly. "It's been strange having you bring me things instead of the other way around."

He grinned. "I hadn't thought of it that way. But we'll reach the island soon, so don't get too used to ordering me around."

A look of consternation crossed her greenish face. "I'm not ordering you to do anything!"

"I'm just teasing." Jin snickered. Bingyoo's dimples appeared, but then she began to retch again. He whirled and scrambled away. "Barfing beasts, I have to get out of here!"

Back on the deck, he breathed a relieved sigh and returned to the prow. The ship sliced through the water, and Jin felt like he was flying. An enormous wave crashed across the bow, spraying everyone on deck with a blast of cold seawater. Jin let out a startled laugh and wiped his face. Though sometimes uncomfortable, ocean sailing was as exciting as he'd imagined. He squinted against the stinging mist thrown up by the breaking waves. In the distance, a blanket of thick fog lay across the corrugated surface of the water, obscuring the horizon and blotting out the afternoon sun.

It was a pity that Bingyoo had to stay hidden in the dank hold, for surely she'd feel better watching the waves and taking in the salt air. But he had a plan. Once they reached the island, he would reveal her and Shishi to the captain, and strike a bargain with him for their passage. Though Jin had no intention of actually doing so, he'd agree to the captain's proposal of capturing extra monsters. Once he was in command of his own monster, as he surely soon would be, he'd need not do a thing the captain said.

Eagerly he searched for signs of land. It wouldn't be long now. The island off the coast of the Three Realms was but a night and a day's sailing from the mainland—less if the winds were good—and they'd reached the open seas last night.

The first mate came up beside him. Leaning over the railing, Wako expelled a jet of red spittle into the churning waves. "You still set on going to Whisper Island? It's not too late to turn back, you know."

"Why would we turn back?" asked Jin, bemused. "I have to go. It's my assignment from the palace."

"The crew's getting jumpy. There's nothing good about going to a forbidden island full of deadly creatures," Wako muttered.

Jin laughed. "They're not all deadly—and if you don't bother them, you should be fine."

"Aren't you trying to capture one?" The first mate squinted at him. "If that's not bothering, what is?"

"You forget, I've been studying to be a Whisperer." Jin tried to sound confident. "The right creature will listen to me."

Wako snorted. "Sure. We might as well go off in search of that lost island that was just rediscovered—Middag? Midaga. The people themselves are said to have beastly powers."

"My ancest . . . I mean, one of the emperors of Samtei

sent an expedition long ago to find that island," said Jin. "He wanted them to find gold and some elixir that promised eternal life. But only a few made it back with stories about the natives there. I'd much rather possess a dragon than be like one. Can you imagine? Having scales and all that?"

A hand clapped on his shoulder, and the captain's voice boomed behind him. "Quite right. Any man with the same powers as an animal would himself be a creature of the in between. Better to have control over a monster than to be one!" Captain Pan chuckled. Then he leaned in and spoke in Jin's ear. "You been thinking about what I said?"

Jin nodded. "Would the crew be helping to handle the extra creatures?"

"Helping with *what*?" Wako regarded Jin and the captain with alarm. "Captain, the men are nervous enough as it is. If they're supposed to wrangle monsters, they might jump ship."

"Well then, leave the creatures to me. I've got Whispering in my blood." Jin squared his shoulders and met Captain Pan's gaze. "I think we can work something out."

The captain's eyes grew keen, and his face split into a red-stained smile. "Excellent."

Wako gave Jin a reproachful look, then turned to the captain. "Sir?"

Growling with annoyance, the captain shouted, "In my

quarters, Wako!" He clomped off, calling over his shoulder, "We'll talk later, boy!"

Alone again, Jin stared out at the misty horizon. For the first time, he wondered how the palace was reacting to his absence. His grandmother was likely apopletic, but if she could see him now, maybe she'd stop raging. Not only was he on his first sea voyage, but he was about to go on his first hunt—and for his very own creature companion, no less! He would prove once and for all that he was truly his father's son, worthy of taking the throne. How different things would be if his parents were still around. As emperor, his father might even be with him now, perhaps with his pet dragon by his side. There would be a grand welcoming ceremony in the village of Whisperers on the island, and then Jin would be sent off on his quest with plenty of supplies and assistance to track down his monstermate. He looked up at the banner of Samtei and gave a wry smile. Maybe this wasn't how things were usually done, but he'd figured a way to go after his birthright in spite of all the obstacles—and that was all that mattered.

"Land ahead! A city on the water!" The shout interrupted his thoughts.

Jin turned his head and stiffened. Out of the approaching clouds of white mist sprawled a fortress of towering spires—a glistening castle. He didn't remember any mention of such a place on Whisper Island. Had they taken a wrong turn? As he squinted, the boat was enveloped in a rolling wall of fog, and the fortress disappeared. A terrible grinding noise filled the air as the vessel shuddered suddenly to a halt. He jerked forward and caught himself on the boat's railing.

A slight breeze blew some of the fog aside, revealing a lagoon where they were grounded. The boat sat unmoving on a flat expanse of shallow water, black as ink and smooth as glass. Just beyond it was a desolate stretch of stone twisted into jagged formations that looked like dragon teeth. The glistening castle was nowhere to be seen.

"Great beasts, where are we?" Jin scanned the rocky shore, and spotted a long-legged crab at the water's edge, waving its claws at them. But it was no ordinary crab. Its shell resembled the death mask of a human face, an open-mouthed rictus of agony rendered on the crab's back. It scuttled farther up the shore to join several other crabs with similar carapaces, a collection of human faces frozen in crab form. "Warrior crabs!" Jin was beside himself with excitement. "This must be Whisper Island!" A shiver of fear ran through him. He'd read that warrior crabs liked to feed on human flesh, and were thought to be the reincarnated spirits of fallen soldiers. But he could easily outrun a crab, he reminded himself. And they were a sign that they'd made it to the island after all.

Ripples formed across the surface of the lagoon. Out of the corner of his eye, Jin caught a flash of white. Around a dozen forms with pale bellies slithered through the water. A few swam alongside the boat, and he followed, moving down the deck with his eyes fixed on them. *Creatures—but what were they?* Jin racked his memory, trying to identify them, but before he could figure it out, they swam off the shallows and dove into the depths of the lagoon.

He turned at the urgent clanging of an alarm bell. As the captain called for the crew to identify the problem, the men raced about the deck. "Out of the way, boy," growled Wako irritably, shoving Jin back against the rail. Several ruddermen stampeded past. Other men swung down the sides of the boat. Jin watched as they inspected the hull and shouted back. "We're stuck on a shoal, sir! A whole ledge right beneath the water!" Captain Pan let out a string of curses, while the first mate threw his hands up. "That was no city—we were fooled by a monster mirage!"

"No apparent damage to the keel!" another crewman reported.

"Thank the gods for that," responded Wako. "What shall we do, sir?"

The captain began to bark orders. "Get the secondary anchor and throw it out that way so we can start kedging the boat. Ruddermen, shift ballast weight back to the stern. Wako, see if you can manuever the leeboards, while the rest of you get to pushing." He looked at Jin. "Whisperer Boy! Make yourself useful. Get down on that rock and push."

Jin followed several crew members to a rope-and-bamboo ladder thrown over the side of the vessel. As he passed by the hatch leading down to the storage hold, he glimpsed Bingyoo peering out through a crack, her face still pale and sickly. He stopped and knelt by the hatch door, pretending a pebble had gotten in his shoe. "Stay put," he murmured. "The ship's stuck, so we're working to free it. Are you okay?"

"Yes," she whispered. He smiled encouragingly, and she shut the hatch door.

The crewmen jumped off the ladder into water hip-deep, standing on an expansive sunken stone ledge that stretched to shore. Half the ship perched just on its lip, the other half over a dark abyss. Jin scanned the waters for the strange fish. He noticed that the ledge was covered in a thick layer of sand. Scattered curved white fragments, looking much like giant eggshells, were embedded in the sand. It reminded him of something he'd seen in the pages of the bestiary. Before he could place it, Captain Pan yelled, "What're you gawking at? Get down there!"

With a deep breath, Jin climbed down the swinging ladder. When he alighted onto the flooded rock, the water came well past his waist. His soaked shoes were heavy weights pulling at his every step as he sloshed next to the boat's hull with the others. He was smaller than even the shortest sailor, but he put his shoulder against the boat alongside them.

The first mate called out. "We're ready, sir!"

"Excellent." Captain Pan nodded at the men down on the submerged outcropping. "Start pushing!"

Shouts and grunts filled the misty air as the entire crew began trying to move the grounded vessel.

"Push, yah! Pull, yah! Push, yah! Pull, yah!"

The men took up the singsong chant as they labored to free the ship. Jin felt his face turning red as he shoved, straining to keep in time with the chant. "Push, yah," he panted.

A shrill scream sliced through the fog. Jin turned. An enormous fish, its head whiskered like a giant carp, emerged from the depths of the abyss, its gaping jaws lined with rows of sharp teeth. As it snapped at the ship's stern, its thick whiplike whiskers lashed out and swept several men off the deck. Its silvery scales began sprouting into glistening gold feathers, while its long, streaming fins morphed into vast wings pumping great gusts of wind with each frantic beat. The rest of the fish continued to transform, becoming a massive bird nearly as tall as the ship's masts, with grasping talons and a tearing beak. Shouts of terror filled the air as the crew scrambled to get out of the way.

"Kunpeng!" Jin gasped. No other creature could change from fish to bird like that. The meaning of the egg-like fragments in the sand became clear. They'd grounded right in the midst of a nest of fish-monster babies—and the mother was not happy about it at all.

Captain Pan called for his men to fight. "Get your

firelances!" he bellowed. "Quickly!"

"No!" Jin cried. The words of the bestiary came to him in a rush. *When this leviathan fish takes the form of a gargantuan golden-winged eagle, the kunpeng becomes the most powerful of birds.* If they angered it further, they'd have no chance against it. "You'll only make it worse! It's trying to protect its young!" But no one paid any attention. His voice was drowned out in the chaos.

The sailors on board raced to grab their weapons. The kunpeng clamped one clawed foot around the long thick handle of the rudder and snapped it like a twig. Splinters of wood flew everywhere. With several flaps of its golden wings, gales of wind swirled about the ship and threw the crew off their feet. Standing in the shallows, Jin struggled to stay upright. The monster snatched screaming men up in its hooked beak and flung them overboard like bits of rubbish.

Firepowder and bullets exploded with flashes of light from the firelances as sailors began shooting at the creature in frantic bursts. Flying through the mist, the lead pellets glanced off the kunpeng's golden feathers and peppered its eyes. It screeched and shook its head.

"More!" roared Captain Pan. "Aim for its eyes!"

As the men reloaded their weapons, the kunpeng dove into the water and turned back into a giant fish, sending massive ripples through the lagoon. Its great tail slapped against the side of the boat with a sickening crunch, smashing open a hole. Jin heard the high frantic yips of a dog barking.

"Shishi! Bingyoo!" he shouted, horrified.

He had to try to get them off the boat. Jin climbed up the dangling ladder, which jerked about as the giant fish tore at the stern with its teeth-lined maw. Peering over the edge of the deck, he saw the captain shaking a mangled trident spear at the creature and yelling insults. The first mate stood beside Captain Pan with a firelance, shooting sprays of lead pellets at the kunpeng as quickly as he could load them. Jin squinted through the fog and firepowder smoke. The hatch to the storage hold was still closed. He climbed partway onto the deck, calling out for Bingyoo and Shishi.

Wako whipped around. "Run, fool boy!" bellowed the first mate. Then the monstrous fish leaped from the water into the air, transforming at once into a gleaming bird. It grabbed Captain Pan with its claws and snatched him off the deck while he screamed. As it flapped away, a huge gust of wind from the creature's wings knocked Jin back into the shallows. With a splash, he landed hard on his shoulder. Cold sea water went up his nose. It filled his ears and eyes with a murky haze. As he thrashed about, his hands brushed rock and he pushed hard. Jin's head broke the surface of the water, and he coughed and gasped, dizzy from his fall.

The screech of the great bird echoed through the air. Jin staggered to his feet and glanced up. The kunpeng had returned to the boat, perched on a railing as the ship listed to one side under its weight. It snapped its beak and ripped off a piece of wood that ran nearly the entire length of the ship, then tossed it like a piece of straw. It flew at Jin and he ducked. The torn wood barely missed him and struck the shallows with a splash.

Heart thudding like the drums of a Monster Festival parade, Jin turned and sloshed away as fast as he could. But the sandy shoal was uneven, and the tide was nearly to his waist, slowing him to an agonizing slog. Something brushed against him and he looked down to see the scaly body of a baby kunpeng swim by, its rippling fins trailing gracefully. Though it was a juvenile, it was as long as a man was tall. Jin yelped and searched about him for more. Were they as fierce as their mother? He didn't want to find out.

Something bumped Jin from behind and he tripped, falling face-first with a splash. In the stinging salt water, his eyes widened as the young kunpeng swam around him. Its eyes were blue, and its whiskers were just beginning to sprout, but its teeth looked sharp and large enough to do serious damage. Frantically he searched his memory for what he'd read.

It's too young to be hunting for its own food, he realized. *Don't panic.*

He emerged spluttering and wiped his eyes to find the shore was within ten paces. The young kunpeng swam a short distance away, then doubled back and circled him. Jin put out a hand and felt its slick body slide by. It swam around him again. A strange sense of wonder came over him. Was this baby monster . . . playing? He wiggled his fingers along the creature's scales, and it rolled over, exposing its white belly. Holy beasts, he was petting a real live kunpeng!

"Over here, boy," said a voice nearby. Several crew members cowered behind a boulder on the rocky beach and waved at him to join them.

A sharp crack sounded from the boat. Jin glanced back to see the enormous golden raptor tearing at a sail while men on deck shouted to each other for help. His heart sank. Bingyoo and Shishi were still aboard. There had to be a way to save them.

He looked down at the baby kunpeng. Impulsively, he reached down and wrapped his arms around its slippery, scaled trunk. Heaving it out of the water, he turned toward its parent. "Hey!" he shouted. The juvenile's long body writhed about wildly, nearly knocking him over as it transformed into an ungainly chick as large as a goat, covered in fluffy pale down.

"Featherheaded fool!" exploded one of the cowering crew members. "What in the name of all beasts are you doing?"

The chick gave an ear-splitting squawk, beating its small, useless wings. The kunpeng turned its head and fixed a glaring yellow eye upon them. Jin gritted his teeth and fought to keep a grip on the bird's fuzzy body, hugging it close even as it kicked and squirmed, scrabbling at him with surprisingly sharp claws. "Yes, that's it!" he yelled at its parent. "Look what I've got here!"

Launching into the air, the kunpeng abandoned the ship with a shove. Jin's heart leaped as he saw the battered vessel begin to drift away, freed from the rock. He inched toward the shore as the great bird flapped into the sky. "That's right, off you go," he said. The juvenile squawked again, and Jin patted its downy belly, trying to soothe it. It nipped his hand with a hooked black beak. "Ow!" The kunpeng circled overhead and let out an answering cry. "No, no, it's not hurt," he called. But then the golden raptor folded its wings and plunged toward him. "Oh, muck."

In a panic Jin released the downy baby bird, which fell into the water with a splash and turned into a wriggling fish. He whirled and raced for land, intent on diving into a crack he spotted between boulders. No monster bird could get to him there. As he glanced up, the kunpeng extended its curved talons, reaching for him. Jin thrashed desperately up onto the stony shore and stumbled, hitting his head hard against a rock.

Then he blacked out.

CHAPTER 12

UNCANNY BEASTS

A SHARP PINCHING SENSATION SHOT through Jin, and he startled awake. He felt another hard pinch and jerked away, then struggled to sit up. "Ouch." He lay back, head throbbing, and shivered in the cool dark. Clicking, skittering noises surrounded him, and he blearily tried to focus on their source. Then something tugged painfully at his scalp. With a yelp, he clapped a hand to his head and scrambled to his feet.

He was on the stony shore of Whisper Island. A full moon glowed like a bright paper lantern, casting its pale light across several warrior crabs, illuminating the eerie angry faces formed on their shells. "Monstermuck!" He must have been out for hours. The crabs backed away, waving their claws. "Get away from me! I'm not dead," Jin growled. He felt a trickle of something running down his temple and swiped at it, leaving his hand dark with blood. "You can't eat me, savage little scavengers. Go on. Get!"

Stamping his feet, he shooed them away. As they scattered and scuttled across the shore, Jin searched the moonlit horizon for signs of the boat, of the kunpeng and its young, of his dog, of Bingyoo. Aside from splinters of wood and a few broken planks floating in the lagoon, all was calm and quiet. Did the boat make it? Bingyoo and Shishi had still been on board. The screams of the crew came back to him, along with the creature's fury as it tore at the hull, and his heart sank.

Walking along the desolate shore, Jin gazed over the glassy black water of the lagoon. He shuddered thinking of the raptor's screech, the sailors flung about, all while Bingyoo and Shishi were trapped in the hold. Was there any way they could have survived? Gods 'n' monsters, if only they hadn't grounded right in the middle of a kunpeng nest.

You featherheaded fool! With a start, he remembered the insult hurled by one of the three crewmen who'd made it to shore, hiding behind a boulder while Jin had tried to lure the kunpeng away with one of its babies. The chick's scrabbling claws had scratched him up badly, but it could have been worse. He'd never forget the kunpeng's baleful glare as it streaked toward him. How had he escaped its fearsome beak and talons? Turning from the sea, Jin saw a path leading inland, away from the stony shore. There was no trace of the sailors. If there were any survivors, they could have gone that way, but if they ran into the wrong sort of monsters, they wouldn't last long.

His stomach roiled. All he'd wanted to do was come to this island. Now he was here, but his wish had come at a terrible cost.

Jin bit his lip. It was salty from seawater, and his tongue felt fuzzy and swollen. He was horribly parched. Desperate for drinkable water, he set off down the path. It was quiet and dark, illuminated only by the moon. The landscape was mostly stone and rock formations, but before long the hard ground softened with sand. It then became soil, and scrubby tufts of vegetation began to appear. But no fresh water was in sight—not even a puddle.

By the time he'd reached a grove of spindly twisted trees, his scratches felt as if they were on fire, and he could hardly think. In a moonlit clearing ahead, Jin spotted the glimmer of a deep pool. *Thank the good beasts!* Dashing straight for it, he hurled himself in without a second thought. The cold shock of it relieved his throbbing skin, and he broke through the surface with a grateful gasp. He pulled himself onto a broad flat rock at the pond's edge and drank, gulping greedily from cupped hands. When his thirst was slaked at last, he splashed his face and neck. A bloody bump on his head stung so hard he yelled in pain. Gritting his teeth, he washed it till the water ran clean.

A yellow-green monster popped out of the water, and

Jin fell back with a shout. Its beaked mouth opened wide and hissed, its red eyes glaring below a bowl-like indentation on its head. The creature was the size and shape of a monkey, its turtle-like shell covered in slime. Though he'd only seen it in paintings and drawings, there was no mistaking what it was. "Water ape," Jin whispered, thrilled but afraid. He recalled the words of the bestiary: *It will attempt to drown anyone who disturbs its habitat. Children are frequent victims.* He retreated with slow, careful steps. "Nice beastie," he croaked. If only he had some cucumbers—he'd read that water apes had a weakness for them. Remembering that they also responded to respect, Jin bowed as he backed away. The creature stared at him intently, then bobbed its head before disappearing into the pond.

He breathed a sigh of relief and examined himself. His lock charm was still around his neck. His tunic was soaking wet and in tatters, and he had angry red welts on his skin, but they weren't bleeding, and the burning sensation had washed away.

Dazed and slapping at mosquitos, Jin wandered through the trees in the night. It wasn't long before he got the distinct feeling he was being watched. Strange hoots, mournful cries, otherworldly shrieks, howls, and clicks filled his ears. Each new sound sent him peering anxiously through the dim forest. Shafts of moonlight pierced the canopy, but they betrayed nothing. Alone and surrounded by monsters, Jin felt utterly lost. What was he to do?

Exhausted, damp, and chilled through, he came across a fallen log and sat down to rest. Though his pack had been left on the boat, his lockpicks and firestarter had remained lodged in his pockets. At least he could try to warm up with a fire. He'd never had to build one or worry about cold at the palace. But how hard could it be, really? He found bits of dead wood around the log and threw them in a haphazard heap. Then he took out the cross-hatched piece of steel shaped like a snake and the chip of quartz stone. Striking them together over the stack of wood, he managed a few wan sparks. But nothing caught fire. Baffled, he rubbed at his lock charm as he poked at the pile. Despair crept through him. Why wouldn't it burn?

He startled at sharp twittering directly overhead. A pair of regal-looking scarlet birds eyed him haughtily from a branch. They resembled birds he'd seen in carvings around the palace, only something seemed to be missing. Then one shook its long curling tail and it burst into flame. "Just as I thought!" exclaimed Jin. "Firebirds!" The other bird's tail also erupted in flames. They launched off their perch and swept toward Jin, the heat and light from their flaming feathers feeling like the sun. Fearing another monster bird attack, he fell back in a panic and threw his arms over his head. But they only circled low once, twice, thrice, before flying away. Panting, he watched their bright forms disappear into the trees. Hearing a crackle, he turned back to see that the fire-birds' trailing tails had ignited the wood, the flames leaping as they grew.

Gratefully, he held his hands to the fire and began to thaw. He couldn't understand why his firestarter hadn't worked, but thank the gods for those monster birds. If only Bingyoo and Shishi were with him. What had happened to them? He'd give anything for them to be all right. That, and a hot meal, plus a whole team of Whisperers to help him.

Wait . . .

The village of Beastly. Of course! How could he have forgotten? It was where the ship was originally headed. Whisperers at the village could equip and guide him. In fact, the ship might've managed to make it there after all, with Bingyoo and Shishi safe.

The maps that he'd so painstakingly copied from the imperial library had been left on board, but tracing the island's contours had helped etch them in his mind. As he remembered, the seaside settlement was at the edge of a valley sheltered by the island's sole mountain ridge. Once he found the ridge, he could locate the village.

It was night and hard to see, but Jin couldn't wait. After he felt sufficiently warm and dry, he stamped out the fire, saving one flaming branch to use as a torch. He waved it before him, squinting to make out what he could in the enveloping dark.

A family of what looked like white foxes darted past, glowing in the moonlight. One of them, smaller than the others, paused to cock its head at him. Chittering, it fanned out a collection of furry tails like a peacock unfurling its glory. Multiple tails! Could it be one of the magical variety known as fox spirits? They were said to bestow wisdom, good fortune, and long life on their captors—quite useful for a monstermate. He took an eager step toward the fox, but it let out a warning snarl. Its face shifted to mirror his own, so that Jin's head glared from atop a fox body. Turning back to a pointed fox face, it whirled and trotted off after the others.

Jin rubbed his eyes, shaken. It was definitely a fox spirit. They were notorious shapeshifters. Despite his devoted study of the bestiary, it was one thing to read about a monster and its traits, and another thing entirely to come across it in person. His pace quickened along with his heart. Angering the kunpeng had been disaster enough, but there were plenty of other uncanny beasts that could do just as much damage if he wasn't careful. Flying ones like the giant bee-like insect known as a stinging duck, so large that a prick from its tail was deadly. Fanged monsters like the piyao that once guarded the imperial treasury—their teeth could tear through metal. Creatures like the haitai with its sharp horn, ready to gore anyone who'd committed misdeeds. It occurred to Jin then that forging imperial papers and lying to everyone from his tutor to the ship's crew could find him at the wrong end of that horn.

Perhaps wandering around at night had been a bad move. Nervously he rubbed at his lock charm and began to hum. *Yawn, beastie; Calm, beastie; Tuck your fangs away.* A rustling sounded above him. Jin looked up to see a flock of hawklike birds perched in the branches above him, hunched beneath their wings in sleep. One remained awake, its eyes fierce and unblinking in an almost human face. What appeared to be a long, bulbous nose was its beak—a mark of ferocious creatures known as tengu. *Tengu are protectors of the forest. They will happily rip apart anyone they catch willfully harming it.* Recalling that bit from the bestiary, Jin looked at the torch in his hand in alarm. Would this count? Even if it didn't, tengu were known to kidnap lost humans and take their memories. Quickly he snuffed out the smoldering branch and scurried away, unnerved. He'd had enough of monster birds. The sooner he could get to the Whisperers' settlement, the better.

At long last, a rosy tinge radiated across the eastern sky, and a looming shape appeared in the distance: the remains of a former volcanic crater. It looked just like a great beast curled up in sleep. Jin smiled wearily at the sight. If he remembered his map tracing correctly, the mountainous ridge rose in the center of the island, and the seaside village of Beastly would be straight to the west. Maybe he wasn't so lost after all.

With the ridge and the sky as his guide, Jin traipsed on. The sun crept over the horizon, bathing the island's features in golden light. As the shadowy dark of night lifted, the prickly feeling of being tracked by unseen eyes eased, though he knew monsters were all around. Peering hopefully into the distance, he saw no signs of the coast or people. He was still too far. Jin licked his parched lips, wishing he had a flask to carry water. His stomach felt hollow in a way he'd never experienced before. Its relentless hunger was painful after a lifetime of having the finest of dishes brought to him. If he couldn't find the village, what was he to do about food or drink? Was he supposed to trap something? Fish with his bare hands? Where could he find a stream? In desperation, he bent and cupped his hands around long strands of dew-covered grass and gathered what water he could into his palms.

But when he straightened, all thoughts of thirst left Jin. There before him stood a real live zouya, a creature that could run a thousand miles in a single day. It resembled an enormous tiger, though its fur was a rainbow of colors, and its exceedingly long tail swirled about its striped body like a ribbon. It took no notice of Jin as it nosed about a tuft of grass, biting at the stalks with sharp teeth. Excitement replaced

Jin's worries. This beast could crisscross this island—no, *the empire*—quicker than any horse. It would make a fantastic monstermate. He crept closer, hand out for the zouya to sniff. "Wouldn't you like to be my beastie?" crooned Jin. The zouya turned and its green eyes glowered. It gave a low warning growl, then appeared to vanish into thin air.

It had run away. Jin blinked, cowed and a bit deflated. He should have known it wouldn't be that easy.

Never mind, he told himself. A dragon would make the best monstermate for an emperor anyway. Once he found the Whisperers, they'd help him capture a worthy creature. Until then, it was better to leave any monsters he saw alone, and hope that they'd do the same. When a poisonspike pig lumbered across his path, Jin kept his distance with a wary eye on its sharp, needlelike quills. They could be shot from the pig's hide with deadly force, as effective as an entire company of archers.

At last he stumbled into a field striped with leafy green plants sporting long, purple fruits that looked familiar. Though it was overgrown and weedy, the field was clearly farmed, and the fruit must be edible. Ravenous, he plucked one and bit into its shiny purple skin. Jin chewed hungrily, but a bitter taste filled his mouth, and the unpleasantly spongy texture felt like it was drying out his tongue. "Blech!" He spit it out, grimacing, and threw the fruit away.

Jin wiped his lips. At least this was a farm. That meant

Beastly must be nearby. He continued west, keeping the towering ridge of the crater, called a caldera on the library maps, behind him. He came across additional signs of civilization: a dirt road, more fields, an orchard of trees planted in rows. As he followed the winding road, he was rewarded with the glimmer of blue ocean on the horizon. He was nearly there! Jin hurried along, convinced that the boat would be docked at the village port, battered but at its proper destination. It had to be. Anything else was unthinkable. Bingyoo and Shishi would be there, along with the captain and crew. They would certainly all have some tales to tell each other, wouldn't they? When Jin came around another curve, he froze. There was the village of Beastly. But it wasn't what he had expected at all.

CHAPTER 13

BEASTLY

THE BLAZING SUN OVERHEAD CAST a harsh light on the village of Beastly—or what used to be the village of Beastly. Jin shaded his eyes and squinted, unable to believe what he saw. As he drew near, his heart sank lower with each step. The Whisperers' settlement had been built around a central square, its buildings spilling toward a small pier overlooking the shore. It looked like a lone finger pointing into the sea. There was no sign of the ship. Worse, Beastly's structures were nothing but burnt husks, some mere piles of ash and broken timber. Not a soul was in sight.

"What happened?" Aghast at the devastation, Jin wandered around the ruins of the Whisperers' village. It had clearly once been a beautiful hamlet on the sea, in full view of deep blue waters, in a verdant valley sheltered in the lee of the volcanic ridge. All that was left were blackened frames and collapsed buildings, cold and still. If there had been survivors, there was no evidence of them now. The whole place was abandoned. But since when? And why had no news of this reached the palace?

Could a creature of fire have gotten out of control and set everything alight? Certainly there were beasts here capable of that, like the firebirds he'd encountered. It couldn't be a dragon. Unless one of the fire-breathing types found in the lands of the Far West had somehow made it to Beastly, dragons were water-bearing creatures. So why weren't the Whisperers able to call on the island's dragons to douse the flames? It was very troubling.

As long as the Three Realms still had creatures of the in between, it commanded respect from its citizens and neighbors. If the last refuge for the beasts was in danger, if there were no more Whisperers to watch over the island, what did it mean for Samtei?

Surely the Whisperers on the island couldn't all be gone. Maybe they'd moved somewhere else after the village burned. But the unkempt fields that Jin had passed made more sense now. And the charred remains of the village were a silent testament to a horrible event.

Which meant he was totally alone—and surrounded by free-roaming monsters.

Despairingly, Jin kicked at a charred piece of wood, flipping it over to reveal intricate carving and bright paint. It was the fallen lintel from a doorway, shaped like a protective dragon. Some protection. He gave it another savage kick, clear across what was left of the village square. What was he to do? He might be able to find food and water—there were springs on the island, and those fields and orchards. He'd give those vile purple fruit another try if he had to. But there was no one here to help him, and no way back to the mainland.

The enormity of the situation hit him at once, and he suddenly felt faint. Dizzily, Jin bent down and put his head between his knees. Even if he managed to find a monster-mate now, how would he bring it to the palace? He was stuck.

Jin groaned. All was lost! What good was a beastie that granted your right to the throne if you couldn't even get it home?

"... oof, he's in a state, isn't he? ..."

"... indeed ..."

"... Haw! Haw! ..."

The murmur of voices floated through the village ruins. Jin's head snapped up. "Hello?" he called. Listening care-fully, he heard only silence. Then the murmuring started again.

Jin straightened and began searching for the source. "Excuse me? Hello? Anyone there? Where are you?" He circled the village square, trying to get a response. He peered into the few burned-out buildings left standing, but saw no signs of life. Had it just been the wind? Then he spotted several monster birds, each with three legs and sleek feathers that shifted from black to emerald as they moved. They were green crows, said to be messengers of the gods. Perched on a charred doorframe at the edge of the village square, they watched him with bright red eyes. Were the voices from them? He halted, frowning. "No, it couldn't be."

"New around here, aren't you?" said one.

"Looking for someone?" asked another.

"What's your business?" queried the third.

Jin's mouth fell open. "I—I'm looking for the Whisperers," he stammered. "I didn't know green crows *talked*."

"How else are we supposed to pass along messages?" asked the first crow, shuffling back and forth on its perch. Each clawed foot took a step to the right, then back to the left in a peculiar dance.

"I thought you carried written ones on your third leg," said Jin.

The second crow let out a little rattle that ended in a loud caw, as if it were laughing. "Sometimes it's easier just to repeat what we've heard."

"Where is everyone? What happened to this place?" asked Jin.

"What happened to *you*?" countered the first crow, strutting side to side.

Jin looked down at his tattered clothes. "I was on a boat that angered a kunpeng. I was hoping the boat had made its way here. I wanted to find a monstermate. I never thought I'd find *this*." He waved a hand at the village ruins.

"You want a monstermate?" The third crow scratched its neck with its third leg. "Maybe you're off to a good start."

"Really?" Jin was perplexed. "How's that?"

The feathers around its neck fluffed up, then settled. "If you want something you've never had, you have to do something you've never done." It launched off its perch, flapping its wings, followed by the other two green crows. Their caws echoed through the air as they flew off.

Though he was mystified by what the crow meant, Jin felt strangely comforted by the first conversation he'd had since awakening on the island. Here he was, actually *talking* to creatures! Then he remembered. He was shipwrecked here. A chat with a few birds hadn't changed that one bit.

He trudged through the destroyed village to the shore, where the solitary pier extended into the water. Jin walked to the end of it and looked out, hoping for a sign of the ship. He saw nothing.

Sighing, he watched waves splash against the pier's wooden pilings and foam up onto the beach. Then he blinked. Were those . . . fresh tracks along the shoreline?

Jin ran off the pier and down to the water to examine them. In the damp packed sand were a set of human footprints—marks clearly made by the soles of shoes. They weren't very big. Could they be Bingyoo's? A flicker of hope flared to life in his chest, and his heart began to pound. Maybe she'd made it to shore somehow, on a piece of drift-wood or perhaps by swimming, though he couldn't recall if she even *could* swim.

"Bingyoo?" he called. He followed the tracks at a fast clip, anxious to find where they led. Soon he was running. There *was* someone else on this island—a person! He wasn't alone.

The footprints left the shore and wound away from the water, disappearing into a stretch of sandy hillocks covered in scrub brush and tall clumps of feathery silvergrass. In the uneven terrain, Jin lost sight of the trail. He stopped, frus-trated, and searched the ground around him.

Another green crow flew overhead and circled. "Lost, are you?"

"I'm looking for a girl—her footsteps led here," said Jin eagerly. "You haven't seen anyone, have you?"

"Anyone—or someone?" cawed the crow. "We see everyone."

The bestiary never mentioned how annoying three-legged crows could be. "What's the difference?" Jin shouted. "Just tell me if you've seen any other people!"

But the crow dipped and whirled away, flashing green in the sunlight. In a fit of temper, Jin kicked a spray of sand into the air. It flew into a clump of silvergrass, whipping through its long, waving strands. A strange buzzing sound erupted, and a round, furry creature scuttled out. Knee-high and winged with six legs, it had no face or tail. "Oh, sorry," said Jin, startled. It furiously flapped its two pairs of feathered wings and buzzed again, sounding almost like it was humming a song. Jin couldn't recall seeing a monster like this in the bestiary. He leaned down to take a closer look. Could there be creatures here he didn't know about?

"Stay away from that hundun!"

The sharp voice made Jin jump. He whirled to see a scowling girl, aiming the spiky points of a farming trident at his throat.

Eyeing the trident, Jin raised his hands in submission. The furry round creature scuttled away, humming and buzzing its wings. He wondered how it could even see.

The girl growled and gave her weapon a little shake to get his attention. "Who are you?" She appeared to be around his age, with a pointed chin and dark eyes that glared from under a ragged, close-cropped fringe of hair. Though she was a bit taller than Jin, her face was gaunt, and her threadbare tunic and pants hung loosely on her frame. Her heels extended over the crushed backs of shoes that she wore like slippers, as they were clearly too small for her. She looked him over from head to toe, keeping the trident's pointed tines in his face. "How did you even get here?"

"It's a little hard to think when someone's threatening to poke your eyes out." Jin recoiled. "Would you please lower that? I'm of no danger to you."

The girl grunted. "That's for me to decide. Answer my questions. Only those with permission from the throne can set foot on this island, and no one's come in years." Her face tightened.

"I have papers with the imperial seal, but they're with the captain." A knot formed in Jin's stomach. "You haven't seen a ship, have you? The one I came on? We grounded on some rocks in the fog yesterday, right on top of a kunpeng's nest. It attacked and I was knocked unconscious. I think it was somewhere on the north shore."

"A kunpeng," said the girl slowly. "How do you know what it was?"

"It was a giant fish in the water and turned into an equally big bird out of it. Either way, it was very angry." Jin poked at the holes in his tunic.

"Goldie." The girl lowered her trident in dismay. "If her nest was disturbed, then she certainly would be." Glowering, she hefted her weapon back up. "Were any of her babies hurt?"

"I don't think so." Uneasily, Jin folded his scratched-up arms, remembering the struggling chick's irate squawks. "But a lot of men were, and the monster tore the ship up pretty badly. I was hoping they managed to get away. My pet dog and a palace servant were still on board."

The girl shook her head. "There's been no sign of a ship around here. But there's been plenty of notice about a strange boy lurking." She narrowed her eyes down the length of her trident. "I'm not sure what to make of you."

A shrill whistle pierced the air, and they turned at the sound. Jin's jaw dropped. Atop a sandy dune was a boy mounted on an immense black creature with two heads— one on each end of its long body. They were distinctly boar-like, each with a set of gleaming tusks, long broad ears, and bristled snouts. The two heads were side by side, watching Jin with two pairs of small dark eyes.

"A bingfeng! That's one of the most stubborn creatures around!" Jin blurted out.

The boy cracked a smile. He looked around Jin's age as well, with dark hair shaved close to the scalp. He had the same sharp chin and wide mouth as the girl. They were clearly related, although the boy's expression was more curious than suspicious. "Did you hear that, Masa? I don't think he meant it as a compliment."

"He wouldn't be wrong," said Masa dryly. "That creature gives new meaning to the word *pig-headed*."

"Don't listen to her, Komengo," said the boy Whisperer to the bingfeng. He slid off the two-headed boar and rubbed each of its snouts. Scrambling down the dune, he joined the girl and tilted his head at Jin. "You seem to know something of uncanny beasts. How'd you come by that information?"

"I know all about monsters," Jin said. "I've studied every one at the palace. Or at least, I thought I had. That fuzzy thing—a hundun? I can't recall it from the bestiary. Anyway, my grandmother has a phoenix. It's pretty bad-tempered, but she seems to like it that way."

Masa raised an eyebrow. "Your grandmother possesses a creature? Who is she?"

"Empress Dowager Soro," said Jin. He drew himself up as tall as he could. "I'm Crown Prince Jin, and I've come to find my monstermate."

"*You're* the crown prince?" Looking him up and down, Masa pointed. "Is that supposed to be an imperial jewel?" Self-consciously, Jin stuffed the worn lock charm under his collar. He had to admit it wasn't helping his case. Her gaze was withering. "Nothing about you says you're royal. You have no permission papers. And shouldn't you have come on the royal barge?"

Before Jin could respond, the boy shrugged in cheerful agreement. "My little sister makes excellent points."

The girl scowled. "We're the same age, Mau."

"But I'm older," Mau shot back.

His sister scoffed. "By five minutes!"

Mau grinned. "And that five minutes makes all the dif-ference."

"Look," Jin interjected. "I told you already, the ship I was on ran aground on a kunpeng nest. I tried to distract it, but it was pretty angry. I got knocked unconscious, and when I came to, the ship was gone. I came to Beastly to get help, but . . ." His voice trailed off and the twins' faces clouded over. "What happened, anyway? Where are all the Whisperers? Are you two the only ones left?"

"Well," Mau began, but his sister put a hand on his arm.

"What makes you think that we're the only Whisperers left?" Masa asked.

Jin shrugged. "You're the first people I've come across so far, and the village is gone. I have to say, I'm relieved to even find you, after seeing what happened to Beastly. Did you lose control of the monsters? If there are other Whisperers, I'd really prefer to work with the most skilled ones here."

"You would, would you?" A gleam came into her eyes, and she smiled sweetly. "Well, Your Highness, that's fine by me." Turning, she started up the slope to the two-headed boar.

Her brother cleared his throat and gave a slight bow. "I think we should go."

"Great, because I'm starving," said Jin. He followed them to the boar and watched as they mounted it. "There's room for me on that beast, too, right?"

"Step back, please," said Masa, pointing her trident at him. The boar turned its two heads at Jin. One gave a high-pitched squeal while the other grunted angrily.

Jin faltered and stepped back. "What?"

She sighed. "You can't just come tagging along with us.

We still don't know who you are, or what you're doing here."

"I told you! I'm the crown prince, and I'm here to find my monstermate," Jin said firmly. "As your future emperor, you *have* to help me."

The twins looked at each other. Mau's mouth quirked. "That's what you think." The boy Whisperer clicked his tongue, and the giant boar turned one of its heads and began to lumber away.

"You—you're just going to leave me?" Jin spluttered.

Masa glanced back. "You managed to make it this far. Good luck, *Your Lordship*!" She waggled her fingers in a jaunty wave.

No one had ever spoken to him like this before—not when he'd been identified as a prince. Jin was dumbfounded. Not knowing what else to do, he broke into a run after the double-headed boar and the twin Whisperers. "Wait!"

He scurried after them. Even as he shouted for them to slow down, ordered them to stop in the name of the Triad Throne, swore they'd be sorry for not helping him, they ignored him. Though the bingfeng's long body had rather spindly-looking legs, it picked up surprising speed, and Jin barely managed to keep the lumbering creature in his sights. Thank the gods, it was so large that even at a distance it was hard to miss. His lungs burned and his legs ached as he followed it out of the dunes and along the shore, and then it took an abrupt turn and sped inland. They were within sight of the ruins of Beastly when Masa glanced back.

Seeing Jin still doggedly on their tail, she threw up her hands and leaned forward to her brother. The black boar came to a halt, the rear head watching placidly as Jin ran up. Masa swung around in her seat and pointed her trident. "Let's get one thing straight. We're not stopping because you ordered us to, and certainly not because you claim to be royal."

"Fine," Jin wheezed. He'd never run this long or far before. Bending over, he leaned on his knees. The great black creature stamped its feet and shuffled a few steps closer. Jin felt a whoosh of warm breath as the rear head of the boar lowered and sniffed him. "Nice piggy," he muttered nervously. He froze as its bristly snout tickled the back of his neck. The front head snorted as if it had just sneezed, and the rear head withdrew. Jin looked up just as a slimy pink tongue shot out and swiped across his face. Spluttering, he straightened up and wiped at his eyes.

Mau chuckled. "Komengo likes him. I guess he's okay."

"Not so fast," said his sister. "Why shouldn't we just leave him on his own? After all, if he's really descended from royalty, he ought to have some abilities with monsters. The first emperors were chosen from the best Whisperers in the land."

"That was nearly a thousand years ago," said Mau. "The royal family has barely any Whispering skill left. If he's really the crown prince, he'll probably get eaten. It's a miracle he's stayed alive by himself this long."

Jin felt a flare of indignation, but it was quickly dashed as he contemplated the boy and girl on the giant two-headed boar. It was true that the imperial family had dwindled in size and power as their hold over creatures had diminished. Once the palace had been filled with monsters, and the emperor hadn't needed an entire ministry of Whisperers to control them. Now there was only his grandmother's phoenix regularly terrorizing the so-called royal Whisperers. He swallowed his pride. "You're right. I suppose you have no reason to believe anything I say." He turned and looked at the ruins of Beastly. "I don't know what happened to your home, but it looks like nothing good. I'd be suspicious of strangers too." Jin took a deep breath. "I truly did come to find a monstermate, but it seems there are more important things to worry about here. If you'll let me, I'll prove to you that I mean no harm."

With a skeptical snort, Masa wrinkled her nose. "How?"

"I can . . . feed the beasts! Or help train them, or . . ." Jin trailed off uncertainly, his mind gone blank. He'd always had servants around. What sort of work did the twins do? "I can do whatever you need. Are you going to rebuild the village? Maybe I can help with that." The destruction would be hard to clean up, but if they sent a messenger bird to the palace, surely his grandmother would send men and materials.

They'd see he was crown prince then.

"Rebuild it?" Mau shook his head. "There's no point in that." He leaned over and whispered to his sister, who shrugged and then nodded.

"Fine, we'll let Ayie decide," said Masa. "But she's not going to be happy."

Jin's ears pricked. *Ayie?* There *were* other Whisperers besides the twins. Hope mingled with his curiosity. "Who's Ayie?"

The boy Whisperer grinned at Jin. "Oh." He chuckled. "You'll see."

CHAPTER 14

THE LAST WHISPERERS

RELIEF SWEPT OVER JIN. THE Whisperers weren't going to leave him behind after all.

"It would take you forever to walk. You can ride with us, I guess," Masa said gruffly. "Hop on." Jin hesitated, gazing at the long body of the two-headed boar, covered in coarse black fur. It was so tall he couldn't even see over its thick, barrel-like back. How was he going to get on that, let alone stay on? She extended a hand. "Here."

As she steadied Jin, he struggled to climb onto the beast. After a few attempts, one of which ended in Jin diving face-first off its far side, her brother dismounted and helped Jin straddle the shoulders of the rear head. "Grab this," Mau said, indicating a furry hump at the base of its neck. "And don't let go." Mau jumped back on and made a clicking noise with his tongue.

The bingfeng set off at a brisk walk, led by the head with

the twins sitting behind it. Jin found himself facing backward along with the rear head, its rough hooves stepping in
tandem with those in front. He clutched the boar's wiry fur
tentatively, afraid of irritating it, but when the boar lurched
over a ditch, Jin nearly fell off. He gripped tighter after that,
looking around him with wide eyes as the creature trotted
along with surprising speed. Soon he was grinning madly.
Not only was he in the presence of a two-headed monster,
he was actually riding one! What great practice for when he
mastered a creature of his own.

They passed by the orchards that Jin had seen on his way
to Beastly, moving through the valley toward the curved
mountain ridge at the island's heart. Clouds of mist blan-
keted the crown, but the rest of it glowed green in the
late-afternoon sun, its flanks covered in vegetation. A herd
of single-horned creatures grazed in a field, their coarse
coats like that of goats, but their legs were covered in sharp
scales. After staring at them, Jin turned and shouted at the
twins. "Are those haitai?"

Masa followed Jin's pointing arm and grunted assent.
"They don't like liars, just so you know."

"I am aware," he scoffed. Inwardly Jin quailed, imagining
one of those wickedly pointed horns piercing him for all the
things he'd done to get to the island. But as they passed by,
the beasts seemed not to notice, and he relaxed. When he

spotted other live monsters that he'd seen in the bestiary or as ornamental statuary at the palace, Jin made sure to remark on each with whatever he could remember from the bestiary, hoping to impress the twins with his knowledge. He searched about eagerly for a glimpse of a dragon, but there was none to be seen. A curiously long-nosed creature the size of a sheep made a trumpeting noise at the sight of them and began trotting after the two-headed boar. Its shape reminded Jin of something. "That's not a dreameater, is it?"

"A baku?" Mau asked. "Yes—we call him Momo."

"I thought they were a lot bigger!" exclaimed Jin.

"The adults are," Masa said with a shrug. "Momo's just a baby."

They plunged into an unkempt field, weeds thick on the ground and tangling with the plants. When Jin asked, Masa identified them as sweet potato. "I saw some long purple fruit in another field," Jin ventured. "Are they supposed to be bitter?"

"You mean eggplant? If you eat them raw, yes." Masa turned and smirked. "You might know a few things about creatures, but you definitely don't know your plants."

The boar squeezed between the rows of leafy greens, cutting through the field before entering a wooded glen. The sound of trickling water and the trills and calls of unseen creatures enveloped them as they moved deep into the woods. Jin caught the smell of smoke with an unusually sharp scent he couldn't identify. "Something's burning," he called to the twins.

"We're almost there," replied Mau. Before long, they emerged into a small clearing, followed by the baby baku. There a woman tended a fire giving off a curious light. She straightened as the baku honked and ran to her side. The bingfeng swung around so that both boar heads faced her. She looked at Jin, startled, and then at the twins. "I see you found the intruder—but you brought him to camp?"

"He's unarmed and appears to be alone," said Mau. "Says he came on a boat that got on the wrong side of Goldie."

His twin sister chimed in. "He *claims* to be the crown prince, here to find a monstermate. But he doesn't have a stitch of proof."

Jin introduced himself with as much dignity as he could muster. "I'm telling the truth, and I'll find a way to prove it to you if you'll give me a chance."

The woman's dark eyes were piercing as she looked Jin over. Lean and browned, she was neither young nor old, and shared the same wide mouth and pointed chin as the twins, though her face was narrower, her cheekbones more prominent. Her ragged hair was cropped as short as Masa's, and there was a fierceness about her as she rested a hand on the knife at her belt. "We don't usually get visitors. If you are who you say, you would know that things have been dire here on the island for a long time, and worse lately. We never got word that anyone was coming from the mainland—not even after we begged for help."

"Begged for . . . what?" Jin blinked, then frowned. "From whom? And when?"

"Months ago," said Masa, her gaze as sharp as the woman's. "And if you were really from the palace, you'd know."

Confounded, he rubbed the back of his head. "That would have been huge news," Jin said. "But I haven't heard a thing about Whisper Island being in trouble." As the twins exchanged a knowing glance, he hesitated, then tried to explain. "To be honest, the palace has no idea I'm here. Empress Soro, my grandmother, forbade me from coming here, even though I'm running out of time to find a creature. I'll be turning thirteen in a couple of months. So I forged some papers and hired a boat."

"He *admits* to lying!" said Masa, triumphant. "I knew it!"

"Not lying, exactly," he protested. "We did ground on a kunpeng's nest, and the papers that I gave the captain really did have the imperial seal on them. I truly am the crown prince, and I'm really on a mission to find my monstermate. Everything else I just . . . left out."

"Which is still being dishonest," the woman said severely. Momo leaned against her and reached his long nose for a jade bangle on her wrist, playing with it. She scratched the baby baku's head but frowned at Jin. "Lying by omission might seem harmless, but it can still have consequences. We don't tolerate that here."

"Understood," said Jin, chastened. "I am sorry."

Mau jumped off the bingfeng and strode to the woman's side. "What do you think, Aunt Ayie? Shall we give him over to the monsters?" He lowered his voice. "I don't believe a word he says, but the haitai ignored him when we passed them."

The woman called Ayie rubbed the bristly snouts of the two-headed monster, eliciting contented grunts from both. "No trouble with him riding the boar either, I see."

"Surprisingly, Komengo seems to like him," said Mau.

She sighed. "Well, prince or not, we could use the extra hands." Ayie nodded at Jin. "You can stay with us, but you'll need to earn your keep. And no promises on a monstermate. Not until we understand who you really are."

"Thank you," said Jin, relieved. Hauling a leg over to the other side, he slid off the creature's broad back and winced. Even though Jin had taken riding lessons before, sitting on a saddled horse was nothing like being astride a giant two-headed boar. His legs were sore, and he stood bowlegged in spite of himself. The woman pointed at the campfire. "We're about to make dinner. Go with the twins to get cleaned up. Then you can help."

Obediently, Jin hobbled after Masa and Mau to a nearby

spring, where they drew water into buckets. It was the first time he'd had a chance to drink anything in hours, so he gulped the cool, sweet water straight from the bucket. He heard a giggle before noticing that the twins were washing their hands and faces. "Thirsty, I see," said Masa.

Sheepishly, Jin put down the bucket. "It's been a while since I've had anything to eat or drink." He splashed his face and winced. "When I was running from the kunpeng, I bumped my head pretty hard. I think there's a cut here."

Masa came over and inspected him. "It's not bleeding, but Ayie can take a look."

"Is she really your aunt?" asked Jin.

"Our mother's sister," said Mau.

"Where are the rest of the Whisperers?" asked Jin.

Masa glanced at her brother and bit her lip. "You're looking at them."

"We're the only ones left," said Mau. "The village was invaded and attacked New Year's Eve. We all happened to be away from Beastly at the time, and by the time the three of us got back . . ." He fell silent and looked away.

Jin suddenly understood why the twins and their aunt all had such short hair—they'd been in mourning. "Bloody beasts, that's terrible. There was a deliberate attack?"

"By boats full of soldiers," Mau said. "From what we can tell, they were from Hulagu."

"Hulagu!" Jin's jaw dropped. His grandmother had been right after all—the empire to the north was a threat, and not just to the borderlands. "But New Year's Eve was months ago. What did you do after the attack?"

"We moved into the forest in case they came back," said Masa. She twisted a jade bangle on her wrist that matched her aunt's. "We sent a green crow with an urgent message to the capital right after it happened, then another, but never heard anything back from the palace. We didn't know what to think when the creatures started reporting a strange boy on the island."

A memory came to Jin at the mention of the green crow— the night of the Monster Festival, the guards at the palace gates were talking about finding a dead bird with three legs. At the time he thought they were telling idle tales out of boredom, but now he realized it could have been a messenger bird from Whisper Island. He shook his head and told them what he'd heard that night. "I'm sorry—I don't think either of the crows ever made it. News of an attack would've set off a huge commotion at the palace. My grandmother's been worrying about the Hulagans for a while now. If she heard about this, she'd declare war."

They went back to the campsite. The double-headed boar had left, but the baby baku remained, its long trunk-like nose delicately playing with feathers while Ayie cleaned a bird. The twins told their aunt about Jin's suspicion that their messenger birds had never successfully delivered news of the attack.

"I was afraid of that. Though it's not like them to fail." The lines in Ayie's forehead deepened. "We should send another, but I hate to risk their lives." She wiped her knife and stuck it in a sheath at her belt. "First, let's get us all fed." She nodded at a pile of bulbous roots. "Peel and cut those elephant-ear corms." She took the bird carcass to the fire she'd been tending. The cookfire was a kaleidoscope of shifting colors, first blue, then green, flashing orange and yellow before turning blue again. Jin was so hungry that he could barely think. He took a small, short-handled knife from Mau and began cutting the rough brown skin off the starchy tubers as fast as he could.

"What are you doing?" cried Masa. "That's not peeling— you're hacking huge pieces off. There won't be anything left if you keep that up!"

"I—I've never done this before," Jin said defensively.

"Maybe His Lordship really is who he claims." Mau chuckled. He showed Jin how to slip his blade under the skin at an angle and wiggle it along. "Shave off just this layer, like so."

Jin went through a couple of tubers before he got the hang of removing just the wrinkled skin, but finally managed to produce one that had most of its purplish flesh intact.

"Not too bad," said Mau. He chopped the peeled corms

into chunks before throwing them into a pot bubbling on the fire, next to the bird his aunt had set to roast on a spit over the colorful flames.

"Is that a monster bird?" Jin asked.

The Whisperer woman looked horrified. "We're not barbarians!" She shook her head. "Our village may be destroyed, but our tie to the creatures we guard will forever be strong." Ayie turned the spit, and a hiss emitted from the flames as fat and juices dripped into the fire. "This is a chicken that's grown too old to lay eggs. We're fortunate that some of the village livestock escaped the attack."

Darkness settled in around them, but the cookfire's colorful flames shone brightly, illuminating their faces. Small lights began to wink on in the trees, until it looked like they were wreathed in stars. Jin looked more closely and was delighted to find they were enormous fireflies that spanned his palm. Who needed butter lamps when monster bugs could provide such light?

While the twins mashed the boiled tubers and ladled the steaming slop into rough wooden bowls, Ayie removed the chicken from the spit and carved it into pieces. The purple mash was starchy and bland, and the old bird was tough and stringy, its meat dry and the skin rather burnt and covered in hairy prickles. But Jin was ravenous and ate it all without complaint.

Ayie seemed pleased. "Hunger is the best spice, especially

with a dash of accomplishment. When you take part in making a meal, it's more satisfying to eat."

"Which helps, since none of us are very good at cooking," said Mau, picking at something stuck in his teeth. He stopped as his sister swatted him. "What? I said we're *all* bad at it."

Masa slumped. "I hate when you're right."

"We've not starved yet," retorted their aunt, but a corner of her mouth twitched. She stroked the head of the baby baku, which had settled itself next to her and was basking in the warmth from the fire. It raised its long nose and patted Ayie's foot. Jin eyed the dreameater warily and edged away when its nose reached in his direction, sniffing.

The Whisperer girl arched an eyebrow and nudged her brother. "What's the matter, Jin? Are you afraid of Momo?"

"No," he scoffed, but the creature blew air from its long nose in a loud honk, and he jumped. "Okay, maybe a little. I've read that you can turn into an empty husk if a baku eats your hopes and dreams—the good ones, I mean. I don't mind it taking my nightmares, but I'd like to keep everything else."

"That's only if it's really hungry," said Ayie. "Believe me, Momo's fed on plenty of bad dreams."

"If anything, we've been keeping him *too* well-fed," Mau chimed in. Dolefully, he scratched the juvenile baku's belly.

"I think I can guess why." Jin hesitated, then addressed

Ayie. "I saw the village ruins, and the twins told me the three of you are the only Whisperers left. I thought this island was a sanctuary. What happened here?"

The Whisperer woman sighed. "It might help to start from the very beginning." She stared into the campfire, its flickering colors casting a rainbow-like display across her face. "Over the centuries, many emperors of the Three Realms abused the creatures in their care, exploiting them and using them to try to expand their empire. It took a toll and their numbers dwindled. The neighboring kingdoms, which Samtei tried to annex, would have turned the tables in an instant if they had known the empire was losing the beasts that made it superior in battle. So this island refuge was a secret attempt to preserve what creatures were left. The Whisperers came and built Beastly, and the beasts they brought thrived.

"Word eventually got out about Whisper Island. Expeditions from other countries as well as profit-seeking poachers sought to find this preserve and capture creatures for their own. The palace sent ships to patrol the waters, our elders worked with the dragons to cloak the island in mist, and over time, the island became almost mythical in people's minds, as if it didn't really exist. But as people stopped believing in the island and its creatures, communications with the mainland ceased. We used to go back and forth to the mainland quite a lot, although by the time I was born, ships were rare visitors. The elders thought it was safer to be isolated. Our settlement had become completely self-sufficient by then, and our duty was to the creatures, first and foremost. We had established a peaceful way of life here and flourished. But we were woefully unprepared for an attack when it came."

"On that night, Masa and I were off racing around and playing games." The boy Whisperer scowled. "But we should have been there, with everyone else."

"We ran back as soon as we realized the explosions weren't fireworks," Masa countered. "We're lucky we weren't killed along with everyone else."

"If we hadn't been away, we could have helped," muttered Mau. "When we arrived, it was too late."

"No, Mau. Your sister is right," said their aunt. Her severe expression softened and grew forlorn. "Had I not been else-where assisting with Momo's birth, I don't think I'd have survived, either." She turned back to Jin. "The creatures raised the alarm all throughout the island, but by the time I reached Beastly, it was on fire, and everyone was either dead or dying."

"Did the attackers escape?" asked Jin.

Mau turned. "The creatures of the island had arrived with us as well," he said fiercely. "And they made them pay."

"Good." Jin felt a rush of vengeful pride. "Is it true the attackers were Hulagan?"

"They wore armor in that style," said Ayie. "There were dozens of them, in small landing craft that had run up onto shore while the village was celebrating New Year's Eve. The island's creatures destroyed their weapons and many of the boats, but some men *did* get away. We've been on edge ever since."

"I noticed." Jin glanced at Masa. She made a face at him. He smiled, but quickly sobered. "Speaking of attacks, I keep wondering if my ship managed to escape." He described the chaos of the kunpeng attack, and the last time he saw Bingyoo and Shishi. "If they or any of the crew did survive, would you hear about it somehow? You'd said you'd heard about me."

"It's possible," said Ayie. "The green crows told us there was an intruder wandering about the island, which is how the twins found you. But if they've sailed back out to sea, it'd be harder to find out."

Jin nodded slowly. He doubted the ship could sail far in its condition, but if they had escaped, there might be word of it eventually. That was all he could hope for, for now. Timidly, he reached out to pet the baby baku and it sighed happily through its long nose. "How have you been managing all the beasts?"

"Barely, to be honest," said Ayie. "With just me and the

twins, we haven't been able to cover much ground. Parts of the island go neglected for weeks."

"I'll do whatever I can to help," Jin offered. "I mean, if you can think of anything."

"If?" For the first time, Ayie smiled. "My dear boy, there is plenty of work for you to do."

CHAPTER 15

MASTER OF MONSTERMUCK

THE PILE OF FRESH MONSTER dung glistened with an iridescent sheen in the morning light. Jin screwed up his face as he bent to collect it, holding his breath while scooping the soft chunks into wooden buckets slung on a pole over his shoulders. He waved aside a buzzing cloud of flies attracted to the eye-watering pungence, then straightened.

"Monstermuck, this is heavy." Steadying his full load with both hands, Jin trudged back to the fields where the twins and their aunt were tending to a patch of beans and squash. Shadowing them was Momo, trumpeting for attention. When the baby baku saw Jin approach, it trotted eagerly toward him. But as soon as it caught a whiff of him, it rolled up its long nose and shied away. "Excuse me if I'm too stinky for you, but some of your own stuff is in here," Jin called.

Mau chuckled. "Smells like you got a good haul."

"I've got a whole mess of dung from Momo," Jin said.

"And some haitai and fire-chicken droppings too."

The twins' aunt glanced over at his buckets. "Not bad," she said briskly. "Make sure you don't add too much water this time."

Jin nodded and tottered to a field where dozens of flat brown rounds were curing in the sun. In a large basin, he dumped the contents of his buckets and added dried grass stalks and water like Ayie had shown him. He mashed and stirred everything together until he had a thick, smelly sludge. "Now that's real monstermuck," he muttered. Who knew it was useful? With a grimace, he scooped up a handful and began to shape the fetid mixture between his palms. Formed into patties and dried, it made an excellent fuel. The dungcakes burned brighter and lasted longer than anything else, giving off white-hot flames with a shifting rainbow of hues at their core. They were what made the campfire so colorful, and it was now his job to pick up after creatures and make the cakes that fueled it.

If anyone at the palace saw him now, elbows deep in poop, they'd be horrified—especially his grandmother. Jin gave a rueful chuckle. In short order, he was becoming familiar with all types of monster dung and where to find deposits. It'd been nearly a week since he'd joined the Whisperer twins and their aunt, and he was starting to carry heavy buckets without having to stop and rest every few steps. His creature cakes were rounder and more uniform now too. But he was never going to get used to the smell. No matter how much he scrubbed afterward, a perpetual scent clung to him as if he were wreathed in a cloud of creature farts.

He was just arranging the last of the fuel cakes to dry when the twins came by, accompanied by the baby baku. The dreameater honked in greeting, while Masa stopped to give his handiwork a once-over. "These look great," she said, sounding surprised. A mischievous smile stole across her face. "His Lordship has a talent, Mau!"

Her brother sidled up to take a look. "They certainly are up to imperial standard," Mau intoned. "His Highness has made the most excellent of dungcakes!" Snickering, the twins bowed extravagantly, bobbing up and down.

Jin rolled his eyes. They still didn't believe he was crown prince, but he wasn't going to waste any more breath trying to convince them. All that mattered was finding his creature—hopefully a dragon. Unfortunately, the closest he'd come to one lately was its leavings, and scooping poop was the only monster-related thing he'd been allowed to do since arriving. The Whisperers had quickly put him to work, and like the twins' aunt had warned, there was plenty of it. Before the attack on the village, the community of Whisperers had grown their own food and looked after all the beasts on the island, which included both ordinary livestock farmed for milk, meat, eggs, and fleece, and monsters, which required particular care. Each Whisperer had been assigned to a certain zone of the island, which was carefully populated with a mix of creatures that could amicably co-habitate. Some needed to be fed or groomed, while others could easily forage for their own food and preferred to be left alone. So long as a Whisperer was around to make sure the various monsters didn't stray from their boundaries, all could thrive and live in peace.

But now, with Beastly destroyed, the harmony of the sanctuary had been disrupted. It was all they could do to keep their livestock alive, for wayward creatures had snatched at so many that there were precious few left. There had been fights between monsters trying to defend territory, while others restlessly wandered, causing havoc in other parts of the island. The Whisperers spent their days trying to patrol different sections, tending to crops and their small flocks of chickens and sheep, as well as taking care of creatures that needed attention, but the three of them couldn't possibly do the work of an entire village, and the island's humans and beasts were suffering for it.

Jin kept offering to assist with the monsters, hoping to get a better look at them, but Ayie wouldn't hear of it. Instead, he was taught to milk the two ewes in the tiny remaining herd, look for eggs from the chickens, and weed the rows of vegetables that the twins and their aunt had planted. Having never been required to do any physical work at the palace, let alone gather and knead monster waste for hours on end,

Jin was challenged as never before. At the end of each day, aching and exhausted, he'd collapse onto a makeshift bed of scratchy straw with a threadbare blanket for cover. And yet, as he lay beneath the trees, the night sky peeking through the canopy, he'd fall asleep within a few breaths, into a deeper slumber than he'd ever had in his royal chambers.

After days of hard work from dawn to dusk, Jin was beginning to think he'd never get a chance to explore the island. But one morning the twins' aunt arrived in their camp with a pair of winged dragon-horses. The horses had scaly hides instead of fur, with leathery wings that reminded Jin of bats. Masa cooed over them, reaching up to stroke their long faces as they snorted and stamped their hooves. They were taller than any horse Jin had ever seen, and when one briefly stretched out its wings, they nearly spanned the entire clearing.

"There's an odd disturbance near the eastern shore," said Ayie. "I was preparing another green crow to send to the palace about the attack on Beastly, when some messenger birds informed me about an unusual presence. I'd like to see for myself, but it'd take all day just to get there on foot."

"We'll come with you," said Mau immediately. "You shouldn't go alone."

His aunt raised an eyebrow. "Why do you think I brought two horses?" She grasped the horse's curling mane and swung gracefully onto its back.

Masa clapped her hands. "It's been a while since we've gotten to fly!" She quickly jumped onto the other horse.

"Can I come too?" Jin blurted.

The Whisperer woman considered him, her dark eyes thoughtful. "Might as well. I'd rather not leave you alone for very long." Ayie held out her hand. "You can ride with me."

Jin waved her off, confident. "I know how to get on a horse." But when he stepped up to the enormous winged creature, he realized his mistake. His head barely reached its shoulders, and the Whisperers rode bareback. Each awkward attempt to mount led to an ungainly slide to the ground, sending the twins into barely suppressed titters.

"Here we go again," Mau said. Taking pity, he laced his hands together and boosted Jin onto the horse's broad back behind Ayie.

"Thanks," said Jin, his cheeks red.

The boy Whisperer grinned and mounted the other winged horse, settling into place behind his sister. "Your Highness is most welcome."

They set off through the forest, the horses ambling side by side through the thick trees, heading for a launch spot where they could spread their wings without tangling in branches. Jin looked around eagerly but found it hard to pick out creatures in the undergrowth. The Whisperers had to point them out first. As they rode by, they were greeted with squawks, grunts, bleats, and barks. Monster birds in the canopy flapped colorful wings and opened beaks of unusual shapes and sizes, calling at them with trills, strange shrieks, and tinny-sounding laughter. From his perch on the horse's back, Jin tried everything from imitating their calls to saying hello to the creatures, but got no response. "How do you talk to monsters?" he asked, mystified. "The only ones that seem to understand me are green crows."

"Well, anyone can speak to the crows, Whisperer or not," said Ayie briskly. "They understand humans in any language. It's why they make good messengers."

"Yes, they mentioned that," said Jin. "But how does it work for Whisperers? Do you actually say words to them, or is there some other way to communicate?"

"It's usually not necessary to speak out loud," said Mau. "But it depends on the creature. Why do you ask?"

"I was just wondering how emperors usually found their monstermates. Wasn't their match the first creature that obeyed their commands?"

The Whisperer woman snorted. "It was never that simple. In a royal creature quest, they had to prove themselves capable of understanding creatures before they were even allowed to go in search of one."

"You mean, understand monster speech?" Jin was uneasy. So far, the only creatures he'd understood on the island were the three-legged crows.

"Not exactly. It helped to have a certain amount of knowledge about creatures and their ways."

"Oh, that I have," said Jin, relieved. He gloated to himself. How many times had he told his grandmother the imperial bestiary was worth studying? "Maybe I can start feeding them—I've read all about monster diets."

Ayie grunted. "It's better for the creatures to be self-sufficient. Our aim is to keep track of their numbers, make sure they're not injured or sick, and encourage them to stay in their designated areas."

"It was different at the Palace of Monsters," boasted Jin. "The Whisperers there had to feed all the monsters at set times. All the cages in the menagerie had feeding troughs."

The twins gave Jin curious looks, as if they weren't sure to believe him. "Cages!" said Masa scornfully. "Creatures run free here—as much like their ancestors in the Uncanny Wild as we can make it."

"But is the Uncanny Wild even real?" Jin shrugged. The ancient forest was said to be the source of all monsters, surrounding a sacred mountain range known as the Stairway to Heaven. Far to the west of Samtei, it belonged to no empire or kingdom. But over the centuries, as wars raged in the region, the forest and the mountains had become shrouded in myth.

"Of course it is," said Ayie. "As real as this place. Many think it's just a fable, but we're still here."

"True," Jin conceded. He told her about the crew on the boat, and how they'd spoken with fear and skepticism about the island. "The first mate wasn't wrong to worry about coming here. I hope they made it to safety." Thinking that Bingyoo and Shishi were gone for good made him queasy.

"We'll look for signs as we fly over the island. We can ask Goldie as well," said Ayie.

A trumpeting sound turned Jin's head. The baby baku ran after them, bleating through its long nose. "Momo's found us." He chuckled. The hairy creature had beady little eyes, small round ears, and quiet cat like feet, but it made plenty of noise. Jin couldn't help but compare it to the colorful painted carvings at the palace, or his stuffed dreameater. After years of handling, his worn toy baku was still bright, in shades of crimson, blue, green, and purple embroidered with gold thread, while the real baku's short coarse fur grew in patches of drab brown and white. "I didn't know bakus were so plain," he remarked. "They're a lot uglier than I thought."

Masa raised her eyebrows. "I think the same thing could be said about crown princes." Her brother guffawed. Jin decided to ignore them.

Their aunt shook her head. "If you're really looking for a creature companion, you'll need to learn how to see. Momo, you can't follow us," she admonished the baby baku. "Be off now. We'll return soon."

With a dejected honk, the baku trundled away, its stubby tail drooping. Jin watched it go, then turned back to Ayie. "What do you mean? What am I supposed to see?"

"It's the same as talking to them," said the Whisperer. "How do you expect them to understand you if you don't understand them?"

Jin frowned. "I don't get it."

"Seeing things differently gives you power. And to conquer a beast, you must first make it beautiful."

He bit back a sigh of frustration. Ayie was starting to sound like one of the green crows. "All riddles, no sense," he muttered. His thoughts were interrupted by Mau, pointing.

"There's a clearing up ahead that should give us enough space."

They emerged into a small meadow. The scaly horses unfolded their leathery wings. Jin yelped and clutched Ayie tight as their horse flapped and reared. Then with a few cantering strides, it sprang into the sky. He could feel every muscle of the horse's body working as its enormous wingspan beat them steadily higher. The ground fell away beneath them till it was but a rumpled green quilt, the patchwork of hill and dale, field and forest stitched with silvery streams. The horse let out a shrieking whinny that rang out in the bright morning air, answered by the twins' horse, which was close behind. Masa and Mau laughed and waved as they flew past. The wind whipped through Jin's hair and made his eyes water, but he didn't care, and grinned madly as their great winged beast rose and wheeled about.

As the horses glided over the island, Ayie pointed out various features. A bamboo grove where fire-chickens known as basan liked to roam. Grasslands dotted with grazing herd beasts like giant aurochs and sharp-horned haitai. An extensive old-growth forest where solitary creatures like the noble kirin and treasure-loving piyao lurked among towering trees. Numerous smaller woodlands filled with monster birds and creatures like the nine-tailed fox and other small, furred beasts. A swampy marshland with mangroves that attracted monster turtles, flying snakes, and vermilion gibbons. The Poison Pass, a ravine where deadly creatures such as the needlenosed viper, the poisonfeather bird, the crested poison rat, and the poisonspike pig found refuge. "I would stick to the bridge if you're ever in that area," she advised as they flew over a narrow suspension bridge that spanned the ravine.

In the distance, Jin recognized the fields and orchards cultivated by the Whisperers. The ruins of Beastly lay just beyond them on the western shore, and he spotted the sand dunes where he'd first met the twins. Farther along the shore were what looked like salt flats, leading to a spit of land where a lone tree glowed with an eerie blue light. "What's happening to that tree?"

"It's a fire tree," said Ayie. "There are four such trees on the island, one for each point of the compass. They're supposed to aid ships when it's dark or foggy. That one's called the Kirin Tree, since it's in the west."

"Curious. We never saw anything like that when we grounded on the kunpeng's nest," Jin said.

"The Tortoise Tree is on a promontory at the northernmost point, and Goldie's nest is in a lagoon just east of it. Either the boat's crew missed its light, or it was blocked by a mollusk monster. They like to project mirages on the water, which can get boats in trouble," said the Whisperer.

"That happened to us!" said Jin. "We saw a shining city—it looked like a fortress—and then it disappeared, and we ran right into the lagoon."

"Yes, the monster mollusks can create spectacular castles from mere sea-foam. They've been doing that more these days, especially after the attack on Beastly."

On the northwest coast, the horses soared alongside tall, sheer cliffs where thousands of monster birds nested. As they approached, the birds cried out and launched into the air all at once, forming an enormous shimmering cloud that danced in the sky around them. The murmuration looked like a single monster instead of a swarm of many. Jin craned his neck, awestruck as the swirling cloud of monster birds swooped about them in intricate patterns, calling as they flew. Their cries fused into a surprisingly beautiful symphony of song, leaving him spellbound.

Ayie glanced back sharply. "Don't go into a trance, now. They've been known to shipwreck unsuspecting sailors." She steered their horse inland, and she pointed to the peaks at the heart of the island. "We call that the Sleeping Tiger." They flew toward the curved mountainous ridge that was once part of an ancient volcanic cone. It was covered in green growth and white stripes like the flank of a giant jade tiger, and a layer of fog hovered as if a blanket of clouds were about to settle on its back. As they drew closer, Jin saw the white stripes more clearly. "Good beasts, those are all waterfalls!" He counted at least a dozen of them, the misty ribbons of water spilling down the ridge into a long narrow lake that fed the island's streams. Jin eyed it warily. "Are there water apes in that lake?" he asked.

"In Dragon's Tears? No, but there are plenty of other creatures," said Ayie. "If you find any pearls on the banks, they're from pearl turtles. There are freshwater fish too. On the Tiger itself, many of the island's dragons make their home. It's why the clouds are so heavy."

They circled the mountainous ridge, flying just beneath the canopy of clouds that shrouded the top. Jin squinted through the mist, scanning the craggy slopes. "I'm not seeing any dragons," he said, disappointed.

"You shouldn't. They're very good at camouflage," Ayie told him. She took in the whole island in a sweeping glance.

"Nothing looks out of order right now." She whistled sharply at the twins, gesturing, and the horses turned in the direction of the north shore. "Let's check on Goldie."

As they sped toward the rocky, barren spires of the north shore, a nervous knot formed in Jin's stomach. More than a week had passed since the disastrous encounter with the kunpeng and its young. Would they remember him? Would Goldie attack again? He set his jaw. If there was any way to find out what had happened to the boat—and more importantly, Bingyoo and Shishi—he'd have to brave the risk.

CHAPTER 16

TRUTHS REVEALED

THE WINGED HORSES CIRCLED THE gloomy northern shore, wreathed in clouds of mist. Though the sun was nearly overhead, it barely penetrated the fog blanketing the stony landscape. Jin searched through the murky haze for the lagoon where the kunpeng had made its nest. "I'm beginning to understand the old saying, 'Thicker than the breath of dragons,'" he mused to Ayie.

"Fog and clouds are a sure sign of their presence," said the Whisperer. "You never have to worry about drought when dragons are around."

A glimmer caught Jin's eye. "I think I see a fire tree—there!"

"Ah yes, the Tortoise Tree. Now we know exactly where we are." With a sharp whistle, Ayie signaled Mau and Masa. They steered their horses past the glowing tree, perpetually aflame with blue fire, and touched down on a large rocky outcropping. Leaving the two winged monsters behind, they picked their way up the craggy rocks overlooking the shallow cove where the boat had grounded. Even though he was with Whisperers this time, Jin's steps faltered as he glimpsed the lagoon, remembering the terror of the kunpeng's attack. He felt for his lock charm and took a deep breath, then forced himself to keep going.

They reached the top of the highest rock formation, its jagged pillars of stone like giant monster teeth, and peered down. From this vantage point, the warrior crabs looked like scuttling bugs on the stony shore, while the kunpeng's babies could be seen lazing about the shallows. Jin counted more than a dozen of them, their long scaly bodies dark enough to blend in with the glassy black water, only exposing their pale glimmering bellies when they turned or twisted. There was also a visible scar in the shoal where the ship's hull had gotten stuck. No wonder the kunpeng had been so angry.

In the watery abyss off the stone ledge, Jin spotted a gargantuan silvery form. "I think that's Goldie!"

"Looks like it," said Mau. He folded his fingers around his pursed lips and gave several long sharp whistles. The great whiskered head of the fish breached the surface of the sea. As the kunpeng's enormous scaled body slid onto the shallow ledge where its offspring nested, the giant fish transformed into a golden-feathered raptor, water dripping from its beak as it stood upright, its eagle eyes level with theirs. It blinked at them and snorted out a cloud of salt-tinged mist, then screeched. Jin cringed.

"Hello to you too," said Ayie.

Mau reached out and stroked the kunpeng's sleek, feathered head, then frowned and put his forehead against it. In spite of his fear, Jin watched the Whisperer boy, fascinated. How was he talking to the monster? After a long moment, Mau looked up. "So a boat really did ground here. Goldie was going to destroy it, but then you started bothering one of her young."

"You what?" Masa whirled and frowned at Jin. "You never mentioned that part."

He gulped. "I was only trying to save the ship. The baby kunpeng let me touch it, and I thought if I just picked it up, it'd be enough of a distraction to stop the attack." Jin bowed his head to the kunpeng in apology. "I would never hurt your babies."

The Whisperer girl scoffed and placed a hand on the raptor's curved beak. She murmured to it, then fell silent, as if she was listening. Masa narrowed her eyes at Jin. "You're lucky you weren't eaten. Some of those men weren't so fortunate. That ratty amulet you're wearing made her leave you alone."

"This?" Jin yelped. He clutched the lock charm, feeling faint. Old Fang hadn't been jesting when he said it would protect him.

Ayie leaned in. "Let me see that." Brow furrowed, she

inspected the amulet closely and muttered to herself. "I wonder . . . could it be?"

"Be what?" Jin was bewildered.

She drew back and regarded him with an unreadable expression. "Where did you get that?"

Looking down at the lock charm, Jin frowned. "One of the palace guard commanders. He said it belonged to my father."

"Moaning monsters, again with the palace stuff," Masa muttered.

Her brother shrugged. "Maybe it makes him feel better," he suggested softly.

"Well." Jin cleared his throat. "Tell the kunpeng I'm grateful she spared me."

A gleam came into Ayie's eyes. "Why don't you try telling her yourself?" The Whisperer woman pushed Jin forward before he could flee.

His knees nearly gave out. Remembering the power of the creature's jaws, he trembled but braced himself as the kunpeng lowered its great head and inspected him. "Please don't eat me," he breathed. "I'm sorry about before. So very sorry." Its feathers slowly rose about its head and neck until the ruffled, glaring bird appeared even more terrifying, but Jin gritted his teeth and stayed put. He had no idea whether the great bird could understand his words, but he kept murmuring them until its feathers smoothed down. Drawing back, it snapped its beak and screeched.

"Interesting," said Ayie. "That amulet of yours is certainly real. She's still not happy with what you did with her young, but you're in no danger from her."

Relieved, Jin gave his lock charm an appreciative pat and tucked it carefully under his collar. A thought occurred to him. "I believe I saw the boat come free. Did Goldie go after it?"

Masa put the question to the great bird silently, looking into its golden eyes, then shook her head. "She chased the boat off but didn't follow it too far—kunpengs stay close to the nest when there's young."

"It got away, then." Though Jin felt shaky thinking about the unfortunate sailors—and how he'd nearly become a monster meal himself—his heart gave a little leap at the news about the boat. Bingyoo and Shishi might've survived after all. But where could the boat have gone?

"Maybe it went back to the mainland," suggested the twins' aunt. "Or perhaps it landed on a different part of the island. The green crows said there was an unusual presence on the eastern shore—but they didn't seem too alarmed, so it might just be a beached whale or a seabird lost from its flock."

"Or it could be that the ship sank on that side of the island," said Mau with a frown. After the Whisperers finished communicating with the kunpeng, it turned and dove into the water, its wings and feathers shifting back into long fins and scales. Mau looked at Jin soberly. "Don't get your hopes up just yet," he said. "Goldie's going to swim around the island to look for wrecks. In the meantime, let's go see what the green crows were talking about."

They got back on the horses and flew along the coastline, the ocean in view. The fog lifted as they drew farther south, and the sun glittered on the water, the sudden brightness hurting Jin's eyes. The rocky terrain on this side of the island was pocked with tidepools and caves, and studded with stone formations of tightly packed pillars spilling steplike into the ocean. In the distance, one jutted out farther than all the rest, a glimmering tree at its tip. "There's the Dragon Tree of the east," said Ayie, pointing it out to Jin.

As the winged horses glided over the shore, Jin watched their shadows dance upon the stony outcroppings and rockstrewn sand. Then he spotted something and clutched Ayie's arm in excitement.

"Down there, washed up onshore," he cried. "Those barrels look just like ones in the hold of the ship!"

"I see them," she replied. The horse circled until it came to a graceful halt on a pebbled beach, followed closely by the twins' horse. Jin nearly tumbled off in his haste to examine the flotsam and jetsam there. Jumping off their mount, Mau and Masa ran after him.

They came upon several barrels sunk partway in sand,

a number of waterlogged crates, and sodden broken wood strewn everywhere. Jin looked wildly about for footprints or signs of human life but saw nothing.

"There's food in these crates!" exclaimed Masa. "Rice and tea, dried fruit, preserved meat, cakes of salted fish roe. Oh, I hope it's not all ruined."

Her brother knocked on a barrel. "This one's still full," he remarked. "Rice wine, from the looks of it. That one's empty."

Ayie examined another crate that had a brand burned into the wood. "I believe there are bolts of cloth and other dry goods in this one. Anything we can salvage here will be useful." A rare smile lit her face.

They set to work digging out the partially submerged barrels and recovering crates. The jetsam was quite heavy, and it took all four of them to drag everything to drier land. The winged horses had wandered farther away from the shore and were cropping mouthfuls of tall grass from the edge of a nearby meadow. Jin collected all the broken bits of wood he could find and threw them in a pile, trying to gather clues. It all had to have been from his boat—he recognized the washed-up cargo from his time in the hold. But what had become of the boat itself? More importantly, what about Bingyoo and Shishi?

"Do you think this is what the green crows were warning Ayie about?" Jin asked Masa.

The girl Whisperer tilted her head, considering. "Probably. Useful items rarely wash up on Whisper Island. And since the attack, we've all been more vigilant."

Her aunt overheard. "Shipwrecks are rare nowadays. When monsters became more of a memory, the island faded from prominence and people stopped trying to come here. But when I was younger than the three of you, it was a lingering problem. Foreign poachers often tried to sneak onto the island and capture creatures, and there were even hunters from Samtei willing to sell parts on the black market for consumption."

"The captain of the ship that brought me wanted a few creatures of his own," said Jin. "He never said anything about eating them, but he definitely didn't have the best of intentions."

"Was Your Lordship going to grant him a royal boon of some uncanny beasts?" asked Mau, raising an eyebrow.

"No, never!" Jin spluttered. "Monsters are sacred to the imperial family. Why do you think I came here in the first place? They're basically extinct on the mainland—" He stopped when the twins started snickering.

"Mau's just teasing!" Masa giggled. "But honestly, while it's a good act, you can stop pretending to be a prince now."

Her brother grinned. "You're fine just the way you are, Jin."

"Some might think a creature's powers can be absorbed

by swallowing ground-up scales or horn." Masa rolled her eyes. "But you're definitely smarter than that."

Mau chuckled. "Smart enough not to eat them, anyway."

"Thanks a whole lot," huffed Jin, annoyed. "Like I'd ever believe that would work. And I'm not pretending!"

"That's enough, you two." Ayie cut a steely glance at the twins, and they sobered up immediately. "I don't want to hear 'Your Lordship' or 'His Highness' anymore, understand? You're being disrespectful."

"Yes, Aunt Ayie," they muttered.

"And you're right," she said to Jin. "You could never become as strong as a dragon by eating one. Monster parts don't offer that sort of benefit. It's a terrible lie that has grown as creatures have become scarce. But that's why our job is so important. You've helped us since arriving here, and that's all that counts."

Mollified, Jin nodded. The Whisperer patted his shoulder, then surveyed all they'd recovered from the shore. "It's going to take us more than a few trips to get everything back to camp. We may have to bring in a few creatures who can help." One of the crates was cracked, with half its lid missing. Ayie called to a saw-toothed monster bird with impressive talons to help them pry the rest off. Once the bird got the crate open, the Whisperer woman sent the creature on its way while the twins and Jin went through its contents.

As Mau and Masa squabbled over what could be salvaged

and what they could carry, Jin pulled out wet bundles tied in cloth, laying them on the ground. "What do you think's most useful here?"

Ayie didn't answer, staring behind him with consternation.

He turned to see the two winged horses backing away from something in the tall grass. They extended their wings and gave low warning roars, baring their teeth. A familiar high-pitched sound reached Jin's ears. "Is that . . . ?" He dropped the bundle he was holding and ran toward the monsters, the twins hard on his heels. "Easy," he shouted as one horse reared. "What is it?"

"Jin, be careful!" called Mau.

Drawing closer, he heard a whine in the grass, and then a rustling. A small dark creature covered in ropy cords sprang out of the wild growth and launched itself at him. Jin lost his footing and fell back. He had no time to think before the monster landed on his chest and began licking his face. He looked at the beast closely and gasped. "Shishi?"

The little lion dog barked. Jin was overcome. "Good beasts, it *is* you! Oh, thank the gods!" He sat up and clutched Shishi to his chest, the dog wriggling with excitement, unable to stop licking his face. He began to laugh. "I can't believe it—you're alive!" Jin looked up at the twins, who were watching with mouths agape. "This is my dog! She was down in the hold of the ship!"

With exclamations of disbelief, Mau and Masa knelt and waited for Shishi to sniff them. They patted her through her tangle of fur matted into dirt-caked cords, and laughed as she licked their hands. "This is wonderful," said Masa. "But how in the realms did she end up here? I wish we could talk to ordinary animals like we do with monsters."

"Is she hurt?" asked Mau.

Jin looked Shishi over carefully. "She looks terrible, but I don't see any injuries."

They were joined by the twins' aunt. "What sort of creature is that?"

As Jin explained, the Whisperer crouched to examine the dog, who wagged her stumpy half-tail. "Perhaps this is the unusual presence the crows meant," she mused. "Your dog must have managed to swim here."

"Maybe she's not alone," said Jin. "Shishi, where's Bingyoo?"

The dog barked, and then dashed off his lap and ran off a little way before halting and looking back. Jin got to his feet. Shishi barked again. "I think she wants us to follow," he said. Shishi turned and trotted off, stopping every now and again to make sure Jin and the Whisperers were just a few steps away.

Leaving the beach and horses behind them, they trekked through the meadow's waist-high growth. The ocean breezes rippled across the sea of grass, and a grazing herd of dancing antelope startled at the sight of them and pranced off, bounding away with peculiar hops and spins.

They trailed Shishi across the field to a small copse of trees. She darted into the undergrowth, then whined. Jin ducked after her, following the sound of his dog until he found her beside a thick-trunked tree. He gasped. Curled beneath it was Bingyoo's small frame.

Heart in his throat, Jin rushed to her side. Bingyoo's eyes were closed, and her clothing was badly torn, stained with what looked like blood. A stab of alarm went through him. Was she even breathing? Shishi whined and pawed at her hair. Murmuring her name, Jin shook her shoulder. The little dog began to lick her nose and cheeks, and her face screwed up as she uttered a groan.

"Thank the gods!" Jin exclaimed. He looked up at the anxiously hovering Whisperers and gave a shaky laugh. "She's alive!"

Bingyoo rolled onto her back and squinted up at him. "Prince Jin?" she croaked. A smile stole across her face. "I didn't think I'd ever see you again!" She sat up, rubbing her eyes, while Shishi barked and ran in circles.

"Neither did I," said Jin. "I can't believe you're here. The last time I saw you . . ." A flood of relief threatened to spill over, and he stopped, swallowing hard. Shishi stood on her hind legs and began licking his face, and he grinned, feeling lighter than he had in a long time. All three of them had survived and were together again. He pulled back and pointed at a large dark blotch on her smock. "Are you hurt?"

Glancing down, Bingyoo fingered it and shook her head. "A couple of cuts. It looks worse than it is." She lowered her voice. "Who's that behind you, Your Brillance? They seem quite . . . fierce."

"That's because they have true skills with monsters," Jin said. He introduced her to the three Whisperers, and explained to them his connection to Bingyoo. "She started working at the Palace of Monsters this year. When she caught me sneaking off to hire a boat, she followed me."

Mau's brow knit in befuddlement. "So . . . you weren't making it up?" He looked from Jin to Bingyoo. "Is he really a prince?"

"His Brilliance? Of course. He'll rule our empire one day," said Bingyoo, perplexed. Her face cleared as she regarded Jin. "Although he doesn't always dress like this. No one on the boat knew who Prince Jin was, either. But at the palace, everyone knows and serves him."

Masa paled. "All this time he was actually telling the truth about coming here for a creature."

"His lock charm is a royal relic, but I couldn't bring myself to believe it," said Ayie, looking mortified. "It's been years since I've seen one." She dropped to her knees and bid the twins to follow suit. "Our apologies, Your Brilliance. After recent events here on the island, we hope you can understand our suspicious nature."

As the three Whisperers knelt in the deepest of bows, Jin was overcome with embarrassment. "Could you please get back up?" he begged. "I think I liked it better when you thought I was pretending. No need for formal address or anything—let's just keep things as they are."

The Whisperers straightened, the twins looking sheepish. "Very well," said their aunt, resuming her usual brisk air. She offered Bingyoo a drink of water from a flask made out of a hollowed gourd. "Let's check you over, if you don't mind." The servant girl's torn smock was stiff with salt and smeared with dirt and blood, her hair a snarled mess.

"How did you even get here?" Jin blurted. "After the monster attack, I thought the worst."

"I thought the same about you!" said Bingyoo. "You were completely exposed. At least we were hiding in the hold." She winced as Ayie poked gingerly at a cut above her temple, crusted with dried blood. "When the attack started, I looked for something that would give us more protection. I climbed into an empty barrel with Shishi and pulled the lid on tight. But I could still hear the screams." She shuddered. "Whatever the monster was, it ended up smashing a big hole in the side."

"A kunpeng," said Jin. "I saw when that happened. I tried to distract it and lure it away."

"It worked, for a moment!" Bingyoo's eyes widened. "But just as I was thinking to get out of the barrel, the whole boat started rocking. The barrel rolled all over the place, and I couldn't figure out which way was up or down. Then all of a sudden, the rocking stopped. I heard the crew yelling about being free and to get away. Only the hole in the side was just above the surface of the sea, and they were afraid it was going to take on water. Some sailors came down and started heaving things out of the hole, and that included me and Shishi."

Ayie stared at Bingyoo, aghast. "They threw you into the ocean?"

"We were still in the barrel. Shishi barked and I screamed when they pushed us out, but there was so much commotion, I don't think they heard us. I don't think they would have understood even if they had," said Bingyoo. "No one except Prince Jin knew that Shishi and I were on board. Fortunately, the barrel landed right side up in the water, and we washed up on shore at some point. I lost track of time and wasn't sure if we were on the island or on the mainland until I saw some monsters. But I sang a song His Brilliance taught me, and it seemed to keep them from bothering me. I've been singing that song ever since."

"Jin—I mean Prince Jin—taught you 'The Beastie Lullaby'?" Masa looked surprised. "That's one of the first things Whisperers learn, when we're barely walking. It's an old trick, but it definitely soothes any creatures that get too close."

"Are you okay to stand?" asked her aunt. "We'll bring you back to our camp."

With a faint smile, Bingyoo nodded. "Thank the gods you found us. I don't know how much longer we could have gone on out here."

"Have you eaten at all?" asked Masa.

"A bit from an open crate down on the beach. Mostly I've just had water from a stream over there, and I found a patch of dandelions in the field. Shishi's caught some odd-looking rats, but I left them to her."

Ayie pulled a piece of dried meat from her waist pack. "Work on this—nibble it slowly—until we can make something at camp. The food supplies we found on the shore will help."

"Just take what can be carried for now." Mau frowned, considering. "Two winged horses will barely be enough for the five of us."

"Six," said Jin, picking up Shishi.

A glint came into Masa's eyes, and she smiled. "Who said we have to go back the way we came?"

CHAPTER 17

THE SLEEPING TIGER

THEY TIED UP SALVAGED SUPPLIES with some rope that had washed up onshore and loaded it onto a winged horse. Mau helped Bingyoo onto the other horse behind his aunt, and Jin handed up his dog. Bingyoo clutched Shishi to her chest, wide-eyed. "So we're going to . . . fly?"

"It's amazing, really," he told her. "Just hold on to Ayie. I've been flying with her all day and haven't fallen off yet."

Bingyoo gave a nervous laugh and nodded, clamping an arm around Ayie's waist.

Masa put her hands around her mouth and yodeled a peculiar call. A big grin stole across her brother's face, as if he understood at once. After repeated calls, Shishi suddenly gave a low growl. A moment later, several monster birds appeared in the field, each as tall as a grown human. Pecking busily at the ground every few steps, they sported helmet-like horns, long necks, wattles of brilliant red, and powerful-looking legs of bright blue. Shimmering purple-black feathers covered their large, squat bodies. Masa greeted them with little hissing sounds as they neared, and they answered with braying honks.

"Here comes our ride," Mau crowed.

"Helmet birds!" Jin recalled what he'd read about them. "I thought they didn't fly." He exchanged awed glances with Bingyoo.

"They don't. But they're great runners," said Masa. "Travel safely, Aunt Ayie. See you back at camp."

The horses stamped their feet impatiently and unfurled their great leathery wings. As they leaped into the sky, Bingyoo gave a little shriek. Jin waved as she flew off.

Masa gestured a command at the monster birds. They blinked and gave a raucous cry, then knelt obediently to the ground. The girl Whisperer smiled. "Hop on," she told Jin.

Gingerly, Jin approached. "Nice birdie." The bird swiveled its horned head and blinked at him, a translucent membrane sliding over its bright yellow eyes. Jin took a deep breath and got on, sitting on the bird's surprisingly broad back. He reached for the bird's neck, but it twisted away from him like a coiling snake. "Er . . . what do I hold on to?" he asked the twins, each settling on their own monster birds.

"Hook your legs over its knees—see where the legs are joined to the body? Then stick your hands in this crook at the top of its wings and hold there," said Mau, demonstrating.

Masa scrutinized Jin's posture. "Whatever you do, don't lean forward. Tip back, more like this." She made a kissing sound, and the monster birds rose to their great clawed feet. "Hang tight!"

The birds began to run, and Jin jerked backward. He gripped the bird's small wings, which were covered in silky feathers, and fought the urge to hunch over. They strode through the meadow and into the woods, the birds leaping over fallen logs and hopping over rocks with their long, powerful legs.

After a little while, Jin got over the shock of being carried by an enormous fowl. More than once he forgot himself and leaned forward, but the bird would immediately take on a terrifying burst of speed and Masa would shout at him to straighten up. Tilting back as far as he dared, Jin clutched the wings, bobbling on the great bird's back as it skittered along. A gleeful laugh escaped him. It wasn't anything like flying, but it was much more fun than he'd expected.

Mau looked over and grinned. "Let's take them out of the trees!" The boy Whisperer steered his mount toward a grassy plain, and Jin and Masa followed. When they reached an open field, Masa yelled, "Race to the other side!"

The birds let out a cry, and her brother whooped along with them. Jin joined in, and then the monsters began to run. Jin hung on for dear life, leaning forward just enough to get his mount to pass Mau's—but Masa's bird bolted past them both. They reached the end of the field, and Mau turned his bird around. "Best two out of three!"

As they sped back and forth across the grass under a shining sun, Jin couldn't stop smiling. He'd never felt more free.

After they'd tired of racing, they continued at a leisurely pace through the island until they'd reached the Sleeping Tiger at its center. The late afternoon sun illuminated the monumental ridge and its many waterfalls, throwing rainbows into the misty air around the steep slopes.

Jin looked up eagerly. While the sun had burned off much of the foggy cover at the top, there were still wispy clouds drifting about. "Think we'll see any dragons?"

"It's definitely the best place to spot one," said Mau, squinting as he scanned the craggy peaks.

His sister urged her monster bird closer. "Let's give the birds a drink at the lake."

They rode their mounts to Dragon's Tears, a long narrow lake at the foot of the towering ridge, where water collected after trailing down the remains of the old volcano. Masa had the birds kneel so the three of them could dismount. Free of their human riders, the creatures sprang back up on their powerful cobalt legs and tramped to the edge of the lake, where they lowered their horned heads and dipped their bright yellow beaks to drink.

A pair of green crows flew overhead, calling in their raspy

voices, then landed nearby and began plucking at snails from a patch of earth. One looked at them with alert red eyes. "Did you find the new arrivals on the eastern coast?"

"We did, thank you," said Mau. "Ayie has taken them back to camp."

The other crow held a snail in its third foot and stabbed at it with its thick beak. "The long-nosed calf is looking for mischief."

A familiar trumpeting noise sounded through the trees, and they turned to see the baby baku headed purposefully toward them. "Momo!" said Masa. "What are you up to? Where's your mama?"

The dreameater came up and lifted its snuffling trunk to Jin's face, patting his cheeks. Jin scratched it gently behind its little round ears. Its stubby tail flicked from side to side, reminding him of Shishi. He looked into the baku's small button eyes. What if he was meant to bond with a dreameater? It wasn't as powerful as a dragon, but it'd be nice to never have bad dreams. "Are you my creature?" he whispered. The baku snuffled and sneezed, then shook its head.

The green crows made a chattering noise that sounded like laughter. "Don't count that as an answer," said one.

"You'll know when you get one, silly boy," said the other.

"I wasn't really asking," retorted Jin, embarrassed. He should've known the messenger birds would overhear and say something. They were exceedingly observant and had no qualms about getting into other people's business.

With an excited honk, the young dreameater trotted over to the lake, where the helmet-horned birds were avidly watching fish dart below the surface. One snatched a size-able fish in its strong yellow beak and shook it, then raised its head as it tried to swallow its catch down its long gullet. In a tussle, the two other birds tried to pluck the fish away, and it fell to the ground, flopping frantically.

"Poor fish," commented Jin.

"So sentimental," said the first green crow. It cocked its head. "All creatures have to eat."

The baku reached out with its long nose and playfully nudged the thrashing fish away from the birds. The fish leaped back into the water with a plop, and the three mon-ster birds turned on Momo, their eyes glaring. Screaming and snapping their beaks angrily, they lunged, and the little baku squeaked in alarm and ran.

"Looks like they're not eating this time," said Jin, chuck-ling.

Mau grinned. "The crows were right about Momo look-ing for trouble, though."

"Trouble is the only certain thing," said the other crow, scratching its neck with its third leg.

"No, the only certain thing is that nothing is certain," said the first. The pair of crows continued to hunt for snails while the baku disappeared into the trees.

Shaking her head, Masa called after the helmet birds. They obediently turned back and lowered themselves before the Whisperer girl.

Back on their mounts, Jin and the twins continued along until they reached a narrow dirt path running parallel between the lake and the Sleeping Tiger. Streams of water plummeted down the steep ridge and flowed into the lake, cutting deep channels. Worn wooden planks laid over them bridged the rushing water. The monster birds picked their way along, their claws scrabbling loudly on the makeshift bridges whenever they crossed a channel. Fine mist blew off the waterfalls, dampening clothes, hair, and feathers. Jin stared intently at the striated green flank of the Sleeping Tiger, searching. Here might be his chance to find a dragon monstermate!

"Something wrong?" asked Mau.

"No, I'm just looking for dragons. Do they come when you call?"

"If I call them just so you can see them, they'll probably ignore me." The boy Whisperer laughed. "Dragons are incredibly smart. Even the best of Whisperers can't easily order them around."

A scream pierced the air, followed by frantic bawling. Mau frowned. "Is that Momo?"

Jin urged his bird into a run. Following the bellowing shrieks, he found the baku stuck in a sinkhole near the lake, its three-toed paws clawing the earth as it was slowly sucked into a thick soupy sludge. Its long nose thrashed desperately about, searching for something to grasp. Its beady eyes met Jin's and it squealed pitifully.

Jumping off his monster bird, he scrambled off the path and flung himself down. He crawled to the edge of the sinkhole and grabbed hold of Momo's front legs. The baby baku was surprisingly heavy and covered in slippery mud. Jin felt himself sliding toward the sinkhole. "Hold on," he gasped, digging his toes into the ground. The baku's trunk wrapped around his arm as the monster squeaked and grunted.

The twins rode up on their birds. "What happened?" cried Masa.

"He's stuck," said Jin. "Help me!"

The ground began to shake. Behind the nearest waterfall, the mountainside moved and an enormous creature—as tall as a house and several times as long—detached itself. It was a dragon, blending perfectly with the surrounding rock and vegetation. Its scales were dark like wet stone, turning liquid green at certain angles, and it sported a pair of twisting dark antlers that resembled leafless branches.

A roar rang out of the clouds of fog overhead, and a second dragon came streaming down like a waterfall, landing in the lake with a giant splash. It was the same size as the first but with pale, silvery coloring. It glided out of the water onto their only path of escape. The two dragons fixed their eyes on the baku, which squealed in terror. "Jin, get out of the way," shouted Mau.

The two dragons approached from either side, their golden eyes full of hunger as they prowled toward them. His monster bird gave a frantic warning call, while the Whisperer twins tried to settle their mounts, both birds flapping and braying. Flat on his belly, Jin struggled to pull the bawling baku out, trying to find purchase in the slippery mud. The twins got off their unruly birds and ran to flank Jin. As the monster birds huddled and hissed, Masa and Mau held their hands up at the dragons, halting their advance.

"We can only hold these dragons off for so long," Masa warned. "If they want to eat one of these creatures, it's hard to stop them."

The two dragons paced back and forth, their gaze fixed on Jin and the baku. One of them was slavering, dragon drool trickling down its long jaws. Stubbornly, Jin tugged at the trapped creature. "Please, we've got to get him out!"

"Oh, monstermuck," Mau groaned. "Masa, I'll help get Momo—keep the dragons in place as long as you can."

She turned and swung her other arm up behind her, as if she were pushing the two dragons apart. "Get no closer," Masa ordered them, her jaw clenched. "Okay, Mau, go!"

Mau grabbed Jin's ankles and pulled. The baku moved ever so slightly.

"More!" Jin urged, redoubling his grip on the trapped creature.

The boy Whisperer grunted and pulled harder. Little by little, he backed up, hanging on to Jin's legs, while the baku inched out of the thick sludge. With a sudden jerk and a loud sucking sound, the baku wrenched free from the sinkhole. Mau landed on his back, Jin's feet in his face, while the muddy baku slid across the ground. It staggered to its feet, bawling all the while.

Panting, Jin looked up at Masa. She was frowning in concentration, head on a swivel, silently communicating with the dragons in that mysterious Whisperer way. As he disentangled himself from Mau and they scrambled to stand, he wished he could do the same. The dragons were stamping their clawed feet, eager to go after the baku. Its long nose thrashed from side to side as it squalled, the whites of its beady eyes showing. Jin could tell it wanted to run, but they were trapped between a steep mountain ridge and the narrow lake, a dragon blocking their path on either side. "How are we going to get out of this?"

Masa turned her head. "Do you trust me?" she barked at Jin.

"Why wouldn't I?" Jin was befuddled. He looked at Mau, who furrowed his brow and shrugged.

"Whatever you do, don't run," she said, and dropped her

hands. Stepping back, Masa nodded at the dragons. The dragons lurched forward, approaching them slowly, their eyes gleaming. What was she doing? The baku whistled in alarm and pressed against Jin's side, curling its trunk up tight. He looked around wildly. The only way out was through the lake. Could the baku swim? If they jumped in, would they be able to escape the dragons that way? He inched toward the water.

"Masa!" said Mau in alarm.

She put a hand on Jin's arm. "It's not what you think," she said encouragingly. "Just hold still."

"What's happening?" croaked Jin. He grabbed his lock charm as the two dragons reached their little group, looming over them. The dragons lowered their great heads until their long whiskered faces were nearly level with his. He could see every iridescent scale on their muzzles, gaze into their liquid gold eyes, and count the sharp teeth in their open jaws. A long tongue snaked out and tasted him. "Holy beasts," he yelped. "It's *me* they want to eat!"

One of the dragons expelled a cloud of mist from its wide nostrils. Jin tensed and squeezed his eyes shut, only to be enveloped in a cool, refreshing vapor that smelled like spring rain. Surprised, he opened his eyes to see the dark-horned dragon inhale the cloud right back into its nose. A low rumble emerged from its throat. Masa smiled. "They're not interested in eating—they just want a taste."

"T-taste?!"

"They have to inspect you," she said. "You're the first new human on the island they've seen in a while. No eating, I promise."

Jin felt a tiny bit better, but it was impossible to relax when a monster big enough to swallow you in one gulp was looking you over, let alone two monsters. "Am I supposed to taste bad or good?"

The silvery dragon gave Jin's face a lick with its shiny black tongue. It reminded him of the two-headed boar. Only this dragon's tongue was nearly the same size as Jin. It licked his face again, and then withdrew with a whoosh of mist from its nostrils. The two dragons turned and went back to their perches—the silvery one ascending back into the clouds, while the dark-horned dragon disappeared back behind its waterfall.

"Looks like you passed inspection," said Mau with a grin. "Crickety creatures, sis—you scared me there for a moment."

"Once I learned what they wanted, it seemed like our best way out. It's hard to tell a dragon what to do for very long." Masa gave a wry smile and patted the baku, which had unfurled its trunk and stopped trembling. "Lucky for this little one they weren't hungry."

"Lucky for all of us," blurted Jin. "Are those the only dragons on the island?"

Masa squinted up into the fog-draped peaks of the mountain ridge. "Oh no, there are plenty more. But don't worry, I think the two you met will signal to the others that you're okay."

"Thank the gods for that." Jin wiped his damp face, deflated. Panic, terror, dread, and spit. *That* was his first dragon encounter? He brushed at his mud-caked clothes, but only managed to smear everything. "If I were to try washing off in the lake, would anything in there try to . . . er, taste me?"

"I've got a better idea," said Mau. "There are hot springs not too far from camp. I say we go for a soak there instead of Dragon's Tears."

"Shishi could use a good bath too," said Jin. He was eager to see his dog and to check on Bingyoo.

Masa called for the monster birds, which had calmed enough to ride. As they knelt before Jin and the twins, the baku raised its trunk and whistled mournfully.

"Couldn't stay out of trouble, could you?" Jin scratched it behind the ears. The beast closed its eyes while its back foot kicked a few times. "We'd better bring Momo back with us."

"It won't keep him out of mischief, but he's certainly had enough excitement for one day," agreed the Whisperer girl. "Want to come along, Momo?"

The creature honked and put a muddy paw on her bird. As it tried to climb on its back, the monster bird turned its helmet-horned head and hissed in warning. Shifting its feathered body, it dumped the young dreameater on the ground and flapped its flightless wings in irritation. The baku gave an excited whistle through its long nose and tried again, only for the bird to squawk angrily and snap its beak. "I don't mean for you to ride!" Masa scolded, steering Momo away. "You're much too heavy."

"You don't learn, do you?" Jin shook his head. "You're lucky we got you out of the mud."

They climbed onto their mounts. As the feathered creatures rose on their powerful blue legs, Mau looked down at Momo and chuckled. "Silly beast. Come on, let's go!" The baku trumpeted loudly, then trotted ahead, stubby tail swinging.

Smiling wryly, Jin leaned forward and gave a rousing yell as his monster bird broke into a run.

CHAPTER 18

QUESTING FOR
A CREATURE QUEST

AS DUSK FELL, JIN AND the twins arrived back at camp, their monster birds down to a sedate walk alongside the baby baku. They found Bingyoo sitting by the fire, her hair wet and slicked back, drinking hot milk. The winged horses were gone, and Ayie was sorting through the new supplies salvaged from the eastern shore. Shishi, whose fur was clean and fluffy again, lay at their feet gnawing a bone. The little lion dog paused only long enough to growl when the baku approached, its long nose sniffing curiously. Bingyoo gave Jin a timid smile. Her face was rosy and free of dirt, and she was wearing a clean set of Masa's clothes that were a bit too big for her.

"What in the name of the realms took you so long?" demanded Ayie. "I was just thinking we'd have to go looking for you three."

"We stopped by the Sleeping Tiger," said Mau. "Did you take Bingyoo to the hot springs?"

Ayie nodded, still looking disgruntled. "I figured the soak would help with her cuts." She peered at Jin. "Good beasts, what happened?"

Looking down at the dried mud smeared all over him, Jin picked off a crusty flake. "Momo was stuck in a sinkhole by the lake."

"Always getting into scrapes," Ayie scolded, examining the muddy baby baku. "What a mess! Did anyone get hurt?"

"We're fine," Jin assured her. "I thought we were going to be eaten by a couple of dragons, but Masa held them off."

The girl Whisperer laughed. "The dragons just wanted to inspect Jin. They gave us a little scare, though."

"You all need a good soak at the hot springs yourselves," said Ayie.

"That's for sure. Mau, you and Jin go ahead. I'm going to see to the birds first." Masa chirruped at the monster birds, and they obediently followed her out of the clearing, the baku trotting after them.

After rummaging through his things, Mau handed one of two bundles to Jin. "A change of clothes."

"Don't take too long," warned his aunt. "Or I'll send a water ape to scare you out of the springs."

They headed out of the camp, hiking deeper into the woods. As it grew dark, Jin stumbled several times, stubbing his toes on exposed roots. Mau clapped his hands. The trees flared with light, as if hundreds of butter lamps had been lit at once. Squinting, Jin reached for a shining winged insect. As long as his palm, it crawled onto his finger, its glowing body cool to the touch. "These monster fireflies are brighter than fire."

"It's quite useful," said the Whisperer boy. "In Beastly we kept nesting boxes for them that doubled as lanterns."

A foul scent wafted over Jin. He wrinkled his nose. "Phoenix farts, what's that smell? Was that you?"

"No!" Mau snickered. "You're one to talk, master of monstercakes. It's coming from the hot springs." They reached a clearing where several dark shapes stood sentry. A swarm of fireflies landed on the shapes in bright clusters, illuminating immense boulders. Picking their way over stony ground to the formation, they found a trio of monkey-faced creatures sitting in one of several bubbling pools. The air reeked of rotten eggs. "Mind if we join you?" Mau asked jovially. The creatures looked at them and curled their lips, then got out, water dripping from their fur. They shook themselves and disappeared without a sound, leaving a wet trail on the rocks. Mau shrugged. "More room for us."

Steam rose from the bubbling water. It ran over a small ledge, forming a small waterfall into another pool that fed a stream. Mau put down his bundle and ducked under the waterfall fully clothed.

"Wash off here," he shouted, scrubbing himself. "Aunt Ayie would have a fit if she saw me bathing in my clothes like this, but it saves time." He sloshed out of the pool. "Give it a try."

Jin waded into the pool, muddy clothes and all, and was surprised by the warmth of the water. He got under the pounding stream from the waterfall and closed his eyes for a brief moment, then watched as the mud and dirt ran off him and swirled away. It was better than any of the sweetly perfumed baths he'd taken at the palace.

"Now we can soak without mucking up the pools," said Mau. They went back up to the larger pools and laid out their newly rinsed clothes on rocks to dry before wading into the water.

"It's hot!" exclaimed Jin.

"You'll get used to it," Mau told him. "And if you're feeling sore, it helps a lot. The pools have healing powers."

Gingerly, Jin immersed himself up to his chin. After a while, the heat made him feel boneless, and he hardly noticed the stink anymore. "Moaning monsters, this feels amazing." Jin felt drowsy and almost light-headed. Finding a large submerged rock, he sat on it and found that the water was still up to his shoulders. He tilted his head back with a sigh.

Before he knew it, Jin felt someone shaking him. "Wake up," said Mau. "It's not good to fall asleep in water."

"I wasn't," protested Jin, but he yawned. He followed Mau out of the pool and put on the dry clothes that the boy

Whisperer had lent him. They were baggy, and he had to roll up the legs. But he was clean and warm, if hungry.

"I'm starving," declared Mau, as if reading his mind. "Let's get back before they accidentally burn all the food."

Upon returning to camp, Jin and Mau found Bingyoo and Masa helping Ayie sort the new food supplies. A cloud of fireflies hovered overhead, illuminating the items spread across the ground.

"We've got some rice and other grains, flour and sugar, spices, dried herbs, and all sorts of beans!" said Bingyoo happily.

"There's dried salt fish that got wet—we should eat that tonight," said Ayie. "But all this should feed us for a good while, especially if we can keep our vegetable crops going."

"Tonight we'll have a feast!" Masa said. "But we'll need more monstercakes to build up the fire."

"Leave that to me," said Jin. He ran off to the sizable stash of cakes he'd made and grabbed an armload. Proudly, he showed Bingyoo his handiwork, adding several to the fire. "See all those colors? Only monster dung burns like that."

"No one at the palace would believe it if they saw His Brilliance now." Bingyoo's eyes were wide as Jin carefully stacked the extra dungcakes in a pile. "I'm shocked you made those with your own bare hands!"

Grinning, Jin stuck a monstercake under her nose.

"Here, get a good whiff!"

With a shriek, she ducked and dissolved into giggles. But when the twins began to argue with their aunt over how to cook the rice, Bingyoo stopped laughing and sat up. "If anyone knows how to cook rice, it's me. It's one of my jobs in the palace kitchen."

"You've made rice for the royal family?" asked Mau, visibly impressed.

Bingyoo's dimples appeared. "Not exactly—only for the other servants. The empress dowager's rice is made by someone with years of training in rice preparation alone. They have to prove they can cook it to perfection even blindfolded." She took the pot from him and nodded at the bag of rice Masa held. "If you're worried about making that last, rice porridge won't use as much. I can stretch it with other things too."

"Tell me what you need," said Ayie. She grabbed her knife. "I'll see what I can harvest."

Before long, Bingyoo had a pot of water bubbling over the fire. She threw in a couple handfuls of rice, and after the grains had swelled and softened, she added chunks of sweet potato and onion Ayie had dug from the fields, and salt fish from the ship, transforming the ingredients into a savory, hearty porridge.

"This is the best meal we've had in months," said Mau, tilting his bowl to get every last drop.

"We've survived so far," scoffed Ayie.

Masa wrinkled her nose. "Barely!"

"There's a big difference between surviving and thriving," agreed Mau.

Their aunt sniffed, but Jin caught her quietly scraping her bowl and licking her spoon. Bingyoo just beamed.

As they sat around the fire in a post-meal stupor, Jin's dog pawed at his arm. "Don't worry, I saved you some," he told Shishi. He fed her bits of fish and sweet potato from his fingers, sending the gods a little prayer of thanks that she'd survived. She licked her chops and flopped beside him. Scratching her belly, Jin found the spot that made her kick ecstatically. "At least I know how to make *you* happy, little beast." He sighed and shook his head. So far nothing had turned out the way he thought. The way things were going, he might never find a monster.

"What's wrong?" Masa eyed him curiously.

Jin shrugged. "I was just thinking about the dragons we saw today. It wasn't quite what I'd hoped."

"What do you mean?" She looked surprised. "I thought it went pretty well. It's not like they attacked you or anything."

He pulled out his lock charm. "Probably because I was wearing this. Your aunt called it a royal relic." Jin turned to Ayie. "You said you've seen one before?"

The Whisperer woman nodded. "When I was young. The last royal visit we had—a prince had come on a creature

246

quest. Didn't you say your amulet belonged to your father?"

"Emperor Jen. That's what I was told." Jin looked down at it. "So you might have seen it on him when he came and found his dragon."

Ayie frowned. "Emperor Jen didn't ever visit. His older brother, Ben, was crown prince, and found a nine-tailed fox here. Prince Jen ascended the throne after both his father and Crown Prince Ben died in a tragic accident while traveling."

"Crown Prince Be— So my father never came to Whisper Island? He wasn't meant to be emperor?" Flabbergasted, Jin paused. "I didn't know I even *had* an uncle. My grandmother's never mentioned him. But she won't talk about my parents either, and doesn't like people discussing them around me. Her personal guard told me it makes her too sad. Sometimes it makes me feel like they never even existed."

"Of course they did," said Ayie softly. "You're the proof that they walked this realm. Even if our loved ones are no longer with us, we honor them simply by going on." Her voice caught and she bit her lip. "As best we can."

The twins exchanged a glance, then folded their hands to their hearts and bowed their heads. "May their spirits be tranquil and free." Their aunt and Bingyoo joined in, and a quiet hush fell, the only sound crackling from the campfire. A moment of reverence honoring those lost. Jin couldn't remember the last time anyone had done that with him. Unexpected tears sprang to his eyes. He blinked them quickly away.

Presently Ayie spoke. "News from the capital was always sporadic, so I don't know exactly what happened with your father. I just remember learning that the emperor and crown prince had died, and that Prince Jen would become emperor when he came of age. Empress Soro—your grandmother, I take it—became regent for a few years."

"Well, she became regent again when my father died," Jin said. Finding out that his father had not been crown prince and that an uncle was supposed to reign floored him. How different would things have been had they all lived? "He was emperor long enough to marry my mother and see me born, but I never knew either of them. How did he even come by a dragon if he never came here?"

"Perhaps the head Whisperer at the palace managed to find one for him," said the Whisperer woman.

Jin got up and poked at the fire with a stick. "Or maybe they got a big lizard and passed it off as a dragon. Nowadays, ordinary beasts are used as stand-ins for monsters all the time. You should see what it's like during the Monster Festival." Recalling the animal fights, he reached down to scratch the base of Shishi's tail stump as she nosed at his feet. "But I can't get away with passing my dog off as a monstermate. Everyone at the palace already knows her. The fact is, even if I wasn't meant to be emperor before my uncle died, I am now, and I came here to find a creature."

Glancing at her brother, Masa shifted in her seat. "We're sorry we didn't believe you before." She looked down and fiddled with her jade bangle.

"But we do now, and we'll help you however we can," Mau added.

Their aunt nodded briskly. "We're still Whisperers. Even if there's only three of us left, our duty is to the creatures— and the Three Realms. You must go on a creature quest, that much is clear. But before you do, preparation is necessary. It's never been as simple as just arriving here and picking out a monster like you would a pup from a litter."

"I realized that after today," admitted Jin. "I don't know what I was expecting when I saw my first dragons. I really thought that there'd be more of a . . . connection. Instead I just felt relieved to survive." He sighed. "So what's involved in a creature quest?"

"It's best done by the quester—alone," said Ayie. "Whisperers have accompanied questers in tracking down their monsters before, and there've been rare instances where monstermates were captured by Whisperers in the name of the royal and bestowed upon them, but the bond was always weak. Secondly, the quester must demonstrate knowledge and understanding of creatures before setting out."

That wasn't as daunting as he'd feared. Jin was heartened. He'd been alone on the island his first night and survived. He had his amulet. And he'd practically memorized the bestiary. "Okay, so when can I—"

Ayie continued. "Furthermore, the quester must be able to fend for themselves for at least three days in the island's interior on foot. Some quests have taken as long as a month, while some find a monstermate before the first sunrise, but such cases are unusual. It's prudent to prepare for at least a few nights alone in the wilderness. No special weapons or tools beyond what's needed for basic survival are permitted."

An uneasy feeling crept over Jin. One night wasn't so bad—but a whole month? "Guess I'll be singing 'The Beastie Lullaby' a lot," he muttered.

"I did that for days," whispered Bingyoo. "If I can do it, you can too."

"Most importantly, the connection with a creature is best formed when one is young," said Ayie. "Past the age of twelve, it's much harder to communicate with uncanny beasts if you've not done it before."

At that, Jin felt his heart drop. Bingyoo caught his look of dismay. "His Brilliance doesn't have much time," she ventured.

"When is your birthday?" asked the Whisperer woman.

"I'll be thirteen by the end of next month."

"Hmm. We're older than you by six months," observed Masa.

Her brother grinned. "You are. I'm older by six months and five minutes."

Masa gave him a shove and he shoved her back. Ignoring the twins, their aunt nodded. "So we've only got weeks left. Before we send you off, we need to make sure you're ready."

Jin leaned forward. "I will be. What do I need to do?"

The Whisperer woman smiled. "You'll be relieved of some of your monstercake-making duties, I can promise you that."

Over the next week, Jin and the Whisperers adjusted to their new situation. Being considered an ordinary boy had forced Jin to do things that he'd never expected. He had developed a few calluses and was certainly stronger than when he'd left the palace, thanks to all the running about and chores he'd done on both the ship and around Whisper Island. But now that Crown Prince Jin was to go on a royal creature quest, the Whisperers were determined to see him succeed—which meant more work than ever.

He could whip up a batch of monstercakes in a fraction of the time it had taken him initially, so it was still one of his duties. But he also accompanied either the twins or Ayie on their rounds about the island, usually on the back of an obliging monster. Without fail, the Whisperers would make him get off and follow them on foot back to camp, where Shishi kept Bingyoo company as she prepared their meals. After one particularly grueling trek back, he couldn't help but complain. "It's not fair that you all get to ride the whole time and I don't."

Ayie gazed at him steadily. "Very well, Your Brilliance. We'll all go on foot, then."

The next day, Jin found himself wishing he'd never said anything. He traipsed behind the twins, huffing and puffing while they strode briskly along. Undaunted by rough ground and steep trails, they chattered like a pair of green crows while Jin worked with aching legs to keep up. Upon returning to camp in the evening, stumbling and exhausted, he approached Ayie. "Maybe we can go back to the way we did it before," he meekly proposed.

But the twins hooted him down. "Don't listen to him, Aunt Ayie!" Mau shouted.

"He's in worse shape than we thought," added Masa. "He'll never be ready in time if we let him ride."

Impassive, the Whisperer woman crossed her arms. "It's up to Jin. If he can't manage the challenge of the island's terrain, there's only so much we can do. Is that what you really want, Your Brillance?"

As everyone turned their attention to him, Jin flushed red and squirmed. "Maybe I'll give it another try tomorrow."

From then on, Jin held his tongue and soldiered along on foot with the Whisperers. Every time he felt like collapsing, he'd stop for a moment and take a deep breath, touching his lock charm. He needed to get stronger to go on a creature quest, he reminded himself. With each passing day, he found that he could go longer without losing his breath, and could keep up more easily with the Whisperers. Walking was slower than riding, but it meant he was getting better at spotting creatures in the wilderness without the Whisperers having to point them out. Once he learned what to look for, he noticed monsters of all sorts, even when they were sitting quietly in the underbrush. He was also starting to recognize individual calls through the cacophony of monster bird song and echoing cries of beasts.

Each night, they'd gather round the fire and dine on fare that was decidedly tastier than before, thanks to Bingyoo and the skills she'd honed in the palace kitchens. Jin had to admit that cooking hadn't been the Whisperers' strong suit, nor his. With Bingyoo, their meals improved not only because they'd salvaged nutritious provisions from the boat, but because there was finally someone who knew how to transform them into something delicious. Eating something satisfying always put everyone in a better mood.

Afterward, the twins would drill Jin on the geography of Whisper Island, the creatures he might find, and what he knew about them. The green crows often visited their camp, and the Whisperers would have them imitate other creatures for Jin to identify. When Jin finally managed to accurately name every creature call mimicked by the green crows, he was relieved and jubilant. "That's it, right? Now I can go on my creature quest! Maybe at first light—I've got ideas for supplies to bring."

The two crows that had been making monster noises opened their beaks and emitted the sound of laughter. The Whisperer twins looked at each other, then at their aunt. Masa ducked her head and began spinning her jade bangle, while Mau cleared his throat. "Getting every creature call right is really impressive, Jin." He rubbed his nose. "I don't think it means you're ready, though."

"But I can keep up with all of you now," said Jin, chagrined. "For the whole day without needing extra rest! So you don't have to worry about me alone in the wilderness. And I just proved that I know enough about monsters—haven't I?"

Ayie shook her head. "It's not just knowledge that you need. It's understanding."

"There's no difference!" Jin argued.

"Actually, there is, and that's why you can't go yet," said the Whisperer woman. "We're trying to make sure you have the best chance at succeeding."

"If you came across a creature now, you wouldn't be able to truly communicate," added Masa. She held out her arm, and one of the two crows went to perch on it.

"The answer is right there in front of you," it cawed.

The other crow barked, sounding exactly like his dog. Jin frowned and picked up Shishi. "Do you mean my dog? Is she actually a monster or something?"

"Not an uncanny beast," said the first crow. "Just a key to one."

The Whisperer woman gazed at Shishi thoughtfully. "The crows are right. If you can understand why you call her yours, then you will have unlocked your ability to bond with a creature."

"Isn't it obvious? She's my dog because . . . she just is!" Frustrated, Jin stopped. It was clear he couldn't convince the Whisperers that he was ready to find his monstermate. Their reasoning sounded like pure monstermuck. Heat blazed up the back of his neck, like a flame on a firecracker about to go off. Abruptly he stood and excused himself. "I'm going for a walk," he said tightly, then stalked off, Shishi at his heels. He'd been working so hard. What more did they want? But his fury was soon overtaken by despair. He'd be turning thirteen in three weeks. Time was running out.

CHAPTER 19

A STICKY SITUATION

TOSSING AND TURNING, JIN GAVE up trying to sleep and sat up. The sky was still dark but shifting from ink black to deep blue. Quietly he gathered a few items around their camp, trying not to make any noise as the others slept. If anyone woke and saw him, he'd just say he was getting an early start on his chores. But as the pale light of dawn turned the sky gray, the sound of snoring followed him as he stole away through the trees.

It was time. If not now, when? He'd been on the island for weeks, and since arriving he'd done more physical labor than in his entire life, had practically wallowed in monster dung for days on end, and had gone on forced daily marches all over the place. The twins and Ayie knew how urgently he needed to find a monstermate. Yet they weren't helping at all. How could they say he didn't understand monsters? The Whisperers didn't understand *him*.

He didn't even require a dragon anymore. At this point he'd take anything, provided it had *some* sort of useful power, and he thought of Momo. The baby baku might bond with him—it liked him already. He'd helped save it, after all. Just like he'd saved Shishi. Maybe that was why the crows said his dog was the key.

So Jin set off in search of Momo, carrying nothing but a gourd of water, his firestarter and lockpicks, a length of rope, and one of Ayie's knives. It had an enameled handle shaped like a dragon's head, jeweled eyes, and a leather sheath embossed with scales, which fit perfectly in his belt. As he got farther away from camp, he relaxed a bit and began softly calling for the baby baku.

Rustling steps in the bushes made him stop and scan them hopefully. "Momo?"

A small furry creature emerged from the underbrush, wagging its stump. "Shishi!" Jin groaned. The little lion dog flopped over at his feet, asking for pets. Jin bent down with a rueful chuckle. "Why can't you be a *monster* dog?" He rubbed Shishi's furry belly as the dog wriggled ecstatically.

A rough caw above startled him. It was a green crow, perched on a branch. "Do you truly wish it were something different?" It looked down at them, cocking its head.

"Not really." Jin shrugged. "It'd be easier. But she's no magical beast—and I never expected her to be. That's why I came to the island in the first place—to find a real monster."

"What happens if you don't find one?"

"Then I won't be crown prince anymore," Jin retorted. "I won't become emperor. Can't rule without a monster."

"So just stay here," said the crow. "Would that be so bad?"

"Stay?" said Jin. "I'm not a Whisperer like the others. If I can't find a creature that will understand me—besides you green crows—what good can I do? Make monstercakes all day? At least back home I know what my future holds."

"You only think you know," said the crow. "But the shape of the future is ever-changing. A full cup one moment can be turned inside out in the next. If you stay alert to the possibilities, nothing will be lost." It stared at him, red eyes unblinking, then flew off.

Jin sighed. "Did you understand any of that?" he asked Shishi. The dog licked his face. "Me neither." He stood, feeling impatient. "Go back to camp," he told her firmly. He gave Shishi a little nudge with his leg, and she took a few reluctant steps. "Off with you. Find Bingyoo. Go!" He waited until she was gone, then went off to search for the baku.

The sun came up, glittering through the canopy, the calls of fantastical creatures punctuating the morning song of monster birds. As he ducked through the trees, a familiar bark and panting at his heels made him stop. "What did I say?" Jin exclaimed, exasperated. Shishi wagged her stump and whined. "Fine, you can come along," he said gruffly, and continued with the dog beside him. "You better hope we find Momo soon."

Yet call as he might, there was no sign of the long-nosed creature. "Is it because I'm looking for him?" Jin wondered out loud. "Fine. Don't follow me, Momo! Stay far away!" He paused and looked around, then sighed and kept on. If not the dreameater, then what? This island was full of uncanny beasts. One of them had to be his. He was determined to search till he found something. If it came to it, he'd make do with a giant firefly, with its useful light, and bring that back to the Palace of Monsters. Never had there been a ruler without a creature companion, and he wasn't going to be the first. But as he pressed on, he caught only frustrating glimpses. Flashes of fur, scales, or feathers would briefly be illuminated by a sunbeam before disappearing into the shadows, as if the island's creatures were avoiding him without the Whisperers by his side.

The light in the forest changed so gradually that he didn't know how long he'd been walking. The canopy thickened and blocked out the sun as the trees around him became taller, the trunks thick and craggy with age. His stomach was hollow, and the air was humid and warm. He swigged some water from his drinking gourd. If only he'd thought to eat beforehand, or bring food along. Wiping the sweat from his brow, he tried to assess his surroundings.

Shishi flopped down, her tongue hanging out. Jin poured

some water into his palm for her to drink, then scooped her up and slung her over his shoulders. "Sorry, girl."

What was he doing? He was halfway through a whole day, and he couldn't even locate the one beast on the island that already knew him and liked him. And even if he made do with a monster firefly instead of Momo, how would he make it listen to him? Shishi didn't even listen to him. How was he to control a creature? He couldn't control *anything*. Maybe the Whisperers were right, and he wasn't ready. With a sigh, he turned and began to retrace his steps to camp. Shishi's stout body grew tense, and she began to growl. "What is it?" Jin halted and looked around.

Barking madly, Shishi scrambled from his shoulders and ran off through the trees. Jin called after her, annoyed. "Get back here!"

A startled yelp rang out, and then frantic crying. His dog was in trouble.

Jin sprinted after the sound, fatigue forgotten. He burst through the underbrush, with thoughts of nothing but Shishi, and as he ran through a curtain of dangling vines, they yanked him to a stop. They weren't vines—he was caught in a haphazard draping of thick, sticky ropes. Nearby whimpers turned his head. His dog was stuck in a wide net of that same rope. The golden strands were tangled around Shishi and pulled at her fur as she struggled. Rope-wrapped bundles hung from the netting, which stretched across their path and high up into the trees. It quivered as Shishi thrashed about.

A flash of movement at the top of the net caught his eye, and as he squinted up into the forest canopy, he realized with an icy drench of horror that it was no net. An enormous spider was making its way down its web to investigate, alerted by their disturbance. Eight long black-and-yellow legs, thick as giant stalks of bamboo, crept along, propelling a dark body the size of a horse. As it moved through patches of sunlight shining through the treetops, bright yellow stripes on its underside glowed.

"Golden earth spider," Jin gasped. As he frantically tried to recall what he'd read about them in the bestiary, the web shuddered with the monster's movements, shaking the dangling bundles. His eyes widened when one shifted to reveal a pair of deerlike hooves poking through. "Oh muck, those are its meals!" The spider had encased its prey in layers of silk to preserve them for later—and if he didn't get his dog out of there, she'd be next.

Shishi whined softly. "Hold on, girl," said Jin. His shoulders were entangled in sticky spider silk, but much of it was ragged and dusty, the remnants of an older web. He managed to work one arm free and reached for the knife at his belt. He hacked at the strands about him, but the spider's silk was stronger than steel itself. Sawing away fruitlessly, he glanced up at the gargantuan spider making its way toward them. He could see its head now, studded with a row of bulbous, shiny, black eyes.

Desperately he slipped out of his belt and tunic, leaving them dangling, and tore himself away from the gummy ropes of silk. He ran to Shishi in the spider's web. Its golden strands gleamed stickily, and his blade nearly stuck fast when he swiped at one. Hearing the clacking of spider jaws, Jin looked up. It had moved halfway down from its perch, close enough for him to see the thick dark bristles covering its head and mouth and the grasping claws on the end of each leg.

"Hold still, Shishi," he said softly, and stroked her nose, trying to calm her. Carefully he cut at her fur, loosening the web's hold on her bit by bit. He began singing "The Beastie Lullaby," and when he stole a glance overhead, he saw that the spider had slowed, though its long legs were still picking their way down. He sang louder, and pulled Shishi close as he shaved away her stuck fur, trying to keep the blade from her skin. The whites of her eyes showed as she panted and whined, and she yelped whenever he nicked her, but remained still. Finally he cut his dog free. "There!" He snatched her up—patchy, bleeding, and nearly bald in spots—and scrambled away from the web.

He'd gone only a few steps when his foot sank through a bed of leaves and he nearly fell flat on his face. His leg was stuck in a hole. When he yanked it out, baby earth spiders the size of his hand came swarming out. "Monstermuck!" He'd stepped in the spider's nest. Turning his head, he saw the giant spider scuttling down the lower reaches of its web, faster now. In a cold sweat, Jin shook off the baby spiders crawling up his shin and ran, hugging his dog to his bare chest.

By the time he reached a stream, his legs were on the verge of collapse and his lungs burned. He stopped and tried to catch his breath and get his bearings. He had no idea where he was. Though he had his knife in hand and the tools he'd stashed in his pockets, he'd lost his tunic and belt, which had carried his drinking gourd and knife sheath. He felt for his lock charm and was relieved to find it still around his neck. Even better, there was no sign of the spider or any of its young. "I don't think it's following us." Shakily, he sank to his knees and put Shishi down so they could both drink from the running water. When he finished, he noticed a strand of old spider silk clunging to his trouser leg. He took a seat on a low rock and wrapped the blade with it, tying the ends around his calf so he'd have one less thing to carry. The thick silk would protect the knife and his leg—it was the strongest stuff he'd ever seen. Shishi huddled by his side, shivering.

"Bit off more than you could chew, didn't you, little beast?" With a sigh, he gathered her in his arms. "I wouldn't have let that monster get you for anything. We belong to each other." As he examined the nicks in her skin and tried to dab away blood, something in him cracked open like the shutters on a window in the dark. All this time he'd been thinking about finding a monster that would be useful to him—the more powerful the better. Shishi was the complete opposite of an imposing creature, and yet it didn't matter. He took care of her anyway.

"It's not about what a monster can do for *me*, is it?" he said to her slowly, rubbing the shorn fur on her back. Jin shook his head. How had he not seen it before?

No wonder the Whisperers had said he wasn't ready. He'd gone about things all wrong, and nearly gotten himself and Shishi turned into spider snacks. He had to get them back to camp before the sun went down.

Jin turned around, trying to remember what the Whisperers had taught him about navigating through the wilderness. He looked at the sparse sunbeams slanting through the thick trees. "We'll follow the sun," he said out loud with more confidence than he felt. "It sets in the west. And water runs downhill, so if we stick by the stream, then eventually we'll get to the sea—or at least the valley."

Slinging Shishi around his shoulders, he set off, hoping he could find their way before it grew too dark. Birds chattered in the canopy overhead, but otherwise the only other sound was the babbling water of the stream and his footsteps tramping across the forest floor. Nervously Jin hummed snippets of "The Beastie Lullaby," and Shishi licked his ear. "No need to tangle with another monster today, right?"

A caw sounded, and Jin looked up to see a three-legged messenger crow land in a tree before him. "Prince Jin. The Whisperers are searching for you."

His heart leaped. "Am I glad to see you! We ran into a . . . little trouble, and I'm a bit lost. Can you tell them where we are? I'm trying to get back to the camp. And . . ." Jin stopped and cleared his throat. "I'm sorry that I ran off. I understand now what Ayie and the twins meant. Will you let them know?"

The crow's feathers flashed from black to green as it cocked its head. "Certainly. If you don't know where you're going, wander no longer. Stay where you are, so you can be found." Flapping its wings, it flew off, cawing urgently.

Jin slumped against the tree and sank to the ground. "Thank gods 'n' monsters!" Help was coming. He and Shishi wouldn't be stranded out here at nightfall. "We'll be all right. But no more running off, understand?" he told his dog firmly. "I don't care what sort of beasts you think you can fight." They just needed to stay put, and the Whisperers would find them.

He leaned back against the tree, which was covered with springy moss that carpeted the surrounding earth, and closed his eyes briefly, exhausted. Shishi curled up next to him, and he smoothed his palm along what was left of her fur. Then he took off his lock charm and pulled out his lock-picks. "Might as well work on something while we wait, eh?"

As he puzzled over the tiny lock, Jin grew so absorbed that he hardly noticed that the shadows in the forest had grown longer until Shishi's body tensed and she sprang to her feet. In the fading light, Jin saw a flash of glimmering, other-worldly blue. Scooping up the dog, he scrambled to stand and jammed his picks into his pocket. He hurriedly looped his amulet back around his neck. A low growl emerged from Shishi's throat, so quiet that Jin only felt it. Peering into the gloom, he reached for his knife, but froze when an enormous four-legged creature emerged. Its massive cloven hooves took delicate steps, making nary a sound. An impressively sharp pair of antlers gleamed atop its dragon-like head, which was framed with a flowing mane of silvery fur.

Hardly daring to believe his eyes, Jin shrank back behind the tree's thick trunk. "A real kirin!"

It looked much like the images he'd pored over in the imperial bestiary, its muscular body covered in irides-cent blue scales and tufts of fur. Its ox-like tail flicked a buzzing insect away from its broad flanks while it bent its antlered head to drink from the stream. When it paused to look around, water dripped from its long, bearded muzzle. Though the kirin was taller and broader than even winged monster horses and had the fierce jaws of a dragon, it moved with a dignified grace. Jin felt calmed just watching it. The bestiary said it was so gentle it wouldn't hurt grass. Forgetting all fear, he leaned out for a better view. Less than ten paces away, it was so close that he could admire every detail.

"Now *that's* a monster," he breathed, awed. Shishi wagged her stump and whined softly.

The kirin turned its head and met his gaze. Its eyes glistened gold, the pupils as dark as polished onyx. It curled its lips, revealing sharp fangs. A rumble emerged from its throat, and to Jin's shock, he heard words.

"We're not monsters. Only humans call us that, because they think they're superior. But they're not." It turned and walked away, its giant hooves treading quietly on the forest floor.

Had he imagined it? Or had the kirin just spoken to him? "Wait!" Jin called. "That wasn't an insult! I meant it as a compliment!" But the great beast never looked back, and soon disappeared. Jin longed to run after it, but he looked at Shishi and stopped himself. They had to stay where they were so the Whisperers could find them. "I'm not ready," he reminded himself. But a thrill ran through him, and he couldn't shake his certainty. He had seen a kirin—his first—and he'd understood what it said.

CHAPTER 20

THE CROW'S WARNING

THE WHISPERERS WERE UPSET, JIN could tell. After finding him gone on his ill-fated and premature attempt at a creature quest, the twins had enlisted the help of a swift-moving zouya to search the island. When they first recovered Jin and his dog, both Masa and Mau threw their arms around him, laughing with relief. But by the time they'd returned to camp on the back of the zouya, the tiger-like beast traveling so fast that it took Jin's breath away, neither Whisperer was smiling. Masa had quieted completely, while Mau seemed stiff and distant, addressing him formally without a hint of teasing. "My aunt would like to have a word with you, Your Brilliance."

Feeling his cheeks warm, Jin handed his dog over to Masa, who took Shishi without a word, and went to Ayie, who sat by the fire sharpening a blade. Jin swallowed a groan when he saw Momo stretched out beside her, his long nose lazily toying with a pebble. Of course the baby baku would show up at camp when Jin was no longer searching for him. "Definitely not my monstermate," Jin muttered. He looked at Ayie and quailed. Darkness had fallen, and the Whisperer woman looked even more severe than usual, her mouth held tight.

"What do you have to say for yourself?" Steadily, she scraped the blade against a flat stone.

Jin knelt and took a deep breath.

"I was wrong," he said. "I thought I knew more than I did, when I really don't know anything." With a bow, he begged forgiveness. Jin explained that he'd gone looking for the young dreameater. "I started thinking he had to be my monstermate because I saved him from the mud pit, and I'd saved Shishi, and you'd said my dog was the key, so . . ." He trailed off lamely as the baku raised its head and blew a little toot through its nose. "Obviously I never found Momo, but Shishi found a monster of a different sort." By the time he finished recounting what had happened with the golden earth spider, Ayie had become very still.

"Why didn't you leave the dog?" she asked. "Why go through so much trouble to save an ordinary beast? Did it occur to you that perhaps you could have gained the monster spider's trust by leaving it a meal? Then you'd have the creature companion you've been longing for."

"What?" Jin was horrified. "No, I couldn't! That never

even crossed my mind. So what if Shishi has no special powers? That doesn't make her any less important. She can't help me claim the throne, but I love her all the same." He looked over to where Masa and Bingyoo were attending to Shishi's nicks and scratches. "That's what you all were trying to tell me, wasn't it? All this time, I've thought only about what a monster can do for me—and that's why I wasn't ready for one." The end of the baku's nose reached out and patted Jin's hand, and he gave it a little scratch. Momo grunted happily.

The Whisperer woman's eyes softened. "You're making progress." Then she narrowed her gaze. "But you disappointed us, Jin. We were very worried about you, and with good reason, I see. You escaped without even the clothes on your back." She tossed him an old tunic, faded but clean. "Put this on—you're shivering." As he meekly did her bidding, she sighed. "But despite your misadventures, you seemed to have learned something."

"I did." Jin nodded fervently. "And I'm sorry. I won't do it again."

"We'd like for you to stay in camp for the next couple days instead of accompanying me or the twins around the island." Ayie went back to sharpening her knife. "You could probably use the time to rest."

But Jin knew it was a punishment of sorts, and that he'd offended the Whisperers. For when he approached the twins and tried to tell them about his encounter with the kirin, they didn't seem particularly impressed.

"It just showed up and spoke to you?" said Mau, raising an eyebrow.

"And you knew what it was saying?" scoffed Masa, tossing her head.

"I did! I thought you'd be more excited." Jin was crestfallen. "I feel like we're back to when I first arrived, and you didn't believe a word I said."

"That's right," Masa snapped. "Because we didn't trust you."

Mau folded his arms. "And when you ran off on your own even after we told you not to, you showed that you don't trust us."

To make amends, Jin volunteered to do all their chores around camp on top of his own. He even offered Bingyoo his help with cooking, though Bingyoo was more understanding than the others. "It didn't surprise me at all, Your Brilliance. Your thirteenth birthday is just a few weeks away now," she said. Her dimples appeared. "And you've never been one to listen when you're told no."

Her support made him feel a lot better. Yet the next day, Jin found that when it came to preparing food, Bingyoo had very decided opinions and was a lot less understanding when he didn't do things a certain way.

"Don't hold the carrots like that—you'll cut your fingers off," she scolded. "Curl your fingertips in." She demonstrated, making her fingers look like giant claws.

"Huh," said Jin, flexing his hand. "Looks like making a proper fist for punching—my knuckles are squared off."

"Yes, but curl your thumb or you'll cut that off too. See, no exposed fingertips! Don't lift the entire blade while you're chopping—keep the tip of your blade against the cutting board so your knife doesn't go all over the place."

"It feels awkward," he complained.

"It's safer," she said sternly. She reached over and repositioned his first finger, which was resting on top of the knife. "Don't put your finger there; it won't help you. Pinch the sides of the blade between your thumb and pointer."

Jin grumbled, but after a while he noticed that it did seem easier to slice things, and looked for other items he could chop up. "Would the palace cooks be impressed?"

"They'd drop their jaws in the soup!" Bingyoo giggled.

That night, upon the Whisperers' return from a day's work around the island, Jin was proud to present them a satisfying meal and a clean camp. It seemed to soften them somewhat. Afterward, as they sat around the fire in drowsy contentment, Jin couldn't stop thinking about his run-in with the kirin. The twins had been dismissive when he'd told them about it the night before, but the exhilaration of seeing the noble creature—and hearing it speak—still buoyed him. "I meant to tell you last night, Ayie—after Shishi and I escaped the earth spider's web, we encountered another monster," he ventured.

"Oh?" The Whisperer woman turned her head, her dark gaze suddenly alert. "What sort?"

Mau and Masa exchanged glances, and Masa rolled her eyes. Jin tried to ignore them. "It was a ki—"

Before he could finish, a dark shape fell from the sky and crashed to the ground in a heap. Bingyoo screamed and Shishi began barking. The twins jumped to their feet, while Jin stared in shock. It was a green crow, an empty bamboo tube dangling from its third leg, which was bent at an odd angle. "Danger! Danger for the island," it croaked. "Beware the dark of the new moon. Invaders will come!"

Ayie rushed to the crow's side. "This is the messenger bird I sent to the capital after Jin arrived." It struggled to right itself, flapping a wing, its feathers changing from black to iridescent green in the firelight. She soothed the large crow with gentle hands and murmurs, while the twins hovered anxiously and Shishi growled, the patchy remnants of fur on her back bristling. The Whisperer woman frowned. "One leg is broken, and your wing is bleeding. What happened?"

"I brought your message to the palace, Mistress Ayie," croaked the green crow. "They tried to capture me."

"Who tried to capture you?" Jin demanded.

With great effort, it reached down with its beak and

yanked out a clump of feathers. It put them in Ayie's hand. "Burn. These. You will . . . see." Its red eyes fluttered shut, and after a moment, it went limp.

A howl went up from Shishi, while Masa cried out. Jin stared in shock. "Is it . . . dead?"

Mau nodded grimly. His sister tenderly took the crow's body into her lap and bent her head, eyes closed. A tear rolled down her cheek. Within moments several green crows flew into the camp, squawking in distress at the fallen crow. More and more three-legged crows appeared, the night air filled with their calls. Bingyoo shrank against Jin nervously, and he tried to say something reassuring, but the thunderous caws of so many monster birds drowned out all speech. They flocked about Masa till she could hardly be seen, then flew off all at once, bearing away the dead bird. After the storm of crows disappeared into the dark, a heavy stillness fell upon them.

"Now what?" whispered Bingyoo, eyes wide.

"We do as instructed," said Ayie. Stoically, the Whisperer woman threw the crow's feathers into the campfire. They blazed up in an instant, shimmering and crackling. As the burning feathers swirled in the heated air over the fire, Jin and the others stepped back until a vision formed above them, and the hiss of the flames became voices.

An enormous glittering room spread before them, as if they were looking down from above. Elaborately gilded ceiling rafters shielded them, and below was a woman seated on a platform in a throne, flanked by men jostling and arguing around her. Jin immediately recognized his grandmother, and realized they were seeing a memory of the throne hall from the crow's eye. It must have sneaked in through one of the old rooftop portals for monster birds.

"Your Brilliant Majesty, if this bird's report is true, then shouldn't we send troops at once?" The voice of the head diviner rang out above the others.

"Yes, but not to the island. We must first punish the attackers," declared the minister of justice, so vehemently that the stiff wings on his tall horsehair cap trembled. "We all know it was the Hulagans—I shall eat my cap if it wasn't!"

"Why not just declare war, then?" shouted a third courtier. "Hang the treaties! We should have finished them off a long time ago."

The head minister of the treasury coughed. "We just raised taxes to pay for the extension of the border wall. Declaring war means another hike—and conscription besides."

"It's the people's duty!"

"They'll be in uproar!"

As the royal advisors squabbled, the empress dowager pursed her lips and pointed her trident scepter at one of her attendants. It was Lady Opal, who bent down and listened as the empress dowager whispered in her ear. The lady-in-waiting bowed and scurried out of the room. Then Jin's grandmother looked around and said querulously, "And what of the three-legged crow that purportedly came from the island with this message? Do we have proof? Has there been any word of Prince Jin?"

"Your Brilliant Majesty," said the head Whisperer. "The messenger bird eluded capture, but palace Whisperers are looking for it right now."

"Such uselessness!" The empress dowager banged the end of her trident scepter against the arm of her throne in frustration, and her phoenix screamed in agreement from its perch behind her.

A man dressed in nondescript dark robes and a plain cap inched away from the knot of ministers and courtiers and slipped furtively out the doors of the throne room, his face obsured by a pillar. The crow hopped through the monster portal in the rooftop and followed, stealthily gliding from perch to perch behind the man as he hurried through the grounds. Jin frowned. Who was that? The man finally stopped in a quiet garden and approached a prominent stone lantern. He passed his sleeve across its glowing window once, twice, three times as if signaling someone, then stepped into the shadows. The crow perched on a rooftop overlooking the garden, sitting among the ceramic guardian figures that lined the eaves. Before long, a uniformed guard appeared and joined the man.

"Good news," said the first man in a harsh whisper. "The village of Whisperers was wiped out after all. Though monsters were set upon our men before they could take over, it's more than we hoped for after all these months of uncertainty. Several monster tamers have survived—a messenger bird arrived from them this week with a report. The empress seems disinclined to act, but we should not delay. Another battalion must be sent as soon as possible."

The guard's guttural voice was so low, Jin could barely catch his words. "After losing almost an entire squadron? What's to keep those monsters from wiping out the next?"

"Hardly any Whisperers are left to command them, and they can be easily overcome," the first man insisted. "This time we will be able to capture creatures. I have gleaned information on these beasts that should allow for our men to hunt down enough trophies for the plan to be fulfilled. Before anyone knows it, the island will be nothing but history for Samtei."

"The soonest we can get men over there won't be for nearly three weeks," said the guard.

"So much the better, for it will be the new moon then," said the first man. "Stealth allowed us to destroy the village of monster tamers, and stealth shall allow us to complete the mission."

A whoosh of flapping wings turned the crow's attention from the two men in the shadows. The empress dowager's phoenix appeared, its crimson-and-gold feathers gleaming in the moonlight. With unnerving swiftness, the monster bird flew straight for the rooftop eaves, its fierce gaze trained on the crow. It opened its serrated beak and snapped at the crow's leg. The crow squawked in pain and stabbed at the phoenix with its sharp, thick beak. The phoenix screeched, and the crow slipped from its grasp and flew into the night sky.

"That may be the messenger bird from the island," cried the first man. "Don't let it go!" A sharp crack tore through the quiet, and then a hail of pellets streaked past. The crow plunged but managed to catch itself before hitting the earth. It flapped and glided away from the palace, and then its vision dissolved into a puff of smoke, leaving everyone sitting around the campfire in stunned silence.

Jin leaped to his feet. "What was all that?" He approached the campfire, searching for the vivid images that had danced above it, but they had dissipated with the smoke. "Did you hear what I heard? Someone from the palace is behind the attack on Beastly?"

"That's what it sounded like to me," said Mau, sounding shaken.

Masa nodded. "And me. Why did the empress's phoenix attack the messenger bird? Why were they even trying to capture the poor crow?"

"It seemed like that guard was trying to kill it," Bingyoo

said. Holding Shishi close, she rocked in her seat, looking troubled.

"Did you recognize either of those men?" asked Ayie.

"I never got a good look at their faces, and their voices were so low that I thought I misheard them. But they said there was a mission, right? They wanted to destroy Beastly— they wanted the Whisperers all gone! Who would do that?" Pacing about, Jin scrubbed at the back of his head, trying to make sense of it all. He recalled the day he'd hidden in the Diviners' Salon, and overheard them talking about spies. Had they meant spies from somewhere like Hulagu? "They're working against my grandmother, that much is clear. I need to warn her."

"I understand your feelings, Your Brilliance, but we mustn't ignore the crow's warning and what it heard," said Ayie. "In little more than two weeks' time, there will be men on our shores. Whoever they are, they won't be friendly—to us or the creatures."

Mau stared blankly into the fire. "And there's no one coming to help." His voice was full of despair.

"I think that's clear," said Masa. Her jaw set and her eyes flashed. "It's up to us to save ourselves."

CHAPTER 21

TRAPS AND DUNGCAKES

THE MOOD THROUGHOUT WHISPER ISLAND was grim. Green crows spread word among the creatures of the impending attack, setting off a few skittish stampedes and wandering swarms that the Whisperers struggled to contain. The dragons generated an even heavier layer of clouds and fog, as if they were trying to shroud the island in a cloak of invisibility. The gray skies and lack of sun made everyone even gloomier than they already were. Huddled in camp that night, they argued over how to face the looming threat of invasion.

"There's but five of us—and you're all mere kits yourself," Ayie fretted. "I can't ask you to fight against a company of armed soldiers."

"You don't have to ask. We'll do it anyway," said Masa stoutly.

Her brother nodded. "If you think we'd ever leave you

to face this on your own, then you have a different fight on your hands, Aunt Ayie."

The Whisperer woman looked away for a moment, biting her lip. "Fine," she said gruffly. "But Your Brilliance, I think we should try to send you and Bingyoo out of harm's way and back to the mainland. Do you think the two of you could manage a winged horse on your own?"

Jin hesitated. His goal had been to return to Samtei with a monster—but not like this. He shook his head. "That wouldn't be right. I can't leave you and the monsters to fend for yourselves." He looked at Bingyoo, who had Shishi in her lap. "But maybe you and my dog could—"

"Forget it," Bingyoo snapped. "I'm not running away. Especially if you aren't."

"Your Brilliance," said Ayie. "We can't guarantee your safety."

"I'm not asking for that." Jin was firm. "Just give me a chance to help."

"And me," chimed Bingyoo. Shishi barked and wagged her stump.

At a loss for words, the Whisperers glanced at each other. Ayie gave a reluctant nod. "What did you have in mind?"

A fragment from Jin's lessons drifted into his memory. "The greatest generals in the history of the Three Realms wouldn't have won against their enemies without a defense strategy." He looked around their little camp in the woods. "We need one too."

They quickly dismissed any notion of fleeing or hiding, for there were too many creatures and nowhere to go. "Even if there were another refuge, we don't have ships or the Whisperers required. There are even more monsters now than when this sanctuary was first established," said Ayie. "And it took months of planning and transport then."

"According to what the crow heard, the attack won't happen till the skies are dark." Jin glanced up and caught a glimpse of the waning moon through a break in the clouds. A sliver was missing from its round glowing face. "We still have some time before then. It makes sense they'll invade when there's no light from the new moon—but maybe we can turn that to our advantage."

"They've already lost the element of surprise," agreed Mau. "Let's surprise them instead."

Masa brightened. "If they're counting on darkness to hide them, we'll take that away. There are so many creatures here that light up the night."

"That's a great idea!" Jin felt a spark of hope. "How about rings of defense that start even before they reach shore? The mollusk monsters—one of their mirages grounded the boat Bingyoo and I were on. We should get them to confuse the invaders with sea-foam forts and ships."

"Sea creatures like the amabie mermaids and lanternfish

can produce light in the water," said Ayie, nodding. "That will make the mirages visible long before anyone even gets near the island, and expose invaders too."

Mau clapped his hands with a chuckle. "Brilliant!"

"But we can't count on that to hold them off completely," said Masa, frowning. "Once they do set foot on Whisper Island, how can we protect ourselves *and* the creatures?"

The campfire spluttered, and Jin went to add another monstercake to it. As he hefted the disk into the fire, a flare of sparks flew out. He stared at the colorful flames, then spun around. "We aren't defenseless," he said slowly. "A lot of the wars fought in the early days of the empire—monsters were what gave Samtei its advantage, right? The creatures could do things that ordinary beasts couldn't—and they also produced things that were like nothing else humans had ever seen. It was only when powdered monster dung was in short supply that firepowder was invented."

Ayie narrowed her eyes. "Yes, that's true."

"We have plenty of monster dung here," Jin pointed out. "And creatures of all sorts. Our attackers might outnumber us people-wise, but they have nothing but themselves and their man-made weapons."

"Do we really have a chance against firelances and soldiers?" Bingyoo ventured.

"Of course we do," said Masa. A smile crept over her face. "All we have to do is make sure they don't get too far."

"Exactly. We won't let Whisper Island go down without a fight," said Mau fervently.

Jin took a deep breath. "We'll just have to be smart about it."

Over the next few days, the Whisperers raced around the island, assembling groups of creatures and marshalling them to help create defensive lines to trap or slow anyone trying to get near. Burrowing monster badgers dug earthen trenches and pits as easily as cutting through butter, while monster birds piled mounds of twigs, leaves, and grasses to hide them. Master Sonsen's interminably detailed lessons in history and war actually turned out to be useful when Jin drew on them to help Ayie and the twins figure out where to set up areas to defend. He wondered about alerting the empress dowager to the traitors at the palace, but after what had happened to the last green crow, he couldn't bring himself to ask any of the Whisperers to send another one.

Putting his skills at dungcake making to the test, Jin found he was glad that his grandmother had insisted he study other subjects and read books other than the bestiary. He recalled an alchemist's finding that certain types of monster dung, like that of the baku, were particularly rich in iron and an essential ingredient in powerful projectiles that could blast through fortress gates. Experimenting with different combinations of creature dung in varying shapes, sizes, and textures, Jin used his firestarter to light them on the beach, throwing sand on them to extinguish the flames when they got too lively.

Monstercakes that hadn't fully dried made exceeding amounts of smoke, Jin discovered, and certain shapes would break into more pieces than others if hurled against a hard surface. When he tried baking a batch of dungcakes in a makeshift pit oven to dry them faster, they became blackened charcoal rounds that burned even hotter and longer than any dried in the sun. After nearly getting set on fire while following Jin too closely, Shishi learned to stay where she was told.

Bingyoo, no stranger with a knife, was set to work on piles and piles of sticks. Some were the size of skewers that she quickly shaved into little points, while others were larger pieces of wood that took more whittling to sharpen into stakes and staves. But as fast as she could make them, the twins and assorted creatures carried them away. To speed things along, Jin went looking for a knife so he could help. He found the jeweled knife that he'd borrowed from Ayie. It was still in the makeshift sheath he'd made for it out of spider's silk, and when he picked it up, he stopped and stared at it. Excitement sent him running to find the Whisperer woman.

"I've got an idea!" he shouted, showing her the blade's cover. Though the grubby silk was coated in enough dust and dirt that it was no longer sticky, it was still impervious to the knife's sharp edges. "That is, if you think a particular monster would cooperate."

When Ayie heard his plan, the severe planes of her face slipped into a rare smile. "Leave that to me," she told him.

Not long after, she returned triumphantly from a visit to the golden earth spider. It turned out that spiders produced many different types of silk depending on their needs: sticky with glue for trapping prey, dry for framing webs, stretchy and elastic, tough as steel, textured and rough, smooth as glass. Ayie had coaxed the spider into spinning bales of silk in all its forms.

With rubbery silk and lengths of bamboo and wood, they fashioned launching weapons that could hurl flaming dungcakes hundreds of paces away with plenty of speed and accuracy. Tacky, gummy silk was carefully strung across traps erected strategically around the island. Solidly durable cables were woven into silken shields and fashioned into armor.

The days and nights flew by in a frenzy of activity as everyone constructed, stockpiled, experimented, and set up all that they could. They were so busy preparing to defend the island and its creatures that Jin pushed the thought of getting a monstermate from his mind. There was no time to waste on a creature quest—they were all in danger.

* * *

One afternoon, with the new moon just days away, the five of them were feverishly at work on finishing a pit trap on the southern side of the island. As Jin carried a bundle of wood out of the forest, Ayie approached Jin with a strange look on her face. "The twins said you told them you saw a kirin when you and Shishi were lost in the forest. Is that true?"

"I was going to tell you, but then that poor green crow showed up with its warning." Jin shook his head and set the branches down. "It appeared after I got Shishi out of the spider's web. I could have sworn I heard it speak, but Mau and Masa didn't believe me. When I called the kirin a monster, it looked right at me and said it didn't like being called that— that it was a term only humans used for creatures."

"Good beasts," Ayie murmured, looking startled.

"For too long all I thought about was getting a monster-mate," Jin said. "I never thought about what the creatures wanted. But their happiness matters too. The only one I've ever known is my grandmother's phoenix, and it's absolutely miserable, but I didn't really understand that before."

"The very word 'monstermate' holds the secret to a successful pairing," said Ayie. "A mate should be viewed as a partner, not a servant."

"I may never find one," said Jin bleakly. "But if we can save Whisper Island, at least there will still be uncanny beasts in the world."

Ayie tilted her head. "All monsters can be tamed, but the

ones we carry within us are the hardest to face," she said, half to herself. "Prince Jin, when do you turn thirteen?"

"Next week." Jin gave a nervous laugh. "If we make it through the attack, that is."

The Whisperer woman snorted. "We will. There's no other choice." She picked up the bundle and nodded at his ax. "We could use more branches."

Obligingly, Jin tramped back into the forest, Shishi at his heels. He headed for a patch of old fallen trees where there'd be plenty of wood he could gather for their defensive positions. It wasn't too far from where they'd run into the kirin, and his eyes darted about, secretly hoping to see a flash of its blue scales. At least Ayie hadn't laughed at Jin's claim of hearing it speak. But her question about his birthday struck a pang of longing. If only things could be different, and he could have gone on his creature quest. It was too late for that now, and they had bigger things to worry about.

As he neared the plot of felled trees, Jin heard a voice he didn't recognize, so low and rumbling it seemed to resonate through his chest. *"Hairless humans! What a bother."* He slowed to a stop, peering through the shadows to the sunny clearing, and stiffened at the sight.

A pale-furred lion, antlers poking through a thick mane crowning its head, sat on its powerful haunches beside a fresh-cut log. It grunted as it licked its front paw, the strands of its forked tail swishing in agitation. An enormous pair of feathered wings shot out and flapped once, sending a gust of air sweeping through Jin's hair, before refolding along its back.

"Gods 'n' monsters," he swore under his breath. "A live piyao!" He'd overheard its voice—Jin was sure of it. Taking care to stay out of sight, he crept closer, his eyes fixed on the winged lion. He could see why this fearsome creature had once guarded the imperial treasury. As it extended its claws and began gnawing between them, the piyao's wickedly sharp teeth gleamed in the bright sunlight. It paused with a huff, nose wrinkled and mouth open, as if it were tasting the air.

"Stop right there, boy!"

Jin froze in his tracks. "Do . . . do you mean me?"

The piyao turned its head, whiskers bristling. *"Who else would I be talking to?"*

At a loss for words, Jin opened and closed his mouth a few times. "I can't believe it," he burst out. "I'm not a Whisperer. But I can understand you! And you can understand me! I knew I wasn't imagining things before. I'm hearing you— perfectly!"

"Well, if you can hear me so perfectly, then stop yammering for a second," growled the piyao. *"Who are you and what are you doing with that ax?"*

"I'm Jin," he replied meekly, recollecting himself. "Ayie sent me to bring back more wood."

The piyao went back to gnawing in between its toes, then put its massive paw down. *"So you're the one making a mess,"* it said, irritated. *"There are sharp bits everywhere."* It began licking its paw again.

"Sorry about that," Jin said nervously. "What's wrong with your paw?"

The piyao stopped and curled its lips, exposing its fangs. *"Nothing!"* It put its paw down, then lifted it immediately with a grunt.

"Are you sure you don't need help?"

It glared. *"Since when do piyao need help? We're the fiercest of all creatures. We give help."*

"Oh, of course! I didn't mean it that way. It's just—I confess I've never had the chance to see a piyao's claws up · close." Jin stepped forward and held out his hand. "May I take a look?"

After a moment, the piyao begrudgingly let Jin examine its paw. It was heavy and bigger than his head, with thick claws the size of curved daggers. Gently Jin searched between its toes, and found several pieces of wood deeply embedded. "Some splinters seem to be stuck," he said. "Would you mind if I get them out?"

"If you must," it huffed. *"But they don't bother me."* Jin rooted in his pocket for his lockpicks. One was a needle-thin piece of metal, which Jin used to pick at the splinters. He worked at one until he was able to grasp the end and pulled it out.

The piyao growled but didn't move. Patiently, Jin coaxed another bit of wood out of the paw, even longer than the first, and the piyao flexed its claws. "Just one more," Jin said. "It's drawn blood—looks like a big one."

"Get on with it, then," grunted the winged lion.

But its forked tail lashed about as Jin picked at its paw. As a distraction, he showed the piyao his knife in its spider silk sheath. The jeweled handle sparkled in the sun, immediately captivating the beast's attention. As it leaned in to sniff it, Jin pulled out the splinter in one swift motion. The piyao roared.

Jin flinched. "I got them all!" He displayed the long slivers, one spanning his entire hand.

Grumbling all the while, the piyao licked at its paw a few times with a silver-blue tongue. Then it tested its weight gingerly, and relaxed. *"That's not bad."*

"I'm sorry you got hurt," said Jin. "We've been preparing defenses for the island and cutting a lot of wood for it."

The winged lion snorted, and its ears went sideways. *"Hurt? 'Twas hardly a scratch."*

"Maybe for you," said Jin. "But small things matter." He remembered something Old Fang liked to say. "One of the palace commanders often told me, 'One loose nail can fell an entire empire.'"

"How so?" The piyao's ears swiveled forward.

"Let's say this loose nail leads to a horse losing a shoe.

Without the shoe, this horse goes lame, and its rider can't deliver a message. Because this message never gets through, troops are never sent. Without these troops, the battle is lost. When this battle is lost, the war is lost. And when the war is lost, the empire falls."

"That sounds quite right." Its golden eyes narrowed. *"Well then. Thanks to you, Jin, when the attackers return, I'll be ready."*

"I hope we are too. But . . ." Jin hesitated. "Do you ever get scared?"

"No."

"Never? But what about when the island was attacked the first time? You didn't feel fear?"

The piyao huffed impatiently. *"Of course I feel fear. What creature alive doesn't? But* scared *is when you allow fear to stop you or slow you down. And that is something we piyao are incapable of."*

"I always thought those two were the same," said Jin.

"They're not." The winged lion's gaze bored into his. *"When you're brave, you go on* in spite *of fear. And piyao are the bravest of them all."*

Jin blinked. "Is it true then, that piyao are the fiercest fighters around?"

"Yes," it growled.

"I've read that some creatures are so gentle they don't even want to bend the grass they step on. Like kirin."

The winged lion snorted. *"I don't know about* that. *But we piyao have no trouble with stepping wherever we like."* It rose from its haunches, as if it were about to leave.

"May I ask you something else?" Jin ventured.

"You can try."

He took a deep breath. "Do you have a name?"

"I suppose since I know yours . . ." The piyao shrugged out its wings. *"You may call me Tao."*

"I'm glad we met, Tao." A thrill went through Jin as he said the name.

"For a human who's not a Whisperer, you're not so bad," Tao grunted. *"Even if you did make a mess here."* Beating its mighty wings, the piyao sprang into the air and quickly flew off, leaving Jin staring after it in a delighted trance.

CHAPTER 22

THE KING OF BEASTS

SNAP! CRACK! RIP! JIN WRENCHED off another branch from a fallen tree and threw it into a pile, not even bothering to use his ax, so anxious was he to hurry back to the others. He couldn't wait to tell them about his encounter with the piyao. He repeated its name to himself like a spell. "Tao."

He gathered an armload of wood and tied it up with a thick length of silk that Ayie had obtained from the golden earth spider. This piece wasn't sticky at all and made for effective rope. Jin heaved the bundle onto his back with a grunt.

An answering grunt in the trees turned his head. Blue scales shimmered in the shadows, then burst into brilliance as the kirin stepped into the sunlit clearing, as if it were sparkling with blue flame. Dazzled, Jin dropped his bundle with a gasp. The great creature picked its way around the felled logs, its cloven hooves deftly treading across uneven ground, its golden eyes fixed on Jin's. He didn't dare move.

"Hello," he whispered. "I uh . . . didn't mean to offend you last time. I meant 'monster' as a compliment."

The kirin glowered. *"That may be, but now you know."*

"Wh—what would you prefer to be called?" Jin stuttered. His heart was pounding. He was talking to the kirin. He hadn't imagined it last time. Its voice was just as he remembered, a low, musical rumble that clearly formed words.

"I am a creature of the in between," said the kirin. *"We uncanny beasts exist in the indefinite space of possibility, belonging to no realm of human, god, or spirit. But defying easy classification does not make me a monster as some would call me. What are you called?"*

Jin hesitated. "Where I'm from, I'm called a prince, and all sorts of honorifics besides," he said. "But here, I'm just . . . Jin."

The kirin tossed its head, its mane of fur rippling in the light. *"Well then, Just Jin. You may call me Chi."*

"It's an honor, Chi," said Jin shyly.

Chi bent down and nosed at the bundle of wood tied with spider silk. *"Preparing for what's to come, I see."*

"We're trying," Jin said. "But we don't know exactly what to expect. I wish we did."

"You may think it is an advantage to know the future," said the kirin. *"But no one would want to shoulder such a burden if they knew how heavy it truly was. You would be unable to move from the weight of it."*

Jin recalled something he'd read in the bestiary. "So is it

true kirins can foretell the future?"

"Not precisely, for nothing is written in stone." The kirin flicked its bushy-tipped tail as if it were an ink brush. *"But we do have a sense for things, and right now the future of us all is balanced on a delicate point. A great struggle lies ahead."*

"Would you ever help defend the island?" asked Jin. "I know kirins value peace above all else, so it's not in your nature—"

The glimmering beast let out a great whoosh of air from its scaly nostrils. *"Just because we don't like to fight doesn't mean we can't. And living with the threat of violence is not peace at all. The dark of the new moon comes in four days, and with it a great menace. Every being on this island, myself included, must be ready for what's to come."*

Heartened, Jin reached for the bundle of branches he'd dropped. "Shall I show you what we've set up so far?"

"No need, Just Jin." The creature's scaly hide flashed green, then back to blue as it dove into the shadow of the trees. *"I already know. Carry on."*

It disappeared into the forest. Jin took off at a sprint, bursting with glee, racing to get back to the Whisperers and Bingyoo. Whether they believed him or not, there was so much to tell them. The jostling branches he carried prickled and poked as he ran, but he didn't care. Breathless and beaming, he finally reached the others, and threw down the bundle of wood. "Two!" he wheezed. "I talked . . . *two* creatures. First . . . piyao. Big wings! I helped. It flew! And I wasn't . . . imagining the kirin—we spoke. Again!" Panting, he collapsed and flung himself onto his back, hardly able to say another word. Shishi barked and began licking his face while he lay there grinning. The twins, Bingyoo and Ayie gathered round and hovered over him, bewildered.

"You helped a piyao fly?" Mau looked concerned, as if Jin were ill.

Bingyoo knelt and nudged Shishi aside. "Are you all right, Your Brilliance?"

A giddy laugh escaped him. "More than all right. I'm 'Just Jin'! And they both told me their names!" Jin sat up, astounded still. "Tao the piyao. And the kirin is called Chi!" He glanced at Mau's worried face and explained. "A piyao's paw was full of splinters and I got them out. When I asked its name, it told me. I watched it fly off, and was rushing to gather wood and tell you all when the kirin showed up again! And we talked—for a lot longer this time." Elated, he flopped back down. "I'll never forget it. Two different creatures spoke to me just now, and I understood everything they said."

"What do you think, Ayie?" Masa asked in an undertone. "The green crows wouldn't have told him the beasts' names, would they?"

Her aunt chuckled. "No. Look at him! He's truly connected with a monster—although I hadn't expected there to be more than one. His little expedition turned out better than I'd hoped."

Surprised, Jin raised his head. "Wait, you sent me in there to talk to creatures? You didn't really need more branches?"

"We certainly could use them, but that wasn't the main reason I sent you back," said Ayie slyly. "After hearing about your kirin encounter, and with time so short, I didn't think we could send you on a formal creature quest, but I figured you'd find out pretty quickly if there were any beasts that would respond to you." The Whisperer woman's smile was startlingly bright, like the sun. "Apparently they did."

"Does that mean you've found a monstermate?" Bingyoo beamed.

Masa knit her brow. "It'd be with him right now, wouldn't it?"

A pinprick of doubt nicked Jin's excitement. "Masa's right. I don't think I have, actually." Staggering to his feet, he brushed off his pants and squared his shoulders. "But that's okay. I'm just relieved that I can communicate with a creature. We've got something more important coming."

With so much to occupy their attention, the last few days slipped through their fingers like water, and the night of a moonless sky was soon upon them. At dusk, Jin and the others donned jackets and leggings spun from giant spider silk. They were strong enough to withstand a strike from a blade, yet light and flexible, unlike any armor Jin had ever seen. He and Bingyoo would be on the lookout on the western shore, while the Whisperers would split off to other posts around the island, all supported with creatures prepared to do battle. Mollusk monsters had formed imposing mirages of sea-foam around the island to help deter ships, while the kunpeng and other sea creatures guarded the northern waters. The dragons had lifted the shield of fog from the island, as Ayie would be patrolling from the air on a winged horse, and green crows would be on hand to relay messages.

Jin looked at Bingyoo, who was pale and quiet as she fastened a coat of protective spider silk around Shishi. "Are you all right?"

"It's torture knowing something terrible is coming," she blurted. "I almost wish it would happen already! Almost."

Masa put her arm around Bingyoo. "I know. The knowledge makes it harder to wait sometimes."

"Waiting is the hardest," muttered Mau.

His aunt shook her head. "Knowledge is both weapon and tool, allowing us to prepare and protect this island." Ayie looked around their little circle. "I believe in each of you. Even if you're scared, it doesn't have to stop you."

"That's just what the piyao told me," said Jin. "We have

the creatures, and the creatures have us. As long as we work together, we have a chance. We're not letting anyone step on this island without a fight."

The others nodded. In that moment, Jin felt less alone than he had his entire life.

A wicked grin crossed Masa's face. "If nothing else, let's make them sorry they ever thought to come back here."

"Sounds good to me," her brother said fervently.

A winged horse touched down, and Shishi growled. Bingyoo shushed her and scooped the dog up. Then a tiger-like beast with a ribbony long tail appeared in their midst, as if it had manifested out of thin air. It was the zouya, which could travel long distances in seconds. In the distance, a ghostly pale creature came flying through the air. Shishi gave a warning bark. The piyao glided down on its silvery feathered wings and landed before them. Delighted, Jin met its leonine gaze. "Tao!" he blurted. "How is your paw?"

"Never better," huffed the piyao. Wide-eyed, the twins exchanged grins, while their aunt nodded with satisfaction.

A pounding of hooves sounded behind them, and they turned to see the kirin galloping up, its powerful muscles rippling below its iridescent scaly coat. Bingyoo let out a startled cry and Shishi barked in alarm.

"Looks like someone's ready to kick some grass," huffed the piyao.

The great beast drew up with a halt. It was even bigger than Jin remembered, its antlered head towering over them.

"It's good to see you, Chi," said Jin. "We're about to head to our posts."

"That's why I'm here, Just Jin," replied the creature. It stamped a giant hoof, and the other beasts responded with snorts, grunts, and growls.

"Are they saying anything?" Bingyoo asked Masa timidly.

The Whisperer girl smiled. "Yes. They're all here to help."

"What do you hear, Bingyoo?" Jin was curious.

She shrugged. "I just hear a sort of . . . rumbling."

"Whenever my grandmother talks with her phoenix, it sounds like it's squawking and screeching," said Jin. "I'm not surprised you only hear rumbling."

"Rumbling!" The kirin gave a derisive snort. *"I'm not just making a bunch of noises. I have things to say."*

"We all do," growled Tao the piyao.

"But most people can't understand beasts, unless they're messenger crows," Jin said. "I can't either, except for you two. Can you understand all humans?"

"Of course," said Chi loftily. *"It's humans who are terrible at understanding."*

The piyao's tail twitched. *"I was just about to say that."*

Ayie greeted all the creatures one by one, silently placing her hand on their heads as if she were bestowing protection. With a pouch of monstercakes tied to her waist, she mounted the winged horse, carrying a dungcake hurler and a silver-tipped conch shell. "I'll sound the alarm as soon as I spot anything. Watch over each other." She gave them all a wave and launched into the skies to patrol the island.

As the Whisperer woman flew off, Masa wasted no time in jumping on the zouya, burying her fingers in its thick, colorful fur. "Be like the beasts," she said, curving a hand in a clawed salute. Jin, Mau, and Bingyoo saluted back. She leaned forward, a hurler slung across her back, and touched the monster's shoulder. With a grunt, the zouya vanished, carrying Masa away in the blink of an eye.

The sun slipped below the horizon, its waning light purpling the sky. The piyao inclined its head at Mau, who mounted the winged lion quickly. "Let's go give those invaders a proper Whisper Island welcome," he said with a spin of his hurler. The monster snarled, its fangs gleaming, and turned its leonine gaze to Jin.

"Remember. Being brave doesn't mean you aren't afraid, but that you try anyway, even when you are," growled the piyao. *"Have courage, Jin."* It stretched out its wings and leaped into the air, Mau clinging to its back.

"Be careful!" Bingyoo called as they flew away. Hugging Shishi close, she bit her lip and looked timidly from the kirin to Jin. "What now, Your Brilliance?"

The antlered beast bent its great head toward Bingyoo. She tensed, watching wide-eyed as it touched its scaly nose to Shishi's. The dog's stump began to wag. Jin smiled. "We give it our best try." He shouldered their dungcake hurlers. "To the lookout we go. Chi, would you mind taking us?"

Once they settled astride the kirin, it took off, racing for the western shore. Bingyoo clutched at Shishi and Jin while he clung to the kirin's thick mane. Its scaly, rippling flanks powered them through the ruins of Beastly, past the abandoned pier, and along the coast toward the jutting spit of land where the Kirin Tree of the west stood. After passing the sand dunes and salt flats, they reached the lookout. With the help of tunneling creatures, the Whisperers had dug a fortified ditch in a slope, camouflaging it with rocks and bushes. From this spot, they would have a good view of the shore.

"Won't the fire tree's light keep attackers from landing here?" asked Bingyoo. She slid off Chi's back and squinted in the distance at the soft blue glow of the Kirin Tree.

"It's bright enough to signal land," Jin said. "But dim enough that the invaders could still evade detection if no one was watching."

The kirin snorted. *"Unfortunately for them, we're watching."*

Jin grinned. He and Bingyoo checked on the supplies at their post, Shishi nosing about helpfully. The kirin moved up the slope to an additional hideout shielded by boulders. Several green crows arrived and perched atop the great rocks, their feathers dark as the depths of the sea. The three-legged monster birds hunkered down, looking like craggy stone themselves, ready to be dispatched with messages.

Time slowed to a painful crawl as they waited in silence. "Maybe the crow was mistaken," said Bingyoo at last. "It must be midnight by now, and nothing's happening. Maybe there won't be an attack."

The kirin grunted. *"The night isn't over yet. And green crows are rarely mistaken."*

"Green crows are *never* mistaken," said one of the crows severely. "The invaders will be here soon."

"I don't know if that makes me feel better or worse," muttered Jin.

As if sensing their fear, the kirin spoke. *"Young prince, bring yourself and the girl here."*

They left their trench to join the kirin in its spot behind the boulders, followed by Shishi. Jin peered into the moonless night, while Shishi sniffed at the air, her ears perked. Beside him, the kirin scanned the horizon in silence, the pupils in its golden eyes grown enormous and black. Finally it turned its dragon-like head.

"Things may get worse, and troubles engulf us," said Chi. *"But hardship is like the night of a new moon. Though we are surrounded by darkness, light will shine again. Hope remains, even when it can't be seen. Think of that when you feel the pull of despair."*

Jin told Bingyoo what the kirin had said. Nodding, she

leaned against the hulking creature, whose golden eyes were unblinking and grave. Its gaze met Jin's. He lifted his chin, though his knees were quaking. Could Chi see how he really felt?

"Close your eyes for a moment," the kirin told him. *"Breathe deep. Wait."*

Reluctantly, Jin obeyed. Then a long low note sounded from above, reverberating throughout the island. It was from the shell trumpet that Ayie carried, warning them all. Jin's eyes snapped open, and he turned his gaze skyward, straining for a glimpse of the Whisperer. Insistently, the call repeated, loud and urgent. Shishi raised her head and howled.

"What's happening to the water?" Bingyoo exclaimed.

Jin whipped around and gasped.

The ocean was lit up from within. Graceful moving shapes darted beneath the surface, some almost like they were part fish, part human. Though the new moon was invisible, the inky heavens glittered with stars, and the sea itself was bright with light, the waves glowing an eerie blue.

"H-how is that possible?" Bingyoo rubbed her eyes.

The kirin gave a brief but satisfied snort. *"Sometimes you must make your own light. The amabie and their lanternfish friends know this well."*

"There are amabie and lanternfish in the water," Jin explained to Bingyoo. "The amabie are mermaids with birdlike beaks, but their scaly, fishlike bodies can give off light, as can lanternfish." He smiled grimly. "The attackers thought they could sneak up unseen again, but this time the creatures were ready. Look!"

In the glowing expanse of luminous water, the dark shapes of sea vessels moved steadily toward the island's shore, their details plainly exposed. Each vessel was large enough to carry at least twenty men and bristled with oars that moved in unison, dipping and pulling at the water like the spindly legs of a bug.

"I see three boats so far," Bingyoo counted.

Jin felt a stirring of hope as he and Bingyoo hurried back with Shishi into their protective trench. With the strategy they'd devised, those men could be defeated. But Bingyoo's eyes were full of fear. "Think they'll see us?"

"Not likely," said Jin. "Plus we can see them, which ought to make a difference. I hope the amabie know what they're doing."

"Why would you doubt them?" The kirin's whiskered, scaly face peered from behind the boulders. *"The water is their home. Land creatures are at a disadvantage."*

"What did the monster say?" Bingyoo asked timidly.

One of the green crows perched on the boulders ruffled its feathers. "Don't call us monsters, girlie," it snapped. "If you must know, land creatures like those men are no match on water for creatures like the amabie."

They were interrupted by a shout in the distance. Bingyoo gasped. "Over there!" Two enormous tentacles shot out of the water and wrapped around a boat, splintering oars and crushing its hull. "Holy beasts, what is that?"

The kirin grunted with satisfaction. *The giant squid have arrived.*

CHAPTER 23

BATTLE FOR WHISPER ISLAND

IN THE SHINING SEA, JIN made out the hulking shapes of two squid, their bodies as large as the boats themselves, each with eight flowing arms and a pair of even longer tentacles covered in suction cups. They quickly latched on to the boats, foiling any attempts to pry them free, though the men on the boats stabbed at them and fired into the water. Within moments, the first boat was pulled into the sea, along with its occupants, and then another as they raced for the shore. "You never see giant squid like this," Jin exclaimed. "They're usually so far down in the depths that they can't be bothered by anything on the surface."

"You can thank the amabie for rallying them," said the kirin. *"I told you, on water they have the advantage."*

Bingyoo clapped her hands. "That leaves just one!"

The remaining boat scraped up onto the beach. "It's in perfect position for our traps," exulted Jin.

Armed men in black, their mail and helmets painted to blend in with the night, jumped out and dragged the vessel onshore. Carrying firelances with sharp long knives attached to the muzzles, they began to make their way up the beach. Bellows of pain rang out as they stepped on the sharpened stakes that Jin and the others had planted in the sand. Some collapsed, hobbled by badly pierced feet, only to fall on more spikes, while others hopped their way across the shore, trying to avoid the hidden points. Some managed to make it through or merely nicked themselves and limped on. They ran but a few steps before falling right into a carefully concealed pit lined with sticky spider silk. Their yelling could be heard all across the beach.

Several furry hundun, the winged, faceless round creature that Jin had encountered his first day on the island, scuttled out to investigate. Their wings beat madly as they sailed over the spiked portions of the sand, and a lively humming emitted from them as they hovered over the injured, gently pawing them. The fallen invaders began screaming and batting at them, wildly swinging their firelance blades and firing shots that went wide, but it only seemed to energize the hundun, and they eagerly flitted from one to another, doing what looked like little dances on the terrified men.

"What are they doing?" Bingyoo asked.

Jin shook his head. "All I know is they're called hundun. I don't remember any images of them at the palace—not even in the bestiary." Whether he missed it or had to write it himself, Jin vowed silently, he'd make sure the imperial bestiary had a hundun entry. That is, if he ever made it back.

"They thrive on chaos, misery, and wickedness," Chi snorted. *"They're feasting right now."* Just then, one of the hundun began to tremble and shake. *"Looks like that one had its fill and is about to divide."* A loud *POP!* from the furry winged blob spawned an identical copy, and the new hundun flitted to another prone man to feed, prancing and pawing.

"What will happen to those invaders?" asked Jin.

"Their minds will empty," said the kirin. *"We need not fear them after that."*

"Gods 'n' monsters." Jin shuddered. "I'm lucky Masa stopped me from getting too close when I first saw one." He explained to Bingyoo what the kirin had told him, then surveyed the scene before them. "So this was the attack we've been preparing for all this time? Three boats, and only one made it to shore! We didn't even get to use our hurlers."

"Don't sound so disappointed," Bingyoo countered. "I'm relieved!"

As the hundun fed busily on the beach, Jin cautiously went to examine the trap that had caught the remaining invaders. When he peered into the pit, he saw nearly a dozen men hopelessly tangled in the gummy spider-silk lining. Some of them had gotten sticky silk across their faces thrashing around and were unable to speak, but those who could began yelling at the sight of him. Shishi ran up beside Jin, barking furiously, just as one of the green crows landed on his shoulder. "I think they're speaking Hulagan," Jin said to the three-legged bird. "What are they saying?"

"They say they have a right to be here," translated the crow. "Apparently they have permission from Samtei to take what they want from the island, and if you don't let them go, Hulagu will declare war."

Jin was taken aback. "Samtei's been trying to *defend* the Three Realms against the Hulagans—my grandmother would never give them access here!" Scorn crept into his voice. "It's an interesting account, I'll give them that. But impossible."

The kirin and Bingyoo joined them at the edge of the pit, and the crow told them what the trapped men were saying. Bingyoo's eyes grew round. "Empress Soro told them to come here?"

"There's no way," said Jin impatiently. "The idea is absurd. She wouldn't even let *me* come, and I'm crown prince."

"Even if the regent of the Three Realms allowed it, which as Jin says is unlikely," said Chi, *"that doesn't mean we creatures would cooperate. I certainly have no intention of going anywhere with these men."*

"Nor I," cawed the green crow. It launched off Jin's shoulder and hopped down beside Shishi, who was peering into the pit and growling at the trapped invaders. The three-legged bird pecked at a tiny sand crab crawling nearby and swallowed it in one gulp.

"You won't," Jin promised. "We'll do everything in our power to make sure that doesn't happen." He picked up his dog and backed away from the pit, just as several loud booms sounded in the distance, like crashing thunder.

The kirin turned its great antlered head. *"Seems like there's trouble in the south."*

"I should have known that it wouldn't be that easy," said Jin, grimacing.

There was a loud caw overhead, and a new green crow came flying into their midst. "The Whisperers need you," it said urgently.

"We heard the explosions," said Jin. "Just lead the way."

"But Your Brilliance, what about them?" Bingyoo gestured at the beach and the pit, both filled with immobilized invaders.

Jin frowned. "They aren't going anywhere for a while. Right, Chi?"

"They're no threat to us now," agreed the kirin. *"You and the Whisperers can decide what to do with them later. Let the hundun feed in the meantime."* The creature stamped its feet. *"Get on my back. There's no time to waste."*

They scrambled to grab what supplies they could carry from their post and mounted the kirin. The green crow launched into the air, and Chi trotted after it. Another distant explosion boomed. Circling back, the green crow dipped with an insistent cry. "Hurry. We must fly!"

The kirin raced across the island, its massive hooves pounding an urgent rhythm. As Chi followed the green crow at a gallop, Jin clutched the kirin's mane and a sack of ammunition while Bingyoo sat behind him on Chi's scaly back, holding tight to him and Shishi. The messenger bird flew ahead and doubled back, trying to keep in their sights as it led them to where the explosions had gone off.

Dawn was nearly upon them, the sky beginning to brighten. They plunged into a forest and the kirin wove through the trees, surprisingly agile given its immense bulk. Taking on a burst of speed, Chi leaped over a fallen log. Bingyoo squealed. With glimpses of the southern shore ahead, the kirin ran down a slope. Emerging from the forest, Chi came to a sudden halt. Jin gasped. "Blazing beasts."

A large ship sat in the water, which glowed with light from lanternfish and amabie. A half dozen launch craft had set off from the ship, and one had already landed. Smoking craters were pocked across the shore, and another explosion sounded as the ship fired a round from a cannon. The projectile hit the beach, and a great boom shook the ground, sending up a spray of smoke, sand, and fire. "They're destroying the traps we set," Jin noted grimly. "It's creating a path for their men to get across."

The green crow circled through the air, which was filled

with monster birds of all sorts—firebirds, phoenixes, poi-sonfeathers, and giant cranes among them—and Tao, the piyao. The winged lion glided high above, then folded its wings and streaked toward the ship. It tore through a sail with its sharp claws and shot back up into the air. Ayie hovered on her winged horse, leading the birds in a charge. They swooped and dove at the invaders in the small craft and on the beach. But the armored men raised their shields, unfazed, and began unloading traps, nets, and cages. Some shot warning blasts in the air with their firelances, while others managed to snag a few birds in fine wire nets. The Whisperer woman wheeled her horse around and flew off to the interior of the island, while the monster birds and piyao continued to fight.

"Where are the twins?" Jin wondered.

Bingyoo pointed. "Over there!"

Not fifty paces away, in a ditch overlooking the expanse of the shore, the twins frantically loaded a bamboo catapult with special monstercakes Jin had formulated from baku droppings. After Masa set them aflame, Mau sent them flying at the invaders coming up the beach, slowing them somewhat. But they were no match for the ship's cannon. The ship launched yet another powerful fireball that rattled Jin's teeth with the force of its explosion. When the smoke blew away, another patch of sand had been cleared of spikes.

Jin took a deep breath. "They need our help—come on!"

With the kirin's scaled bulk providing cover, they made a dash for the ditch and joined Mau and Masa, whose faces lit up with relief.

"Thank the gods you're here," said Mau.

"Get your launchers," Masa ordered, lighting another round of dungcakes with a burning ember stick.

Rooting through his sack of supplies, Jin grabbed the hand-held hurlers they'd fashioned from stretchy spider silk and bamboo. Dropping a hard puck into Bingyoo's launcher, Jin touched a smoldering ember stick to the dungcake till it caught fire, flaring with bright blue flame. "Go!"

Taking careful aim, she fired. The burning monstercake soared in a high arc. It struck the edge of an invader's shield and exploded into flaming pieces, some of which slipped beneath the man's gear. He stopped in his tracks and began clawing at his face.

"A direct hit!" cheered Jin. He slapped Bingyoo on the back.

"Not bad," observed the kirin. *"But more are coming."*

"I see them." Jin loaded another round. As fast as they could, he and Bingyoo lit and launched baku dung-cakes, bombarding the attackers with fiery projectiles that exploded on contact and sprayed white-hot splinters all over. Dungcake explosions bloomed across the sand like flowers of flame, scattering men as they struggled to get across the beach with equipment to capture creatures.

A shouted command sent the invaders into a tight formation, raising their shields so they resembled an armored beetle. They headed straight for Jin and the others, who launched flaming monstercakes that glanced harmlessly off the shields. Closer and closer the men marched. A flare of light appeared from the back of the formation, and a dark object came flying through the air, trailing bright burning embers and hissing smoke.

"Get down!" cried Masa, and she yanked at a sheet of thick spider silk folded at the edge of the ditch. The kirin leaped out.

"Where are you going?" Jin shouted, just as the protective silk shield swept over them. The smoking ball bounced off the shield.

BOOM.

The projectile exploded in a blast of flame and firepowder, sending them tumbling to the ground while shards of metal rained on the spider silk. Over the ringing in Jin's ears, he thought he heard bellowing. "Chi's hurt!"

Urgent shouts and terrified yelling led to a clash of metal and firelance blasts. Jin moved aside the silk shield and stuck his head out. Chi was still standing—and had charged the invaders. The kirin tossed its antlers, sending the men flying in all directions, then whirled about and pawed at the ground with its cloven hooves, snorting. Several men ran up behind Chi with a large net, preparing to throw it over the kirin.

Before Jin could shout a warning, the piyao swooped down, snarling. The kirin bucked its back legs and kicked the men so hard that they flew more than twenty paces, tangled in their own net. The piyao alighted near the kirin and roared, glaring at the attackers. With the two great beasts back-to-back, sneaking up on them was impossible. Though several men boldly tried approaching with snares, intending to rope the creatures, the winged lion speedily dispatched them with a quick swipe of its massive paw.

"Should we help them?" wondered Bingyoo, plucking at the stretchy silk of her dungcake launcher.

A snare landed around the kirin's antlers, but the creature merely charged and butted the man so far that he skidded halfway across the beach.

"I think they can handle themselves just fine," Jin said with a chuckle.

Alarm bells filled the air, and they all turned in the direction of the ship.

"Look!" cried Bingyoo. "The squid are back!"

Sure enough, the giant squid that had helped defend the western shore had appeared, their long arms and thick bodies silhouetted against the glowing waves. One got its tentacles on a landing craft that was nearly to shore and pulled it into the sea. As the other squid went after the ship, the sailors on board turned their cannon in its direction. With terrible booms, they shot fireballs into the water that forced the creature to turn back. When the smoke cleared, a severed tentacle dangled from the ship's anchor line. Bingyoo gasped. "A poor squid lost one of its limbs!"

"It's okay," Mau told her. "The squid's arm will grow back. Sometimes they break off their own arms as a distraction."

A dark cloud in the water pooled around the squid's bodies, obscuring them in the glowing water. "And sometimes they use ink," Masa added. "But that won't help them get past four cannon."

"We need to take those out," said Jin. "I have an idea. Where's the sticky stuff?"

"I've got some right here." Masa grabbed a bag and filled it with leaf-wrapped balls of monster dung that Jin had carefully mixed with pine resin, sulfur, and glue extracted from the giant spider. Her brother stuck several glowing ember sticks in a pouch of spider silk lined with firebird feathers.

"Be like the beasts," Mau said with a grin, handing both to Jin.

Jin raised his hand in a claw salute, then leaped from the ditch, calling the piyao's name. It remained nearby with the kirin, the two creatures on guard after forcing the invaders to retreat back down to their launch craft.

Tao turned. *What is it?*

"I need to drop something on the ship's cannon," said Jin breathlessly, the bag and pouch clutched to his chest. "Will you help me?"

With a grunt, the piyao shook itself. *"Hop on."*

Jin settled the bag between Tao's shoulders. Grasping the piyao's ruff with his free hand, he swung onto its back.

The kirin stamped its foot. *"Be careful out there."*

With a nod, Jin twined his fingers deep into Tao's mane. "Let's go." He felt the creature's muscles bunch up beneath him and its feathered wings unfold. They sprang into the air and the piyao's wings beat a steady rhythm as they rose higher and higher into the sky. The tops of the trees fell farther beneath them, the wind ruffling Jin's hair as they circled and headed in the direction of the sea.

The morning sun had risen over the horizon, throwing its rays across the water and making it glitter. Jin squinted. From the air, the ship looked like a toy in the palace lake. Several sails were shredded, thanks to Tao's claws, but flashes of cannonfire lit up its deck as it continued to fire into the water at the squid.

"Now that the sun's up, they'll see us coming," Tao growled. *"We'll have to move fast."*

Jin glanced down at the sack he carried. "We have to drop burning dung directly on each cannon in order to take them out."

The piyao homed in on the ship. *"Understood. Get ready to light it."*

As they flew out over the water, high enough that chilly wisps of low clouds and fog dampened hair and fur, Jin

319

pulled out an ember stick. It blew out, as did the next, till none were left. "No!" In desperation, Jin dug in his pocket for the firestarter from the fortune-teller. With difficulty, he struck it again and again, but the sparks quickly died and flew away as Tao dipped and soared in the air currents above the ocean.

"Are you ready?" asked the piyao. With a single flap of its wings, they surged toward the ship.

"Wait, I'm having trouble with lighting it! Can you slow down at all? There's too much wind and fog!" Hunching over to create a sheltered space with his body, Jin opened the bag and stuck his hands inside. Tao held back to a hover, and Jin tried again with the firestarter. Sparks flew and landed on several fuses made of twisted dried grass. He cupped his hands around them as they smoldered. "Come on," he urged. Finally, tiny flames flared. Jin waited for them to take hold, then shut the bag. "Okay, we can go!"

Tao's wings beat powerfully. They rose even higher, and then the piyao folded its wings and pointed its maned head toward the ship. *"Hold on!"* Jin's stomach flew up to his throat as they plunged at high speed, the bag of dungballs going up in flame, scorching the burlap. With his teeth, he yanked the pouch of spider silk and firebird feathers over his hand, then reached for a burning ball. As they drew close, Jin saw the cannons straight ahead.

"Now!" snarled Tao. Jin aimed and hurled the flaming

orb, which smacked against the base of one cannon and burst open in a sticky smear, just as the men on the ship pointed their firelances at them. The piyao pulled out of its dive and streaked from one side of the ship to the other. One by one, Jin dropped burning spheres of gluey dung on the other cannon. Shots rang out, and fireballs whizzed past as they swerved about.

The burlap sack was fully aflame, with two dungballs left. Jin threw the whole thing at the last cannon. "Pull up," he shouted.

The piyao streaked from the ship, its wings beating madly. A series of giant booms sounded behind them like a chain of firecrackers as the fiery dungcakes exploded, one by one. The blasts knocked Jin forward and he flung his arms around Tao's neck, just as the piyao nearly tumbled into the sea. Right before they hit the water, the winged lion flapped hard and managed to gain control, righting itself.

Jin looked back over his shoulder. Towering columns of smoke billowed into the sky. On deck where each cannon had sat, there was now a smoldering hole.

"Did we get them?" asked Tao.

Unable to contain himself, Jin slapped the piyao's shoulders. "Yes we did! We did!"

Tao roared and then flew up away from the water. The wind stung Jin's eyes and whipped through his hair. He raised a fist and cheered.

But their celebration was short-lived. From the sky, Jin saw that the invaders on the beach, while diminished in number, were still fighting to snare monster birds and the kirin, even as the twins and Bingyoo threw lit monstercakes. At the same time, men were coming off the ship and making their way for shore.

The piyao turned back. *"This isn't over."*

"Monstermuck," Jin swore. "I threw all the dungballs I had. How are we going to finish this?"

A low growl rumbled from Tao. *"I believe we have reinforcements."*

An enormous silvery fin burst from the sea, flinging men in all directions. It was Goldie. As the kunpeng slammed its great tail against the ship, a half dozen of its young went to work on the landing craft in the water, knocking them about as easily as if they were driftwood, and yanking oars away. Meanwhile, Ayie reappeared in the sky, just as several large dragons emerged from the forest, looming over the beach. With screams and shouts, the remaining invaders on the sand abandoned their traps and snares and retreated, running from the great scaled beasts for their boats.

The Whisperer woman urged her horse higher into the air, and the monster birds followed in a huge dark cloud. The cloud shifted into a form resembling an arrowhead before plummeting toward the beach. Pecking and clawing monster birds plunged from the sky, some attacking the men, others tearing captured creatures free from nets and snares.

The piyao landed near the edge of the forest, not far from where the twins and Bingyoo huddled in the shelter of the ditch, having run out of monstercakes. Before them stood the kirin, keeping watch while Shishi closely guarded its great hooves.

Transfixed, Jin watched as prowling, snapping dragons swept the shore clean of invaders. The lucky ones pushed back into the ocean and rowed as fast as they could, pursued by baby kunpeng. Goldie's tail flashed as she dove deep. The ship's anchor flew out of the water, trailing its line and landing on the smoldering deck of the ship with a splintering crash. The kunpeng transformed into a great bird and sank its mighty claws into the ship's bow. Flapping its enormous wings, it dragged the battered ship away from the island's shores. With a mighty shove from the giant squid, the invaders' ship was sent back to sea.

Not long after, Ayie and her winged horse alighted by Jin and the piyao. As the Whisperer woman dismounted, the twins and Bingyoo came running up, weary and relieved. "You brought the other creatures in the nick of time," Mau told his aunt. "We were down to our last monstercakes."

Masa threw her arms around first her aunt, then Jin. "You were absolute beasts, both of you."

He grinned back. "It was easy." The piyao gave a great snort and then hacked as if it were a cat trying to cough up a hairball. Jin rolled his eyes. "Don't choke laughing, now."

Bingyoo jumped about, clapping her hands. "That was so amazing."

"Well done, everyone." A rare smile flitted across Ayie's face. "Word will spread, and people will think twice before breaching this sanctuary. If the Hulagans ever try coming here again, they're bigger fools than I thought."

Jin sobered at that. "Actually, there're still a few tied up on the shore near Beastly that we'll have to take care of. They were saying the strangest thing about having permission to take creatures." He told them what the trapped men had claimed and shook his head. "It would destroy Whisper Island and hurt the creatures, and my grandmother would never allow it. She might have barred me from coming here, but her intentions were good," said Jin. "I need to go back to the palace. I have to face my grandmother and carry news to her about this attack. She needs to know the truth."

The kirin turned its golden gaze to Jin. *"In that case, young prince, I shall go with you."*

CHAPTER 24

THE PRODIGAL PRINCE RETURNS

THE SUN BEAT DOWN ON Jin and the kirin as they sped across the sea toward the mainland. They were in a boat moving faster than any ordinary boat could, for they were being carried along by the kunpeng, its giant scaly body skimming just beneath the surface of the water while it balanced the boat on its broad fish head. Jin squinted against the rushing wind and the salt spray thrown up by Goldie's trailing fins. Even folded close to the boat's hull, they broke through the waves and sent up a fine mist.

"There!" Jin shouted to Chi, pointing to the mouth of the river. "The Horned Serpent!"

Behind him, the kirin shifted uneasily. *I hope people do not panic at the sight of us. I doubt many on the mainland have seen uncanny beasts before, if ever.*

"Panic? If anything, they'll be thrilled to see true creatures of the in between," scoffed Jin.

Chi's whiskers twitched. *"We shall see. Perhaps you're right. I was just a wee calf when the Whisperers moved us to the island."*

"How old are you?" asked Jin.

Blinking its long eyelashes, the kirin pondered the question. *"I've seen more than a hundred and twenty summers on the island. Beyond that, it's hard to say."* It shook its mane. *"But as kirins go, I'm quite in my prime."*

The kunpeng turned, steering them into the wide river delta from the sea. The boat was an unmarked vessel, one of those left behind by the invaders on Whisper Island's shores. Originally propelled by oarsmen rowing with long paddles, the boat was being nudged at a speed that no ship could ever match, and was sure to draw attention for that alone, though the immense fish and kirin would cause even more of an uproar. Jin rubbed at his lock charm. He didn't want to admit it to Chi, but he was nervous. He scanned the river and its banks, but there was no one in sight. He wondered how his grandmother would react to reports of him spotted with not just one creature, but two. For so long, he believed that all he needed to win her approval was a monster, but now that he was returning to the capital, he wasn't so sure.

"Living your life to please someone else means your life will never be your own," said the kirin, as if it had read his mind.

Jin made a face. "My life has never been my own. It's always been about preparing for the duties of the throne."

"Fulfilling your duties doesn't mean you can't make choices for

yourself," Chi said. "*Trying to please others won't sustain you for long. You need to know what brings you satisfaction as well.*"

With a shrug, Jin leaned over the bow and watched the waves breaking over the kunpeng's head. "How am I supposed to do that?"

"*I think you already know what makes you happy. Embrace it instead of wasting energy fighting it. You'll be all the stronger.*"

Jin shook his head skeptically. His obsession with the bestiary had finally served him well, but would his grandmother agree? Perhaps once she saw Chi—a kirin, the king of beasts—by his side.

The trip up the river was much faster than the one Jin had endured downriver on the ship. They were soon in sight of the ravaged villages, which caught the kirin's attention. "*These ruins remind me of the one on the island.*"

"It does look a bit like Beastly," Jin said. "But these settlements were destroyed and abandoned over years of neglect and disaster."

They cruised past the mill town, the river blackened by the waste spewing from the mills. The kunpeng shuddered and made to move out of the water, but as its head transformed into a bird shape, the boat began to tip off and Jin grabbed hold of the side. The kirin stamped a warning. "*We won't stay on if it turns into a bird.*" The kunpeng lowered itself but speeded up, as if it could not get through the murky water fast enough. They passed a few fishing boats, a barge, and several cargo ships, and Jin caught numerous people pointing at the sight of a near-empty boat powered along by a gargantuan fish, a kirin standing calmly within. He heard cries of astonishment as the kunpeng swam them up the river. But they were going too fast for anyone to do more than point and shout.

"We've been spotted dozens of times over," the kirin observed. *"By the time we get to the palace, it may not be a surprise."*

"Good," said Jin. "That just might make things easier."

Dusk had fallen by the time they reached the juncture of the two rivers around Shining Claw. The lights of the city winked on as lanternmen went about illuminating the streets and butter lamps were lit in homes. At the riverfront docks, the bustling activity of the day was winding down as crews tied in their vessels for the night and went off to tea houses and inns for their evening meal. The kunpeng slowed and dropped lower in the water, surfacing only to bump the boat along to the far end, sliding it into an empty spot at a quiet dock. In the growing darkness, Chi looked like a statue. Few people even looked their way as Jin jumped out with a rope and tied the boat to a piling.

The kunpeng's head surfaced just enough for its golden eyes to blink, birdlike, at Jin. He nodded his thanks, and Goldie disappeared into the water. The kirin stood and shook itself, then took a graceful leap over the side of the boat, landing lightly on the dock with its giant hooves. As they stepped off the wooden pier and moved into the streets of the capital, Jin heard gasps and squeals.

"Is that real?"

"What is it?"

"Holy beasts, I think that's a real-life kirin!"

"Monsters do exist!"

A rapidly gathering crowd surrounded them, gawking at the kirin ambling alongside Jin. "You're causing a bit of a stir," Jin whispered.

Chi snorted. *If this keeps up, we'll take forever to reach the palace.* The creature raised its front leg. *Climb on so we can get there faster.*

With a grin, Jin grasped the kirin's flowing mane and swung onto its back. To exclamations of wonder, the kirin tossed its head and moved into a brisk and stately gait. Jin directed Chi toward the main boulevard of the city, while growing throngs trailed after them. As the beast's massive hooves clopped through the streets, people emerged from homes and storefronts to see a monster in the flesh. "That's the crown prince!" someone shouted. Murmurs went up from the crowd.

People began to bow as Jin passed by on the kirin, bending their heads low like stalks of ripened rice. If the palace hadn't known his exact whereabouts, they surely would now. He kept his back straight and his chin high, his hands clutched in the kirin's mane to keep from trembling.

"Steady, Just Jin," said the kirin. Jin relaxed his grip a little, but his stomach churned as they drew closer to the palace. Upon reaching the central square, where the Monster Festival took place, Jin took a deep breath. They approached the palace's towering Phoenix Gate, topped with a sweeping two-story pavilion where guards kept watch. Thick wooden doors barred the arching main entrance.

Jin looked up at the guards peering down from the watchtower. "I am Prince Jin, Crown Prince of the Three Realms, heir to the Triad Throne," he shouted. "Let me in!"

The guards exchanged a glance and murmured to each other. Finally a senior commander appeared. It was Old Fang. "Your Brilliance!" He turned to the guards and barked at them. "What are you waiting for? Open the gate!"

Scurrying to do his bidding, the guards rushed out of sight. After a moment, the wooden doors swung open with a groan. The kirin stepped forward, its hooves tapping against stone tiles as it moved through the arched entrance and into the first courtyard of the palace. They were met by a phalanx of guards standing at attention, firelances in hand instead of their usual tridents. As Old Fang came down from the gate tower to meet them, Chi stopped and waited, tail swishing from side to side as if annoyed. The Beaststalker bowed to Jin, unable to take his eyes off the kirin. "Welcome home, Your Brilliance," he said. "You've caused quite the commotion."

Jin looked back as the wooden doors closed, taking one last glimpse of the crowds that had followed him to the great square outside the palace gates. He gave the commander a wry smile. "It's sort of hard to hide a kirin."

The old guard chuckled. "Oh, I'll bet." The mirth quickly faded, and his craggy face creased into a grimace. "But I meant here in the palace. Your grandmother has been on a rampage ever since you left."

"I imagine it hasn't been easy on any of you," said Jin. "But I had to go. You can see why." He patted Chi's scaly shoulder.

Old Fang raised his eyebrows. "Impressive, to be sure. I never thought I'd ever see one in real life."

"Beats any sculpture or painting, that's for sure." Jin sat up straighter. "Now, if you don't mind, I must see the empress dowager immediately."

"With . . . that?"

Jin eyed the commander sternly. "It's a kirin. Of all places where the king of beasts has a right to go, the throne hall is one of them."

"Of course, Your Brilliance. Er . . . permit us to accompany you." The Beaststalker turned to one of the guards and spoke in an urgent low voice. "Inform the court that His

Brilliance is on his way there with . . . a very large monster."

Nudging Chi onward, Jin and the scaled creature moved past Old Fang. The grizzled commander and a contingent of guards fell in behind them, following at a remove. Though their weapons remained resting on their shoulders, Jin could tell that all the men were uneasy. Even Old Fang.

But he couldn't worry about them right now. He was about to face his grandmother for the first time since running away. Chattering nervously to Chi, Jin pointed out various buildings and structures as they wound through the palace grounds, noting the carved and molded creatures eternally standing watch on rooftops and aside doorways. "There's the imperial treasury—behind it is an attached den where they used to keep piyaos—and over there the kitchens are guarded by a pair of bronze shachi on the roof, to protect from fires."

The creature saw the haitai statues flanking the entrance of the throne hall and grunted. *"A bit flashy with all that gold, but not bad. If actual haitai saw those likenesses, they wouldn't ram them with their horns."* With a shake of its mane, it strode into the building and into the ornate chamber where the empress dowager sat waiting amid all her advisors and courtiers, her back stiff and straight on the Triad Throne. It was the moment Jin had dreamed of all his life. From his vantage point on top of the kirin, his grandmother seemed surprisingly small in the great chair—almost frail. Despite his fears, Jin felt a rush of confidence surge through him. There was no shame in what he'd done. If anything, he was proud.

"Grandmother!" Jin jumped off the kirin and bowed low with ceremonial flourish. "I've come straight from Whisper Island, which was just invaded by Hulagans. I helped the surviving Whisperers fight them from taking any monsters. And as you can see, I've returned with a kirin!"

There was a silence as she regarded him with a flinty stare, her face impassive. "Is that all you have to say?"

"I—I'm sorry that I went against your wishes," Jin began.

Her lips drew back in a snarl, showing her blackened teeth. "Yet again."

"But I did it because of you, Grandmother. You said I had a lot to learn. By going there, I learned so much more than if I'd stayed behind these walls. I've seen our people's need. Hiding all the monsters away was a mistake. It's affected the land, our rivers, our way of life. Let's bring the creatures back—I believe it will restore our empire if we do it in the right way. It will help the people."

The empress dowager's face pinched. "You disobeyed me, failed in all your studies, caused endless trouble, and ran away. And you dare come prancing back as if nothing happened."

"What about the attacks on the island?" countered Jin. "You must've known Beastly was destroyed months ago, because the survivors sent a messenger bird here—several, in fact. I know at least one was received, because it came back with a report. Instead of help, Hulagans showed up on the island, trying to capture beasts." Jin produced a charred snare. "And they claimed that you had given them permission to be there, which I find hard to believe. Perhaps one of your advisors acted in your name." As murmurs and whispers rippled through the room, courtiers and ministers in various states of shock and outrage, Jin wondered which one had sent the secret order. "Fortunately, we were prepared for them. Otherwise, a ship full of creatures stolen from the sanctuary would be headed for the empire of Hulagu right now."

The empress dowager frowned at one of her advisors. "Minister Taru, I've heard nothing from you and your prophetic stars about treachery in the ranks, nor about collaboration with our enemies. What say you?"

"Prince Jin's accusations are outrageous," the court astrologer spluttered. "I'm sorry to say this, Your Brilliant Majesty, but he's obviously trying to distract from his transgressions. Those who are loyal do not go against the commands of the throne—and we are all loyal here."

The room buzzed with agreement and nodding heads. Jin spotted Master Sonsen standing near the throne. Blinking owlishly through his spectacles, his tutor gave him a faint smile. Encouraged, Jin beseeched the empress dowager. "Do you honestly think everyone here is to be trusted?"

"Like you?" His grandmother pointed a spiky finger-guard at him. "You've brazenly defied me again and again. If you don't trust my judgment, how can I trust yours?"

A flare of anger ignited in Jin. "I've done my best to study all that you required, do as you wanted, to follow your every wish. And it was never enough for you!"

"You think it was . . . *for me?* That shows how little you understand, boy. Everything is for *us.* For the enduring greatness of the empire. Always." She leaned forward, ever so slightly. "You've shown that to sit on this throne, you will lie and steal. But there are severe penalties for thieves."

Jin felt a chill go through his body. "What do you mean?"

"Don't pretend you don't know." She held up a crumpled piece of mulberry paper stamped with a crimson mark. It was the defective forgery Jin had left in his room. "You stole my seal. You trespassed on a forbidden imperial refuge." Her mouth set in a grim line.

"I *borrowed* your seal, and it was for a good reason," protested Jin. "And if I'm part of the imperial family, then how can the island be forbidden to me?"

She barreled on as if he hadn't spoken. "Most importantly, that kirin is not yours. You stole it!"

"I stole this kirin?" Jin repeated incredulously. "The king of beasts doesn't just reveal itself to anyone. I thought you'd be happy it found me worthy. I brought back a creature. You no longer have to worry about my taking over."

"Worthy? Take over? You are not fit to rule," she spat. "Astonishing that you think you can just flit back and claim the throne as it suits you."

"How can you say that?" Jin felt stung. "I'm the son of an emperor. A creature of the in between willingly chose to accompany me here. And not just any uncanny beast, but one of the most noble. By those measures, I've fulfilled the requirements to rule. Everything else is stuff you made up."

She gestured at the kirin. "Dragging a monster in here does not mean you get this seat."

"Excuse me, but there are no chains binding this creature to me," Jin argued. "It carried me here of its own free will. It's as willing to be by my side as your phoenix is with you."

The phoenix let out a cry and the empress dowager turned to it and hissed angrily. "Don't you start." It cried out again, and she began scolding the monster bird. The kirin nudged Jin.

"Young prince," said Chi in a low murmur. *"Something isn't quite right. This woman on the throne is your grandmother?"*

"Yes," Jin whispered back. "I know the way she talks to me is harsh, but she's always like that. Nothing I've ever done has been of any value in her eyes."

The kirin let out a soft whoosh of air through its nostrils. *"There's an unsettling darkness about her. The phoenix too. As if they're surrounded by a cloud of lies. Stay close to me."*

A cloud of lies? About what? As for being unsettling, everyone feared his grandmother. When did she ever make anyone feel comfortable? Uncertain, Jin put a hand on Chi's scaled flank, gaining courage from its solid warmth.

The monster bird had quieted. The empress dowager's gaze returned to Jin, cold and hard. "As I said, you have broken commands, lied, and thieved, but I shall give you one last chance to atone. Turn that beast over to me, and I shall consider allowing you to remain in the line of succession."

Jin shook his head. "Absolutely not. The kirin came with me." A thought occurred to him. "Grandmother, you never answered me about the Hulagans. You didn't . . . give them permission to take creatures. Did you?"

"How dare you!" she thundered. There was a deadly silence, and then she spoke more softly. "Take him away and lock him up. The monster he brought is mine."

Instinctively, Jin made to run, and Chi moved to go with him. The empress dowager flicked her hand at the phoenix. With a shriek, it launched at Chi. The kirin tossed its head, antlers slashing at the monster bird, whose extended claws scrabbled for the kirin's scaled face. In a frenzy of feathers and screeching, the phoenix attempted to peck out the great beast's eyes.

Strong hands grabbed Jin from either side, pinning his arms behind him. Looking wildly about, he saw that they were surrounded by guards, their firelances pointed warily at the kirin. "No, don't!" cried Jin. He kicked and struggled to get free.

"You mustn't make this harder, Your Brilliance," muttered a familiar voice. Old Fang gave him an apologetic look as he clapped restraints on Jin's wrists.

Jin shook his head. "You don't understand. Kirins hate to fight. Leave it alone and it will settle down, I promise."

"The empress dowager wants the monster," said Old Fang dolefully. He looked at the guards holding Jin and nodded. "Take him to the palace lockup. But give His Brilliance his own cell."

As he was dragged away, the remaining guards circled the kirin, still fighting off the phoenix, and Whisperers from the Bureau of Divination approached with monster snares and special netting. Jin shouted a warning. "Watch out!"

He watched helplessly as the phoenix flew toward the rafters just as the royal Whisperers cunningly entangled Chi's feet, bringing the kirin to a crashing thud on the floor. A net was quickly thrown over its great form, and armed guards swarmed about. Jin's voice stuck in his throat and his vision blurred as he was hauled out of the throne hall.

Stumbling to keep up, Jin found his footing and managed to right himself as the guards hustled him to the stark stone quarters that housed those who'd displeased the empress dowager. His eyes widened as they passed several of the accused suffering punishment out in the open yard, serving as a warning. There was a man struggling to keep his head above water in a deep tank, another whose arms were awkwardly trussed and left to dangle from a bar with his feet barely touching the earth, and a couple of women who wore heavy wooden collars around their necks, looking as if they'd caught their head in a door.

Screams came from the back of the building, where someone was being caned, and Jin shuddered, remembering his own beatings. A knot of dread tightened in his stomach. Even when he'd been punished for angering his grandmother, he'd never been taken to the lockup before. What was going to happen to him? And what would happen to Chi?

CHAPTER 25

LOCKED

JIN PACED ABOUT HIS TINY cell, so narrow he could almost touch the stone walls on either side when he stretched out his arms. The room confining him was just long enough to hold a worn mat of woven straw, a stump of wood for a pillow, and a stinking wooden bucket that smelled rank even with its lid shut tight. He walked six steps from the window, a barred rectangle high up near the ceiling, to the heavy wooden door. Then six steps back to the window. Six steps to the door. His thoughts churned.

It was his second night in the lockup. He was turning thirteen in a few hours, but so far no one had come to see him—not his grandmother, not his tutor, not even Old Fang. How was he to get out of this? The empress dowager had ordered his arrest before the entire court and accused him of stealing the kirin. What had the ministers from the Bureau of Divination done with Chi? He prayed no harm would come to the creature. If Chi was hurt, he'd never forgive himself. He'd thought that his grandmother would finally be impressed and believe in him. Instead, she'd locked him in a cell. Given what he'd glimpsed of other prisoners' suffering, he wouldn't be surprised if he never saw freedom again.

He searched his cell once more, fruitlessly hoping to find a way to escape. At least his hands were no longer restrained—likely because it was impossible to break out of the cell. The door was featureless except for a cut-out slot at the base where they'd passed him a small wooden bowl of soup and a row of fixed metal slats angled so that the guards could look in on him. He'd attempted to peer out of both, but was unable to see anything but the floor and rafters of the corridor. The lone window was open to the outside elements, but barred in iron and out of his reach. The floor was hard and cold, its chill seeping through whenever he tried sitting on the thin straw mat. So he paced, rubbing his hands to keep warm and pondering what to do.

A thin sliver of moon, curved like a hooked end of a lockpick, was high enough in the sky to be glimpsed through the bars of the window. If only he still had his picks—or something, anything, to help him escape. Before throwing him in the cell, they'd confiscated them, along with the jeweled knife from the island and his firestarter. At least they hadn't taken his lock charm, but if it was supposed to protect him, it was doing a terrible job. Jin fiddled absently with it, staring up at the window. His eyes narrowed as he gauged the distance. Experimenting, he jumped, one arm outstretched. If he could reach the window, maybe find a way to pry the bars loose . . . he crouched down and leaped again, tapping one of the bars. What if he had a running start? He moved back and took two strides before springing for the window, and caught the bottom ledge with his fingertips.

"Yes!" he whispered. Grabbing the window ledge with both hands, he scrabbled at the wall with his feet. The stones were rough enough that the soles of his shoes found purchase, and he seized first one bar, then another, and hauled himself high enough to look out the window. There wasn't much to see but a windowless storehouse, an expanse of gravel, and the high wall of the palace compound. He took a closer look at the bars bolted into the window frame. Welded in a grid, their bolts were solid as rock.

His arms were beginning to tire, so he jumped back down. Jin picked up the chunk of wood that served as a pillow and examined it. The bark had been worn off, but it seemed sturdy enough. Bringing it to the window, he set it in place, then stepped up. Muckety muck, it was too short to help.

A sudden wave of exhaustion overcame him. He hadn't slept, had barely been given anything to eat or drink, and despite all his efforts, he was trapped. He lugged the stump back to the mat and lay down, resting his head on it. After tossing and turning for a few minutes, he fell into a fitful sleep.

In the morning, loud clanking and a splash announced a guard's presence outside his cell. "Mealtime," barked a rough voice. Jin crawled to the door and peered through the cutout at its base. A sloshing bucket and a pair of booted feet were in view. "Where's your bowl?" asked the guard. "Give it here."

"Are we not allowed utensils?" Jin demanded. He slid the wooden bowl to the man's impatient hand. "I only got a little soup yesterday morning, and there was no spoon."

"Sounds about right," the guard grunted. He ladled something into the bowl and shoved it back through the slot. "Meals are once a day. Make it last." He moved on down the corridor, whistling through his teeth.

Jin was indignant. Didn't the guard know who he was? But at the sight of the filled bowl, his stomach growled. He snatched it up and slurped thirstily, crouched on the spot. It was little more than grayish lukewarm water with a few mushy grains of rice and a dozen beans, their centers hard and half-cooked, but he tilted the bowl to get every bit. There was a lone chunk of old boiled turnip, bitter and tough. He chewed it down to a wad of woody fibers, then swallowed that too.

With the gnawing in his belly eased, he went to use the

chamber pail in the corner. Its wooden lid had a rope handle secured with a twist of wire on the underside. His eyes lit up upon seeing the wire. Carefully he worked it free, surprised that the stink of the uncovered bucket didn't knock him out. All that dungcake making had paid off in more ways than one. Jin straightened the scrap of metal into a makeshift lockpick and felt better having a tool in hand, even if there were no visible locks to spring.

The floor was paved with hard tiles, the grout between them stained and cracked. He scratched at a section of crumbling grout with the end of the wire, blowing away powdery fragments, loosening the tile. After a while he was able to wiggle one free, then another, revealing hard-packed earth beneath. He spied his empty wooden bowl, and excitement coursed through him. Prying up enough tiles to expose a good-sized patch, Jin got to work. He chipped at the earth with the edge of a ceramic tile, scooped out dirt with the bowl, and emptied it into the bucket. It was painstaking, tedious work, but eventually the bucket was overflowing, and he took to hiding the excavated dirt in an even layer beneath his straw mat.

All day, as a striped patch of sunlight crossed the floor of his cell, Jin diligently dug away. Occasionally he'd hear the footsteps of a guard coming by to check on him, and would sweep his tools into the deepening hole, throw the lid over the bucket of dirt and sprawl on the floor, covering up his little project. He'd prop his chin on his hands or lay his head on his folded arms and look as listless as possible. Then, after the guard had walked away, he'd get right back to work.

By the time the sky outside the window had turned dark, with only slivers of light from the corridor to see by, Jin had burrowed so deep that when he stood in the hole, only his head and shoulders stuck out. Yet as far down as he dug, there seemed to be no end to the stone wall of the cell. With a sinking feeling, he realized he had no idea how deep it extended into the ground. His arms ached and his hands were blistered raw, and he was no closer to tunneling out than he'd been when he started. He pulled himself out, then collapsed on the floor of his cell, exhausted and defeated.

Something hard dug into his cheek. Raising his head, he saw it was his lock charm. He pulled it off and stared at it. A royal relic, according to Ayie. Old Fang had meant to give it to him when he turned thirteen, and claimed it would protect him. Well, today was the day, but how was he being protected? Jin tried to insert his makeshift lockpick into the tiny keyholes. Maybe if he finally managed to unlock the charm, something good would happen. But the wire was too big, and the shackle between the dragon's head and tail remained firmly in place. "What a load of monstermuck." Throwing the amulet and lockpick across the cell, Jin buried his head in his arms.

Then he heard whispers and creeping footsteps.

"I'm telling you, Jin's in this building. The piyao says the scent is strong. And look at Shishi—she smells something too."

Jin's head snapped up. Was that . . . the twins? He got to his feet and flung himself at the window ledge. Gathering what strength he had left, he grabbed the bars and pulled himself just high enough to stick an arm through. "Masa! Mau!" he hissed, blindly waving his hand. He heard a familiar whine and Shishi's snuffling as the dog neared his window.

"Over there!"

"That must be him!"

"Your Brilliance!" Bingyoo's voice sounded both relieved and horrified.

A low growl announced the presence of the piyao. It placed its enormous paws on the edge of the window and peered in. *"It's Jin!"*

"Tao!" Weak with relief, Jin fell back to the ground. He looked up at the winged lion. "Thank the gods you're here. I've been trying to dig out, but I've gotten nowhere. The wall goes down deep."

"I see. Give us a moment." The piyao disappeared from the window and there was a mumuring as it discussed what to do with the twins. Jin strained to hear.

Bingyoo's voice piped up. "I'll do it. I'll take Shishi—she can help with the diversion."

"Take these!" said Mau. There was a rustle, then the crunching sound of gravel as someone's footsteps hurried off.

"What's happening?" asked Jin, trying not to sound anxious.

"Hold on, Jin—you'll know when it happens," said Masa.

"When *what* happens?" The clomping boots of the guard on duty echoed down the corridor. "Hush—a guard's coming!" he warned. Throwing himself over the hole, he tucked an arm beneath his head and turned his face to the door. He closed his eyes as if he had fallen asleep, and when the guard stopped outside his cell, he let out a tiny snore, and then another. After what seemed like an agonizingly long silence, the guard moved on. Jin waited till the sound of footsteps was no more, then scrambled up. "Okay, he's gone. But you've got to hurry. Someone comes by every hour to look in."

A sudden boom rattled the door of his cell like an earthquake. There were shouts and pounding boots as guards ran through the lockup. "What in the forsaken realms is that?" bellowed one as he passed Jin's cell. Jin went to peer through the slot at the bottom of his door. Bells rang out, pealing a warning across the palace complex.

"Stay back, Jin." The piyao's great jaws appeared in the window, its sharp teeth tearing through the iron bars as if they were pulled sugar. Jin watched in fascination. Piyao were able to eat metals like gold and silver, and now he

could see how. Making a face, Tao spit out a piece of iron. *"This tastes burnt. Too bitter and lumpy."*

"So don't eat it—it's not supposed to be cake," hissed Masa.

Once the window was clear, the twins' faces popped up, and Mau gestured to Jin. "Come on!" Glancing around his cell, Jin saw his lock charm and the wire he'd thrown. Guiltily, he scooped them up, then turned and jumped for the window ledge. Mau and Masa grabbed his arms and hauled him through the shallow window. He kicked and wriggled, trying to speed his escape. The twins were standing on Tao's back, and when Jin tumbled out, the two strands of the piyao's forked tail quickly caught him before setting him carefully on his feet.

"I can't believe you came," said Jin, dazed. The piyao sat back on its haunches, eyes narrowed in satisfaction. Though it was quite dark behind the lockup, there was no mistaking the glimmer of the twins' smiles. A strange lump came into his throat. His eyes were suddenly scratchy, and he blinked hard, then rubbed at them with a quick swipe of his fist. "Where's Bingyoo?"

Masa nodded in the direction where the explosion had come from. "Didn't you hear that? That was her doing."

Her brother glanced about, then spoke in a low voice. "We should go—as soon as they notice you're gone, guards will surely swarm."

"We have to find Chi," said Jin urgently. "When I was arrested, they captured the kirin as well."

The piyao raised its nose and sniffed. *The kirin is still here on the grounds somewhere. We'll fly over the palace and search. It's how we found you.*

"If that's the case," said Jin, "there's really only one place that would make sense to keep an uncanny beast. We have to go to the old menagerie."

The piyao stretched its wings. *"Get on, then,"* Tao said. *"Quickly."*

"All three of us?" asked Jin. "Won't we tire you out?"

"How weak do you think I am?" growled the winged lion. It shook its mane. *"I brought three humans and that dog of yours all the way from Whisper Island."*

They clambered onto Tao's back, Jin sitting up on the lion's shoulders, while Masa squeezed between him and her brother. Flapping its mighty wings, the piyao sprang into the air. Alarm bells urgently clanged away as guards rushed in the direction of the explosion.

Jin stared at the plume of rising smoke curling into the night sky. "Dungcakes?"

Masa laughed. "Turns out there were still a few left. We figured they'd be useful. Isn't that a great distraction?"

The piyao circled over the palace grounds, careful to stay high enough that they wouldn't be spotted. From the air, the grand buildings appeared like doll houses, their windows glowing with light, and lantern-lit pathways crossed the grounds like strings of shining jewels.

"Look at all those people!" Masa said.

The sprawling square before the palace's main entrance teemed with movement, appearing even busier than it had been during the Monster Festival. "When I rode Chi through the capital, we were followed by crowds all the way to the palace gates," said Jin, astounded. "But it's been a few days. Surely they couldn't have stayed?"

"We saw them on our way here," observed Mau. "I think they never left. Maybe they want to see you and the kirin again."

As they passed over the severe outline of the lockup in a remote part of the grounds, Jin located the other side of the palace complex and pointed to a darkened patch of unlit pavilions and unkempt gardens. "Over there," he shouted to Tao. "That's the old menagerie."

"The scent of the kirin is growing strong," grunted the creature as it glided closer. They touched down in the grounds of the abandoned menagerie, and Jin slid off Tao's back. He had a feeling he knew exactly where Chi was locked up. As he drew closer to the old kirin pavilion, he saw a faint glimmer in the moonlight. He began to run, the twins hard on his heels. Jin reached the barred enclosure and found the kirin inside. It was lying down, its antlered head flat on the ground. Jin felt a stab of fear.

"Gods 'n' monsters," he said. "Please tell me Chi's not dead."

The kirin's ears twitched listlessly and it turned its head. *"Just Jin."* It raised itself slowly, as if it were in pain.

"We're here!" he said breathlessly. "Are you all right? Did they hurt you? I'm getting you out right now."

The twins and the piyao arrived at the kirin's cage. The winged lion growled. *"I don't like this place at all."*

"I've got a couple of dungcakes left," offered Mau. "We can blow the door off."

"No need." Jin reached into his pocket. "That'll draw more attention than it's worth." He brought out the piece of wire he'd pulled off the waste bucket in his cell, and found the lock on the cage's barred door. Working as quickly as he could, he sprang the lock with a snap, then yanked open the door.

"Oh, good." The piyao licked its chops disdainfully. *"I was afraid I'd have to bite through it."*

Slowly, the kirin shuffled through, then stamped its great hooves and shook itself. Jin threw his arms around its neck. "I'm so sorry. This shouldn't have happened to you."

The twins examined Chi carefully, while Tao touched noses with the kirin's scaly muzzle. *"Never thought I'd be this glad to see you,"* grunted the winged lion.

The kirin snorted. *"Strangely, I feel the same way."*

A new round of bells began jangling an alarm across the

351

palace. "I think they've discovered me missing," said Jin.

"We'd better get out of here, then," said Masa. "But we can't fly out with the kirin. Tao is strong, but not that strong."

Jin waved them off. "You two go with Tao and find Bingyoo. I'll go with Chi—I know the grounds well enough. Give me a dungcake and I'll make enough of a distraction to let us sneak out."

But the twins crossed their arms and shook their heads. "No more splitting up," said Masa.

Mau's expression was stern. "We stick together from now on."

"All right, then." With a resigned shrug, Jin pointed. "The entrance to the menagerie is that way—I'll need to unlock it."

They hurried down the winding paths of the menagerie grounds to the gate. To his surprise, Jin found it was slightly ajar. "Strange. It's usually locked."

The kirin blew out a whoosh of air through its nostrils. *"Those so-called Whisperers that serve the empress dowager—they've come to see me quite a few times."*

"They must have left it open for easier access." Jin cautiously peered out. Seeing no one, he gestured to the others. "It's clear." They streamed through the gate, and Jin led them away from the menagerie through the quiet garden courtyard and down a deserted colonnade. A high-pitched cry and a furious round of barking stopped them in their tracks.

"That's got to be Shishi and Bingyoo," said Masa, ashen-faced.

"It's coming from that way." Jin bolted into a run. "Come on!"

CHAPTER 26

THE KEY

THEY CHASED AFTER THE SCREAMS, which grew louder as they neared the Temple of Gods and Monsters. Rounding a corner, Jin saw Bingyoo in the center of the temple courtyard, dangling precariously from the towering dragon statue. At its coiled base, Shishi stood on her hind legs, barking anxiously. High above hard marble tiles, Bingyoo clung to the nose of the stone dragon, trying desperately to find her footing. One hand slipped off the dragon's nostril and she swung lower, hanging by one arm. "Help!" she called.

"She's going to fall!" exclaimed Masa.

Sprinting into the courtyard, Jin stretched out his arms. "I've got you!" Bingyoo lost her grip and fell with a shriek. Jin caught her, but they both tumbled to the ground. An overjoyed Shishi began licking his face, while the twins tried to help Bingyoo up.

"What happened?" asked Masa.

Mau was confounded. "What were you doing up there?"

"Get away, get away!" Bingyoo cried, waving them off.

The kirin leaned down and sniffed her. *"She's unhurt,"* Chi said. *"But in shock. That was quite a spill the both of you took, Just Jin. It would have been better to let me catch her."*

"I could have easily nabbed her before she fell," said the piyao, swishing the sections of its split tail.

Jin rolled his eyes. "Excuse me for not thinking of you two. I was just trying to get to her before anything bad happened."

"No, listen to me," said Bingyoo frantically. "They've been waiting for you." She pointed over their heads at the temple. On a balcony overlooking the courtyard was the empress dowager along with a retinue of court ministers, royal Whisperers, and her Beaststalkers. Her phoenix sat on the railing. It opened its serrated beak and let out an ear-splitting shriek.

Tao growled and sprang into the air. The piyao unfurled its wings just as great big nets hurtled down from guards stationed on the temple roof. They fell on Tao and the kirin, which reared and shook its head, trying to free its tangled antlers. The sound of running boots filled the air as a large contingent of palace guards surrounded them, their fire-lances drawn.

"Stop right there!" said Old Fang. He nodded at the royal

Whisperers, who filed off the balcony and came down into the courtyard. They set to work tightening the monster nets around the trapped creatures and roping their limbs till they could barely move. Chi bellowed and squirmed, while the piyao roared as its ensnared wings were crushed. It struggled to rip at the net with its teeth, but the mesh was too fine for it to get a good grip, and its paws were bound and immobilized.

"Leave them be!" Jin shouted as Shishi barked furiously. "Get back from them!"

The empress dowager's powdered face was ghostly white and impassive as she stared down at them. "I should have dealt with you properly the moment you returned from your misadventures, prancing in on that beast. The impudence! It was clear you were beyond saving. But Commander Fang and your tutor convinced me not to." She glared at the two men, then waved a dismissive hand at Bingyoo. "Fortunately, this kitchen rat was caught sneaking around the grounds with your filthy barking cur. I knew you'd be lured out to help. The problem is you've always been too soft. She's just a servant!"

"No, she's not," Jin said fiercely. He looked at Bingyoo, who'd scooped up Shishi, and at the twins, standing beside him. "She's my friend. They all are."

"Don't be a fool," snapped the empress dowager. "There

are no such things as friends in a palace. Friendships cannot survive in the halls of power. There are only those who serve and those who rule. All creatures, whether of the in between or this realm, exist to serve. Whisperers, ministers, tutors, and guards—they serve. None of them are friends. It's nature's law."

Jin frowned. "That's monstermuck—it's just what *you* think. Having a creature doesn't mean you're better than anyone else. And it doesn't give you the right to do whatever you want. Rulers are servants too. They must serve their people."

"What do you know about serving people? Your every need has been attended to since birth—you've never had to make difficult decisions." The empress dowager pointed her trident scepter at him accusingly. "You don't understand how I've tried to protect you."

"Protect me how? By keeping me from what I love? By never telling me anything about my parents? Why didn't you ever talk about them? Did my father even have a real dragon? I learned he never went to Whisper Island—but only when I got there myself. And that's where I found out about Father's older brother. I never saw any records of Crown Prince Ben in the royal archives. What happened to my uncle and the nine-tailed fox that was his monstermate?"

The phoenix let out a cry. The empress dowager pinched its beak shut and held the tines of her trident scepter to the monster bird's neck. "Stop squawking or I'll make sure you can't." She glared at Jin. "What good is it to dredge up family tragedies? My husband, your parents, your uncle, who was my oldest son—they are gone. But I refuse to be beaten by loss or to wallow in sorrow. We must always look forward, not back. The Three Realms have been changing for a new age, and I've been trying to prepare you. I wanted you and this empire to find greatness again, not to be stuck in an archaic bind with monsters!" She let go of the phoenix's beak with distaste.

"You made a deal with the Hulagans, didn't you?" said Jin slowly. "You really were going to give them Whisper Island."

His grandmother's lips tightened. "What if I did?" Several ministers around her exchanged startled looks. She drew herself up. "Trying to conquer monsters can only bring ruin upon the Hulagans in the long run. They are welcome to try, but I would never have agreed to it if it gave them an advantage."

Jin was speechless, as was everyone on the balcony. The empress dowager waved her scepter. "I'm not an unreasonable person, boy. I believe in giving people choices, including you. That way, you may decide your own fate."

"What do I need to do?"

"Turn these beasts over to me. Renounce your claim to the throne, and take a vow of monkhood at a monastery. If you do, the monsters will be allowed to live." The empress dowager glanced at the twins and Bingyoo, who clutched Shishi so hard that the dog yelped. "As will those you insist on calling friends."

Jin's stomach churned. "And if I don't?"

"Then you'll be tried for treason and executed, along with any accomplices." Looking at Master Sonsen, she added, "And sympathizers." The empress dowager murmured to him. Looking ill, he bowed and scurried off the balcony.

"What do you want with the kirin and the piyao?"

"That is none of your concern. If you truly desire what's best for them, you'll surrender them. If you refuse, they die along with you."

"But . . ." Jin's protests died in his throat. He glanced over at the two beasts, wrapped so tightly in the nets that they were unrecognizable. A strained rumble emerged from the kirin.

"A moment ago the empress's bird said something I didn't quite understand," said Chi. *"But your grandmother is not being truthful."*

At that, Mau turned his head. "Did you catch what the phoenix said?" he muttered to his sister.

"It sounded something like 'Right before you,'" Masa whispered.

"Your Brilliance!" Master Sonsen rushed out of the temple into the courtyard. "You have the chance to save lives." He wrung his sleeves. "I beg of you to choose the right thing. Your grandmother is willing to show you mercy."

"That's mercy?" Anxiously twisting the jade bangle around her wrist, Masa scowled. Mau shook his head at Jin.

What were they trying to tell him? Did he even have a choice here? He looked up at his grandmother. "They were only trying to help me. I'll do whatever you tell me—if you want to send me to a monastery, so be it, as long as you release my friends." Jin took a deep breath. "But please, won't you let the creatures go free too?"

"So you still try to change the terms." The empress dowager bared her blackened teeth. "Very well." She turned to the grizzled commander of the guard, standing on the balcony beside her. "Commander Fang, arrest them all at once. We shall hold an execution in the public square tomorrow. Like the Monster Fights, a good show ought to pacify those lingering crowds."

Old Fang shifted uncomfortably. "I—I don't think . . ." He stopped and pressed his lips together.

"But the prince agreed to renounce his claim, Your Majesty!" Master Sonsen shouted.

"I never said he could select only the bits he could stomach," said the empress dowager. "True leaders bear the hard parts too. Well, Master Sonsen. This means you must take responsibility for your failings as well." She gestured to her court Whisperers. "Leave the creatures bound. It'll be easier to dispose of them that way." Contemptuously, she pointed her trident at Jin and his friends. "Judgment is rendered, and the Haitai has decided. Commander Fang—don't make me repeat myself."

The commander swallowed, then slowly saluted. As he raised his hand to give an order, the phoenix leaped off the balcony and snatched the trident from the empress dowager's hand. It flew around the courtyard with the jeweled scepter in its talons, screeching at the top of its lungs. The Whisperer twins looked at each other. "Did that monster bird just say what I think it said?" asked Mau in a low voice.

As if in answer, the phoenix swooped onto the stone dragon statue, the jeweled trident grasped delicately in one clawed foot, and screeched again.

"'Use this key to set them free?'" Masa murmured, sounding confused. "The trident? On what lock?"

"Does it mean the kirin and piyao?" Mau sounded just as puzzled.

"Get back here!" shrieked the empress dowager. With a flurry of wings, the phoenix launched off the dragon, dropping the scepter. The empress dowager gasped. "No!" The golden trident hurtled toward the marble tiles. Then an arm clad in a long trailing sleeve shot out and caught it. Master Sonsen clutched the trident scepter close and turned to the balcony.

"I fear you are making a grave mistake, Your Majesty," said the tutor. "Crowds have been camped outside the palace since witnessing Prince Jin arrive on a monster. They are well aware of the significance of the crown prince with an uncanny beast. Executing him will not solve your problems. They'll only become worse."

"How dare you?" seethed the empress dowager. "Bring me that trident immediately, and perhaps I'll stay your sentence." Her furious glare darted to the phoenix, which was still circling about. "You wretched monster bird—if you don't return at once, I shall have you blasted with every firelance here!"

Landing back on the dragon statue, the phoenix answered with a long, piercing cry, louder than nearly anything Jin had ever heard. Everyone in the courtyard clapped their hands to their ears, even the empress dowager. As the monster bird's call subsided, they breathed a sigh of relief and uncovered their ears, and the phoenix obediently flew back to the balcony. But the Whisperer twins fell to their knees, while Shishi began howling.

"What's wrong?" Bingyoo asked in alarm.

Masa pressed her temples, as if her head hurt. "The

screaming! There's so many of them."

"So many of what?" demanded Jin. All he heard was a faint ringing in his ears from the phoenix's sharp cry.

With a grimace, Mau looked around. "The creatures of the in between," he said through gritted teeth. "They're calling to be released."

"They've been awakened but are trapped." Masa doubled over with a gasp.

Master Sonsen touched Jin's arm. "Your Brilliance, look over there." He pointed to the towering dragon statue. "See anything that could . . . use a key?" Smiling faintly, he pressed the scepter into Jin's hands.

Carved in stone was a chain that looped around the dragon's neck, ending in a lock at the base that looked strangely familiar. Jin grabbed the lock charm at his neck. It was a miniature version of the one on the dragon. Then he stared at the jeweled trident in his hand, heart pounding. Impulsively, he made a run for it.

"Guards!" shouted the empress dowager. "Bring back that scepter this instant!"

One lunged in his path, prepared to tackle him. Jin skidded to a stop. Without even thinking, he hauled back, his work-roughened hand in a proper fist, and punched him square across the jaw. The guard's head snapped to the right, and he fell flat on his back, unconscious. "Sorry," Jin muttered.

"Nice hit," exclaimed Old Fang.

Jin leaped over the knocked-out guard to the dragon statue, diving for the stone padlock carved at its base. On the side of the padlock where there would normally be a keyhole, three slits were chiseled into the rock. Holding the trident's points to the slits, he saw that they aligned exactly. Jin pushed them in and held his breath.

Nothing happened.

He thought his heart would stop.

Then a cracking, snapping sound filled the air. Fissures crazed across the stone dragon in a widening web. Jin scrambled back. Shards clinked to the ground as the giant statue in the courtyard began to move. Sheets of stone scales fell to reveal luminous azure-blue ones underneath. The dragon's limbs flexed, and its clawed feet stomped off bits of rock. Its long, fringed tail unfurled with a snap, while the golden-finned ridge along its back bristled. A whoosh of air came out of the dragon's nostrils, and then it shook itself vigorously. A cloud of dust and stone flew all over the courtyard, sending everyone from guards and ministers to the empress dowager ducking for cover. The dragon, freed from its stone casing, gave a thundering growl that shook the earth.

Bingyoo clutched Jin's arm. "Look!"

It wasn't just the dragon. On the temple and all around the palace grounds, the statues and carvings of creatures on rooftops and walls, flanking doorways and gardens, and standing watch over the royal residence were coming to life. Thunderstruck, Jin watched as dozens of creatures leaped from the rooftops and ran off. An entire flock of phoenixes took to the skies, stretching their wings in flight for the first time. They were joined by a pride of piyao, the flying lions roaring as they soared over palace grounds. The air was filled with strange hoots, shrill whistles, and haunting cries—the sound of newly awakened creatures calling out to each other. It reminded Jin of Whisper Island, and it sounded like music.

CHAPTER 27

FINDING FREEDOM

THE CREATURE CARVINGS AND STATUES around the Palace of Monsters had all come to life. They leaped from their long-held positions on rooftops, doorways, and walls, tasting freedom. Only the giant dragon remained, standing in the temple's courtyard with its nostrils flaring as it swiveled its bearded head and surveyed the scene. The terrified palace guards all backed away, pointing their firelances at the newly awakened creature.

"No one shoot!" Old Fang shouted.

"Tell them to attack, you fool!" said the empress dowager. "What are claws and scales against weapons?"

"Begging your pardon, Your Brilliant Majesty," said the Beaststalker tersely, "but we've never had to fight a real dragon before, and we're in close quarters here. I know dragons come sacred to the throne, but I don't know how they react to being attacked. I don't want to accidently make things worse."

Her mouth pinched tight as if she'd tasted bad vinegar. The empress dowager glared down at the royal Whisperers clustered around the piyao and kirin. Frozen in place, the trembling men eyed the dragon with alarm. "You're supposed to be the greatest diviners in the land. Don't just stand there," she charged. "You've trapped those two already— trap this one!"

"Forgive us, Your Majesty." On the balcony beside her, the head minister of the divination bureau cleared his throat. "W-we're not prepared for a monster of this size." His long beard quivered.

"If my scepter had been returned to me, you wouldn't have needed to be. Guards!" She pointed at Master Sonsen. "Take him away before he meddles further."

"Wait, no!" Jin blurted.

With wary glances at the looming dragon, two guards inched toward Master Sonsen. He held up his hands. "No need to restrain me, sirs. I'm coming." He glanced at Jin and smiled. "It's all right, Your Brilliance. You know, loss is not the same as defeat." Calmly, he allowed the guards to lead him from the courtyard.

Surrounded by the royal diviners and painfully entangled in nets, Tao and Chi began bellowing with renewed vigor, as if calling to the dragon. It approached the knot of Whisperers from the Bureau of Divination, towering overhead. The royal Whisperers cringed and huddled closer, while the palace guards backed farther away, their weapons still trained on the great creature.

"Stop," croaked one of the royal Whisperers, holding up his hands. "Nice . . . dragon. Good beastie." The dragon cocked its head and hesitated.

Another royal Whisperer stepped forward, emboldened. "That's right. Stay. Stay," he commanded. "Now, monster, sit."

The dragon made no move to sit. Instead, it sneezed, spewing a thick, slimy spray over the diviners. They moaned in fear and revulsion as dragon snot dripped down their faces. "My silk hat," one said mournfully. As the azure-and-gold-scaled creature moved closer, the royal Whisperers hastily shuffled back, giving it a wide berth, while a few turned and ran, flapping their slime-covered hands.

"Useless, all of you," fumed Empress Soro.

Delicately, the dragon used its enormous talons and sharp teeth to tear open the nets and ropes that bound the piyao and kirin, and the creatures staggered to their feet and shook themselves. The three legendary beasts bowed to each other, and then the dragon turned and stalked about the courtyard, its sinous body rippling as it inspected everything. Upon coming across the balcony, it raised its head, looming over the empress dowager. "You don't scare me," she seethed. "I rule here." Her phoenix gave a strangled-sounding cry.

The dragon jerked back and snorted as if it had smelled something bad, its breath whooshing through its nostrils in a fine mist. Its eyes met Jin's, and it brought its shaggy whiskered head close. The Whisperer twins moved a step closer, flanking him protectively.

"Steady now," murmured Mau.

"This is the crown prince," Masa said softly to the dragon.

Jin gulped as it sniffed his lock charm, careful to hold still as the dragon evaluated him. The great scaled beast went and nosed through the pile of stone fragments that had once encased it. When it raised its head, the golden trident was in its jaws. It presented the scepter to Jin, who took it gently. "Thank you," he whispered.

The dragon curled its long body around him, the twins, Bingyoo, and Shishi, shielding them. Chi and Tao flanked the great azure-and-gold creature, staring down the palace guards. Shifting uneasily, the armored men tightened their grip on their weapons. Jin thought fast. While the scales of both Chi and the dragon were quite tough, and Tao's teeth could tear through metal, the piyao's furry flanks were vulnerable. But he couldn't let the guards know that.

"I wouldn't use those firelances if I were you," Jin called out. "Old Fang is right. Attacking these creatures will only make things worse."

The commander nodded grimly. Empress Soro snapped at Jin. "Shut up, boy! You know nothing!" She turned to the Beaststalker. "Enough stalling. You and your men will bring those monsters to heel. That dragon is nothing but an enchantment, and the flesh and bone of those other two are nothing against firelances if you aim for the eyes."

At that, the twins grabbed each other's hands and reached for the dragon. It reared its crested head and let out a long, sonorous cry. It was so unexpectedly beautiful that all the humans in the courtyard were overcome. The dragon's song washed over them, leaving them slack, their mouths open with wonder, unable to do anything but listen.

In a blaze of bright feathers, sharp claws and snapping fangs, hundreds of newly freed creatures descended on the courtyard. A herd of deerlike kirin, smaller-framed than Chi, galloped into the courtyard, their scales in a multitude of shades. They were joined by dozens of dragons in varying sizes, monster birds, bleating bakus with their long noses and their ability to eat dreams, and fearsome haitai with their singular pointed horns that could skewer wicked men to death in one stroke. Winged lions that looked just like Tao, only in myriad colors, landed on the rooftops and crouched watchfully, ready to pounce. And lastly, four immense dragon turtles that Jin recognized from the palace water clock dragged themselves into the courtyard, still carrying stone blocks on their backs and looking particularly snappish.

"I'm afraid we're outnumbered, Your Brilliant Majesty," said the commander steadily, though his grizzled face was ashen.

"Don't be ridiculous," Empress Soro spat. "They're illusions! Just like the dragon!"

"And the children? Illusions or not, the crown prince is in the midst of all that!"

Her head jerked and she hissed at the commander. "He is crown prince no longer—and not on the throne. I am. I am your master. Question me again, and I'll throw you off this balcony and have my phoenix tear you from limb to limb. Fire upon them now!"

With a resigned expression, the commander addressed the guards. "On my signal, first unit, train your sights on the dragon!" he barked. "Second unit, focus on any creatures you see on the eaves! Third unit, take out the beasts on the ground! Ready!" He raised a hand, and the guards positioned their weapons. "Aim—"

Before he could finish his command, the creatures of the in between set upon them in a frenzy. Monster birds swooped down and snatched the firelances from the guards' grasps. Charging haitai lowered their heads and aimed their spiky horns straight at the backsides of the royal Whisperers, who ran about, wailing. Smaller dragons, some no taller than knee-high, swarmed over several guards, ripping at their armor with their claws and teeth. Winged lions leaped from the rooftops, pouncing on other guards. The men's screams were drowned out by fearsome roars.

From the protective coils of the giant imperial dragon, Jin and the others watched as a full-sized baku the size of an elephant knocked a guard to the ground and placed its long nose on the man's forehead. The guard howled until his eyes rolled into the back of his head and he went limp. The baku then placed the end of its long nose into its mouth and seemed to swallow something. "It's dream eating," breathed Jin.

As Chi stood watch nearby, an intrepid guard approached and struck at the kirin's flank with the blade on his firelance. The metal glanced off Chi's scales, sending up a shower of sparks. Lowering its head, the kirin scooped the guard up in its antlers and flung him like a doll. The herd of palace kirin, smaller than Chi but with impressively sharp antler racks, galloped after a group of armored men, chasing them toward the snapping jaws of the four surly dragon turtles. Up on the balcony, the empress dowager was paler than ever, the phoenix had begun tearing its breast feathers out, and Old Fang shouted helpless orders at his men.

Jin turned to Mau and Masa. "I think they've gotten the message," he said. "Maybe we should call them off."

The twins nodded, and Masa clapped her hands, while Mau gave a sharp whistle. The creatures immediately halted, dropping guards from their jaws or abandoning their pursuit. Some beasts glowered at their intended prey with slaver dripping from their fangs, but refrained from attacking further. As guards and royal Whisperers cringed and gibbered, Jin stared up at his grandmother.

"Now will you believe in me? The time has come for you to step down, and for me to do my job. With or without your approval, I will." He took a deep breath and squared his shoulders. "And I can."

His grandmother's lips curled in disgust, but before she could say anything, a gate guard came running into the courtyard and skidded to a stop before the balcony. He saluted. "Commander!" he said to Old Fang. "The crowds in the imperial square have started banging against the gates. They've seen all the strange new monsters flying above the palace and they're calling for the crown prince! Sir, what should we do?"

Silence fell over the courtyard at the gate guard's words. In the distance, the rhythmic chant of thousands became clear, followed by a percussive sound that echoed across the grounds of the palace.

"Crown Prince Jin!"

Boom. Boom. Boom.

"Let his reign begin!"

Boom. Boom. Boom.

"Er, perhaps we should allow Prince Jin to address them, madam?" ventured Old Fang.

Glowering, the empress dowager nearly vibrated with fury. Instead of replying, she stared down at Jin. "What a stain you are on the imperial family," she sneered. "We may share a bloodline, but you will never be good enough to rule."

Mau grunted. "How sweet. Nice grandmother."

"With family like that, who needs enemies?" Masa murmured.

"Don't listen to her, Your Brilliance," whispered Bingyoo.

Jin flashed a smile at them, then turned to the empress dowager and lifted his chin. "These friends of mine are more family to me than you've ever been or ever will be." He held up the scepter, pointing it in the direction of the palace gates. "My duty is to the people of the Three Realms—not to you."

"Insolent boy!" With a hiss of frustration, Empress Soro snatched up the phoenix. "Take their eyes out, one by one. Go! Fly, now!" She pitched the monster bird into the air.

The phoenix shrieked in response, then circled around. It dove down, straight at Jin. But instead of attacking him, it landed on the trident and stared at him with its golden eyes. It darted its head and snatched up the amulet he wore. With its serrated beak, it bit down on the leather cord and jerked back.

"Hey!" Jin protested. "That's mine!"

With the lock charm in its jaws, the phoenix sprang into the air with a flurry of flapping wings and flew off into the star-flecked sky. Empress Soro followed its flight with narrowed eyes. "Oh no, you don't!" To gasps and exclamations of shock, she leaped over the balcony. With surprising agility, she landed on the hard marble tiles as easily as a cat. Straightening, she turned and pointed a long gilt fingerguard at Jin. "This isn't over. I promise you that."

Then the empress dowager ran out of the courtyard, calling after her phoenix, disappearing into the night.

"Crown Prince Jin! Let his reign begin!"

Outside the palace gates, the gathered crowds shouted their demands, while those within remained dumbstruck, speechless for what seemed like ages. Standing before the palace temple, Jin gawked at the empty space on the balcony where his grandmother had been. Had she really jumped from that height? Shishi pawed at his leg and whined, breaking the silence.

"Now what, Your Brilliance?" asked Bingyoo, scooping up Shishi.

"What should we do with all these creatures?" asked Mau, gazing about in awe.

"Some of these men don't look so good," Masa observed.

One glance at the injured guards and their shaken commander and Jin realized it was now up to him to take charge. He bowed to the imperial temple's dragon, which had kept him and his friends safe within the protective circle of its coiled body, and the enormous dragon gracefully unwound itself so that Jin could get to work.

The first thing he did was approach Old Fang. The grizzled commander dropped to his knees and pressed his forehead to the ground.

"Have mercy, Your Brilliance," said Old Fang. "I never meant to place you in danger. Your grandmother . . ."

Jin leaned down. "I know." For a long time, Old Fang had been the only one who'd actually seemed to care about him. He placed a hand on the man's shoulder and helped him up. "I should really say thank you."

"For what?" asked the commander, looking surprised.

"For teaching me how to make a fist—and when to use it." Jin flexed his hand and grinned.

A flush came over the commander's face. "Forgive me, Your Brilliance. You are the crown prince. You should never have had to do that."

"But I was ready for it," said Jin. "Knowing how and when to fight is everything. Especially if others are depending on you." He glanced around. "Now let's make sure your men are okay."

After confirming that Bingyoo was unharmed, Jin dispatched her to find the palace healers. She returned, smiling, with the healers in tow and Master Sonsen carrying a chest of medicines. "The guards didn't take me very far before a stampede of monsters sent them running," he said merrily.

"I'm glad," said Jin. He held up the scepter. "Thank you for giving me this—and for the clue."

His tutor's eyes crinkled behind his spectacles. "Always work backward from a problem."

As they saw to the injured guards and royal Whisperers, setting broken bones, patching bite wounds, and administering remedies for pain and shock, various ministers and courtiers timidly approached Jin, swearing that they knew nothing about his grandmother's deal with the Hulagans. Meanwhile, the twins hurried about corralling the monsters, cataloging and counting the formerly inanimate creatures that had come to life on the palace grounds.

But the chanting outside the palace gates continued. Another gate guard arrived to ask the commander what to do.

"Your Brilliance?" said Old Fang. "The people are asking for you."

Master Sonsen looked up from where he was assisting a healer with the preparation of a poultice, weighing out dried herbs and precious elixirs. "You should address them, Your Brilliance."

"Yes, Your Brilliance," said the head of the diviners' bureau. "You should address your people. After all, you're clearly ready to." He nodded at the kirin and the piyao, both keeping watchful eyes on Jin amid all the activity in the courtyard. The other ministers chorused in agreement, maintaining a respectful distance from Jin while nervously glancing at the two beasts.

Feeling uncomfortable, Jin walked over to Chi and Tao. "They want me to speak to the crowds at the gate. But I have no idea what to say."

The kirin regarded him, its golden eyes unblinking. It lowered its scaly nose to the jeweled trident in Jin's hand. *"Tell them that the woman who held this scepter has gone, and that you are prepared to take it up."*

"Tell them you will lead," growled Tao. *"And anyone who doesn't fall in line will have to answer to me."*

At that, Jin couldn't help but smile. But he quickly sobered. "I've thought about this moment for as long as I can remember. But now that it's here, I don't feel ready at all."

"I shall come with you," offered Chi. *"Half the city's seen me already."*

"Then how will he impress them?" The piyao shook its mane. *"I say you fly in on my back for a grand entrance!"*

"If it's a grand entrance you want, then he should appear on the imperial temple dragon's back," Chi snorted. *"It's a lot bigger than either of us."*

The piyao folded back its ears, affronted. *"I suppose."*

"It would mean a lot to me if you both appeared with me," said Jin. "Please."

There was a pause while the creatures sized each other

up, then the kirin blew out a breath through its nostrils. *"In that case, I shall meet you at the gate. Might as well fly in on this winged cat—it* would *make a good show."*

"Thank you," said Jin, relieved. He turned to the commander, who was waiting to hear his answer. "I'll go right now."

Old Fang saluted. "Very good, August One."

Jin started. It was the first time he'd ever been addressed with such an honorific. As the commander told the guard to prepare at the palace gates, Jin was joined by the twins and Bingyoo, curious about what he was about to do. He filled them in briefly, twisting the jeweled trident in his hands. "I think I was less scared when we were up against the Hulagans."

"You'll be fine," said Mau with a wide grin.

"More than fine—he'll be great," Bingyoo declared stoutly.

"Be like the beasts," added Masa, her fingers curved in a claw salute.

The commander called to him across the courtyard. "Your Brilliance! Shall we?"

With a nervous smile at his friends, Jin took a deep breath and nodded. He got onto Tao's back and asked Bingyoo to lead the kirin to the gate tower. Then he waved Old Fang on. "I'm going to fly," he told the commander. "We'll meet you at the Phoenix Gate." Tao sprang into the air and flew over the palace grounds till they reached the main gate and its two-story tower overlooking the imperial city square. As Tao circled above the gate tower, which was lit from top to bottom with lanterns, the teeming, chanting crowds packed in the square began to cheer in excitement. The piyao dipped its wings and swooped over the throngs of people to gasps and squeals. Then Tao landed on the top story of the gate tower, gracefully depositing Jin on the balcony, where he was handed a loud-speaking horn by a guard. As Jin waved and took in the crowd, he was joined by the kirin, which sent up even more excited cheers. Flanked by the two creatures of the in between, he held up the jeweled trident, and the crowd quieted.

"People of Shining Claw, of Samtei, Empire of the Three Realms," he shouted through the horn. "I am honored to hold the scepter wielded by my forebears—most recently by my grandmother, Empress Dowager Soro. She is no longer here, and so I will be ascending the Triad Throne in her place. I promise to do my best by you, and to always put the interests of Samtei's citizens first. As you can see, great beasts have returned to the Palace of Monsters, blessing us with their presence. It is a good omen!"

He nodded at Tao, and the winged lion gave an impressive roar. Jin turned to the kirin, which obligingly reared on its hind legs and bellowed. The crowd went into a joyous, cheering frenzy. Jin waved and caught sight of his friends.

The twins were grinning ear to ear. "Perfect," mouthed Masa, while her brother gestured with wild enthusiasm. Bingyoo held Shishi in her arms, a proud smile on her face.

Jin waved at the crowd one last time, then led the kirin and piyao off the tower, while the throngs of people in the square broke into song and spontaneously began dancing. The commander of the palace guard was waiting for him at the bottom, along with Master Sonsen. "Well done, Your Brilliance," said his tutor. "You said exactly what they needed to hear."

Surprised, Jin scratched his head. "I didn't say all that much."

"You didn't need to," said Old Fang. "You spoke from the heart, and it showed. You've given everyone hope for a fresh start."

Master Sonsen nodded fervently. "It's just what the country needs."

CHAPTER 28

A NEW SAMTEI

THE EMPRESS DOWAGER AND HER phoenix did not return to the Palace of Monsters. Rumors flew for a while, with people reporting odd sightings around the empire, like at a field of rice, or on a steep hillside of tea bushes, or in a tangled wood at night. It was as if she'd become a spirit. Sometimes it was just the glimpse of her companion phoenix, or the tinkle of the long golden ornaments she'd worn in her hair. Parents took to warning their children: "If you don't behave, the empress dowager will come and her monster bird will peck your eyes out in your sleep!" It was an effective threat that kept many a Samtei child obedient.

Those who'd served her without question, like her loyal ladies-in-waiting, were treated more kindly by Jin than many had expected. In the olden days they might have been fed to the palace monsters, and now that there were creatures in the palace again, some thought the tradition would be restored. Instead, Jin allowed them to retire quietly, as long as they stayed away from the capital.

Meanwhile, preparations were afoot for Jin's coronation, which would take place as a late celebration of his thirteenth birthday. As the residents of Shining Claw swept and scrubbed the streets, the main square was set up for festivities in honor of the upcoming event. Much like the Monster Festival, there would be games and food stands, and a parade of fantastical creatures—real ones this time. But no animal fights would be allowed. Jin made sure of that. The only fighting would be for a prize in a dance competition for teams of lion-dog acrobats and dragon dancers.

Jin spent much of his days meeting with not only the ministers of his grandmother's court, but also receiving congratulatory messages from governors of far-flung provinces, as well as lord mayors and magistrates across the land. He promised them that he would visit them all on a tour of the empire, to see for himself what needed to be done for them. Often he stayed up late poring over maps and going over ledgers. It was dizzying and tiring, but fortunately he wasn't alone. Master Sonsen had been made his chief minister, Old Fang was always there to listen and offer advice, and courtiers who'd struggled under his grandmother found new confidence as Jin asked for their honest opinions.

As for the Whisperers, Jin sent supplies to Ayie so that she could live more comfortably on the island, along with a number of court Whisperers who'd expressed interest in training with a true Whisperer. He'd asked the twins to stay on at the palace and help with all the creatures now freely roaming the grounds. Mau and Masa had free rein to redesign the menagerie to better suit resident beasts, and Jin pledged to search for young people with Whispering abilities so that their ranks could be rebuilt. The twins had their hands full but were slowly adapting to court life. Of course, it helped that the new head of the court was their friend.

Bingyoo was promoted. No longer a mere kitchen drudge, she was given the important position of assisting the Whisperers with the creatures' diets, preparing meals for all the different beasts. When Shishi wasn't snuggling with Jin or chasing after monsters on the grounds, she was often seen trotting by Bingyoo's side.

At times it was all rather overwhelming, and Jin would wonder whether he was up to the demands of the throne. But then he'd see a magnificent creature ambling the halls or quietly guarding a doorway and get a thrill that pushed him to keep trying.

It was customary to have one's monstermate be part of the coronation ceremony, and that worried Jin, for he was still unsure whether he actually had one. For so long he'd hardly dared to hope for connecting with even one monster, let alone two. Was he now supposed to select a creature companion? Ask them to choose between themselves? By the night before the ceremony, he still didn't know. After tossing and turning for hours, he got up and paced the halls of the palace. The kirin and the piyao found him frowning up at the throne in the throne hall, festively decorated for the morning's ceremony.

"We heard you wandering about," said Tao. *"You should be in bed. Tomorrow is an important day."*

"I couldn't sleep," said Jin. "I'm supposed to be crowned with an official creature companion, but I don't think that's been settled."

"Just to remind you, kirin aren't called king of beasts for nothing," Chi huffed.

The piyao bared its fangs in a leonine grin. *"Actually, piyao are the best and most loyal protectors a leader could ever have."*

"Yes, I know—I've read all that in the imperial bestiary," said Jin, smiling at the fantastical creatures before him. He'd once dreamed of finding a dragon who would rule with him, but these two were his friends. How could he ever do without either of them?

As if hearing his thoughts, the kirin's golden eyes met his. *"But to lead well and effectively does not require you to know such things. It only requires that you know your heart, and respect those of others."*

"You may be right. But emperors of the Three Realms have always done things a certain way." He shrugged. "I don't want to mess it up."

"Doing things differently doesn't mean you're doing them wrong," growled Tao.

Jin hesitated, then shyly posed a question. "Well, what if *both* of you were my companions?"

The winged lion sniffed Jin's face, touching its surprisingly moist nose to Jin's, and the scaly kirin licked the back of Jin's head with a warm tongue.

Laughing, he tried to smooth down his hair. "I'll take that as a yes."

The next morning, Jin awoke and got ready, washing up before getting dressed. He'd moved into larger quarters, as befitting one about to be crowned emperor. There was enough room for the kirin and piyao to sleep there, although they were free to come and go and explore the palace grounds. But they were both by his side on this most important day, and when he reached for his usual simple garb, Tao made an involuntary hiss, and the kirin stamped its foot.

"I want to feel like myself today," Jin said, a trifle defensively.

The piyao wrinkled its nose. *"You've also wondered if you're ready for this. Dressing for the part can help."*

"You might even feel like a better version of yourself," said Chi. *"At least put something on that will make you stand out."*

"Why would I need to stand out when I've got the two of you with me?" Jin rolled his eyes, but he put on the splendidly embroidered robes that had been prepared for his coronation. They were far more substantial than the silks that his grandmother had made him wear, almost like a coat of armor. As he looked in the mirror, he had to admit that his creature companions were right. He threw his shoulders back and raised his chin. "How do I look?"

"Better," said Chi dryly.

"It'll have to do," Tao growled.

Jin snorted. "Your compliments will go to my head." He was too nervous to eat but gulped down a little tea. The water clock in his room announced the approach of the hour. It was time. "Ready?"

The beasts accompanied him to the Hall of the Jade Hai-tai, where the throne room was resplendent in banners and garlands, butter lamps everywhere ablaze with light. Officials and dignitaries from all over the empire were there, as well as the entire court. Many of them looked uneasily at the fantastical beasts in attendance, dozens of which were perched on the rafters and lined the walls. But the creatures themselves were unperturbed, watching the activity in the room with placid eyes. The Whisperer twins stood in back, making sure the beasts were comfortable and staying out of trouble. Mau was dressed in fine silk, Jin saw with surprise, as was Masa, her short hair pinned in a semblance of formal court style. She caught Jin's expression and made a face at him. She nudged her brother. He grinned and gave Jin a claw salute.

A bell chimed, and a hush fell over the room as everyone bowed low. Jin approached the throne platform, where a host of his newly appointed ministers was lined up. In front of the Triad Throne, the crown, Royal State Seal, and jeweled trident were displayed on raised stands of gold lacquer. Master Sonsen—no, Chief Minister Sonsen—began the sacred coronation ceremony. After the trio of imperial regalia was formally presented to the gods, Jin was asked to take his oath to the empire. He took a deep breath.

"I pledge my life in service to the Three Realms," he recited, his voice as loud and clear as he could muster. "I pledge my creature companion—*companions*—in service to the empire, for as long as they will allow."

The Imperial Scroll of Succession had been unfurled across a long table and awaited his mark. With reverence, he approached and placed his own personal seal onto the paper. Then he picked up the imperial seal from its stand and smiled to himself at the familiar weight of it. There was no need to break into the royal treasury this time. Jin inked it carefully and placed it on the scroll featuring the stamp of his father, his grandfather, and all other rulers before him.

Chief Minister Sonsen lowered the crown onto Jin's head. The elaborate headdress felt strange and heavy, but Jin held his chin up, his back as straight as a steel rod. He caught sight of Bingyoo, her dimples deeper than ever. Jin grinned back.

"If you please, August One—rise and meet your subjects," said the chief minister.

Jin got to his feet and turned. The assembled crowd in the throne room bowed as if one. Even the creatures of the in between, lined in the back with Mau and Masa or perched in the rafters, lowered their heads in salute along with the twin Whisperers.

"May the emperor live ten thousand years!" cried Chief Minister Sonsen.

"Ten thousand years!" The crowd chanted it three times as both a wish and a blessing before erupting into cheers. Bells rang out from the palace, across the city, and the land. The Empire of the Three Realms had a new emperor, and it was time for celebration. The hall emptied as the guests headed for a great banquet given in Jin's honor, while outside the palace in the main square, strings of fireworks wrapped in bright paper went off in a loud cacophony, signaling the start of coronation day festivities for the people.

With the twins keeping the creatures in line, the monsters of the palace paraded down the main boulevard. While Tao stalked before him like a fierce personal guard, Jin rode the kirin once more through the streets of Shining Claw, waving to his new subjects as they cheered, threw flower petals, and gasped at all the fantastical beasts. Though it was a brief route, the roadside was packed, and by the time they returned to the palace, Jin's head was spinning.

Once safely back through the gates onto palace grounds, the monsters scattered, scampering off in all directions to their favorite perches and hideouts. Masa shook her head. "Crickety creatures, I didn't dismiss them yet! We're going to have to work on that."

Her brother chuckled. "For their first time out on parade, I think they did just fine."

Jin slid off the kirin and stroked its scaly muzzle, and gave the piyao a scratch. Instead of running off like the other beasts, the two creatures stayed close, ambling alongside him and the twins. As they neared the pavilion where the banquet was taking place, Bingyoo hurried out, Shishi at her heels. "Oh good, you're back. There's a whole table full of food waiting for you!"

"Just lead the way," Mau said cheerfully. "I'm ready for it."

"Me too," said Masa. She scooped up Shishi and pretended to bite the little dog's neck. "I'm starving!"

"You all go ahead—I'll be there in a bit," said Jin. "I just need a moment after that parade."

With a nod, the twins went off with Bingyoo for the feast,

while Jin and his monstermates remained in the quiet garden courtyard. He took off his royal headdress and rubbed his neck. "It's a lot heavier than I thought," he remarked, and sighed. "And there's so much to fix and change."

"*You've said that before. But now you're in a position to do something about it,*" said Chi.

The piyao grunted in agreement. "*Taking action is better than just talking. And even if you're scared, try anyway.*"

Turning the crown in his hands, Jin watched it sparkle in a beam of sunlight and felt himself brighten. He wasn't alone anymore. He had friends and not just one, but two magnificent creatures to help him. "I guess you're right."

"*There's no guessing about it,*" Tao growled. "*Look at the heavens, young emperor.*"

He glanced up. The sun was shining brightly through a lacy scrim of clouds generated by the imperial temple dragon, and a brilliant arc of colors had formed in the sky.

"*It's a very good omen, Just Jin,*" the kirin told him.

"*Want to see what it looks like up close?*" asked Tao. "*We could go for a quick flight.*"

Jin laughed. "I thought you'd never ask."

"*Let me take this for safekeeping while you're flying about.*" The kirin delicately picked up Jin's crown between its sharp teeth.

There'd be no better guard for it. With a grin, Jin patted

Chi's scaly flank in thanks. Then he swung onto the winged lion's back and curled his fingers into its thick mane.

"Hold on!"

They sprang into the air, the rainbow in their sights. Jin let out a whoop.

THE IMPERIAL BESTIARY OF THE THREE REALMS

(Abridged excerpts translated from Samtei and annotated)

AUTHOR'S NOTE: One of the most sacred and important texts in the Empire of Samtei (also known as the Three Realms), *The Imperial Bestiary of the Three Realms* is vast. Here I've pulled just a few entries on creatures that appeared in the story, as they also appear in the stories of many countries in our world. Hopefully this will give an idea of the long history and wide reach of these fantastical beasts, and inspire you to learn more!

AMABIE | **Preferred habitat:** Sea | **Characteristics:** Scaly fish body, multiple legs, a beaked mouth
Special ability: Glows in the water, protects against plague, predicts the harvest
Translator's notes: Amabie are a type of mermaid—some have been pictured with long flowing hair and three legs in addition to their scaly fish bodies and beaked bird heads.

In Japan, they're said to prophesy famine and plague, and images of the amabie are supposed to provide protection against illness.

BAKU | **Preferred habitat:** Land | **Characteristics:** Long nose, small eyes, tiger like paws
Special ability: Devours nightmares. If called upon too often, the dreameater may also consume one's hopes and desires.
Translator's notes: Known as *mo* in Chinese, *baku* in Japanese. Carvings of this creature adorn temples in Japan and were used as talismans by children in Meiji-era Japan against nightmares. The Japanese *baku* originated from the Chinese chimerical creature called the *mo*, which was also what giant pandas were once called. Nowadays in Japan, *baku* refers to both the mythological creature and the Malaysian tapir.

BINGFENG | **Preferred habitat:** Land | **Characteristics:** Giant boar with a head on each end
Special ability: Roots out trouble with its exceptional scenting power
Translator's notes: The early Chinese writings in *The Classic of Mountains and Seas* (or *Shan Hai Jing*), describe the piglike bingfeng as black in color, and its two heads are thought to make it particularly stubborn. The dual heads have also been thought to represent male and female genders.

DRAGON | **Preferred habitat:** Land, sea | **Characteristics:** Scales, whiskers, beard, mane, fangs; number of claws and legs vary, from zero to many. Wings, horns, and antlers may appear. Size is variable.

Special ability: Controls weather, namely rain and fog; controls bodies of water

Translator's notes: The dragon is one of the most revered creatures in Asia, associated with kings and emperors across the continent. Every supernatural power has been attributed to dragons, and there are many types, in all shapes and sizes. Since Neolithic times, when dinosaur bones were discovered in China and attributed to dragons, the creature has been seen as a symbol of prosperity, good fortune, harmony, wisdom, benevolence, and excellence.

FOX SPIRIT | **Preferred habitat:** Land | **Characteristics:** White or golden fur, multiple tails (usually in odd numbers up to nine)

Special ability: Shapeshifting, enchantment

Translator's notes: The fox spirit, or nine-tailed fox, is often called *hulijing* in Chinese, *gumiho* in Korean, *kitsune* in Japanese, *hồ ly tinh* in Vietnamese. It can be benevolent or evil, depending on the situation, and is known primarily as a trickster and shapeshifter. Fox spirits are highly intelligent, long-lived, and have magical powers.

GOLDEN EARTH SPIDER | **Preferred habitat:** Land |
Characteristics: Giant spider, striped with yellow
Special ability: Produces silk of incredible variety, texture, and strength, as well as strong glue and venom
Translator's notes: The earth spider, known as *tsuchigumo* in Japan, is a legendary monster that can catch and eat prey as large as humans and livestock. It builds its nest in the ground, and its web is constructed like that of ordinary spiders, but with silk of far greater size and strength. Whether from giant monsters or ordinary ones, spider silk can be five times stronger than steel and can stretch up to four times its length.

GREEN CROW | **Preferred habitat:** The sun, heaven |
Characteristics: Three legs
Special ability: Brings messages, offers guidance
Translator's notes: The three-legged bird, usually depicted as a crow, is known as *sanzuwu* in Chinese, *samjogo* in Korean, and *yatagarasu* in Japanese. There is also a three-legged bird called *qingniao* in Chinese, which means green bird, that serves as a messenger for an important goddess known as the Queen Mother of the West. In Korea the *samjogo* is regarded as even more important than the dragon and phoenix.

HAITAI | **Preferred habitat:** Land | **Characteristics:** A single straight horn on its head

Special ability: Discerns evil and dispatches of it with a thrust of its horn

Translator's notes: Known as *xiezhi* in Chinese, *haitai* in Korean, *shinyo* or *kaichi* in Japanese, *giải trãi* in Vietnamese. This creature is described as either being lion-like, ox-like, or goat-like, often with scales on its body. But the one constant is the long single horn and its sense of justice; it instinctively knows who is innocent or guilty, and will ram the wrongdoer with its sharp horn before devouring them.

HUNDUN | **Preferred habitat:** Land | **Characteristics:** Faceless round furry body with multiple legs and wings

Special ability: Feeds on wickedness; sows chaos and confusion

Translator's notes: This creature is known in early Chinese texts as one of four fiends that were banished by Emperor Shun, a legendary ruler in Chinese lore. It's said to be drawn to unvirtuous people. Though it has no mouth, ears, or openings of any kind, it hums, sings, and dances. It's been suggested that wontons (dumplings in soup) take their name from the blobular shape of the hundun.

KIRIN | **Preferred habitat:** Land | **Characteristics:** Scaly ox-like body, antlers, a dragon-like face

Special ability: Protects the righteous and brings good fortune to rulers

Translator's notes: Called *qilin* in Chinese, *girin* in Korean, *kirin* in Japanese, *gilen* in Thai, *kỳ lân* in Vietnamese. This chimeric creature is considered one of the most noble, often appearing as a good omen or a sign of a great ruler. In Japan it's ranked above the dragon and the phoenix. In modern-day Korea and Japan, the word *girin/kirin* is also used to refer to the giraffe. Early sightings and descriptions of giraffes by fifteenth-century Chinese explorers sounded like the mythical creatures had been found in Africa, and that connection made its way to Korea and Japan.

KUNPENG | **Preferred habitat:** Sea, heaven | **Characteristics:** Giant winged fish
Special ability: Transforms into a fierce bird out of water
Translator's notes: This creature shapeshifts between two Chinese mythic monsters from which it takes its name. Chinese literature describes this creature's fish form, or *kun*, as being so enormous that its body spans miles. Its bird form, or *peng*, is thought to be derived from the Indian bird god, Garuda, and is described in a Buddhist mantra as the king of birds, so great and powerful it eats dragons.

LION-DOG | **Preferred habitat:** Land | **Characteristics:** Sharp teeth, fierce eyes, with distinctive mane
Special ability: Guards portals against evil elements and people

Translator's notes: Though in English these monsters are known as *lion-dogs* or *fu dogs*, they're really a type of guardian lion. Typically found in male-female pairs, statues of these guardian lions are found at entrances to palaces, temples, gardens, and other important spaces all over Asia. They are called *shishi* in both Chinese and Japanese; in the countries of Thailand and Cambodia, they are known as *singha*; in Sri Lanka, the Sinhala name is *simha*; and in Tibet, they are known as *gangs-seng-ge*, or snow lions.

MOLLUSK MONSTER | **Preferred habitat:** Sea | **Characteristics:** Giant shellfish resembling a clam or oyster
Special ability: Casts illusions/mirages on the water; builds cities and fortresses out of sea-foam
Translator's notes: This sea monster is said to be shaped like an enormous clam or oyster, and can create vast structures with its bubble breath on the water's surface. Traditionally it was thought to be the source of mirages. In East Asian countries, the word for giant clam monster (*shen* in Chinese; *shin* in Japanese and Korean) is found in the words for mirage (*shenlou* in Chinese; in Korean, *singilu*; in Japanese, *shinkiro*).

PHOENIX | **Preferred habitat:** Land, heaven | **Characteristics:** Sharp talons, strong beak, long, showy tail feathers in multiple bright colors
Special ability: Strength, loyalty, perseverance

Translator's notes: This mythical bird is known as *fenghuang* in Chinese, *ho-oh* in Japanese, *bonghwang* in Korean, *phung hoang* in Vietnamese. As a symbol, it's often seen as the complement to the dragon, and is associated with royalty—specifically empresses and queens. It stands for grace, virtue, and heavenly power. It is also a symbol of justice, fire, and the sun—but is not known for eternally regenerating in fire like the phoenix of Greek mythology.

PIYAO | **Preferred habitat:** Heaven | **Characteristics:** Winged lion with antlers and a split/forked tail
Special ability: Fights fiercely, can eat its weight in gold and silver
Translator's notes: The winged lion is more commonly called *pixiu* in Chinese, although other names include *piyao*, *taoba*, *tianlu*, and *bixie*; in Korean it's known as *bihyu*; the Japanese call it *hikyu*; in Vietnamese it's called *tì hưu*. Its wings allow it to fly between heaven and earth, and its love of jewels is legendary. In the practice of feng shui, they're oft-used symbols of good fortune and wealth. In China until the end of the Qing dynasty (1912), there was a long-standing law forbidding anyone but the emperor to possess a winged lion. They're considered great guardians of treasure because they love to eat gold, silver, and jewels but are unable to defecate—so whatever they eat is secure.

SACRED BEASTS OF THE COMPASS | Preferred habitat: North (tortoise), south (phoenix), east (dragon), west (kirin) | **Characteristics:** Black (tortoise), vermilion red (phoenix), azure blue (dragon), white (kirin)

Special ability: Guard and guide the four cardinal directions of the compass

Translator's notes: This quartet of creatures is known by many names across Asia, including *Four Guardians/Gods* (China, Korea, Vietnam, Japan), *Four Auspicious Beasts* (China), *Four Holy Beasts* (Vietnam), and *Four Symbols* (China, Korea, Japan, Vietnam). They symbolize the four directions on the compass (north, south, east, west), the four seasons (spring, summer, fall, winter), and four parts of a day (dawn, dusk, midday, midnight), and are significant elements of Chinese astrology that originated thousands of years ago.

SHACHI | Preferred habitat: Sea | **Characteristics:** Head of a tiger, body of a fish

Special ability: Summons rain; retains large amounts of water; protects against fire

Translator's notes: In Japan this monster is called *shachihoko*; in Chinese, it's known as *chiwen*, a type of dragon. Said to be able to control clouds, summon rain, and swallow/hold volumes of water, this scaly fish like creature with fearsome jaws is often found in the form of sculptural ornamental tiles on rooftops in many parts of Asia as guardians against fire.

Nowadays in Japan, the term *shachi* is used to refer to orcas/killer whales.

TENGU | **Preferred habitat:** Land | **Characteristics:** Raptor-like body, with distinctive long beak that looks like a bulbous nose and gives the creature's head a humanlike appearance
Special ability: Tears apart human offenders; kidnaps people and steals memories
Translator's notes: This fierce protector of the forest is a well-known creature in Japanese folklore. They come in various forms that usually combine bird, monkey, and human traits, but a long nose is the most popularly recognized feature. Tengu can be viewed as beneficial spirits but are also depicted as malicious troublemakers.

WARRIOR CRAB | **Preferred habitat:** Sea, tide pools | **Characteristics:** Carries the mark of a human face on its back
Special ability: Scavenges human flesh
Translator's notes: In Japan, a species of crab known as *heikegani* have shells that resemble angry faces. They are said to be the reincarnated warriors of the Heike samurai clan that were defeated in a famous sea battle.

WATER APE | **Preferred habitat:** Bodies of freshwater | **Characteristics:** Turtlelike shell and beak, webbed hands and feet; has an indentation on its head that holds water
Special ability: Drowns people and animals many times its size
Translator's notes: The water ape is primarily known as *kappa* (river child) in Japan, though it's also called *kawatora* (river tiger) and *komahiki* (horse puller), among other names. It is infamous for drowning people and livestock. This creature is often used as a warning symbol on caution signs in Japan. In Chinese folklore, the *shui gui* (water ghost) or *shui hou* (water monkey) is similarly dangerous.

WINGED HORSE | **Preferred habitat:** Land, heaven | **Characteristics:** Wings can be either feathered or batlike; body is covered either in fur or scales, depending on species
Special ability: Flies great distances
Translator's notes: The winged horse is also known as the thousand-li horse (*qianlima* in Chinese, *chollima* in Korean, *senrima* in Japanese, *thiên lý mã* in Vietnamese), because it can travel a thousand *li* in a day. A *li* is also known as the Chinese mile. It's said to be too fast and beautiful for ordinary people to ride, and is an important symbol of national pride in North Korea. Other types of winged horses include the dragon horse (*longma* in Chinese, *ryuma* in Japanese)

and heavenly horse (*tianma* in Chinese), which have scales instead of fur.

ZOUYA | **Preferred habitat:** Land | **Characteristics:** Herbivore; tigerlike in shape but much larger; striped fur (in up to five colors); a tail far longer than its body
Special ability: Travels great distances at high speeds
Translator's notes: In Chinese mythology, the zouya, also known as *zouwu* or *zouyu*, is a gentle creature that can traverse thousands of miles quickly. Despite its fierce feline appearance, it is a plant-eater.

ACKNOWLEDGMENTS

The world turned upside down in 2020, and everything I knew as normal disappeared. So much was lost, including my mom. In such turbulent times, I found a measure of solace in writing this story. It has been a lifeline in many ways, and a balm to see it become a book.

Many thanks to my prince of an agent, Josh Adams. I'm so grateful to you and Tracey, and the tireless efforts of Cathy, Anna, and Adams Literary.

To my lovely and amazing editor Kristen Pettit—a true queen. Your insights and instincts are invaluable to me, making me better and more sure-footed as a writer. I can't imagine getting to this point without your guidance. I feel so lucky to be working with you.

Deepest appreciation to the team at HarperCollins and their incredible talents. Thank you to associate editor Clare Vaughn, copy editor Maya Myers, designers Catherine Lee and Alison Klapthor, cover artist Daniel Chang, production editors Jessica Berg and Gwen Morton, production managers Sean Cavanagh and Vanessa Nuttry, marketing director Delaney Heisterkamp, and publicist Lauren Levite. Your magic touch has conjured this book into my hands, and I couldn't be more thrilled.

Even in isolation for months on end, I never felt completely alone, thanks to priceless calls, chats, emails, socially distanced visits, Zoom meetings, and messages from community and friends such as Arti Panjabi Kvam, Aurora Gray, Elizabeth Barker, Elizabeth Ross, Hilary Hattenbach, Jason White, Josh Hauke, Kristen Kittscher, Lilliam Rivera, Mary Shannon, Laura Ling and Li Clayton, Paula Yoo, Erin Eitter Kono, Ken Min, Mike Jung, Rita Crayon Huang, Sher Rill Ng, Carmen Wong, Amie Kaufman, Erin Kieu Ninh, Oliver Wang and Sharon Mizota, Joven and Leslie Matias, Krystal Swaving and Mark Villanueva, Xinh Le, Elise and John Cheng, Emily Liu Foy, Evie Jeang, Gene Rhee and Helena Ku Rhee, Kathee Lin, Jackie Park Kim, Juliet Lee and Roger Fan, Stefanie Huie and David Lee, Tina Hua Sun, Sherry Berkin, Ed Mun and Aileen Han, Ted Lai, Carol Young and Peter Kim, Eileen Cabiling, Eileen Kim and Devin Jindrich, Fatimah Tobing Rony and Tim Hoekstra, Harry Yoon, Helen Yoon, Helen Lee and Todd Jones, Jo Odawara and Kathy Green, Marle Chen and Amy Chang, Mayumi Takada and Warren Hsu, Raina Lee and Mark Watanabe, Shuntaro and

Asaki Shinada, Vivian Bang, John Cheng, Rosa Yan, Darcy Fleck and Holger Imler, Tiina Piirsoo, Trish Dacumos, Amy Briede, Deb Frank, and many others. Though we can't always be together in person, the presence of your friendship has provided much needed comfort and strength.

To my beloved family, your endless care and support keeps me going, even when things are difficult, scary, and uncertain. Much gratitude to Wendy and Dennis Chang; to Amanda, Nicole, Lindsey, and JP; to David and Michelle Lin; to the extended Chang clan, including Karena, Carl, Timothy, Joshua, Christina, Dave, Kadence, Tiffany, Harvey, Amelia, Devin, Steve, Virginia, and Grace; and to my Hou and Lin relatives in Taiwan, including Aires, James, Pauline, Nick, Paul, Mimi, Henry, Vincent, Sherry, Andy, Wen-Tung, Wen-Pin, Wen-Chien, my aunts, uncles, great-aunt, and so many other cousins. Thank you to Steven's parents, Rosa and Koo Pak, for being my bonus parents. Most of all, thank you to my father, Paul Lin, for his fortitude, kindness, wisdom, and the loving example he sets. You're the best dad anyone could ever ask for, and I love you more than words can say.

Lastly, I am grateful to all who've read my stories. I've received some wonderful letters from young readers that fill me with joy and make this dream of putting stories into the world feel fully realized. Thank you. I hope to bring you many more.